WICKED GAME

ERIN CAINE

ISBN: 0692402063
ISBN-13: 978-0692402061

This book is dedicated to Mom, Dad, Claire, and Conor. Without the support of my family, this book would never have been possible.

ACKNOWLEDGEMENTS

I'd like to thank my family for supporting me and for offering their thoughts and revisions on *Wicked Game*—particularly my aunt, Julie Halter, for having the eye of a hawk when it comes to editing; my grandparents for reading the early versions of the book; my uncle, Chris Halter, for all the publishing know-how; my mom for taking the time to read and edit the final two drafts; and my dad for always bugging me with, "So when's that book getting published?" I'd also like to thank my current and former English teachers who believed in my writing and believed that I could make something from it, and all the teachers who've assured me that one should never be ashamed of a good work ethic. Thanks also goes to my sister Claire (photography wizard), everyone from tenth grade Creative Writing (for being crazy, unique, and enthusiastic human beings), my father's friend and coworker (and author) David Swinson (for his kind words and interest in seeing *Wicked Game* succeed), thesaurus.com (seriously, thanks), and anyone who has ever said to me, "Hey, you're pretty good at this whole 'writing thing.'"

WICKED GAME

"I was not born to be forced. I will breathe after my own fashion. Let us see who is the strongest."

— Henry David Thoreau

PROLOGUE

JENNY

My memories never seemed to leave me, even if I wanted them to. Mine was a memory so willfully precise I could remember exactly how tightly my mother had clutched me to her after the shouting had ceased and given way to the kind of silence that felt like a weight on my chest. I could close my eyes and picture us there by the window as she brushed her thumb back and forth across my damp cheek, whispering words of comfort into my ear so that maybe the image of my father as he walked out of the house and into the rain would disappear with him. The door had slammed hard, the crack of wood against wood jarring to the bone, loud enough to make it clear—even to a girl of barely nine—that he wasn't ever coming back.

"Don't cry, Jenny," my mother murmured, not looking at me but at the rain that slanted across the window. "It's over now."

A strangled noise escaped me, and I tucked my face into the crook of her arm. The argument between them that had conjured me from my bedroom still rung in my ears, electric and stinging. "B-But Daddy…"

"Daddy's gone now, baby. You understand that, don't you?" Her voice had taken on a soft, chanting resonance, like praying. "And he's been needing to leave for a long time now—"

"But *why?* Why would Daddy want to leave us?" I demanded, feeling anger bubble inside of me. She'd asked if I'd understood but really I didn't understand any of it at all.

"He didn't want to leave us, Jenny." After a pause, she added, in a firmer voice, "He had to. Sometimes people *need* to do things they don't

1

want to do to make the people around them happy. Or, at least…to make the people around them better off. If someone couldn't give anything up for the ones he loves…Jenny, it wouldn't be love."

Oddly, something about that made more sense to me. I looked up at her, my chest still rising and falling irregularly with the last string of hiccups that always came after a fitful storm of tears. After a moment's hesitation, I dragged my sleeve across my eyes, trying to imitate her expression, mimic some element of composure there. I could still remember the set of her brow—so determined, always determined.

She smiled. "That's my girl."

For so long after that night, all I wanted was a little sense of jurisdiction over my own life. All I wanted was to not lose the people close to me to things outside of my control. All I wanted was to feel as if the reins weren't slipping from my grasp more and more each day. Little did I realize, when I finally *got* what I wanted, suddenly a thoughtless decision or word or action could throw everything out of balance and hurt the people I never wanted to hurt, and what was worse was the fact that all of it would now be a product of my own doing, and my own doing alone.

I had become unintentionally, yet irreversibly, entangled inside of this world, and it wasn't long before I would come to understand that the only way to stay afloat amongst these people of greed and power and bloodlust was to know how to play the game.

And it was a very wicked game.

1
WHEN DUSK FALLS

Gray blotches pockmarked the hillsides, rolling on seemingly forever into the horizon where the weary gold sun still clung to the edge of the tree line.

Gravestones. But I was really only looking at one of them. If I shut my eyes, I could still see the words as if they were hewed into the very backs of my eyelids.

Heather Halford, it said. *Loving Mother. 1971 – 2015.*

It almost struck me as ridiculous, how brief and inadequate that inscription was, how empty. Less than a month ago, when St. Ambrose cemetery had existed only through a car window, I'd observed the orderly marble rows with nothing beyond an offhand thought to the effect of, *Thank God I'm here and not there.* I didn't feel that way anymore. The school's guidance counselor had done what she could with me in the weeks after the funeral, but I didn't seem to be following the "Five Stages of Grief" identified in any health textbook. Everything that I wanted to do—crying and breaking down and getting inexplicably furious, among others—I stopped myself from doing. There was always in my mind a feeling that it would be an unforgivable thing to do, letting myself break down when she had always been so strong, strong even when she could hardly stand up on her own, even when the sleeves of her sweaters started to hang off of her wrists.

In the stillness of approaching nightfall, I found I wasn't in denial or depressed or angry or bargaining or accepting at all. I was just...numb, I guessed, left drained from countless blows to an already exhausted emotional reservoir.

Her illness was never a battle that could be won, really, only fought. In retrospect, childishly expecting her to go on fighting it forever, as if she even *could* fight it forever, was a waste of energy and time. And time was the most valuable thing to me in the world after she told me she was dying. I remembered most graphically those last few months, right when things had really started to take a worse turn. The drugs. The chemo. The fevers. The sickly smell of hospitals pervading every bad dream, and—post-funeral— the sicklier smell of roses soon beginning to take its place.

But I wasn't so hasty to pin the fault on cancer. No, I knew better than that. I knew better than to assume, as everyone else had, that my clever, quick-minded mother had simply *overlooked* her illness.

It wasn't the *cancer* that had killed her; it was my self-absorption, it was my negligence. And it was my father's pride. For reasons entirely unbeknownst to his nine-year-old daughter, Michael Cable had one day abruptly departed, to pursue a life separate from his wife and child, to never contact them again except to argue ineffectively over the phone regarding, from what I could gather, things like where I would stay, who would get what, and et cetera. Legal terms were notched and loosed over the phone like arrows, and I had to watch as my mother's face grew gaunt from sleeplessness and strain. I came to understand that she was so preoccupied with the divorce that she didn't realize how sick she was until she was nearly overcome by it. I didn't think I would ever forgive either of us, not my father or myself. I didn't think I *could*.

Guilt was a curious thing, an entity that both enlightened and blinded. It had a way of making someone wonder what could have been, ponder the dreaded "what-ifs". Unwillingly, I found myself forming these scenarios in my head, scenarios involving parents who loved each other and mothers who never died and fathers who never left.

Still, in spite of everything I hadn't really cried since the funeral. What was more, I *refused*. I'd cried enough already, sapped that emotional reservoir dry a hundred times over. Mom wouldn't want me feeling sorry for myself. A week before she'd passed, she had taken my hands in hers and had told me that she could feel that it wouldn't be much longer, and that we'd been preparing for this for a long time. She told me I shouldn't worry. "You still have so much left in you," she'd said, but I had doubted her then, and I doubted her now.

And I hadn't just doubted her; I'd been *angry* at her. I'd been angry that she'd given up. Only now did I realize that it hadn't been a decision she had made, but a fate she had accepted.

"I figured I'd find you here." I was startled from my thoughts, Taylor's voice cutting through them in a way that brought to mind daybreak filling a dark room, chasing off the lingering shadows. He smiled down at me, and it was a relief not to see pity in his expression (characteristic of people who didn't know how I felt but pretended they did.) We'd been friends for some time—if memory served, nearly a year—but even from the first moment I'd ever laid eyes on him I'd *known* somehow that he was the very sort of person one could invest one's faith in.

"Nice sunset, yeah?" he asked, running a hand through his hair, his attention for a moment diverted by the object in question. I took the opportunity to study him, more frequent a habit than I cared to admit. There was something about his smile, a persistence about it that I couldn't help but admire. He was long and lean, more on the slight side, really. His eyes were sometimes blue, other times the color of the cornflowers my mother had always planted in her garden. *Yes,* I thought, *exactly that color.*

I shrugged, following his gaze. The sun itself was almost gone, just a fingernail of amber, the sky around it ringed in bruise-like purples and washed-out reds and oranges. It was beautiful. Or it would've been if not for the circumstance, if not for the fact that this wasn't the scenario in my head where mothers never died. "I guess."

He sat down beside me. "You guess? Well, it's a nice change from all the black from these past few weeks, isn't it? I mean—"

I shuddered, my mind evoking images of black suits and black veils and shiny, black shoes and black words on paper signing me over to a virtual stranger. "Yeah," I interrupted, sharper than intended. "Yeah, it's a change."

Taylor didn't seem to have anything to say in reply, his lips thinning into a straight line. I didn't know why I insisted in always making things harder for him than necessary. All I'd really had to say was that the stupid sunset was *nice.* I took the opportunity to change the subject.

"It's getting late," I said, peering sideways at him. "Tarek starts getting anxiety attacks past seven, you know."

Tarek was Taylor's roommate, a twenty-something college student with the air of an Indian prince and a temperament that reminded me of a rubber band pulled too tight. It made me wonder sometimes if he'd been born with his disability or if something horrible had happened to *put* him in that wheelchair, though the thing itself seemed of little issue to him, outwardly, as he made quips about it whenever he got the chance.

They were two of a kind, Tarek and Taylor, neglecting general disposition. Neither of them seemed to mind too much the lack of specificity concerning their respective pasts and families. Taylor had divulged to me roughly *two* facts about Tarek, and I was beginning to think they were the only two things I would *ever* know about him. These facts were: 1. His family lived somewhere in India and 2. He hated cilantro. And then there was Taylor, himself, who never mentioned his family *at all*, not even to me, and out of respect for his privacy I'd never broached the topic. Still, I found myself wondering about his peculiar sensitivity about the subject, his openness with almost everything except his family and where he'd come from. I supposed it was no more peculiar than my *own* family situation. For almost nine years my father had been a ghost to me, and yet starting today I would be living with the man indefinitely.

Taylor waved away my concern. "Tarek's mental instability will continue on regardless of when I get back. I wanted to squeeze in a last goodbye before you left."

My mouth quirked up at the corners. "You already said goodbye. You've been saying goodbye for days. It's not like I'm moving to some distant country, Taylor. Really, I'll just be a few hours away."

He muttered something I couldn't hear, looking at his bitten nails. Audibly, he said, "I guess it's just that I…I'll miss you, you know."

I smiled, taking his hand. His skin was warmer than I expected it to be, especially in the briskness of October. He looked up at me, surprised. Usually the only form of affection I ever extended to him was a not-so-gentle punch on the arm. "I'll miss you, too." I gripped his fingers tighter, lowering my voice. "You have to promise me something."

"Of course."

"You have to promise to come visit *all the time*. Swear you will."

I heard a new tone of seriousness under his characteristic humor as he said, "You know I will, Jenny." There was something forceful in his look now, in a way that made my heart twist in my chest. I fully recognized the fact that I didn't deserve him. For a straight month, I had been renting his shoulder and I could only assume he wanted it back.

"I know," I said, softly. Then I added, with a contemplative tap on my chin, "You don't think Tarek would let me crash for a few days with you guys, do you?"

He laughed, hopping to his feet, tugging me along with him. "Probably not. He's a little unsettled by you, I think. When I tell him you're coming over, he curses in Hindi and hides in his room." I shoved his shoulder, but it only seemed to encourage him. "Unless your old man's become some sort of serial killer in his spare time. In which case, I would have to come rescue you from his *dastardly* clutches."

I couldn't resist playing along. "Dramatically?"

"Is there any way else?" he asked, feigning offense at the question, though when our gazes met he couldn't keep himself from smiling. Taylor always had a way to cheer me up, even at my lowest point, even if it was just for a moment.

I sighed, noticing for the first time that the sun had dipped well below the belt of the forest, and that the shadows hadn't wasted any time soon afterward in settling on the grounds of St. Ambrose. "We should go. The *serial killer* will be here soon."

Twilight fell quickly, and the townhouses lining Sentinel Avenue, crowded together and in a motley of sun-faded colors, looked to me then like crooked, discolored teeth. My own house was entirely a pastel blue, and I had a clear memory of helping my mom repaint the front door when I was little. It'd been a couple months after my father had left, and she'd been in her "rebuilding" phase, which was both literal and not. She'd taken me to get ice cream afterwards, and I'd watched her as she ticked off the things to do and to repair next on her slim fingers.

There was that same door before me now, dull and peeling in some places, just ahead. I used to find it unsettling to live so close to a graveyard, but now I just found it sort of…*tragic*, I supposed was the word for it. It was a particular word a lot of people around town liked to use to describe *me*, as it happened. *Did you hear about that poor girl, Jenny Cable?* they would murmur, too loudly. *The whole thing is just tragic, you know. Simply tragic.*

Taylor walked beside me, unspeaking. I preferred it that way, the two of us absorbing each other for a moment, as if saying good-bye was like soaking up the last of the sun's rays before it disappeared. I looked up into the lightless sky, realizing it was exactly like that.

My eyes found Taylor again, examining his face, where the skin was tight with anxiety. "Well, there's your dad, I guess, probable mass slaughterer. Here to take you away forever," he said. He nodded to the parking space in front of my house, where I saw, as my gaze followed his, a black car waiting at the curb. The car itself was startling, sleek and stylish, certainly not like any type of car my father could afford. I could just make out the faint purr of its engine. It was idling. Whoever was inside hadn't been here long.

Before I could come up with something to say to comfort Taylor, or at the very least trip him for being so melodramatic, someone stepped out of the car.

There was the dark shock of hair first, and then the young, trim figure. I tensed. Something didn't feel right about this guy, a guy who very obviously was not my father. Something was...different. Off. My mistrust was only deepened by the way the hairs on the nape of my neck stood on end, the pang of deep suspicion turning my stomach. "That's weird," I murmured. "My father should be here by now."

I looked at Taylor again. Apparently, he felt it, too, whatever it was that was so inexplicably *bizarre* about this stranger. He had gone very still, his face darkening, and he took my hand very abruptly, pressing his palm to mine in a grip like iron. It wasn't like before, when I had been comforted by the contact. Now it sent only a bolt of panic up my arm. "Jenny, we should go inside."

I couldn't quite manage to tug my hand from his. "Taylor, you're freaking me out. What's going on?"

"Just go inside, Jenny," he said, urgency both in his voice and in his stride now as the boy stepped away from the car.

I turned around to face him, forcing him to stop. "Taylor, *explain to me* what's happening right now. What's wrong? Why are you—?"

"Jennifer? Jennifer Cable?"

I whirled, and there was the dark-haired stranger not ten feet from us. He was about my age, I supposed, and for a boy decidedly lovely. Maybe it was the high cheekbones, the fullness of the mouth. Maybe it was his eyes, the color of honey. Though when I glanced at Taylor he didn't appear as though he shared my opinion of the guy.

"Jennifer?" he said again, much closer now, reaching into the inside pocket of his jacket. I could feel Taylor tense behind me as if he expected the boy to pull a gun or something.

I finally found my voice, stepping toward him. "Yes? Can I help you?"

He withdrew an envelope from his pocket, handing it to me without a word more. After a moment of hesitation, I accepted it, tearing away the seal. There were several crisply folded documents within, and as I smoothed out the creases I noticed my name and my parents' names several times. "I suppose," the stranger said, "you've already gathered by now that I'm here to escort you to Mr. Cable's."

Hm. British. His accent was British, though faded some, a quality seeming to imply that he hadn't been back home in a long time. Of course. *Of course* he was British. "Why didn't *Mr. Cable* come, himself?"

He blinked, as if surprised by the bitterness of my voice. He plucked the envelope from my hands, returning it to his inside pocket. "Busy man, you know."

I eyed the black car from over his shoulder, and then the boy, himself, in a nice button-down shirt and slacks and shiny shoes. It didn't take a genius to realize that my father had, in the interval of nine years, come into a fortune by some circumstance or another. "Clearly," I replied, folding my arms.

The stranger looked amused, nodding his head a little as a wry grin lifted one side of his mouth. After a pause, he clapped his hands and rubbed them together. "You're all packed, then?"

"Yeah, why don't I just...I'll be right back. Let me just go get my bags. They're in the living room."

"By all means," he said, with a generous wave of his hand.

As I started up the steps to the front door, I heard Taylor begin to speak to the other boy in a low voice. Maybe they knew one another, I thought. Though nothing about the interaction seemed to suggest to me that they were acquainted in any *friendly* way. "I think she'd feel more comfortable if *I* drove her, instead. It'd make the transition easier for her, you know? Just give me the directions, and I'll be happy to—"

"Yes, I'm sure you would be happy to, wouldn't you?"

I turned, barely even through the doorway, surprised at the new note of contempt souring the boy's response when before he'd been all listless civility. Taylor's eyes flickered to mine and back again to the stranger's, and he stepped closer to him, lowering his voice so I couldn't hear. I thought it sounded something liked, "Don't do this," and after that his mouth formed soundlessly over the words, "Not here."

"She's completely in the dark, isn't she?" was the smug reply. The full mouth curled at both corners, now, and there was suddenly another tone to his voice that was impossible to mistake, one that held the undercurrent of a threat.

Taylor's gaze moved toward me again, and he stepped away from the boy. "Why don't I go get your bags, Jenny?" he asked, with an abruptness that destroyed whatever nonchalance he was attempting to pull off.

"Oh, okay. Sure, if you—" But he was already starting up the steps, brushing past me and disappearing around the corner.

The other boy ambled after him, putting his hands in the pockets of his slacks with a good-natured grin at me. He paused in the doorway, his shoulder nearly touching mine. "I think I'll go lend him a hand." He stared at me a little longer than necessary.

"You really don't have to—"

But then he was gone, too, vanishing just as swiftly as Taylor had.

I exhaled in a huff, dropping onto the top step, crossing one leg over the other as I leaned back onto my palms. Five minutes had passed before I realized that they seemed to be taking an awfully long time just getting luggage in the next room. For all I knew, one had taken a kitchen knife to the other while his back was turned.

I stood, brushing my hands on the front of my jeans, turning into the hallway. I heard no sound within, which I supposed either contradicted my prophecy or validated it, depending on the timing. "Taylor? Are you in here?" I walked into the kitchen, heading toward the living room. Everything was dark. "Where—?"

They stood facing each other, my bags still strewn about their feet. Taylor's back was to me, and before I could even entirely understand the scene in front of me he was dropping like a weighted doll, striking his head on the corner of the coffee table as he tumbled to the floor. The stranger stood over him, rolling his sleeve back down to his wrist, looking just as bored as he'd looked before.

"Taylor." I went to him, sinking to my knees. Dragging him halfway into my lap, I saw that his eyes were closed and that there was a spot above his eyebrow starting to swell and turn purple. My hand shook as I lifted it to

my face.

"I'm sure he's fine."

My gaze snapped up to the stranger's, and I glared at him. He didn't appear apologetic in the least. "Fine? You think he's *fine?* He could have a *concussion.*"

"Doubtful." He scratched at his chin. "Besides, he's breathing, isn't he?"

I slid Taylor from my lap and stood, and the boy backed away hastily, throwing his hands up in front of him. "Hey, now, no sense in *that*, is there? He wanted a fight, and I gave him one. Nothing to be done about it, really."

"Normal people *discuss* their problems. You know, like *adults.*"

The boy cracked each knuckle on his right hand individually. "Well, I suppose you're right about that." He bent and seized both of my bags from the floor, slinging them over each shoulder. "Move him onto the couch, if you like, but in five minutes I'll be leaving."

As he left, he called brightly from over his shoulder, "With all your stuff."

I sighed, sliding my arms underneath Taylor's and dragging him over to the couch. Smoothing his hair away from his face, I wondered just what it was that had happened between them to make them hate each other so fervently. An old girlfriend, maybe? I hoped not, though it was hard to say exactly *why* this was the case. The sound of a car horn made me lose the train of thought, and I straightened, still not taking my eyes from his face.

Almost four minutes passed before he regained full awareness, his eyelids fluttering open halfway as he groaned, his gaze sliding to a spot on the ceiling. I ran into the kitchen to retrieve a small, plastic flashlight from one of the drawers, and he flinched when I shone the beam into his eyes. To my relief, the pupils contracted, and with another forbearing sigh I tossed the flashlight onto the table and sat back on my haunches.

"You idiot," I murmured. At least he wasn't an idiot with a concussion.

His gaze slowly came to rest on mine, and he pouted his lips a little. "I think that's literally adding insult to injury, Jenny."

"Yeah, well—" He was saved another of my insults as Vince leaned into the horn again, cutting off my reply. I glanced at the door. "I really have to go now. Call me soon. And I mean *soon,* okay?"

"Okay."

I stood to leave, but I hadn't taken a step before I felt Taylor's hand on the inside of my elbow. I turned to look at him, and saw that there was now desperation in his face, barely suppressed. "Jenny?"

"Yes?"

"Just..." His grip loosened, and he seemed defeated in some way. "Just be careful around him, alright?"

I brushed his hand from my arm. "I'll be fine."

The blurred, twilit city from before had somehow transformed itself into a midnight arrangement of trees, half-dismantled barns, and decaying cornfields, the stark absence of streetlights and concrete leaving me only with a sense of complete vulnerability. I supposed I'd just expected to at least be able to say a proper goodbye before I left. And now all I had left were these questions, these questions and these fears that overshadowed everything else.

What happens now? I thought. *What kind of man is my father? Has he changed at all? Has he stayed exactly the same?* I couldn't be sure which would be worse.

The same words echoed around inside my head, ceaseless in their rotations, yet not a single question ever met with an answer. We had driven for hours—almost three, according to the backlit numbers across the car's dashboard—when we finally rounded a bend and were met with an enormous Victorian, nearly a castle, perched at the top of a steep driveway. The mansion, tucked away in the middle of Nowhere, Maryland, seemed more out of place than my *escort* did in his high-class get-up. He turned around to face me as we pulled up in front of the house, catching me staring up at it in awe.

"Welcome home," he said.

He came around to open my door for me, which would've been rather gentlemanly if not for the look of boredom and dry condescension still plain on his face. He looped his arm through mine, and in this manner we approached the house, which looked so much more intimidating when one stared up at it from right under its eave. The place was as beautiful in its age as it was daunting in its dimensions, with its turreted roof and dark red shutters and countless windows. The front doors were enormous, arched things that belonged to a palace. Twin gargoyles, grimacing, adorned each door, as if whoever owned the place hoped to scare off company. The boy barely hesitated, turning the knob on one of the doors and shoving it open with his shoulder.

"Don't you bother to lock up?"

He just laughed, leading me inside.

If I'd thought the outside was grand, the inside of the mansion was…simply breathtaking. It was decidedly Gothic-era, ancient furniture placed artfully around the open space, everything done up in red and black, a color scheme I thought unusual. The floors and tables were ebony, worn around the edges like the steps on the sweeping staircase, which dominated the view from the front door, splitting in two before curling up to the upstairs. The walls showed little signs of age, a vibrant red to rival the black of the drapes, which were filmy and fluttery like a butterfly's wings. The bottom floor was essentially all one room, lit warmly by the sconces on the walls and by the chandelier overhead. The antique comfort of the atmosphere, as I imagined to be much like visiting a grandparent's home, seemed *wrong*, somehow. It seemed wrong that I almost *wanted* to be here. My eyes paused on a grand piano, collecting dust in the corner of the room.

"The name's Vincent Hallows, by the way. Call me Vince," the boy said, eyes wandering around the room like mine. The lighting of the room softened his features a little. He looked in the direction of the piano, where my gaze had come to rest on again. "Do you play?"

I shook my head. "No…it's just…" *What are the chances of me being a concert pianist, do you think, Jenny?* I recalled the night when Taylor had said that to me with ease. We were sitting in a little café we often visited, Taylor and I, in the early hours of the morning. He had been staring at the low, crooked smile of the moon, talking to me about destiny and fate and how some people were doomed to be exactly what people expected them to be. Remembering that now, it felt like someone had punched me in the gut. God, how I missed that idiot already. "Nothing. I'm Jenny," I added, not to be rude, which I found to be a little ridiculous when I thought about it. "Cable. But I guess you knew that already."

"Do you like it? The house, I mean." He glanced at me, for a moment appearing expectant of my answer, as if he was a little less *bored* than before.

"I guess. I mean, yeah, it's nice," I said, going over to sit in the chair by the window across the room. "It's beautiful. And…*roomy*, too. Do you really live here?" I couldn't imagine what one could do with so much space.

"My father and I do, yes—uh, I mean…*you're* father." He sat in the opposite chair from me, looking uncomfortable. "Well, he's kind of my father. Actually, he's not really. He took me in when I was very young."

I stared at him for a moment, filled with a sudden cold sense of dread at the thought of possibly sharing any amount of blood with the insufferable Vincent Hallows. "Kind of?" I echoed, plucking a petal from the rose on the table between us, stuck in a gorgeous glass vase. I crushed it between my fingers, staining them red. "Or not really? Which one is it?"

"He's not my biological father," Vince clarified, to my relief. "He just raised me. I'm more of an…apprentice to him, really."

"Apprentice?" I wiped my hand on the frayed knee of my jeans. "What's the trade?"

"The trade?" he asked, smirking, as if in on a secret I didn't know. "It's a bit complicated. I may or may not explain later. Right now, though, I think it'd do you well to wash up a little, maybe get some rest for tomorrow. First impressions are everything, after all." *Hmph. Indeed they are,* I thought, as my gaze slanted to the side to cast him a withering look. He ignored it, casting his voice loud enough to echo throughout the foyer. "Laura!"

A thick, elderly woman with watchful eyes bustled into the room, seemingly from out of nowhere. "Sir?" she asked, glancing back and forth between Vince and me with a narrow gaze.

Vince nodded in my direction. "Show Jenny up to her room. Liam will be home early tomorrow morning."

"A maid?" I asked, raising an eyebrow. How old-fashioned. I felt like I had somehow been thrust back in time, transported to 19th century London.

He shrugged. "It's a big house."

"Liam? My father's name is Michael."

"A lot's changed in nine years."

I sighed, following the maid up the wide staircase as Vince leaned his chin into his hand and watched me go.

We stared at each other, our faces almost touching. She really was a pathetic looking thing, with tangled, reddish blonde hair and miserably sleepless eyes. She was of an average stature, but she was also slight, all angles and planes. There was a hole in her jeans and the sweater she wore seemed several sizes too big. Somehow, despite her state, there seemed to be a certain stubbornness about her, a certain stubbornness that undoubtedly never did her much good.

"Jennifer."

I turned away from the mirror, reproachful of the elderly maid. She seemed kind enough, grandmotherly almost, but I couldn't trust anyone in this *house*, if one could simply call it that.

She huffed impatiently, taking my arm and hauling me over to an open door on the other side of the bedroom. I could hear a noise from within like falling beads. Poking my head around the frame, I was struck by the humidity and the smell of shampoo first and the size second. I had never seen a bathroom so big. It was a room all by itself, and every surface a startlingly intense and sterile white. How did one old housekeeper keep everything so *clean*?

"Determination and a somewhat exorbitant wage among other reasons," said the maid—Laura—from behind me.

I turned to ask her how she knew what I'd been thinking so exactly, but she slammed the door leaving me alone in the cavernous bathroom.

Midnight quickly melted into dawn, within the flutter of an eyelid, it seemed. I stared out of a foreign window, at the unfamiliar stretch of driveway lined at even intervals with alien trees. I pulled my legs up to my chest pressing my chin into my knees. The clothes I'd found neatly folded on the sink fit perfectly. They were also outrageously cozy. It was odd, being so…*comfortable,* I guessed one could venture to call it.

Though I wasn't at all content in my mind, my emotions compiled into an uproar of contradiction unable to be stifled. On one hand, selfishly, I considered the fact that I had never had so *much*. But at the same time, I guessed I still had nothing. I had nothing because Taylor wasn't here on the window sill next to me making jokes and imitating Vince's crisp accent as his long legs dangled over the edge. I had to find him. This place was no home, and I was no prisoner.

I looked around. No incongruous shadow to rumple the darkness. Maybe I didn't even have to *tell* Vince where I was going. Maybe I could just...

I padded over to the door as quietly as I could, the cold, empty floors making me shiver, spotting a worn pair of brown leather boots that were a little strange looking in a house so elegant and tidy. My own shoes were still upstairs, and I couldn't risk going back for them.

I had just pulled on the first boot when: "I hope you aren't planning on leaving, Jenny."

I raised my chin a fraction before slipping on the second one and standing up, not wanting to feel inferior. Though, as it happened, whether I was sitting or standing made very little difference at all. It was all about presence and how one held oneself. Vince had a daunting, disdainful air about him, whereas I only came across as slightly resentful and actually a little uneasy. Okay, a lot uneasy. I shook my head, cursing myself for being afraid of him. I retrieved the keys to his car from the hook by the door, twirling them around an index finger. "And if I am?"

His eyes flashed like trees rushing by in a car window, and I could have sworn they went a more sinister green color than hazel then. "Then I'd have to stop you."

"Really?" I asked.

"Really."

I bolted toward the door, scrabbling for the handle and flinging it wide, the motion bringing with it a rush of crisp autumn air. A cold-fingered breeze reached in and brushed my cheeks, sending a shiver from my toes to the roots of my damp curls, and I vaulted through the doorway, leaves crinkling under the heavy soles of the boots. My feet, in untied shoes a few sizes too big, slid around inside of them, the left one threatening to slip off completely.

Then I was hurled to the ground, a solid mass pinning my face and body into the dirt. Vince's elbow dug into my back between my shoulder blades. He grabbed my wrist as he stood, pulling me up with him as he wrestled the keys from my hand.

Laura came bustling out of the door, frowning so deeply the lines in her face seemed to grimace, as well. She stopped in front of us, smelling strongly of cleaning product, staring at my feet. "Can't say those suit you, Jennifer."

2
PERSUADER

I squirmed in the tall, mahogany chair, wrists starting to ache, rubbed raw and red by the twine securing them to the wide arms.

Vince sat again in the opposite chair, not taking his eyes off of me. I would've probably felt a little uncomfortable if I actually cared what he thought of me. I shifted, trying to kick off the tight rope around my ankles. No such luck.

"Your father will be home soon," Vince said, casually, sounding as uninterested as usual. I wondered if nothing short of a third World War could even manage to get a reaction from this guy.

"Fantastic," I said, allowing the highest amount of sarcasm to drip in. He most certainly deserved it. "If I wasn't tied down, I'd probably be *jumping* with excitement."

"When he gets here," he muttered, finally glancing away from me, "you should at least *attempt* to keep that mouth of yours in check."

"Why? Do I *bother you*, Vince?" I found I suddenly had a new object of entertainment before me.

"No." He stared hard at me with those eyes of his. Even barbed as they were, those eyes were almost disturbingly captivating. I always found my attention drawn back to them.

I sat back in the seat, smug now in my confidence. He was born for the stage, without question, but the whole "slick criminal" persona didn't quite seem to fit him. I could see that the costume sagged in places. "Sure."

That surprised him. The cut-glass look he had on faltered, and he bent forward, toward me, his voice carrying a lightly challenging tone. "You don't believe me?"

"Nope." I cast him a sidelong glance, my eyebrows lifting.

Vince didn't respond. He leaned back in the chair, ignoring me.

"Come on, admit it," I said, with an odd conviction this time. "You can keep up that surly attitude all you like, but you're not fooling me."

Without warning, he leapt up from the cushioned seat, bracing his arms on either side of me. He gripped my forearms painfully, his face frightening in its composure, his words like ice in their precision. "Don't act like you know me. You don't. I'm not like you, so don't pretend to have any idea what you're talking about."

"What is it that you think makes you so much better than me?" I demanded, finally finding my voice. "Your fancy clothes? Your big house? I have news for you *Vincent Hallows:* You're not better than anyone. You're just a spoiled jerk with some serious issues. Not much else."

"Is *that* what you think?" His eyes narrowed. "You don't know anything." He stormed over to the center of the floor, holding out his hand, fingers splayed, toward the unsuspecting glass bowl on a bookcase across the room.

Everything seemed to slow. I watched the bowl as it rattled slightly, entranced by the impossible. Stars of light glittered off of its surface, and I could hardly follow the bowl with my eyes as it blurred across the room and shattered against the edge of the staircase. Snow-like shards of glass bounced down to the floor, and I looked up at Vince, who looked as surprised as I felt. He tore his eyes away from the glass dust to look at me. His expression was one of someone who had awoken from a trance to discover he had done something horrible.

His chest heaved up and down, his hair a dark tangle in his eyes. "Why did I just do that?" he whispered, to himself mostly. The sound carried, resounding in a room that was once again graveyard quiet.

"*How* did you just do that?" I interjected, feeling like I was going to hyperventilate or pass out or worse. Oh, God, I was going to be sick and—damn these constraints—there was no helping the case if my stomach decided to suddenly and violently rid itself of its contents.

"I believe," he said, with a mocking tilt to his head, instantly calm and suave once more, "it's called being *better*, darling."

Impossible. It was *impossible*. There had to be some sort of wire... It had to be a magic trick of some kind, an illusion.

But the worst thing about it was that in my heart I knew that what I had seen him do was no illusion. It seemed more conceivable than it ought to have seemed, and that scared me most of all.

My hands clenched and unclenched on the armrests of the chair. "First," I said, surprised at the levelness in my tone, "you're going to untie me. And then, you're going to give me an explanation. I deserve that much."

He only looked at me for a second, a strange expression twitching at the corners of his full mouth, but the look vanished as he stooped to unbind me from the chair, oddly compliant. Of course, this was done not without grumblings under his breath along the lines of, "Demanding, aren't we?" I rubbed my wrists, pressing my fingers into the flushed, chafed series of lines across my skin as I threw him a glare.

"Sorry," he murmured. "I tend to get a bit theatrical, at times. 'All the world's a stage', after all. 'And all the men and women merely the sociopathic captors.'"

"It's 'all the men and women merely the *players*', you pretentious idiot," I snapped, still somehow finding the capacity for annoyance. "Now tell me what you are. Tell me how you just did that."

"Most would call us freaks. Some call us villains." He glanced at the door, as if expecting someone to be listening in on what he would say next, and lowered his voice to a conspiratorial whisper. "We call ourselves Persuaders."

"Persuaders." I tried it out on my tongue. Spoken aloud, it struck me as an odd mixture of being both foreign and familiar. "Whom do you persuade, exactly? And to do what? Something tells me that it isn't especially pleasant, whatever you do. You seem like the opportunist type. Coldblooded, self-justifying…" My eyes swept over him head to toe once, a crisp assessment. "Volatile."

He chuckled. "Don't think I'm the only one who's transparent here. Perceptivity. That's a particular Persuader habit. I notice things, too. You get judgmental when you're nervous, did you know? Right now I'm guessing it's because of…me?"

I bit the inside of my cheek. "No," I lied. "And you're avoiding the question again."

He shook his head. "What do you mean by it? Do you mean that in a romantic way? In which case, I am *very* persuasive." He winked, his expression almost playful, except with that ever-present wicked edge that made him appear immediately untrustworthy.

I grimaced. "You're absolutely horrible, you know that?" He shrugged, indifferent. "I was asking what a Persuader *is*. So, you're telekinetic. You move things with your mind—"

"We call it Shifting," Vince supplied, somewhat unhelpfully. He shrugged at the blank look he received. "Among other things. Persuaders are *human*…just…not." He winced, running a hand through his hair, pushing it off of his forehead. "I'm not explaining it right. We've evolved in such a way that we can cause physical changes around us by psychological means."

"Is that what happened with you and Taylor?" He started, clearly not anticipating the question, but I pursued it anyway. "It didn't look like you hit him. It looked like he just…*fell*. For no reason."

Vince glanced away, evasive. "Well, it's not as simple as all that."

"Then explain it to me."

He sighed, appearing both irritated and grudgingly impressed by my persistence. "When a Persuader like myself runs into…*conflict*, he finds it in his best interest to settle things quickly and cleanly. Think of it as a gentlemen's duel. When we close our eyes and take each other's arms like this,"—his hand curled around my upper forearm to demonstrate—"we can see into each other's minds. You can imagine anyplace, any*thing* at all, and the end result possesses elements of both *your* visualization and of your opponent's. The object is to mold the world around you to your advantage until there is a victor. Traditionally, the 'victor' is the one not *dead* by the end of it. It's a lot less messy than the alternatives. No incriminating evidence. No blood. No traceable cause of death. Understand that it's considered *civil*, in our culture, a way to settle disputes."

I considered this for a moment. He'd said our culture. But…but he couldn't mean to say that *Taylor* was one of them. It had to have been some kind of a mistake. "Why didn't you kill Taylor, then? You had the chance." This new revelation didn't make me any less wary of him, however.

"Oh, yes, I certainly *did* have the chance, didn't I?" He still hadn't released my arm.

"Vincent," drawled a slick voice. He stepped away from me hastily. The speaker had only spoken it softly, but the acoustics of the room carried it to the point where it sounded like a shout. "I see you've brought our guest home safely. Congratulations on not frightening her away."

I was about to make a comment about how I had actually tried to escape once or twice and I was, in fact, vaguely petrified of Vince, but the snide remark caught in my throat the moment I saw him.

Liam. As in Michael Liam Cable. My M.I.A. father.

He looked about the same. Clean cut, with wavy dark blonde hair and greenish eyes. His clothes were more expensive looking than I remembered them being, but of course they were. He was wealthy now. He lived in a *mansion.*

Still, there was something about his appearance that seemed—well, that seemed *haggard.* He looked pale, almost translucently so, as if he hadn't seen the sun in years. Liam stopped short when he saw me, as well, surprised but in an almost indefinably repressed sort of way. "Jenny?" he whispered, staring in quiet wonder at his own eyes replicated back at him. He ventured a step forward, inspecting me. His expression became a less-than-careful blend of anxiety and what looked very much like *pain.* Not the customary way a father greeted the daughter he hadn't seen since she was a child, but then again he hadn't been any real *father* to me since I was nine years old and too young to understand the reason why he had left in the first place. A big part of me still didn't understand. "Dear God." His voice was hoarse. "You look so much like your mother."

At that, all the feelings of hatred and blame and disgust I had attributed to him in the past suddenly rose up and burned the back of my throat, begging to be verbalized. "How could you?" I said at last, almost without any inflection to my voice at all.

He looked taken aback. "I don't understand what you mean—"

"How could you?" I snapped, finally losing any semblance of control. "You left us without ever writing or keeping in touch. Not one letter. Not one email or phone call or *anything.* You didn't even come to the goddamn *funeral.* But you didn't care! Just as long as you could finally rid yourself of us and start your life again. News flash: There's no reset button you can push to make it all go away, no matter how badly you want to believe that!"

"Enough!" Liam boomed, the door opening and slamming as he did. All the curtains flapped upward, like a bird's frantic wings in a storm. "I loved your mother. And you. But Heather and I were both too different and too proud to admit it. She told me that I couldn't be half-involved, and that my only two options were to leave completely or to not leave at all. And so I left. I *left* because I was afraid of what might've happened if I had stayed."

"You're not telling me anything I didn't know before," I said, in a low voice. "I always knew you were a coward."

I shoved past Vince—who had stood there, looking bewildered the whole time—to the staircase, taking the steps in twos to get to the top, running toward the first open door I saw and slamming it shut behind me. My hands shook as I turned the lock.

I should've known better than to think that I wasn't a prisoner in this place, and with this revelation I realized that I wasn't the only one, either.

3
SENTRY

TAYLOR

I awoke to the sound of birds outside the window, my cheek pressed into the crook of my elbow.

My eyes snapped open, and I found that my arms were angled awkwardly against my side; I winced as a lance of pain pulsed through my temple at the movement and ricocheted around in my skull. I blinked against the feeling, trying to collect my thoughts and recall why I was here, in Jenny's house, on her couch.

And then I remembered.

The Persuader boy's mind had been cold, colder than any I had ever felt before. I had imagined in my mind's eye a dense forest, muted light slipping through the small breaks in the trees. The Persuader hadn't *imagined* anything. He had used a memory from a time in his distant past. One could always tell the difference. Everything was so sharply defined, so specific. Under the heterochromatic sky—a sky comprised of warring shades of cobalt and crimson—we faced each other from a distance, in some sort of clearing. The forest I had envisioned was around us, albeit icicles hanging from the limbs of the trees and tinkling softly like wind chimes. But, in the center of it all, we were standing knee-deep in rubble, the charred skeleton of a sizable estate surrounding us. And there was snow. A lot of it, too, maybe a foot deep, mixed in with the ash.

Neither of us moved an inch for a moment, as I surveyed my

surroundings and he sized me up with the eyes of a hunter, as if I was an animal about to step right onto a foothold trap.

Then he lifted his hand, and with it a hunk of glass and blackened wood compressed itself into a tight ball and floated just over his head. He smirked. "Your move, Ross."

I didn't stop to consider how he knew my name. I Shifted quickly, sending a charred piece of what was once probably part of a floorboard at him and took off running into the forest.

He cursed as he ducked away, and I heard the collision of the snow and wood with a tree just behind me as he returned the greeting, but I didn't stop running. I kept going and going, deeper and deeper into the forest. I probably would have been able to get farther, and at a faster pace, had the snow not been so deep. It clung to the fabric of my jeans in clumps, melting into my socks.

I finally stopped, clinging to the trunk of a small tree, cold sweat seeping under my collar and dripping down my temples. I spun around in a full circle, painfully alert to every sound, every minute movement of the forest around me.

It was so silent; not even the wind chime icicles on the trees made a sound. When I was very young, long before I had run away, I remembered a storm had caused all the lights and appliances to shut off. I remembered being so amazed that the absence of sounds I had overlooked before, like the hum of a refrigerator, made everything so much quieter.

It was like that as I stood shivering and alone and vigilant in the snow, the branches above me like clasped fingers, keeping me cupped between their palms.

Then the silence erupted and a branch came swinging erratically toward my head.

I ducked just barely in time, the claw-like twigs scratching the back of my neck, icicles breaking off and landing in the snow. Vince broke out of the black trees, skidding to a stop several feet away from me.

We were back where we started, it seemed. I stood, brushing off snow from my jacket, raising my hands.

A bouquet of icicles whistled through the air, and I rolled forward to avoid impalement, throwing out both of my hands as I sprung to my feet again. Two leafless boughs on either side of the Persuader swung toward him simultaneously, fissuring where they nearly broke away entirely from their respective trunks. He leapt high into the air, the branches coming together with a sound like several bones snapping at once as he evaded them unscathed. Though he was an outcross, it was evident that he had the discipline of any full-blooded Persuader—his one noble quality, perhaps, if he had one. Even so, he had known from the start that I was stronger. I raised my hand toward him, a movement so nearly devoid of effort it seemed impossible that it would send his body a moment later slamming against the broad base of the tree at his back. There was a crunching sound as he struck, and I tried not to flinch at it.

The Persuader fell to the snow in a heap, using his elbows to prop himself up, slowly, to a kneeling pose. He spit a mouthful of blood into the snow, his head bowed, coal-black hair hanging over his eyes. "Do as you will," he said, faintly. For a moment I felt complacent in my victory, but that feeling was quickly overwhelmed by shame. I took no pleasure in an unfair match, even if the Persuader was the one who had asked for it in the first place.

And it was during this momentary hesitation that I heard her voice. Disembodied as it was, it sounded almost otherworldly in my ears. *Taylor?*

I straightened at the sound, looking to the sky, caught by surprise.

Apparently, my opponent wasn't too keen on sportsmanship. Before I knew what was happening, or could even look back at the boy, the icy bow of the tree behind me swung right at me, impossibly fast, cracking against the side of my head, and I was out before I hit the snow.

Now conscious, I shook my head to clear it, forcing myself to my feet, ignoring the rush of blood that whooshed in my ears and nearly threw me off-balance. My own bleary-eyed expression stared back at me from the mirror that hung on the wall. I glanced down and with a start saw that Jenny had left her cell phone underneath the coffee table, and realized it must've fallen out of her pocket when she had crouched down next to me. *Call me soon,* she'd said. The task would've been much simpler without this new dilemma, I thought, and I swore under my breath as I bent to retrieve the phone from the floor.

I would have a lot of explaining to do if I saw her again. *When.* I gritted my teeth, and the face in the mirror contorted into one of hard-jawed resolution. *When* I saw her again.

I'd just have to ask around, figure out if anyone had heard anything of a "Mr. Cable" in the area. Near-untraceable as Persuaders tended to be, especially a Persuader as reclusive as Jenny's father was, I had my own ways of finding people.

I'd promised Jenny I'd look out for her, and I didn't intend to go back on that now.

JENNY

My father had looked at me like I was an intruder, nothing more than a trespasser in his carefully reconstructed life, bringing him back into the harsh reality that, yes, he'd had a *different* life before this, a life he had all but managed to escape.

And Vince. That part had stung most of all, the part where I realized that he was, in a sense, my *replacement*. His lovely, cruel face flashed behind my lids. I honestly couldn't see how anyone, even Liam, could live with someone so dark and brooding and narcissistic.

A light rap came on the door, followed by Vince's voice, soft as a cat's purr, yet obviously forced. "Jennifer," he murmured, sounding as if his lips were pressed right up against the wood. "Please open up. Liam's in his office; it's just me."

I didn't believe him. I refused to. "Go away, Vince. It's *your* fault I'm here."

"It's nobody's *fault,*" he said, his tone hardening. "I had an assignment and I carried it out, nothing more. Now open this door or I'll kick it down."

I scrambled away to the opposite wall, just in case his words had any merit to them. "Then I'll just—I'll just..." I looked around frantically for any sort of leverage, and my eyes fixated on the wide, tall window at the far side of the room. "I'll just escape out of the window. It's not so long a..." The curtains were drawn back, and as I approached they revealed a dizzying view of the lawn twenty to thirty feet down. "Fall." My voice was a squeak. I shuddered. Well, scratch that plan.

"You'd better not," he warned, as if he cared if I broke both my legs or not.

I strode over to the door, not daring to open it, but leaned into it instead. "Why *am* I so important to you, Vince? And don't tell me it has anything to do with my father. I'm not stupid."

"Open the door and I'll tell you."

I gritted my teeth. A clever maneuver, granted, but one that only served to further my distrust of him. My hands fumbled for the bolt, and I turned the brass knob slowly, like I was six and about to face the monster in my closet. He leaned casually against the frame, shadows dancing across his secretive eyes, looking nothing like the hideous, ghastly creature I had once imagined inhabited my room. "Why are you keeping me here?" I demanded, and—feeling in a particularly dignified mood—I added, "I find my being forbidden from leaving completely unjustified, by the way. I have my rights. I'm a human being."

"Human being, huh? I wouldn't bet money on that," he said, not kindly, moving around me to stand at the window. "And I don't think you want to know the answer."

"I do," I insisted. "I need to understand."

"The boy—the one you were with—" he began.

"His name is Taylor," I said, slitting my eyes at Vince.

"Whatever." It was as if the name was some vulgar word he didn't care to repeat. "He lied to you."

"Taylor wouldn't lie to me," I said, automatically. Taylor wasn't the kind of person who was dishonest with me if it was important. At least, that was what I had always believed.

"Well, he didn't tell you the truth. That's no different than lying." Vince turned to face me, eyes blazing out of the dimness of the unlit room beneath dark, curving lashes. "He's a Sentry."

"A Sentry?" I asked. "Sorry, I'm not exactly up to date with your fancy Persuader terminology."

Vince rubbed his face, hairline to jaw, clearly annoyed. "A Sentry is like a Persuader, only…more concerned with the morals involved in our lifestyle, I suppose. Or lack, thereof. You see, they don't like what Persuaders do to get all this." He waved his hand in a semi-circle to elaborate.

I suppose I should've been upset with Taylor for not telling me what he was, but that all depended upon if Vince was even telling the truth or not. Still, the evidence that my best friend was possibly something more than human was hard to ignore. "How come?"

"Well," he said, rubbing the back of his neck, "we swindle them, you know, regular people, through the use of our…particular skillset. Keep in mind, we run a rather involved system here. Target any sort of lucrative business—electronics, cars, weapons, drugs, you name it—and I guarantee there's a way to con the unsuspecting out of their life savings within a week. I could walk up to someone right now, on the street, and return with all the money in his pocket. Their minds are so fragile, really. As soft as clay, and just as pliable."

"So...like mind control?" I took a step back. "That's not right."

He pointed an accusing finger at me. "Careful. You're sounding a little too much like a Sentry." Vince threw an arm over his face dramatically. "Oh, the *poor*, innocent people, cheated out of their excess unknowingly." He lowered his arm and rolled his eyes. "It's not as if we're robbing shoes off of the homeless. What's it to the *haut monde* if they lose a little money?"

"But do you return some money to the poor? Like Robin Hood?" Some part of me hoped for at least one, redeeming quality in my father.

"No," Vince said, at length. "We're a business, not a charity foundation." His voice sounded clipped. "They do what they can, the Sentries, to stop us. Ever since they broke away into a separate faction centuries ago, they've become rather...militant. Killing and fighting and bleeding over *nothing*. So much unnecessary violence over regular humans, people they don't even know, people who don't even *deserve* their help. They let their superiority go to waste."

"Is it really a waste?" I asked, quietly. "Defending the powerless?"

Vince looked taken aback. "That hardly has anything to do with the matter at hand," he replied at last, sidestepping the topic altogether.

"Exactly, to which 'matter at hand' are you referring?" I asked, half-heartedly. There seemed to be so much I didn't know about the world now, so much more I needed to know, so many questions I needed answered. It hadn't escaped my notice that, while Vince had freely answered my later enquiries, he had yet to give a clear answer to my original question of why I was so important to him. It was still unclear to me what he hoped to gain from all of this.

He turned toward the window again, his hands folded behind his back. "Your father is a Persuader. Do you know what that means?"

"No." But in reality I had a growing idea, a thorn bush unfurling deep in my chest. I suppose I just didn't want it to be true, and chose to deny it as vehemently as my father had chosen to deny my existence for nearly half of my life.

"It means," he said, angling his face to the side, white teeth flashing from the shadows, "that you'll be one, too. Very soon."

4

PROMISES TO KEEP

There was a knock on the door and, if the trend of the past few days continued, it could be only Vince or Laura. Never my father. He was always in his office downstairs. "Jenny. Please come out. We need to talk."

I had all but nailed myself shut into my room since the day I arrived, refusing to come out or let anyone in except Laura, who pitied me and brought me food and fresh clothes to put in my dresser. *The* dresser, I reminded myself. Silently, I scolded my referencing it as *my* room. *My* room no longer existed. To *have* a room, you needed a home, not just a particularly and unreasonably large house that you were stuck living in. If I really thought about it, did I really have anything at all in the world that was mine? "Get lost, Vince. How many times do I have to tell you? I *don't* want to see him."

"You don't have to see Liam," Vince said, almost soothingly. "It's just me again. Alone. Look, I'm sorry about earlier but someone needed to tell you the truth. If you'll only open the door, I'll tell you anything you want to know."

I scoffed. "Why don't you just kick it down, *darling?*"

"Do *not,*" Vince said, tautly, "mock me. And I respect your privacy to some degree. I prefer to wait. You'll have to let me in sometime. It's either that or I'll tell Laura to stop bringing you your morning coffee."

"But—"

"Worse," he warned, gravely. "I'll tell her to start brewing decaf."

I hopped off of my—*the* bed, turning the lock and springing away just as quickly, distancing myself from him. Vince walked in, and I was surprised to see he wasn't dressed to the nines like he had been before. He folded his arms, the material of his close-fitting gray t-shirt pulling tight around his shoulders and biceps—*not* that I noticed his shoulders and biceps in any particular way. I raised my eyebrows at him. "Jeans?"

He looked down at himself. "What? You think just because I live in a Victorian mansion with imported furniture and a maid, I don't own regular clothes? That's bigotry, and I will not stand for it. Besides, it's not as if you're even attempting at *decent,* much less regular." He gestured to my rumpled pajamas.

"I don't care about looking nice," I informed him curtly.

"You should." He took a step toward me, his expression mild yet drawn inward some, his brow furrowing. "Persuader society is one that concerns itself about *image.* You have to learn to fit in."

"But I'm not a Persuader!" My outburst was abrupt enough to visibly startle him. "You said—"

"No cause for alarm," he amended, quickly, hand outstretched as if he meant to comfort me. "I only meant that someone of your background shouldn't dress in such an...*unbecoming* way."

I ignored the way he said "unbecoming", knowing it was really an only slightly nicer way to say "unattractive". "Background," I repeated. "Huh. Background I wasn't even aware of a week ago."

"You're plenty aware now, though. That's what matters." He cleared his throat lightly. "Perhaps I should tell you about a little something called an Embracement, now. Yes, that's a capital E, before you ask. It's quite literally the most important event in the life of a Persuader, so listen up because I will *not* be repeating myself."

I scrunched my nose suspiciously. "Did Liam put you up to this? I didn't ask to be schooled on the oh-so-important cultural highlights of Persuader life, you know."

"You'll either learn these things the easy way or the hard way. Little piece of advice: The latter option includes you most likely having to spend a lot more quality time with Liam." I was silent. "As I thought."

He fell backward on the foot of the bed, patting the space next to him. I remained standing, eliciting only a shrug from him. "Just figured this was something you needed to be sitting down for. At some point it involves…things about your mother."

I rocked back on my heels as the word "mother" found a way to bite at me. But I didn't sit down.

"The Embracement," Vince began, leaning back onto the silk sheets and tucking his arms beneath his head, "is a very old ritual. Think of it as a coming of age gathering. What you know up to this point is that there are Persuaders and that there are Sentries. You know what each stands for and you know that somehow you're one of us. What you *haven't* been told is that the Adjudication demands that all Unavowed—that's you, by the way—when they turn eighteen must align themselves with one circle or the other. There's no way around it."

"What does this have to do with my mother?" I considered clamping my hands over my ears, but that seemed both pointless and childish.

"Well, you see, your mother was a Sentry—"

"I'm sorry," I interrupted, holding out my arm to stop him as the world took a sudden, violent tilt around me, "but did you just say my mother was a Sentry?"

Vince smiled grimly. "Quite the Romeo and Juliet story, really. A Persuader and a Sentry. I'm surprised they lasted for so long together at all."

"She never told me…" I sunk to the floor then, my legs unable to hold me up anymore. My fingers curled into my palms, making scratching sounds against the cold wood.

"Of course she didn't." I blinked and Vince was there, kneeling at my side. I was too dazed to move away. "She never wanted any of this to affect you. This war. She experienced it first-hand. People didn't exactly *approve* of their marriage or…really, you existing."

"Vince?" I asked, mindful of the wary look he tossed me. "There had to be another reason other than your little assignment for Liam for you to be keeping me here, or you wouldn't have attacked Taylor. You wouldn't have stopped me when I tried to run away. And don't avoid the question this time." I turned my head, unflinching as I met his gaze only inches from mine. He didn't move away, either, I noticed, though he was hardly the type to back away from a challenge. "Call it Persuader intuition, but I suspect you aren't telling me everything."

"I should've expected that." Vince nodded to himself. "I suppose

Taylor didn't mention to you that he's on the Most Wanted list of every Persuader within a two-hundred mile radius? Not too popular with the Wardens, either."

He didn't seem inclined to reveal to me what a Warden was, so I moved to the subsequent question in my head. "Is Taylor a criminal?"

"Not exactly," he sighed. "A lot of people want him found. You see, his parents are Persuaders, ones that hold rather high status. Particularly his father, who works with the government. When he turned eighteen, he defied three generations of Persuader ancestry and went Sentry, and not only that but failed to align himself with a stronghold. Which makes him what we call a *rogue*. Things like this don't happen every day, so he's almost as much of a rarity as you are. We would prefer him imprisoned. Or dead." I winced. "Sentries, on the other hand, see great potential in him. Those under the age of eighteen—the Unavowed, like you—aren't usually privy to a lot of information, but Taylor was high up on the social ladder, even for a Persuader, so he overheard...many important discussions, which is why the Sentries want him. Information. That's always the incentive, isn't it?"

I glanced off to the side, so Vince couldn't see my eyes begin to tear up. Taylor, a Sentry and a hunted man. Aloud I said, "Everyone I trusted...*every one of them* has lied to me for all this time. No one ever told me any of this."

"If it helps, I just told you *a lot* of things. I'm very particular about honesty at all times. Well, most times, anyway," he offered, and then he shifted so he was sitting on the ground. He didn't seem to be able to stay in one place or position for any extended amount of time. "Back there I...I saw who you were with, recognized his face. Taylor Ross, Sentry rogue extraordinaire. I realized it was an excellent opportunity to draw him here, to the mansion. I admit, the thought of being the one to catch him was an enticing one. It's not every day something like this happens, you know. Especially not here. Sue me if I wanted a little excitement."

My brow creased. "Before...how did he know that you...well..."

"That I had ill intentions in store for him?" Vince finished, not without a tinge of humor. It wasn't like Taylor's, which came as naturally as his smile. Vince's humor was darker, more strained than anything else. "You know we can sense one another? From quite a distance away, actually. Something to do with intercepting the signals another's mind emits; it's all very boring. Anyway, I'm sure he knew what I was almost immediately."

"Then he knew that I had Persuader blood from the moment we met. He *knew* and he never told me."

"If you live with a secret for long enough, it starts to change you. Define you. Make you act a certain way. Try not to judge him so harshly; there are plenty of people who will do that for you." Vince smiled cheerfully at this, but after a moment it distorted into more of a slanting leer. "In all honesty, I thought you were his girlfriend. He looked at you...like you were. I figured that I could draw him to this house, where I would have the means to apprehend him, by making *you* the damsel in distress."

"As if," I scoffed, finding the capacity to be indignant, yet something else about what Vince said before unnerved me. "What did you mean when you said he looked at me a certain way?"

"Come now, Jenny," he crooned, his mouth curling up at the corner. "He was nice to you. He was there for you. He brought you under his wing. If that doesn't create...*special* feelings, I don't know what would."

I flushed, straight up to my hairline. I tried in vain to come up with something to fire back at him. "You don't know anything about him...how could you even...?" I stopped, taking a deep breath, realizing this was a battle I could not win. "So you think he's coming for me right now?"

"I know it."

It grinned at me with black and white teeth, a sly smile that held an unnatural gleam in the dim lighting. Somehow I ended up right in front of the monster, brushing off dust from its oil black hide, trailing my fingers along the inside of its gaping maw, never daring to press too hard.

"I could teach you, sometime."

I whirled to see Vince, back in his formal attire, hands clasped behind his back inquisitively.

"No, thank you," I huffed, turning back around, still idly brushing keys.

Two hands slipped around me and came down over my own, fingers directing mine where to go. A familiar song poured from the piano, soft yet in its sparse melody somehow capable of filling the room. I could feel how close he was. He was so near his chest was almost against my back, his arms like an embrace around me. I wanted to move away, but when I turned to tell him to stop, his viper's gaze caught mine. My mind began to fuzz around the edges. I blinked rapidly, trying to form a coherent phrase. "Vince…"

"Moonlight Sonata," he murmured, eyes darting about my face. "*Quasi una fantasia*. Granted, a little cliché. It's possibly Beethoven's best-known piece, yet no one ever seems to appreciate it as it should be appreciated." He looked down, finally releasing me, backing away with an upward tilt to his lips. "Which is to *learn it*. The growing lack of musicianship in this country continues to put me at unease."

I smiled a little at that, avoiding his gaze just as intensely as he appeared to be avoiding mine. "Well, it *is* cliché, but it's also beautiful. Sad."

"You should get ready," he said, so abruptly my hip struck the piano, causing a cacophony of sour low notes.

"For what?"

"We're going out." His smile was that of a villain and a gentleman combined.

The dress looked ridiculous on me. I wanted to laugh. No, I wanted to hide. The thought of anyone—especially Vince—seeing me in something so *gaudy* was downright humiliating. It was too *shiny*, for one. The material was gray, but with silvery sequins parading all about it in a sweeping swirl up the front, casting off blinding flashes of light whenever I moved. It was also one-shouldered, and the hemline was awfully short for a "formal" event, leaving me with more skin exposed than I particularly cared.

Laura sat back after she was finished her work on my stubborn tangles, moving in place the last of the opal pins, which pinched my scalp uncomfortably. "Don't you look nice," she sighed. "I knew I saw a pretty girl underneath that mess who came to us only a week ago." As if I were an abandoned puppy. I tried to conceal my scoff of irritation.

The old woman smiled, her face wrinkled particularly around the eyes, like an old handkerchief crumpling. She must have smiled a lot, or she used to smile, in her younger days. I couldn't begin to imagine why.

She made a sort of chuckle then, grinning down at the corner of the bathroom mirror as she splashed me—attacked me—with an odd smelling perfume in a round, blue glass bottle. It didn't smell *bad* or anything, just…odd. Not like my mother's perfume. She smelled like gardenias. If I closed my eyes, I could almost imagine her scent—or the memory of it, at least—around me. Then I started, realizing something peculiar. "What's so funny?" I knew I sounded rude and demanding, but I couldn't help it. Was it my imagination, or did she have a habit of responding to my *thoughts?*

Laura just shook her head a little. "Nothing, dear, nothing."

I decided to risk it. With a deep breath I asked, "Can you...read minds, Laura?" She went very still, so still she didn't appear to be breathing. "I was just wondering. I mean...since everyone in this house can do such unusual things, I thought it wouldn't be crazy to ask."

I was starting to wonder if I had given her a stroke when she, very brusquely, realigned all the perfumes and make up kits and jewelry boxes. "I suspect Vincent is, ah, anticipating your reappearance. Best that you make your way down."

Without another word, she left.

She had been right, of course. Vince was waiting for me, standing with his hands behind his back—oh-so-formally—in the yellow-white sphere of the porch light. It was chilly outside, but I was afraid Vince might grow impatient with me if I went back to get something more substantial than the light jacket I had found and thrown on last minute. I had seen his temper; it was best to remain on his good side. He turned as I shut the front door behind me, eyes cloudy for a moment, as if reminiscing. They cleared as his gaze swept over me from head to toe. I didn't know if I should've been embarrassed or annoyed by his lazy, up-and-down glance. I cleared my throat. He looked back at my face, head slightly tilted, his assessment complete. "Shall we go?"

Did I imagine a challenge in his tone? Typical. "We shall."

The car ride was silent.

Well, silent until I finally lost my patience. "It's been hours! Where are we *going?*"

Vince sighed, my outburst obviously interrupting his precious quiet. Did the sound of my voice just annoy him right off? "It hasn't been that long." He rolled his eyes at my childish anxiety. "Think of this as a kind of...field trip. Educational. You'll see where we're going soon enough. We should be entering Baltimore in a bit."

"Baltimore." I nodded, wondering what Persuader wonders could possibly wait for us there. "Okay, why?"

"You'll see."

"You know what?" I snapped. "I think you enjoy being cryptic."

"Perhaps," he admitted, not looking at me, though I could see his mouth twitch.

"You're impossible." I ground my teeth, staring furiously out the window.

"Perhaps," he repeated, a wry smile threatening to spill over onto his face. Was he ever serious? "I often find myself wondering how Laura's put up with me for all these years."

"Laura's certainly one of a kind." After a long pause, I asked, "Can she…is Laura some kind of mind-reader? I mean, *actually* one." It was an abrupt, unprovoked question, but for some reason I needed to know. It was like solving a mystery, playing detective.

Vince blinked in surprise. "Laura? Read minds? No…no, only the very strong and very experienced can read another Persuader's mind. We were told Laura is of a weak parentage. Only a quarter Persuader."

I sat back in my seat, not pushing the subject but still not entirely convinced. "Even so," I said, "I think Laura merits a little more credit than you're willing to give her."

Vince looked ahead, a line forming between his eyebrows. "I—" He stopped, peering at a large building looming to our right, doors gleaming in the bronze light of the streetlamp, very inviting. The car crawled into an open space several blocks away. "We're here. Seems packed," he noted, looking behind us at the queue of cars lining the sidewalk and then in front of us at the queue of people.

He slid out, coming around, the perfect gentleman once again, to open my door and offer a hand to help me out. I ignored it. The door slammed roughly behind me, almost snagging my dress. I turned to glare at Vince, but he was already down the block. I hurried—as fast as I could in the stupid heels—to catch up with his long strides and take my place beside him in line. When we got to the door, Vince inclined his head to the man standing there, beefy arms crossed over his chest. A doorman. He looked more like a bouncer. "I hope you're on the list," I murmured in his ear.

Vince smiled good-naturedly at him, clearing his throat. "Vincent Hallows."

The man stiffly consulted a clipboard in his hands. "Welcome, Mr. Hallows." The doorman's voice was more polite than I thought it would be, though it didn't hold any warmth, either. We were prepared to go in when the man stopped me. His gaze bore into mine, darkening under heavy brows. "Wait. Who's this?"

"It's okay. She's my," he paused to look at me, his face filled with so much affection I almost lost my balance, "date."

I choked and would have remained standing there had he not taken me by the arm and led me inside. When we were past the prying eyes of the doorman, I turned to him. "Since when am I your date?"

His eyes had lost the warm glow they had held before, and I realized he was simply a very, very good actor. What other emotions did he pretend, I wondered? "Since now. You have to go along with it tonight. Can you do that?"

"Well, I didn't vomit at the mere suggestion of it," I replied, enjoying the quick flash of annoyance sweep across his face. "Not yet, anyway. So I think we should be good."

He shook his head, taking my hand and leading me to an elevator off to the side of the lobby. I rapped a fingernail on the glass of the doors, which covered the ornate bronze underneath. Suddenly—irrationally, maybe—I was afraid to see the main event, afraid that it would be...too much. But the doors slid open and Vince all but shoved me inside. I took a moment to admire the plush red velvet lining the interior, the reflective white and gold walls around me. Then Vince spoke, all business. "Okay, remember this: You are not to speak until I tell you to. Don't talk about your parentage. Don't say anything about yourself or who you are besides your first name. Understand?"

"Sir, yes, sir!" I stood at attention, saluting him. "And here I thought we were here to have fun."

"It may seem like a party," he said, "but it's really just a way for other people to decide if you're a threat to them or not. If we meet a man named Samuel, don't speak to him except to exchange a few polite words. Got it?"

"Why, is he some sort of creep?"

Vince sighed. "If only it was just that. Think of him as a sort of...tyrant. He has money. He has power. He has friends in high places. No, worse. He *is* the friend in a high place. You don't cross him. Especially if you're practically his next door neighbor like we are."

I nodded. "Okay. Don't speak much. I got it."

"And don't forget it," he warned. "You are the *epitome* of brainless arm candy."

Before I could think of a way to inflict an appropriate amount of pain upon my "date", the doors dinged open and I had to stifle a gasp.

The room was huge and seemed to be effortlessly keeping up with the red, gold, and white themes I had observed before in the lobby. The carpet was the color of rich, red wine, sweeping under mahogany furniture and silken sofas and gold curtains pulled open to reveal a dizzying sight of the city below. We were higher up than I originally thought. Chandeliers hung like pendulums above us. And the people. There were so many people. All dressed in attire particularly superior to mine. Of course. I didn't see many Persuaders my age, mostly just adults with faces that looked like they had tried and failed to look *closer* to my age through painful, expensive means. They took the time to scan the room every few seconds as if hoping for a new person to skewer. Dozens of eyes found Vince and me, pinning us to the wall like butterflies. "Vince," I whispered. "I'm a little terrified right now."

He turned his head slightly to look at me, eyebrows raised as if he was offended that I doubted him. "Just stick close to me and you'll be fine."

I breathed in deeply through my nose. "Okay." I grabbed his arm, and we dove headfirst into the wolves' den of a party.

Many people spoke of their "profits" and "investments". "Oh, yes, I see this business going very far for us in the future...I did enjoy the look on her face as she handed me the check...I can't believe how easy it was to convince him to give me complete and utter ownership...!" Some bragged of their wealth in a way that made my skin prickle with irritation. "Yes, the ebony I had shipped from Indonesia...I fired the idiot because he tore a hole in my $10,000 dress...These chandeliers are just *darling*, much smaller than the ones I have at home..." To someone who hadn't had much growing up, these people dismissing grand things as if they were children bored of their toy dolls made me hate every single one of them.

A hand came down on my shoulder, and I looked up in surprise to see a girl, maybe a little older than myself, smiling at me. At first all I could focus on was the circumference of her eye shadow, and felt a prickle of annoyance that somehow she pulled it off. Further assessment discerned that she was very pretty, with pale brown hair, a decidedly aristocratic face, and a general ambiance about her that invited members of the opposite sex like the glow of electricity drew in moths. Her dress was a deep burgundy, with a hemline that tumbled to the floor. I tugged at my own dress self-consciously. Also noted: Her eyes wouldn't stop darting over to Vince, at my shoulder, who was studiously ignoring the girl.

"Haven't seen you here before," she said, voice raised to be heard above the insipid noise. "What's your name?"

I glanced at Vince. He nodded, almost imperceptibly. "Jenny."

The girl smiled. "I'm Gwen." Her eyes flickered to Vince again. "Are you a friend of Vince's?"

She looked so tragically hopeful that I *was* just a friend, and for a moment I deliberated dismissing the whole date alibi altogether, but Vince made up my mind for me. "Actually, she's my date for this evening."

The girl's face fell just the slightest bit, but she recovered, rather impressively, and looked at me again. "Oh. Well, you two look good together. Vince must be really," she paused to stare at our linked arms, *"serious* about you."

She melted back into the crowd and I turned to him. "Have a falling out with her?"

He disentwined our arms to rub his jaw, looking very tired. "We dated once upon a time. She's a good person, she is. But she's just as vapid and self-absorbed as the rest of them. She just wanted to have the most expensive things and go to the most prestigious events. I told her I needed to find someone more…serious."

"I don't think she's self-absorbed," I said, looking toward the sofa where she'd sulked off to. "Otherwise she wouldn't have been so *absorbed* with you the whole time we were talking. I think you may have broken her heart."

"You think I don't know that?" Vince demanded, looking upset for the first time since her appearance. "I didn't mean to. I don't blame her for how she is. She was raised that way. But I just…I can't feel anything particularly special about someone so shallow. I'm sure she'll get over it eventually."

I nodded. "You want to date for love, not money. That's actually kind of admirable."

Vince coughed, astonished. "Never thought you'd use that adjective to describe me."

"Don't get used to it," I said, not wanting him to get any ideas about—I shuddered to think it, even—*friendship*. It would not be unlike Rapunzel befriending the witch who locks her away in the tower. "Why'd we even come here if you knew she might show up?"

"So you can see how Persuaders interact in a real setting."

"I don't like it." I scrunched my nose, trying to tune out the plump man beside me with a shiny, sweaty, bald head who was busy talking about his eleven or so cars.

"Figured you wouldn't. Look, why don't we get out of here and step out on the town for our next lesson?"

I nodded fervently. "Yes, let's. But you should tell me now if there's any more ex-girlfriends I should be on the lookout f—"

"Vincent Hallows. How good it is to see you." The voice was calm and low, but it still managed to glide across the room to where Vince and I stood, quieting all the Persuaders within earshot. A man emerged from the tightly packed bodies, walking toward us through a sudden gap that had formed in the crowd. He reached us, smiling, but in a contemptuous way that I hated immediately. His hair was a light copper color, slicked back, not a strand out of place, his eyes very, very dark. His suit was expensive looking, the shirt underneath a deep maroon. "And who is this?" He eyed me with half suspicion, half curiosity.

"This is Jenny," Vince said, equally composed, which was an impressing accomplishment in itself. The man, though average in outward appearance, had a sort of palpable authority circulating around him that chilled me.

"Jenny," he echoed. "You look…familiar. Have any parents I might know?"

"No," Vince said, quickly. "They're both dead. Terrible accident." I went along, trying my best to look sad and pathetic.

"Of course," the man said, a tick in his jaw. "That would make sense. Two of a kind, rather." I gawked at Vince, wondering why he had never told me his parents were dead. But I guessed one *rarely* spilled one's tragic life story on a first date. "I am Samuel Locke, by the way, Miss Jennifer." He extended a hand.

I stiffened. Samuel. It couldn't be the same…

I looked at Vince, his face tense and guarded. It could. Fighting the tremor radiating throughout my entire arm, I reached for his offered hand.

His fingers curled around my wrist in a sudden movement, and I had to smother a gasp at the painful jolt that went through me, as if he had stuck needles into my skin. Samuel's eyes narrowed, like he knew we were

WICKED GAME

lying. I released his hand, grabbing Vince's for support instead. "If you don't mind, Mr. Locke," I said, the tremor now in my voice, as well, "we really must be going."

Samuel regarded me with something disturbingly keen for a moment. Then he turned his bottomless, black-brown eyes on Vince. "You haven't heard anything regarding...a rogue Sentry, have you? David Ross's son. Taylor. There've been rumors recently. Forgive me for asking, but...oh, you know, with Liam's inclination toward the lesser faction."

To his credit, Vince seemed unfazed. I, however, couldn't stop the light shudder that passed through me. "No, sir."

As we turned to leave, Samuel stopped us, speaking again, "For future reference, Jennifer, you look too much like your mother to pass as anyone else. I don't know why you two are keeping things from me, but I find it rather...suspect. And I would think your parents would be ashamed of your behavior, Vincent, were they with us now."

Vince's back stiffened, as if Samuel had just dumped ice water down his collar. Without thinking, I turned, livid, on a faintly surprised Samuel and said, "Yes, I think they would be ashamed. Ashamed that he's wasted even a second of his time speaking to someone like you. If you'll excuse us."

The din had died down a little at my outburst. Samuel appeared to not know quite what to say. I'd completely disoriented him, and that had made him...angry. I could see in his eyes his astonishment start to dissolve into rage, and I snatched Vince's sleeve and hauled him toward the elevator.

"I didn't know you had a sharp tongue on you." Vince finally said, in a conversational tone. I stared out the window, at the rows and rows of decaying cornstalks flashing by, curled in on themselves and spotted brown. "Never mind, yes I did. In any case, it was nicely done. It was *stupid*, but it was still nicely done. He did not expect *that*. Probably plotting retaliation as we speak." Vince chuckled.

"It's not funny," I grumbled, burying my face in the crook of my arm. "I just seriously pissed off a tyrannical psycho who I'm sure could easily have me 'taken care of' in a heartbeat if he wanted to." After a mournful pause, I added, "This is why I don't go to parties."

"Why'd you stand up for me, anyway?" he asked. "You owe me nothing."

41

"True," I said. "But I just…I don't know…I sympathized. And I also really, really hated that look of his. I wanted to smack it off."

"Sympathized," he echoed, hands flexing on the wheel. "Because of your mother."

I swallowed. *Don't cry. Not here.* "How come you never told me about your parents?" I demanded, pushing the subject back at him.

"Why does it matter?" he seemed to be puzzled by my sudden urgency.

"I don't know. It's just that I might…well, it might've—"

"Humanized me," he finished. "Is that what you were going to say? That you might've hated me less if you'd known that I feel pain, too? That I haven't been just some sheltered brat sucking on a silver spoon my whole life?"

For a moment I was at a loss for words. Then I said, quietly, "Is that why you're different from them? So…isolated from everything? Wait, no, I didn't mean to say that."

"No, it's true," Vince sighed. "I am a little distant from it all at times. To them it's all about money and notability, power and decadence. None of them care about anything of any worth at all. They haven't been through anything close to what you and I have been through."

I wasn't sure if I liked being clumped with Vince in the same group or not, as some part of me still didn't fully trust him. I didn't respond.

"Aren't you coming in?"

Vince stood in the doorway, suit jacket slung over one shoulder carelessly. I shrugged, trying my best to look nonchalant. Trying my best not to look as rattled as I felt. "I think I'll stay out here for a little while. I need the air."

He yawned, nodding a few times as he waved his hand at me dismissively. "Suit yourself if you want to freeze." He moved as if to go inside the house and close the door, but at the last moment he paused and turned back to me, holding out his jacket stiffly. "Here, take it."

His voice was curt, and he shut the door firmly behind him before I could get out so much as a "thank you". I turned and started off down the road, aimlessly. At least the jacket as I wrapped it around my shoulders was warm, but the night was cold. It was so infernally cold, and I shivered as the breeze threaded through the insubstantial material of my dress and numbed any area of skin exposed. Leaves scraped against pavement, the sound of their rustling the only sound. I wasn't sure where I was going, just as I wasn't sure why I took comfort in the numbness in my hands and the loneliness of the stars.

Up ahead, I saw twin beams of light, the only illumination so far aside from the glow of the near-full moon. I shielded my face, trying to see through the glare. There was a rumbling, like distant thunder. Maybe not so distant as it came closer—

I barely had time to scramble out of the way as a sleek, black car growled past me, a blur of motion and metal. There was the squeal of brakes, and the car came to a halt, so still it was like it hadn't been moving at a demonic speed just a moment before. Two people got out, both dressed in black. The taller of the two had a beaky, crooked nose and an equally crooked smile. The slender Hispanic woman beside him had something in her hand, shielded by her body. The thin man still smiled his charlatan's smile, his teeth oddly sharp-looking. He reminded me of a rat.

"Oh, good. We didn't have to drive *all the way* up to the mansion. Better not to have to deal with Liam getting in the way. Wouldn't you agree, Cira?"

"Much better," the woman agreed in a voice somehow at the same time like silk and like barbs stuck in the flesh. She pulled out the object from behind her back.

It was a knife.

I froze, not making a sound, not even as the two stepped closer to me, not even as the man produced a crowbar in his scarred, long-fingered hand. He brought it down, lightly, over and over again in his palm. I stayed where I was, though every thought that tore through my brain screamed at me to do the opposite.

The woman, with a sadistic smile, raised her knife in a flash of liquid silver. Absurdly, all I did was lift my hand toward her, as if to block it.

I watched, with a horrific-roadside-accident fascination, as she went flying, slamming into the back window of the car, the glass spider-webbing beneath her. I hadn't even touched her. She tumbled to the ground, landing hard on her elbows, and the man's eyes flew wide, his mouth forming around the word "impossible".

He abandoned the crowbar—sending it clanging against the ground—for a gun tucked away in the waistband of his black pants.

The woman lifted her head, seeing the weapon held in her partner's shaking grip, her eyes wide. "Thom!" She attempted to drag herself to her knees, wincing. "We were told to just scare her!"

"We were told she was harmless, too." His pale, flat eyes flashed to my face. "Apparently we were misinformed."

It was then that I took in a huge, gasping breath, my heart stuttering into double-time. *No!* I wanted to scream. *No, I'm not dangerous! Leave me alone!* But once again, any basic self-preservation skills abandoned me in an instant. My tongue felt like a gag, my lips like two pieces of cloth stitched together. The man took aim, and his index finger moved to rest on the trigger. Time moved on like syrup, and I realized that this wasn't a dream or a hallucination or a game. This was real. I was going to die. A new figure moved into my peripheral vision, and I heard the sound of the gun as it fired.

And then...and then there my attacker was, in that same instant on the ground as flashes of light cartwheeled across my vision. My own legs gave way shortly afterward, and I saw him just a few feet from me, someone leaning over him, the crowbar clutched in the figure's hand. Thom held his side, groaning in agony.

Then the pain registered, and it was as if someone had injected hot metal into my veins. I cried out as I attempted to move my head, trying to catch a glimpse of the source of the pain. I saw the blood first, much darker than I'd always thought blood was, freckling the ground beneath me.

I could feel the rest of me go cold, absolutely still, as I saw the wound. It was a small hole, but just the sight of the ragged flesh—and was that *bone?*—within it made me want to faint. Blood bloomed, like a grotesque sort of flower, around my leg, staining the expensive dress.

There were thwacking sounds, and sharp cries, and then nothing else except a clattering as the crowbar was hurled against the side of the car. I heard footsteps drawing near, but the most I could do was turn my head to the side. Distantly, my gaze came to rest on my arm, startlingly pale against the asphalt, fingers clawing spastically as bits of rock got up under my nails.

I felt myself being hoisted up and cradled into someone's chest, and my head lolled back to take in two very blue, very clear, very familiar eyes. The uneven brown hair. The crease of concern between the brows. I knew it all. Taylor. He'd come at last. He had come to rescue me at last.

5
WITHOUT EXPECTATION

TAYLOR

The morning light inched forward, slithering off the windowsill and onto the cold floor. It then crawled dimly and with great subtlety to the bed, where it grabbed hold of the blankets and hoisted itself up so it lay across the sleeping girl beneath the covers. It reached out with cautious fingers to brush her face with a possessive deliberation.

She stirred, mumbling something incoherently. She sighed, a single word able to be heard more distinctly than the others: "Taylor."

I straightened, startled out of my half-unconscious state. I had thought she was asleep. "Yes?"

She went back to mumbling, her chin tucking down into one shoulder. I blinked. She *was* asleep. I stood, unable to help the slow grin stretching across my face. A sleep-talker, eh? Interesting. In a few strides I was kneeling at the side of the bed, chin propped in my hands. "What is it?" I whispered, wondering if she was going to answer like she would consciously, or if it was going to be something slurred and nonsensical like "unicycling goldfish".

"Liam…" she sighed, almost too soft to hear.

Someone cleared his throat behind me and, at once, I shot to my feet, spinning around. Liam stood, arms crossed over his suited torso, perfectly still with a ramrod-straight posture. His face was both like his daughter's and not. Hers had softer lines to it, a trace of gentleness that his didn't have. But there was no denying that the identical shape and color of their

45

eyes, their similarly defined cheekbones, and their analytical demeanors undoubtedly marked them flesh and blood. Liam spoke, his voice deep and controlled, yet still tense, like a distant roll of thunder. "I thought I told you to wait outside the room."

I swallowed. He certainly possessed a formidable presence. I felt like he would send me flying out the window with a flick of his wrist at any moment. I didn't doubt his capability—or willingness—to do just that. The only thing that kept me safe at that moment was the fact that I had kind of saved his daughter's life. "Sorry. I-I just wanted to make sure she was...okay."

Liam scoffed, stalking past me to stand at the foot of Jenny's bed, hand over his mouth. "*Okay*. As if any of this is okay!" He whirled on me. "Who did it?"

I blinked, rocking back a little on my heels. "Sir?"

Liam glared at me with a dry sort of impatience, as if I was the biggest idiot he had ever laid eyes on. "The attack, boy. Who attacked my daughter?"

"I-I didn't see their faces too well," I stuttered. "But I think they were Persuaders."

For a moment Liam was silent, then he went back to glaring at me. "Persuaders? Impossible." He grabbed me by my collar, and I fought the urge to flinch from the contact. "Now, without your lies, *tell me*—"

"It's the truth," mumbled a groggy voice over his shoulder.

He released me, and we both turned to look at Jenny, elbows gathered under her as she tried to sit up. Her eyes were in slits, the sunlight paling the crescents of color within.

Without much conscious thought, I had moved to her side, helping her prop herself up. She cast me a grateful, if not slightly bleary, look before saying, to Liam, "He's...not lying. They were from Samuel." She paused to catch her breath, as if the subject matter was exhausting her. "Samuel Locke."

Liam's face turned white. He went very still, fists clenching and unclenching at his sides. Then his brow drew low, and with a voice that barely masked his incredulity, he simply said, "I'll be sure to have a word with him" and bolted from the room.

I looked at Jenny, her at me, both of us startled and very confused. She ran a hand through her hair, fingers threading through the strands until they hit knots, then she just dropped her hand back into her lap. "Well, good morning," she sighed, heavy on the sarcasm.

"How's the leg?"

She looked down at herself, eyes large, as if suddenly remembering she had been *shot*. "You tell me. I've been out cold."

"Your maid, Laura, was a nurse back in the day, I guess. Or…something. She says that the bullet just nicked you. You were lucky." Maybe "lucky" wasn't really the word for it. "No bones fractured."

She breathed a deep sigh of relief. "That's good. Still hurts like hell, though."

We sat there in silence for a moment, not looking at each other. I had a feeling I knew what was on her mind. "You're mad at me, aren't you?" I asked at last, bracing myself for her reaction. "Look, I'm sorry I didn't tell you I was a Sentry and all—"

"Taylor," she interrupted. A small grin spread across her face, and she punched me in the arm. "I think you more than made up for it by *saving my life*, dork."

"Oh, good. Good." I rubbed my palms together and smiled back at her for a moment, but the smile faded when I remembered what Liam had said, before. "What your Dad said… It didn't strike you as a little, I don't know, *odd*? I guess I just expected him to be a little more upset by this." Even a father like Liam cared about these things, right?

She laughed and then winced as the movement seemed to make the pain in her leg flare up again. "Are you kidding? *Liam*, look unrestrained in front of a Sentry?" She leaned back against the enormous headboard, staring at her hands as they folded together in her lap. "Besides, he doesn't care about me, anyway."

I spluttered. "But he's your father."

Jenny shook her head, gaze still stubbornly downcast. "I thought that, too, once. When I was eight. Now I know better. He's only after his own self-gain. Whatever he thinks will fill that void in him, he strives to have it. He thought my mother would do the job. She didn't. He left. Guess it wasn't Romeo and Juliet after all."

I blinked, taking a seat at the edge of the covers. "What did you say?"

Jenny stared at me, perplexed. "My mom…was a Sentry. I know it's kind of unheard of—"

"No," I interrupted, as faces and scraps of conversations flashed across the front of my mind, culled from dim childhood memories I hadn't even known I'd possessed. But, then again, a Persuader's brain was capable of clinging to memories even from as far back as infancy. That phrase 'Romeo and Juliet'…it called to mind certain things. "I remember hearing about your parents. I was very young. They had just separated, and their marriage in the first place was…quite the scandal. Everywhere. Sentries were outraged. Persuaders were furious. I remember my father…he said, 'That child of theirs—'" I broke off, aware of Jenny's mildly panicked expression.

"What?" she demanded, leaning forward without thinking again, eliciting another twinge of pain across her face. "What did he say?"

"'That child of theirs…'" I let out a slow exhale. "'It'll be too powerful for its own good.'"

"Powerful?" she repeated, eyebrows arching into her hairline. "Me? But I…I don't understand. I literally just realized I had these powers last night. How could I be powerful?"

I tried to grab another sentence my parents had exchanged, but all I got was a word. Undiluted. "Your parents are both full-blooded. Like mine. So you *are* powerful, in the typical sense. But you have something I didn't have when I went rogue."

"A decision without expectation," she said, sitting back again, suddenly looking exhausted, as if the whole world balanced carefully on her shoulders.

"How did you—?"

"Vince told me about my parents, and the Embracement. He didn't go into specifics about what that meant for me. I get it now. People want to sway me."

"Under the laws of the Adjudication, all Unclaimed have a right to decide where they want to belong, but in reality people never really anticipate that Persuaders would ever want to leave a life of luxury or that Sentries would ever abandon their strongholds. I chose what I had to, knowing there was no stronghold that would take the son of David Ross in as one of its own, and I have to face the consequences of that. *You* have a birthright to either one."

"I wish I could give this all back," she murmured. "Give back all this nonsense and trade it for my old life. I wish everything would go back to normal."

"I've wished for things to be normal ever since I was a kid. But then I guess we would never have met." Her hand slipped into mine, an almost automatic gesture, and I allowed myself to take comfort in it.

After a few moments she nodded off again, her head against my shoulder. I stood, moving gingerly, clasping her hand in both of mine. "So I guess I stopped wishing that a while ago," I added, softly.

I made my way over to the door, trying to shut it quietly but abandoning the effort entirely when it squeaked with an ear-scraping sound. The door remained open a slit.

I spotted an armchair a little way down the hall, and with a long sigh I sat down, wishing I could stay in Jenny's room and look after her, make sure she didn't need help with anything. But no, she needed her rest. Someone watching you while you slept didn't exactly leave you with a *soothing* feeling when you closed your eyes.

I knew I wouldn't be able to sleep for two or three nights, at least. Memories undid me in a way nearly nothing else did. My parents had always been the most persistent of the ghosts that haunted me, but even the bitter memories *they'd* left behind seemed to pale in comparison to the sound of a single shot against the night air and the dark stain spreading across Jenny's dress and the whites of her eyes as they rolled back into her skull.

I didn't know what had come over me as I turned to the man with the gun. A violent rage had filled my head, and all I could think was: I will kill him. And I was certain that I almost *had.* What I *wanted* to do was break a couple more of his ribs with that crowbar, but I stopped myself because of Jenny, because I needed to carry her home. Just carry her home.

When I'd lifted her into my arms, she had felt so delicate I thought she might drift away with the wind, like ashes. Yet she was strong, I knew that. I knew she was strong. The fact that she had so quickly harnessed her powers at a moment of need—as an Unavowed, to boot—made her more than strong. She was powerful, and that made me worry for her more than ever.

"Hello, there."

Coming back to myself, I twisted in the chair a little to see a boy, arms crossed, a sly grin across his face. No, he was *the* boy. The boy who had knocked me out. The boy who had taken Jenny away. The boy who I seriously wanted to push into moving traffic sometime when nobody was looking.

"I don't believe I got the name of Jennifer's *heroic* rescuer, did I?" he asked with a drawling, accented voice, maybe British. I scoffed. As if he didn't already know my name. Taylor Ross: The notorious Sentry rogue, hunted by any able Persuader from south of Virginia to the Mason-Dixon line. He extended his hand, amber eyes flashing with contempt. "Vince."

"Taylor," I said, gruffly, not taking his hand.

"So nice to meet you. Again." He raised a dark eyebrow in a particularly unpleasant expression. "I do believe you're lost. You see, the front door is"—he gestured lazily behind me—"that-a-way."

"I'm not lost," I said. "And I'm not leaving."

Vince straightened, still smiling politely, but his eyes turned from glittering and fluid into solid, bronze plates. "You won't be able to feed off of your immunity for long, Taylor."

"I know," I said, looking at Jenny's half-closed door.

He barked out a laugh. "In fact, if I were to estimate how soon she'll tire of your company, I'd give you about a week. Maybe less."

My hands clenched into fists. "Funny, I've already tired of yours." The words were biting, too defensive, maybe.

Vince raised his hands, taking a step back. "Whoa, there. Didn't mean to get you all worked up. I can see you're...quite fond of her, aren't you? Truly adorable."

With a cheerful smile, he sauntered off down the hall in the way he had come.

I had sensed Jenny's aura in the doorway the moment she had crept out of bed, though I didn't think she was aware of that fact. With exaggerated casualness, I walked toward her and opened the door the rest of the way, nearly knocking over Jenny as she leaned into the doorjamb. "How much of that did you hear?" I asked, not sure if I should feel slightly embarrassed or not.

"Um..." She tilted her head, contemplating. "All of it?" she said, having the dignity at least to sound *a little* ashamed of her eavesdropping.

"So what's up with that guy? How do you stand him?" I glanced off down the shadowed hallway.

"Who, Vince?" she asked. I didn't like how natural and familiar the sound of his name sounded when she said it, as if they were old pals. "Well, I wouldn't exactly call him an open book, but I *do* know that he's hiding something. I don't know what, but I'll find out."

I motioned for Jenny to follow me down the dimly lit hallway, taking in the smell of old carpet and the deep red of the walls and the old-fashioned gaslights that lined both sides at intervals. I looked back to see two wavering shadows following us in synchronized steps. "Maybe not everyone is a puzzle—" I began, but looking down at her I stopped myself, blinking. "You're limping. You aren't in too much pain, are you?"

Jenny shook her head. "I'm fine. And I *know* something about him is off. I mean, isn't that always the thing with his type? My guess is, *his* story is probably just as depressing as yours and mine—"

"Do *not*," I said, holding up my hand to stop whatever horrible thing she was going to say, "compare me to him."

She glared off down the hallway, jaw set, obviously stung by my snapping at her. "Fine."

I touched her shoulder, hesitantly. She didn't shrug me off, which I took as a good sign. "I'm sorry," I said. "I didn't mean to be so harsh with you. It's just...you have to understand how it is—"

"Taylor, come on," she interrupted, turning to skewer me with that ever-intuitive look. "Is that really *how it is*, or is it just how the two of you—and everyone else—makes it out to be?"

I looked down at my worn sneakers, so out of place as they treaded heavily on the burgundy carpet, a carpet probably imported from somewhere halfway across the world. "It's how it has to be, Jenny."

She didn't respond, just stared angrily ahead. I wanted to smooth out the seriousness from her face, like creases from paper. "Whatever," she said, tersely.

Together, we went down one of twin staircases that curled into a foyer-like area, where the main stairs led down to the bottom.

I grabbed Jenny's hand, pressing my thumb into her palm. I didn't exactly feel like confronting Liam again. "Hey..." She looked up, surprised. I nodded to the opposite staircase from which we had come. "How about we do a little exploring?"

Jenny immediately lit up at the thought of adventure, as I knew she would. "Sounds fun."

Grinning ear to ear like misbehaving children, we inspected each room of the west wing with the care of crime-scene investigators, to our disappointment finding only old knick-knacks and dusty, moth-ravaged furniture in most of them. In the fourth room we found a framed photograph, maybe from the seventies or eighties. It was of a girl, very pretty, with long, ghostly hair to her waist and a pensive expression. She was perched at the edge of a dock over the brownish water of maybe a pond or a lake, hand trailing in a distracted manner through it. "Look familiar?" I asked, yellowed parchment held lightly between my fingers.

Jenny looked over my shoulder at it. "No," she said. "I have no idea who she is."

We both stared at it for a while, puzzled. "You think it might be someone related to you?"

"If she is, I don't see the resemblance."

We moved on, giving up on the peculiar picture shortly after, finding the majority of the other rooms to be either nondescript guest bedrooms or gutted, open spaces, like looted tombs.

Finally, we reached the last door at the end of the hallway. I found myself suddenly caught up in the mystery of what awaited us beyond this black door, so tucked away from visitors' eyes. I encircled the cold, brass knob with one hand, laying the other one against the splintering wood. The knob stuck at first, then turned, the door creaking open, louder than any of the others. Light spilled through the doorway, as if we were stepping into the sky.

When the entirety of the room became visible, Jenny put her hand up to her mouth in astonishment. This wasn't a room. It was a balcony.

Unkempt potted plants and natural vegetation intertwined along a wrought iron balustrade, and on the floor were more cracked, clay pots, overflowing with white flowers. So overflowing, in fact, that most of the floor beneath us was ivory petals and snarled vines. Jenny and I made our way carefully to the edge of the balcony, both of us a little guilty as we crushed delicate flowers underneath our heavy footfalls.

Beside each other at the banister, we overlooked a glittering pond and a forest line pressing against its farthermost edge. I held my hand above my eyes to block the sun's glare, trying to see more clearly the statue that dominated the center. It depicted a man, or something of human form, his face tucked into the crook of his arm, snakes wrapped around his wrists and legs as if they were ropes pulling him downward. Wings, slightly battered looking, sprouted from his back, his expression contorted by both the agony of falling from grace and by an unspoken vow to take vengeance upon those who had cast him down.

"An angel falling from Heaven," Jenny whispered, softly.

I was about to respond when I felt a faint aura and heard an elderly voice from just behind us. "This sculpture Liam had based off of a statue in Madrid. *La Fuente del Ángel Caído*, I believe it's called. It depicts Lucifer, cast out of Heaven because of his quest for absolute power." Jenny and I turned to face her, and then glanced at each other. Laura smiled grimly. "Liam likes to remind himself of the dangers of trying to take from someone in a position to take more."

Jenny blinked. "Did you—"

"Come to find you two for a reason?" the robust maid finished, folding her arms. "Yes. Liam wishes to discuss…living arrangements for Taylor."

Jenny's eyes widened in horror, and she grabbed the banister, as if for support. "Oh, no, Laura. He can't *kick him out*—"

"That is something to discuss with him, not me. Come along, you two. He's in the dining room.

The "dining room", as it'd been referred to, was not really a "room", either. Attached as it was to the east side of the mansion, it was like a building all by itself.

The perpetually busy Laura, who claimed she had work to do somewhere else within the mansion, abandoned Jenny and me at the doorway. In the center of the room was a polished, solid-looking table, easily the length of a limousine but almost completely bare. I noticed here and there little smudges of color, a red one at my feet, a purple one across Jenny's face. She blinked, looking around, as if in a dream.

Jenny gasped suddenly, grabbing my arm, pointing at the ceiling. I looked up with her, feeling my eyes bulge a little. A large circular skylight made up a portion of the ceiling above our heads, composed of panes of multicolor glass. It reminded me of a stained glass window, like in a cathedral, only it was directly over us. Soft light filtered through, throwing the splotches of color I had noticed earlier across the room. "So beautiful," she breathed from beside me, awestruck.

The room, I decided finally, was something halfway between a ballroom and the cavernous gut of a haunted castle. I sat down in one of the heavy chairs and Jenny wandered away from the banners of light to sit across from me, face immediately glum as she remembered why we were here. I attempted a smile, but even *I* could feel it was a weak one. "Everything will be fine," I said, though it was the very sort of comforting statement that was more reflex than truth. "I'm not leaving you."

She opened her mouth to speak, but an arrogant, irritatingly amused voice cut across the room. "Well, look at this. I'm among one of the last to show. What does that say of my punctuality?"

Vince strode, eternally confident in everything he did, over to where Jenny was sitting, having a seat beside her. I bristled at the way he looked at her, a detached appreciation, if that was even possible. I doubted that she noticed it. Vince glanced over at me, confident grin turning quickly into something more of a sneer, like butter melting. "Ah, Taylor. You know, I think I just might miss you when you're gone."

"Don't expect a goodbye kiss," I returned, leaning my chin against my hand.

Jenny kicked me under the table with her good leg and frowned at both of us. "There's no need to carry on your stupid fight with each other. It's childish."

"Yes, why don't we all just get along," Vince scoffed. "Not that I can *begin* to even understand why you insist on your odd, little friendship with that...*traitor*—"

"There's nothing wrong with extending kindness on occasion, Vince. Even to a Sentry. Especially a Sentry who saved my only daughter's life."

Liam walked in, casting Vince a scolding look as he sat down at the head of the table. Vince scowled, folding his arms. "Sorry I'm late. I had a bit of business to attend to." He shot a look at me. "Actually, it was about finding a stronghold willing to accept you so you don't have to live as a rogue anymore. But it's always difficult to get a word across with our Sentry neighbors, especially when the leader of the stronghold and I have a bit of a bitter history." He paused, his normally clear eyes darkening, darker memories swimming within them. He shook his head, continuing, "They suspect underhandedness of some sort. You all really are an untrusting lot, I must say." With another vilifying shake of his head, he spat, "For a faction that prides itself on its martial competence, one would think you would dare to come out of the shadows once in a while."

Vince was staring at me, lips twisted upward. "Oh, yes, I agree."

I looked over, for assistance, at Jenny, who had flushed angrily at her father's blatant predisposition against people he had just claimed deserved kindness. A predisposition against me. And Vince really wasn't helping. "Liam," she snapped. "Maybe you're forgetting, but they have every reason not to trust you. I mean, think about what you *do*—"

"They are not the heroes you make them out to be, Jennifer." Liam rose to his feet and braced his hands against the table. "This isn't a situation of good versus evil, of martyrs and villains. This is a world on the brink of war. You're either on one side, *or the other.*" He wasn't speaking to me, but I found myself recoiling from his vicious snarl. Even Vince looked speechless, for once. "Maybe your beloved Taylor isn't what he seems. Perhaps he just wanted to insinuate himself into our home. Glean valuable information!" His hands flailed wildly, and I was afraid for a moment that he would accidentally bring the ceiling down in a hazardous downpour over our heads.

Jenny stood now, fists clenched at her sides. "Taylor saved my life. Show some gratitude! And you're wrong about this world, Liam. This *is* a situation of good versus evil. It's as simple as this: If you throw him out," she said, staring him in the eye unflinchingly, "you couldn't *possibly* be good."

She went out of the room, the limp mysteriously out of her gait, not throwing a backward glance at any of us.

Liam rubbed a hand down his face, taking a seat again, looking decades older than he was. "She still calls me 'Liam,'" he said, flatly, to no one in particular. "Never 'father.'"

My gaze on him was cool and even. "With all due respect, Mr. Cable, I don't think you deserve to be called that."

I left to find Jenny.

6
A SHIFT

VINCE

I excused myself from the table, leaving my adoptive father and mentor alone in the dining room, head pressed into his hands. I didn't attempt to comfort him because I didn't particularly know *how* to do that, anyway. When I was young, my parents hadn't paid me enough attention to realize when I needed to be comforted, and Liam had never exactly been the sentimental type, either. All my life I'd centered a livelihood on my ability to manipulate people into feeling exactly what I told them to feel. A woman on the street, a man in the park…no one needed to be *convinced*, really, to do these things. No one ever needed a pat on the hand or a few words of consolation, and that left me in a bit of a rut when I finally found Jenny on the balcony, gripping the banister so hard her fingers were bloodless. Taylor was posted several feet away as if giving her space. I stepped toward her and leaned an elbow on the banister, silently watching her as she turned her face to me.

Her frustration quickly dissipated into a cold resentment, and she took her hands off the banister with a hard enough look in her eyes to catch me off-guard. "I can't believe you did that."

"Did what?" My claim to innocence seemed to only aggravate her, and her expression darkened visibly. With a glance over my shoulder, I saw even Taylor throw her a look, his brows creasing over his violet eyes.

Her fingers twitched unconsciously, and I heard the slight groan of metal as the banister tilted slightly, though no one had touched it. "I *can't believe* you would just stand there while Liam ripped into him like that! And when you did speak, it only made things *worse*. You sided with Liam even though he—"

"Of course I did!" I snapped. "He's my father. I've known you for, what? A little over a week?"

She didn't look angry now. She just looked wounded. "I don't know. I guess I just thought we were…"

"What?" I demanded, sharply, cruelly. "Friends? Please don't deceive yourself, Jennifer." I didn't regret the words, not then. It seemed the only way I could make her see how things really were, however unpleasantly the news was delivered. "Look, I don't know what sort of *fantasy world* you've been living in, but I think it's time you realized that Liam and I are *Persuaders*. We don't make friends, we make enemies. And, thanks to your carelessness, we have one under our roof now."

There was a sound of anger and incredulity from Taylor and, before I could react, he'd Shifted, and I was on the ground, my head smacking the unforgiving iron of the balcony. A burst of pain swelled above my eyebrow.

I leapt to my feet as swiftly as I had been forced down, whirling on Taylor, Shifting him into the banister at his back. His arms flailed like the wings of a lawn decoration, and he almost toppled right over the edge. I held up my hand a second time, but Jenny grabbed my arm and tried to push it back down to my side. "Stop!"

I turned my head to tell her I wasn't planning on actually letting him fall and that he would have caught himself, anyway, but Taylor had sent a large, black flower pot spiraling at my head. I dove to the side, just barely avoiding the heavy object as it hurtled over the opposite banister. I could hear the faint shatter as it crashed into the stone walkway below. I lunged for him, he started for me, and Jenny stepped between us with her hands held out, as if to separate us. To my complete surprise, separate we did.

I was lifted off of my feet and tossed, like a doll thrown by a child, across the balcony. I landed heavily on my backside, the overgrowth beneath me barely serving as sufficient padding to the impact, and I looked across the space in time to see Taylor get thrown as well. He landed on his spine, exhaling sharply as the breath was knocked out of him.

Jenny stood in the middle of the floor, back straight, hands still out, grinning triumphantly. She looked admittedly extraordinary like that, bright hair curling around her face. She looked like a true Persuader, I realized, and somehow she'd managed to gain a passable degree of control over her powers just a few days after realizing she *had* them.

I forced myself to my feet, with some pain, head tilted as I stepped closer to her. "Not bad," I said, feeling a smile turn the corners of my mouth. "Not bad at all. I think proper training would do you some real good. Help you develop your technique."

Jenny turned her head to me, the pale sunlight backlighting her hair, turning the edges gold, as if she were burning. I looked away. "Training? Who's going to give me that?"

"I will," Taylor and I said at precisely the same moment.

Taylor gave me a patronizing look from over Jenny's shoulder. "No offense, pretty boy, but we can do just fine without your help. I'm a little more qualified than you are, after all, being—" I could see the word "full-blooded" on his lips, but at the last moment he discarded it for: "Being older than you and more experienced."

I scowled. "Well, I live here. If she trains in *my* house, *I'll* be the one doing the training."

When he saw that I wasn't budging on the subject any more than he was, his eyes narrowed. "Think rationally. You can barely even hold your own in Cavea."

"Cavea?" Jenny asked, looking slightly mystified. "What's that?"

My gaze slid to hers, and I exhaled slowly. "It's just a word we have for the inside dimensions of the mind. Latin, I think. It was a term used for the seating sections in Roman theaters, though it also refers to the underground cells where they kept animals for the arenas—"

"If you want my opinion," she interrupted, evidently disinterested in the etymology of a dead language, "I think you two should split the work. Since Taylor is apparently more capable in…in *Cavea*, he should be the one to train me there."

"Okay, sure," he conceded, though he cast a wary look in my direction. "But can you really trust *Vince* to train you? I could always—"

"I trust him," she said, after a moment's hesitation. I tried not to look at her too quickly in my astonishment, certain it would betray me somehow.

I always felt as if every expression and gesture I made without thinking betrayed me to her in some small way. Maybe that was why she trusted me so readily, because with an eye as discerning as hers she could see through even the most opaque of characters.

7
CAVEA

TAYLOR

The door shut with a soft click behind me, and I scanned the room. The floor, warped by age, possessed a dull gleam to it, and scattered across it was an assortment of cardboard boxes and plastic bins shoved into the corners where wispy spider webs crisscrossed the wooden support beams. For our training, Liam had relegated us to the attic, accessible through a hatch in the ceiling of one of the east wing's rooms. It was a large space— not that we needed it—and there was quite a chill to it, more so than in any other place in the mansion. The chill seemed to reach up through the floorboards and into the bare soles of my feet, seemed to squeeze through the cracks in the wall, leeching all the light and warmth simultaneously. The only brightness came filtered through a little, shaded window high in the far wall. Jenny's teeth were chattering with an audible sound as I made my way over to her. I offered my arm for her to grasp, and she accepted it, fingers slipping around my wrist.

"Okay." I closed my eyes. "I'm not going to do anything at all. I want to see what you can do with this. Ready?"

"R-ready as I'll ever be, I guess…" she began, but trailed off.

For a moment all was black, as it normally was, behind my eyelids. Then a burst of color exploded like a firework in the corner of my vision, and instinctually I knew that we were in Cavea.

Yet when I opened my eyes again and I glanced around, I saw nothing but a blank landscape with a purple-black sky above me. The

59

ground beneath my feet was only an ankle-high layer of fog. I began to wonder if maybe I had done something wrong, and we weren't in Cavea at all, but in some sort of weird limbo.

Then Jenny suddenly materialized from the backdrop, glancing about her dazedly. I lifted my arm above my head, waving to her with a smile and a light shiver. As she walked toward me—the edges of her were blurry, I noticed—I said, "Explain to me, Jennifer, why it's *s-still* freezing!"

She looked remorseful. "I f-forgot to think otherwise?" Seeing the look I tossed her, she added, slightly defensive, "What? The attic was the last thing I was thinking about."

I sighed. "No, the temperature was the last thing," I corrected her, with a loose, semi-circle of my hand. "Honestly, I guess I just thought you'd be a little more…specific!"

Jenny laughed, the sound ringing through the blackness, the sole source of warmth. "Okay. Hold on. Let me think of a place more *suited to your liking, sir.*" She did a curt, little bow to complement the terrible British accent and I smirked at her, folding my arms as she closed her eyes in concentration. Before I could ask her where she was sending us, I found myself standing not ankle-deep in mist, but in fine, sun-scorched sand, so hot I found myself hopping from foot to foot. It was somewhat disorienting, the shift from nothingness to the sun glaring down on pale sand and bottle-blue water, and I felt the beginning of a headache bloom against my temples. Then I looked up and saw Jenny, and I felt like a kite yanked back to the earth. The pain subsided. Glancing around me, I saw that we were on a beach, glass-clear waves lapping the shore, the ocean darkening to turquoise further out. The sky above us was strikingly violet, the color of an Unavowed. I tried to imagine it more blue than red, but failed. It was perfectly undecided, a color so precise as to be utterly unfavorable toward either circle. Just purple. Just Jenny.

"Now," Jenny said, her smile dazzling in the new brightness, the edges of her eyes turned to rings of peridot, "since anything goes here, I was thinking we should start with creating a race of shark-human hybrids."

"Whoa there, champ," I said, laughing. "Cavea is a complex place. It's probably best if you just get used to your surroundings first and learn to shape it to your advantage."

She sobered, the smile dropping. The sky above us began to grow hazy, cloudy, the waves getting choppy. "Advantage?"

I swallowed, tugging at the collar of my t-shirt. What did she think Shifting was ultimately for? Rearranging knick-knacks? "Well, you have to be prepared in case you ever run into trouble..."

"But I don't want to fight anyone!" The ground rolled beneath our feet at the cry, as if we were standing on the back of some giant serpent.

I moved toward her, but something in her face stopped me. She looked ready to explode or, worse, prepared to inadvertently conjure a place to match her emotions—like an active volcano.

"I know you don't," I said, as soothingly as possible. "But I can't be there beside you twenty-four seven. You need to learn to defend yourself as a precaution. You do realize that, right?"

She looked unhappily out to sea, visibly withdrawn into herself, and I noticed that the water was quickly turning into a shade as gray as lead, waves as brittle.

"Hey," I called, making an effort to make my tone light. She glanced over at me, the angry slant of her brow and the thin set of her mouth alone communicating a deep and toxic infirmity in her mind. I remembered that the same lost expression had been on her face at her mother's funeral. I remembered that it was the last time I had seen her cry, and ever since that day it had just been that withdrawn look, just the clouds but never any rain.

I extended my arms to her, and Jenny leaned her head against the inside of my shoulder, allowing me to hold her as she rarely let people do. I took at least some pride in the fact that she permitted me to be her solace, if nothing else. And despite this imbalance, the unfairness of her tethering me to enemy territory—though I wouldn't ever leave her to face the Persuaders alone—I felt that I owed it to Jenny to at least *try* to help her. Or...to make her see that she *needed* help in the first place. She could be stubborn, at times too rooted in her convictions, so getting her to realize that she was hurting herself and the people who cared about her would undoubtedly prove more challenging, even, than avoiding my own discovery.

The lapping waves were still gray, the sky still hazy. Further out to sea, I could see the beginnings of a storm. I sighed. "Why does the ocean look so dangerous?"

She didn't reply.

8
THE DIFFERENCE

JENNY

It was decided, after I had emerged more or less victorious from Cavea, that Vince would instruct me in the "back yard" or, more correctly, the ring of property around the oval-shaped, brownish pond that dominated the center of the yard. The statue of Lucifer rose from the dark, sludgy water, a steel gray slash against the green wall of trees at the edge of the lawn.

Vince stood several paces away from where I was, facing me, lazily tossing an apple into the air and catching it. Maybe it was just my overactive imagination—or I was still a little fuzzy from my little mind-trip in Cavea—but I thought that possibly it hung suspended in the air for a longer time than the laws of gravity usually permitted.

His gaze cut sharply to me, eyes gleaming like a viper's, mildly humorous. He was waiting for me to fail horribly, I realized, to make a complete fool of myself just so he could get a cheap laugh out of it.

I wrapped my arms around myself, shivering not just from the cold. "Okay. What now?"

Vince shrugged, turning his attention back to the apple. It orbited like a tiny, red moon around his head. "Now you Shift."

I glared at him. "But you said you'd teach me technique."

"I know what I *said*," he snapped. The apple dropped into his upturned palm and he bit into it, continuing with his mouth full. "But this isn't something you learn on the spot. It takes patience, discipline." He swallowed with a patronizing smile. "Though it may take some time, in your case, to *acquire* these traits."

Something inside me snapped, and I flung my hand out, watching as the apple shot from Vince's grip, a red blur slicing through the air, to mine, all in the flutter of an eyelash. He blinked several times, and I waved the apple tauntingly at him. "Enough of this, Hallows. You promised you would help me. I intend to hold you to that."

"Alright, alright." Vince's smooth indifference slipped—a rare occurrence—and I noticed he was trying very hard to conceal an impressed, crooked grin. "First, you need to focus. Nothing else matters apart from Shifting itself and the ultimate goal you're trying to reach. Second, you need to relax your shoulders and level your breathing—"

"What is this? A yoga exercise?" I interrupted, my arms falling to my sides heavily. "What next, the high lunge?"

Vince cast me a look that could've perhaps silenced the roaring jet engine of a Boeing 747. "Third," he went on, tersely, "is to pray you don't do something terribly wrong."

"Not that *you* have to worry about that one," I muttered. "You're Mr. Perfect."

"One mustn't talk under one's breath, Jenny," Vince called. "So if you're quite done…" He held out his hand expectedly, fingers curling twice.

For some reason, this infuriated me more than anything else. *Oh, I'm quite done, all right,* I thought. *Quite done listening to you talk to me like I'm a child.* How could I trust what he said when it was clear he wanted me to fail? I tensed my shoulders, breathing quickly and shallowly. I could feel pressure begin to build around me, could feel it against the back of my eyes, at my temples.

Vince's eyes widened, and he looked about to shout something at me, but either he never got the chance or I just didn't hear him, because the apple wasn't what was Shifted.

I felt myself lifted off of my feet violently and suddenly, sailing backward, hair whipping into my face as all the air in my lungs rushed out.

I hit the water, and all other thoughts froze in place, ceasing to be relevant, as the chilly, gritty water enfolded me into its heavy embrace. My eyes burned as I looked up, completely submerged, at the rippling surface, becoming increasingly father away. *Why does the ocean look so dangerous,* Taylor had asked? I hadn't answered because, for me, any body of water that I couldn't stand up in—the ocean, the deep end of a pool, a lake—terrified me more than anything else, terrified me because I had never learned how to keep my head above the surface.

One typically learned to swim in one's childhood, I supposed, in the back yard kiddie pool with floaties encircling one's tiny, chubby arms, being partly held aloft by Dad while Mom snapped a few pictures with the camera. I'd had no such childhood. I remembered going to the beach with them at the age of six, trailing behind them on the sand as they argued about things I didn't understand, looking out at the vast, dark ocean and wondering what would happen if I tried to swim away into the horizon.

I knew the answer now. I would sink like a rock.

Frantically, I tried to visualize what someone swimming looked like. Did they kick their legs? Move their arms? I did both in wild movements more akin to thrashing than swimming. But there was hardly time to think, and I was quickly running out of both air and time. I managed only once to break the surface, spitting water before I dipped back below. A few more failed attempts, and my limbs started to burn, and with this exhaustion of the body came a revelation in the mind: I was dying.

The edges of my vision blurred, lungs ablaze, my mind screaming as thoughts were turned from questions to demands, demands to pleas.

Suddenly, a figure darted into my line of sight, cutting through the water like a lance, grabbing me around the waist. I lashed out at my attacker with all the strength I had left, drawing blood, which mixed with the murky pond like poison.

Still, the figure didn't release me, slowly dragging me deeper into the muddy bottom of the pond. I twisted in its hold for a moment, but then stopped, noticing a bit of hair that was not my own, as black as ink, and feeling a warmth that didn't usually strike me as the clammy temperature of a sea monster.

I wasn't being dragged down, I realized. I was being pulled up. My face broke the surface of the water, and I gasped, drawing in a ragged breath, my throat as raw as if it had been scrubbed with sandpaper. I turned in the pair of arms that secured me to its chest, seeing Vince, his curls sticking to his forehead as he glared at me with his head held just above the water like an alligator's. I could feel the heat of his anger rolling off of him.

In a single, smooth motion, he tossed me onto the ledge around the statue, pulling himself up beside me, as if it were effortless. I looked toward the shore, in my humiliation wishing almost more than before that I could reach it alone.

"What the *hell* were you thinking?" Vince demanded, not even giving me time to catch my breath.

My voice was little more than a frog's croak as I snapped, dripping sarcasm, "I thought I'd just take a swim, I guess!"

"You deliberately did the exact opposite of what I told you to!" His chest heaved as he shouted. "When you tense up like that, extra energy builds up around you, energy that snaps back at you like a rubber band."

I looked down, face dripping, at my soaked sneakers. "I think that explanation would've been better if you'd said it five minutes earlier."

Vince growled something that sounded like "Unbelievable!", tugging at his saturated hair manically. "I didn't know you were going to try to *drown* yourself!" he burst out.

I recoiled from him as if he had hit me, scowling and turning my attention back to the edge of the grass, arms folded.

Vince noticed the change, however slight, swiveling surprised tawny eyes to me, thick, dark brow drawn low over them. "Wait. You don't…you never learned…?" He took a breath and asked, unusually serious, "You can't swim?"

My scowl deepened, and I answered, curtly, "No. I was never taught how. Big 'oopsie' on Liam's part, I suppose."

I tried not to show any emotion on my face, attempting to imitate the jaded evenness I always saw in Vince's. Apparently, I did not succeed.

Vince clasped his hands, leaning forward and peering at me, obviously reading my expression as plainly as words inked across my face, I thought. His jaw clenched and unclenched once. "Quite the limitation, no? I would've never guessed that *you*, of all people—" He looked away. "Never mind. Let's head back."

I looked sharply at him, unable to decide if I was annoyed by his ambiguity or curious about what exactly he'd meant by "you of all people". Vince didn't give me the chance, either, slipping back into the pond and offering me a hand to take while the other firmly gripped the stone ledge. I complied, allowing him to help me into the water, put his arms under mine, and towboat me back to shore. I was impressed at his strength, his speed, as he swam us back. The pond was not small, and the water was not thin, but somehow he managed to get us to the grass without looking too winded. *Of course* Mr. Perfect had saved the day. All the talk about how "powerful" I was, and yet I was starting to grow *sick* of feeling helpless. I was like a little girl kicking around in a kiddie pool, suspended on a pair of floaties, partly held aloft by everyone else.

My soaked clothes clung to me as tightly as a second skin, beginning to itch uncomfortably as we trudged back to the house. The back door was beneath the balcony, and some tendrils of vines had started to work their way down the wall.

Vince stood at the door, already reaching for the handle, when he turned to me so quickly I all but slammed into him. I straightened, looking up into his face to see that he was regarding me with the light humor of before, but without the malice, eyes raking my muddy, tangled hair and the smears of dirt across my skin.

He chuckled. "Just wait until Laura sees us."

9
A SPARK

SAMUEL

I was a patient man, well accustomed to employing my particular...*skillset* when it was necessary, ebbing back into the shade when it was not. I was meticulous. I was careful. However, patient as I was, I could not stand to see the ruination of the Persuader world for long. I could not let the blight of a once proud race fester to a point where the damage could no longer be reversed. It was these thoughts that plagued my mind at night and kept me from sleep, as it seemed too often as if I carried the burden, alone, of maintaining any semblance of purity in modern society. The interbreed, Jennifer Cable—her sudden appearance seemed to be the very writing on the wall I'd always feared would one day materialize, her existence a menace to the concept of a pure world I had for so long imagined. I decided I detested all who bore and associated with the name "Cable", vehemently. Each of them would have to answer for his depravity, eventually, whether that punishment was delivered through my own actions or not.

Two, wiry figures burst through my front door, uninvited, stupidly stumbling about as if drunk or insane. I recognized them to be the pair of ruffians I had hired to pay a little visit to the Cable child. I'd expected them back sooner, and in a better state.

Thom's arms were wrapped around his ribcage and the side of his face had a sizable welt on it just above the temple, and Cira was hobbling, putting most of her weight on the right leg.

I made my way calmly down the staircase, hand trailing the banister. Thom was looking at me with spiteful eyes. He scowled as he spoke. "You told us she was harmless," he accused.

My eyebrows lifted as I folded my hands behind my back. "Don't tell me a little girl did this to you."

"There was someone else with her—" Thom began to say, but Cira stepped forward and spoke over him. "She's strong, Samuel."

A single, severe look was enough to make her look at the ground and retreat back to her place beside Thom. A wise decision on her part. Her hotheaded partner was not so judicious. He growled, fists clenching at his sides. "Well, she *is*. You said she was untrained. You said—"

Thom went sailing backwards at the twitch of my fingers, slamming into the floor with a sharp cracking noise. He writhed there for a moment, gurgling, his back arching as a fine spray of red dribbled down his lips and onto his shirt. I kneeled at his side, grabbing his collar in one hand, making him look me in the eye as I spoke to him. "Know your place," I hissed, regarding him with contempt. I released his shirtfront, and his head dropped back to the floor, turning to the side, his jaw working. "You outcrossed vermin always seem to forget it."

Wiping the bit of blood from my hand on Thom's sleeve, I stood, coolly observing Cira, who was frozen where she was, eyes very wide and frightened, looking down at her unfortunate friend. "Cira," I snapped, enjoying the look of pure terror flash through her face at the mere sound of her own name. "Assist this idiot."

She scrambled to help prop Thom into an upright position and hauled him shakily to his feet. Thom no longer looked at me with anger. In fact, he didn't look at me at all. "It appears as though Jennifer is someone to keep an eye on," I said, staring out the door into the cold night. "If we do not smother this little, bothersome spark now, I'm certain it'll grow and grow until it becomes something we can no longer handle, a wildfire that will destroy us and the Cause altogether."

Cira's forehead creased, and she shifted Thom in her grip. "Sir? You mean we should kill her?"

"No," I said, smiling a little to myself. "No, not yet."

Cira slung her comrade's arm around her own shoulders, as if preparing to leave, but I held up a hand to stop her. "Wait a moment. Leave him here. He needs a little more…lecturing."

With a visible movement of her throat, she silently unwound his grip from around her and settled him back onto the floor. He rested there on his knees, head hanging low into his collarbone. I cracked my knuckles. "Do take care in the future to remember, Thomas. You make things *so* inconvenient for both of us."

TAYLOR

After training in the attic, we made our way down a little staircase leading into a room on the east wing and out into the hall. There had been something...*off* about Jenny then, obvious in the compulsive way she tugged at her shirtsleeves and how she worried her lower lip.

"Taylor."

I had started to wander away from the set of glass doors where I'd left her, but she grabbed my arm, causing me to turn. She cast an apprehensive glance toward the manicured lawn just beyond the doors. "I'm not so sure about Vince training me, anymore. I want to learn proper technique, and all, but just not..."

"From him," I finished, grinning. "Well, unfortunately, this seems to be his level of compromise. I'm not exactly in a position to be making any demands around here. Besides, you're a natural. You'll do fine."

"A natural?" Jenny looked doubtful. "For most of my life I thought I was just a totally normal human being, and it was only a week ago I found out I *wasn't*. I don't think I'm really all that cut out to be a Persuader at this point, Taylor."

I knew that she had only meant "Persuader" as in the collective term for both Persuaders and Sentries, but some part of me still recoiled inwardly from the words. With effort, I smiled and choked out a generic adage of encouragement. "It'll just take a little time. You'll see."

After she had gone, I'd taken it upon myself to further investigate my surroundings. Liam had shut himself into a dusty office room, as I was informed he did often, and it didn't appear as if he would emerge any time soon. Put frankly, it was the perfect time for a little reconnaissance. I supposed it was only in my *Sentry nature,* as the Persuaders liked to say, to revert to the habits of one held prisoner in enemy territory. Not that I would ever consider Jenny my enemy, not even if she one day soon chose to wear a title that said she was.

The downstairs, I discovered, was nothing remarkable, save for

Liam's office. The space in front of the staircase was a large lobby, a Baldwin grand piano grimacing silently in the corner, and adjacent to it were the doors leading to the dining hall. The tables and the frames of the mirrors hanging on the walls were made of ebony, ornately carved, probably imported from somewhere, and had definitely cost no trifling amount, I was sure. At least there was only *one* huge, gaudy chandelier. Not like in my old home, where there were three or so, maybe four. My recollection of the Ross mansion had become somewhat indistinct, perhaps due to a certain phenomenon Dr. Freud liked to call "repression". From the day I'd left home, I hadn't cared to revisit it much in my memories.

The back sections, to the sides of the stairs, seemed to be split in two. On one side was Liam's office and bedroom. That side was darker and with only one door leading in and out. The door was locked. The other side was not concealed from view by a wall. It was open, like the foyer. It served as a kitchen and a sitting area. The transparent doors Jenny had gone through to the backyard were in the back, spilling tawny light onto the floor before it. I began forming a visual layout in my head of the mansion—a habit from my childhood developed out of necessity, as I often got lost in one of the many hallways of the Ross estate. Like a puzzle, the whole Cable mansion began to take shape piece by piece as I filled in new information. I realized there were still some pieces missing.

I was starting up the staircase, following it left instead of right, toward the west wing. The locked door from before had been a nagging thought in my mind ever since Jenny and I had discovered it, and I'd been reluctant to use Shifting to open it in her presence. Within me there was some anxiety that she would think less of me for picking locks or doing anything that struck one as morally gray. I didn't want to be morally gray to her; I wanted to be someone she trusted completely.

It squealed open under my touch almost immediately after I had Shifted the lock, so loudly I thought that Liam would hear and come charging up the stairs at any given moment.

A moment passed undisturbed. I blew out a gusty sigh of relief, walking through the door, flipping the light switch on as I did.

It was a bedroom. A rigid-looking, queen-sized bed sat in the corner of the room, made up as neat as a soldier's. The walls, like the bed sheets, were black, and really the only notable source of color to be found was in the spines of the books lining the shelves. All else was dark.

70

I also noticed that not a speck of dust or a rogue sock was visible anywhere on the floor or on the nightstands or chairs or tables. Not a dent in the frightening cleanliness was to be seen. I would've assumed that it was unoccupied had there not been an upside-down book splayed open across the bed. I picked it up, studying its much-abused pages, some torn, some punctured through with a pen. I squinted at the sharp, frantic handwriting across the page I held in my grasp.

I've been having the same nightmare for weeks now. I'm stepping through a doorway, and James is calling out for me as smoke fills the hallway. For some reason, in my dreams James isn't doing anything but calling my name, and I always wake up just before I reach him.

It's been ten years and I find I can't even remember their faces— and yet I can still remember the strangest things about them. Like the way James used to laugh, rapidly, with a hitching sound. And I remember that my father once pressed the burning end of a cigar to the back of James' hand, though I can't remember the reason for it. I remember my mother, with her scarves and hats, how she seemed to buy a new one of each every week or so. It's silly, I know, remembering that. Strange to think how something precious or something valued or something *alive* could not even exist the next day or the next hour or the next moment.

I scowled at the entry, tossing the notebook back on the bed. It seemed Jenny had been correct in assuming that there had been something in his childhood to make him how he was. I thought back to when we were fighting in Cavea, the odd memory, the ashes, the snow. It made more sense now...

I straightened, shaking my head several times as if clearing it of an ugly thought. Horrible tragedy didn't justify horrible behavior. Yes, it was sad; I pitied him. But Jenny hadn't allowed tragedy to be an excuse for unkindness, and so I found it hard to muster much of that same inclination she felt in regard to him, that impulse to "fix" him, somehow. If he wanted to wallow in the past *I* was more inclined to let him.

The hairs on the back of my neck prickled, and I heard heavy, swishing footfalls outside the room. It wasn't Jenny. The aura she generally emitted was strong, almost overwhelming to the senses. The one drawing nearer to me reached me slowly, as if being dragged through murky water, not nearly as powerful as Jenny's, yet ten times sharper, as if it would cut me if I got too close.

Vince.

I flicked off the light and looked about me frantically, seeing the closet door, diving for the handle and slipping inside. The door shut me into the dark with a soft click. I heard the footsteps come through the door on the other side of the room, could hear Vince muttering something about stupid girls and stupid ponds and stupid wet socks. I contained my laughter as best I could. *Training must've gone well,* I thought.

The muttering suddenly stopped, and I sucked in a sharp breath, waiting for him to march across the room, fling open the door, and Shift me out into the hall with a string of threats following the arc of my descent.

But then something else hit me, another aura, only this time it struck me in the gut like an iron weight, and I knew who it belonged to before I even heard her speak. "Vince?"

I risked cracking the closet door open the tiniest bit. Jenny was standing in the doorway, dripping wet, wringing out a lock of her hair in an almost guilty way. Vince had his back turned to her, and I caught the weirdest expression flash across his face, like little cracks forming in ice, ripples across water. It was gone in an instant, and he whirled on her, folding his arms across his chest. "Oh, what do *you* want?" he snapped. I seethed silently behind the door, wishing I could leap out and hit him for talking to her like that. But some instinct told me to wait, to listen. As long as Jenny's aura was overlapping mine, I would go unnoticed. In actuality, a Persuader or Sentry only really ever noticed an aura when he was consciously expecting it or if paranoia was causing him to expect it *un*consciously.

She flinched, looking down at the tiny puddle of water forming around her shoes, picking at the doorframe. "I, uh, I wanted to…apologize. For causing you so much trouble." I sighed inwardly. Leave it to Jenny to attribute the blame to herself and not to the person who most deserved it.

Vince didn't say anything for a moment. Then he sighed, and his shoulders sagged a little. "Look," he said, sounding unusually defeated, "I'm sorry I wasn't a very good teacher back there. You were right. I should have explained. And—"

"Whoa, whoa, whoa," she interrupted, holding her hands up to stop him. "Did you just say the words 'you were right?'" She smirked at him, taking a few steps into the room.

I could imagine the glare he threw at her, the resentful twist of his mouth. "I think," he said, uncrossing his arms, "that you must have imagined it."

"Nope!" she said, clapping her hands together. "You definitely said it! No taking it back!"

"You're such a child," Vince accused, throwing up his hands. He turned away, toward me, and I caught a slight smile tugging at his lips.

Ah. So that was it, wasn't it? *This* was why Jenny wanted to *figure out* Vincent Hallows. When alone with her, he didn't seem quite so two-dimensional, didn't seem quite so cold and reticent. I wondered what it was about Jenny that pared people down to their centers.

She walked up to him, placing a hand on his shoulder. "Hey—"

"Jennifer."

All three of us snapped our attention to the doorway, where Liam's tall, thin shape lurked like a shadow. Vince and Jenny sprung away from each other, and I just stared, from behind the door, trying to gain control of my breathing.

Liam stepped into Vince's room, looking between his sullen apprentice and the daughter who more or less harbored a long-standing and intense hatred for him. "Why are you two dripping wet? You both tracked mud all the way from the back door to here. Laura, I think, will be very displeased."

Vince rubbed his arm like a four-year-old caught scribbling on the walls with crayon. "We had a little...mishap."

Liam looked to Jenny for confirmation, but she was ignoring him. He only raised an eyebrow, sighed, and said, "Well, you two better get cleaned up. Especially you, Jennifer."

She glanced up at her father, confused. "Why?"

"Because," he said, slicking back his hair with both hands, "we are going to be spending some quality father-daughter time together. You need someone to train you in a *real* context."

"I'm not going anywhere with you," she said, frowning, chin raised defiantly.

Liam looked down at her, matching her obstinacy with a sternness in his expression. "You have a lot to learn about this world, Jennifer, and splashing around in the pond will hardly cut it."

Vince flushed visibly. Jenny turned her face to the side, and I could see the frustration and anger burning in her eyes even from where I was. "Look, I know you're trying, and all, to *reconnect* with me or whatever, but if you ask me it's a little late for that. You should've taken an interest in me when I actually *needed* you to."

The rigid lines of Liam's face softened with remorse, and it made him look like another person. "I know. *I know* what I did to you, all the mistakes I made. But whatever your feelings are, you can't ignore the fact that staying cooped up here won't help you. Please, Jennifer. If not for me, for yourself."

She looked at him, and I saw the stiffness go out of her posture, and her hands slacken at her sides. It seemed to me a gesture somehow impossibly significant. It was the first time in nine years Liam had really made any progress with Jenny, and the first time she had let him.

JENNY

I wound a strand of my hair around my finger for about the twentieth time and released it. Liam's car was as flashy as, if not flashier than, Vince's. In the sun, pinpoints of light glittered off of the hood as if laden with garnet. The interior was, obviously, black, complete with smooth leather seats that were stiff with neglect, which only reinforced my belief that Liam didn't get out of the house much.

"It's in top condition," said a voice beside me. Liam leaned an elbow on the passenger side door, running a hand along the glossy roof of the car. "It's yours if you want it, in case you were wondering."

"I wasn't." I shut the door hard, facing forward, sinking low in my seat.

Liam removed his hand from the car, actually looking miffed by the action. I scoffed under my breath as he made his way over to the driver's side. He turned the key and the car purred to life immediately, clearly pleased to finally be driven.

At first there was only silence between us, but after a while Liam began fiddling with his cuff buttons and tapping his fingers on the steering wheel. He didn't seem to know exactly how to make small talk with me. I doubted he even remembered my middle name, much less anything significant about me.

He cleared his throat, unbuttoning and re-buttoning his sleeve cuff one more time for good measure, before saying, "Well, to be honest I thought you'd be more curious to know where we're going."

I looked unseeingly out the window for a long while before saying, "If Vince is anything like you, I assumed you'd just be patronizing and mysterious about it. Figured I wouldn't waste my time."

Liam laughed lightly, though there was a forced quality to it. "It's true he's developed certain…characteristics that have a likeness to mine."

"Yeah," I returned, suddenly more annoyed at my father. "Must be great, finally having a kid just like you who can live up to your great legacy."

Liam gripped the wheel harder, his knuckles whitening. "Jenny." I was surprised to hear him call me "Jenny" instead of the impersonal, ill-fitting "Jennifer" this time. I turned to him. His face was lined with frustration. "Please. Let me explain this to you. You have no idea how much I wanted to bring you with me, but Heather would not be separated from you. I wrote to her at first. I tried to see you—"

"Well, you didn't try enough!" I shouted. I could feel tears prickling at the backs of my eyes, and I bit my tongue to hold them back.

Liam was stunned into silence for a moment, green eyes wide and intent on me. "I see," was all he said, turning his attention back to the road.

But I knew he didn't.

VINCE

"You look absolutely pathetic," was the first thing I said to Taylor when I saw him at the windowsill, one leg dangling absently. "Don't you have something else to do, other than wait for your girlfriend to get back? Any hobbies at all? Wait, don't tell me. You have a secret passion for crochet."

I stepped further into the room as he swiveled his head toward me. After a moment, he returned his gaze back to the window, as if deciding a response wasn't necessary. He seemed faintly purposeless, I thought. Lonely. I bit back the tide of empathy, trying to come up with some other meaningless thing to say to quash the feeling. It wasn't hard. "Tell me, what do you Boy Scout Sentries do for fun? Help out the elderly? Pick up trash along the highway? You know, your whole *circumstance* is rather pathetic. You do realize that she's going to be a Persuader one day, a Persuader who will soon realize how dangerous you are to her. Who knows? Maybe she'll even grow to hate you."

"What's your problem?" Taylor demanded, swinging his legs and jumping down from the window's ledge.

"I'm just feeling chatty today, I suppose—" I stopped myself when, out of the corner of my eye, I caught sight of something through the glass pane of the back door, a dark figure heading toward the side of the house.

Taylor started forward, wary yet utterly unafraid of confrontation (as Sentries were), standing at the threshold of the kitchen. "Who's there?" he called.

The figure heard him, paused for the briefest of moments, and broke into a run. Taylor sprinted after him, throwing out his hand to Shift the back door open hard enough to cause a long, vertical crack to appear along the glass. I followed, approaching the two just in time to see Taylor tackle the figure to the ground and grab the man's collar—I could see now that it was a man, probably in his early thirties. Taylor hauled him to his feet, twisting an arm behind his back, and proceeded to drag the trespasser back into the house, brushing past me without a word. Without much ceremony, he threw him to the floor, kicking the man over onto his back. Now so close, I could see that the man already appeared to have been beaten severely. There were old bruises on his swollen face. With effort, he drew himself up to a kneeling position and lifted his head.

Taylor's eyes widened. "*You.*"

A delicate vase the color of a robin's egg trembled once, twice, and then flew at Taylor's head. I lurched forward, Shifting it away. It crashed into the wall, raining down like sharp, blue hail.

Taylor nodded to me in thanks, then turned to glare back at the man at his feet. "What is it with you?" he hissed. "Don't you know when to quit?" Taylor sounded almost bitterly amused, but mostly angry.

"You know him?" I asked moving to stand next to Taylor.

He barked out a noise that was somewhere between a laugh and a snarl. "This clown is one of the two Persuaders who attacked Jenny."

At that I, too, glared down at the man. "Is that so?"

The man stood, holding up his hands in a gesture of surrender, eyes wide and frightened. I noticed his face creased with pain as he did so. He lifted his head, licking his lips nervously. "What are you going to do, then? Kill me?"

"Well, that all depends on *you,*" I replied, serenely. A chair slid across the floor, hitting the backs of his knees. With a cry, he fell back into it. I dropped my hand. "Tay—" I caught myself before I said his name, not taking my eyes from the intruder's. Close one. "Find something to bind him. We need to have a little chat with this guy."

"We aren't so different, you know. The two of us."

I stared down at the man, scowling with all the contempt I could muster. When was Taylor going to reappear with that rope? *"Really?* Oh, go on and explain how you've come to *that* conclusion. Please, I insist."

"Sure, sure. Feign ignorance all you want, but we both know what I mean." A crooked-toothed smile stretched across his face. He looked like a rat. "We're both outcrossed. Your friend knows that. And he despises you for it, you know. He thinks himself better. All the pure-bloods do."

Oh, he despised me, all right. But not for the reason the man was thinking. Taylor at that moment walked back into the room holding a bit of twine in his hands, saving me from the obligation to reply. "Will this do?" he asked.

The man squirmed as I tied him down, thin frame straining against the rope. He soon gave up, slouching against the chair.

"Wise," I remarked.

"Jenny and Liam will be back soon, I think." Taylor leaned against the wall, flicking on the kitchen lights. The room was flooded by a soft yellow glow. "So what do we do with Asinine Assassin, over here?"

I shrugged. "Try to get information out of him. What else? It's worth a shot."

Taylor whirled on the man, sticking a finger in his face in an accusatory fashion. *"Who do you work for?"* he demanded, but a smile was tugging at the corners of his mouth. He half-turned to me with a satisfied snicker into his hand and said, "I'm sorry. I've just always wanted to say that."

I sighed impatiently, pushing him aside, looking down at the man. "What," I asked, slowly, "is your name?"

"Thom," the man gasped, his head beginning to slump, as if the one syllable was a major exertion on his part.

I regarded the man—*Thom*—with a sneer. "Who told you snooping about here was a good idea?"

"I was only following orders," Thom murmured, a tick in his jaw.

"*Whose* orders?" I asked.

Thom looked extremely alarmed by the question, as if we had just asked him to dive from a plane without a parachute.

Taylor took a step forward to stand at my shoulder, shaking his head. "Samuel. Samuel Locke. He's a psycho. And he's targeting Jenny."

I regarded the man with a new wariness. "What did he say he wanted you to do?"

"Basic reconnaissance. He wasn't specific."

"Of course he wasn't," I said. It was impossible to tell if the man was lying or not. "Did he tell you anything else?"

"Nothing." Thom did not look pleased by this. If anything, he looked very pale. He was staring at the ceiling.

Taylor looked poised to say something else when the overhead lights abruptly shattered and the kitchen went black. I put my arms over my head as splinters of glass rained down over the three of us. Taylor shouted something, but it was lost in the confusion.

When I lifted my head again, I saw that the chair was empty, its only occupant a bit of broken twine.

Taylor cursed, turning to me. "Aren't you going to go after him?"

I couldn't answer. All I could think about was the man's rasping voice. Maybe punctured lungs, maybe something worse than that. He couldn't get far.

With a scowl, Taylor ran to the door, throwing it open to see only the empty backyard and the gray smudge of the pond beyond it.

JENNY

I looked out at the Chesapeake Bay, recognizable mostly by its usual indiscernible color that seemed to be a mixture of brown and gray and yellow all at once. I recognized the narrow and infamous Bay Bridge, as well, and started to form an idea of our destination.

I sat upright, so quickly Liam looked over, a small smile at his mouth. "I see you're awake. Figured out where we're going, yet?" I stared out at the Bay, brow creased. "Patience is a virtue, after all."

"Why D.C.?" I demanded, more sharply than I intended.

Liam seemed unfazed by my tone. "I told you. To learn by experience. I'm going to show you what it is we do, but…on a relatively small scale."

"What would a small scale be?" I mused aloud. "Wreaking havoc upon the unsuspecting? Pillaging? Murder?"

Liam smiled in a way that was decidedly devious. "You'll see. No pillaging or murder will be necessary."

My father leaned against a wall, stretching his arms out in front of him before knitting his fingers together behind his head. "I take it your training's going well? Only a few hiccups?"

I wondered if Liam considered almost drowning to be one of those "hiccups". I chose a place on the wall several feet from him to position myself. "Yeah," I said, knowing it was mostly a lie, twisting the cuffs of my shirt. "It's going well."

"It seems you've only really flexed your *telekinetic* muscle so far," he said, slanting his eyes toward me. "But I'm sure you're not ignorant to the fact that you possess within you...*other* abilities."

I stiffened. "So...what? You want me to *pickpocket* someone? Is that your sick idea of father-daughter bonding time?"

He lowered his hands, noticing the shift in my demeanor, in the same instant reaching for me. "Jenny—"

I pulled away quickly, placing myself farther away from him on the wall. I felt my own anger begin to bring heat into my face. "This might come as a shock to you, but I'm going to have to take a rain check on your little crime spree today. Try me on Tuesdays."

To my astonishment, he laughed. It was a brief sound, more of a bark, really. "Who said anything about crime? You won't be *pickpocketing* anyone."

I paused. "I won't?"

"Pickpocketing it for petty thieves and thugs. It's for humans, Jenny. Our kind, a race of *greater beings*...we don't pickpocket." His gaze leveled on a passerby, a man in a nice suit, the lenses of his glasses flashing as he stepped out of the shadow of the building. Liam smiled. "We persuade."

He slouched away from the wall and fell into step with the man, clapping him on the shoulder. "Long time no see, George."

The man blinked, stopping in the middle of the sidewalk as a stream of irritated pedestrians parted around the two of them. He pushed his glasses up the bridge of his nose as if to get a better look at the unfamiliar person before him. "Oh, you must have me mistaken for someone else."

Slowly, Liam removed his hand from the man's shoulder. "I don't think I do, George. I think you're the person I want to talk to." As he spoke, his face angled downward and the hollows in his face darkened. He looked more like a villain to me then than he ever had before.

"I…" It was immediately evident that the man's mind had deserted him. He echoed Liam's words in a voice that sounded like an automated recording. "Yes. I'm the person you want to talk to."

My father smiled. "How's the wife, George? Linda, right?"

"Yes, Linda. How did you—?"

"A marketing manager? Not bad, I suppose. What is it that you make, one-hundred and twenty thousand? One-hundred and thirty?"

"Thirty-five," George said, and then blinked again as if he didn't know why he'd said that.

"What have you got in that wallet, George, right now?"

The man reached into his pocket and withdrew the object in question, and Liam plucked it neatly from his fingers. I detached myself from the wall, finally interfering when I saw that the man had no intention of asking for it back, and seemingly not even an *inclination* to do so. "Wait a second, I thought—"

Liam sighed, rolling his eyes as if the whole thing was ridiculous, as if it was just a game. "No need for alarm, Jennifer," he said. "It's just a demonstration."

George's face changed as Liam spoke, and he pointed to his wallet, still in my father's left hand. "Is that mine?"

"Yes, it is. You dropped it." Liam tossed it back to him, and the man fumbled to catch it. "You should be more mindful of it in the future."

The man left us and I folded my arms at Liam, frowning. "You're expecting me to pull that stunt on someone else? What makes you think I can do it?"

"Well, we'll just see if you can do it." He crossed his arms over his chest, as well, a challenge in his tone that he made no efforts to conceal. "Won't we?"

If there was one thing I couldn't stand, it was that look on his face as he spoke, the thought of him thinking me incapable of something. My hands fell heavily to my sides and balled into fists. "Yeah. We'll just see."

A clique of aggressively attractive teenagers ambled around the corner in that same instant, two boys and a girl. It was plain to see that the ringleader was the one in the middle, a square-jawed hipster-looking guy with a shoulder bag and a face that seemed elongated past what was proportional to the rest of him. As I approached them, it appeared to me that this boy was incapable of withholding his opinion on anything his companions said, and he was in the middle of explaining exactly why both of them were so mistaken when I interrupted his speech with, "Hey! Where've you been? I've been waiting here for you all day."

The boy came to an abrupt halt, and the other two barely managed to avoid running into him. "I…do I know you?"

I recognized that this was the part where I would use my, as Liam had termed it, *other abilities.* "Of course you know me," I said. Without realizing exactly how, suddenly I was in the guy's mind, rifling through his thoughts as one might rifle through alphabetized manila folders in a file cabinet. "Come on, Calvin, quit joking around. You called an hour ago and said you were on your way. Remember?"

I could feel the word "no" rise to the surface of his thoughts, and again without much effort I repressed it and substituted it for the answer I wanted. "Yes, I remember," he said. As the ill-fated victim of my father's manipulations had done just a moment before, the boy—a Mr. Calvin Meyers—blinked slowly, and I felt the influence of confusion on his mind, and saw that it left a place vulnerable and exposed. With a jolt, he looked at me and ran a hand through his hair, looking mortified without knowing fully *why* he was mortified. "I guess I just…I guess I must've forgotten."

The girl who had been standing behind Calvin made a noise of impatience, flicking her hair from her face. "Cal, who is this girl, anyway?"

Still looking at me, he replied immediately, "Jenny. This is Jenny."

I glanced at her, sensing her indignation and bafflement, and beneath it a startling twinge of envy. Ah, so *that* was how it was. "Emily, could you give us a second or two alone?" I asked, keeping my expression even. Fish-like, she opened her mouth and closed it again several times, and I ignored this and looked over at the second boy. "Why don't you go with her, Tyler?"

The two backed away from Calvin as if he was some unknown and dangerous species of insect, turning to head in the opposite direction. I moved toward him a few steps until I was right under the boy's chin, lowering my voice. "Let's see. An only child in a well-to-do family. That right?"

"Yes," he said, and he swallowed with visible difficulty, like his throat had swollen to a point where it was hard to breathe.

"How much do you have on you right now, Cal?" I murmured, and even before I'd finished the question Calvin was digging in his pocket.

He handed his wallet to me like some sort of religious offering. "Here," he said. "Take all of it."

I stared at the wallet for a moment, faltering. I recognized the particular stumbling block to be my own moral objections, and the hesitation had an almost immediate effect. His hand shook as he started to resist my influence, his expression likewise sharpening in increments as he slowly became more cognizant of what was happening to him. I noticed Liam inching toward us in my peripheral vision, certain to intervene if things got too out of hand.

Without warning, I planted a hand in the center of his chest and shoved him roughly away. Shock registered on his face, but only faintly—like a pencil sketch partially erased. "Go catch up to your friends and forget this ever happened."

He nodded stupidly and obediently, spinning on his heel and sprinting away from me, returning his wallet safely back into his pocket as he did. Liam came up behind me, laying a hand on my shoulder. "Nicely done. Though I do have some confusion concerning your choice of a subject."

"He's a conceited teenage boy who thinks he's the smartest guy ever. Where's the confusion?" I brushed his hand from my shoulder, for whatever reason still hearing the phrase "greater being" ringing in my ears. "Okay, so I did what you asked me to. Can we go now?"

"Jenny." My father's tone softened unexpectedly. "You've been learning and improving much more quickly than I could have imagined. You...you do know how proud I am of you, don't you?"

I turned to look at him, my eyes widening. "You're—?" I broke off before I said something I would regret, clearing my throat and trying to look indifferent as my gaze slid away from him. "Well, how would I know? That's probably the first time you've ever said anything like that to me."

"I know. But that doesn't mean I haven't..." He trailed off, and unwillingly I understood—possibly for the first time in my life—that we were the same. We were the same, and the irony was that neither of us could tell each other what we both knew to be true. I could see the words that he hadn't said as plainly as if he'd written then down.

That doesn't mean I haven't always been proud of you.

I shoved my hands in my pockets, putting on a scowling face to hide these dangerously touchy-feely reflections. "Whatever. Can you just take me home now?"

"Sure," he said, and that startling softness in his tone was, seemingly against all reason, still there. The sun had started to turn orange in the sky, burning like the end of a cigarette as it edged toward the tops of the gray office buildings. "It's getting late. Let's go home."

10
STRONGHOLD

JENNY

When I stepped into the threshold of the mansion it was immediately evident that something had happened. There was a shattered vase in shards and a dusting of glass across the floor which Taylor was crouched over and carefully sweeping into a pan, and in the center of the kitchen a chair with broken twine draped around it. I thought I could also see a crack in the glass door behind them. Vince glanced up quickly when he heard the door open, looking pale. "I thought you two would be back later—"

"Jenny is a rather quick study," Liam said, raising an eyebrow at both boys.

"*Is* she?" Vince muttered, tugging the rope off of the chair. I made a face at him, which he ignored studiously.

I turned to Taylor, who stood, brushing glass from his knees. "Did something happen?"

He went the opposite color from Vince as a shadow of disquiet passed over his features. "We were attacked."

What followed afterwards was an exhaustive account of whatever new catastrophe had taken place during our absence. Liam asked questions twice, some of them seemingly irrelevant, and we were all a little spent by the time his extensive inquiry had run dry, even Liam himself.

He blew out a long breath, one that managed to sound both anxious and fatigued. "I suppose I always knew that you would one day be targeted, Jennifer." He looked down at me with dark eyes. "I just didn't anticipate it coming to these measures, not so soon. It'll be tug-of-war from this point onward. I hope you're ready."

I hoped I was, too.

In the morning, I awoke early to a light rap on the door, followed by a muffled whisper. "Jenny? Are you awake?"

The door opened a crack and Taylor stuck his bed-mussed head in, bright smile just visible in the muted light.

I threw a pillow at him, but he ducked back out into the hall. I seethed for a moment in vengeful dismay as he came fully into my room, shutting the door softly behind him. A few hours later into the day and I would've been thrilled to see him. But this early, I wasn't nearly so thrilled. "What," I began, fighting to keep my voice even, "could you possibly want at six in the morning?"

"It's almost seven," he said, as if there was some enormous difference between the two. "Besides, you've known forever that I'm a morning person."

"Incurably so." I sat up and, blinking rapidly and thinking I must still be half-asleep somehow, I set my hands to my leg and realized that I wasn't in pain anymore. I wasn't in any kind of pain at all.

I swung my legs over the side of the bed, deciding to investigate. "I'll be right back," I called over my shoulder at Taylor as I made my way across the room to the enormous bathroom.

I shut the door behind me, closing myself into the too-bright space, sitting on the edge of the sink. Carefully, slowly, I pulled up the hem of my shorts and began peeling away the layers of bandages circling my upper thigh, dreading seeing the wound and not exactly knowing why. Absurd hypochondriacal anxieties streamed through my brain, and I wondered what I would do if it turned out to be infected, or if it had worsened, or if the skin around where the bullet had grazed had simply gone…dead.

Yet there it was, or where it *had been*, no ripped flesh or puss or blood or thick, jagged scar to indicate that anything had ever happened to me. There was only a faint, pink mark in place of a once pronounced wound. I touched it lightly with my fingertips. It felt smooth, not raised like a scar. Also, it was painless and—to my relief—not inexplicably desensitized.

I sat there for a long time, still blinking, beginning to imagine myself in a dream, where things could not make sense and it was okay.

But then Taylor spoke from the other side of the door. "Are you alright in there?"

"Yeah." My voice came out a weak, unconvincing croak. I cleared my throat and tried again. "Yeah, I'm fine."

"You don't sound fine." The knob on the door rattled as he tried to turn it. "Why is it locked? Can I come in?"

I looked down at the pink mark across my leg, biting my lip. "Okay. If you promise not to freak out."

There was a scoff on the other side of the door. "What, a third arm I don't know about?" he asked.

I was silent.

A sigh. "Okay. I promise."

I held out my hand, feeling more experimental with my powers after my outing with Liam. For a moment I felt almost victorious as the lock on the door turned by its own accord with a metallic click. But when Taylor walked in and his eyes immediately flicked to the ghost of a wound that should have been there, I just felt sick.

He stopped, midstride, shaking his head as if he thought this was a dream, too. "Am I seeing things," he began, "or is your leg…all mended?"

I shrugged helplessly. "I don't know! I woke up without any pain so I went to unravel the bandages and *poof*, it just wasn't there."

"Well, it's not as if it was too serious to begin with," Taylor mumbled, as if trying to convince himself more than he was trying to convince me. He moved forward to stand over it, head tilted as if that would change the way he saw it. "It was just a scratch, really…"

"A *scratch?*" I repeated, incredulous. "You've seen it, Taylor. You know that's not true."

He reached down, pressing his thumb on the spot. "Does that hurt?" he asked, looking back up at me through the hair hanging in his face. He still had bedhead. Then again, he always had bedhead.

I stifled a laugh at the failed clinical way he tried to look at me. He could never cover up his emotions very well; in all the time I had known him, he'd always been an open book—well, a *mostly* open book. I thought, oddly, of Vince, with his secrets and his unyielding expression. "No," I said.

He pressed his palm against my leg, pushing down lightly. I felt pressure—and heat, which I, in vain, tried to not think about—but there was no pain. "Still nothing."

Taylor shrugged his shoulders, as I had done, moving to sit beside me on the counter. "I guess it's all healed, then."

"Thanks, Captain Obvious. I got that about five minutes ago." He made a face at me, and I laughed. "Hey, be comforted by the knowledge that you aren't some mutant freak like I am."

At that he turned toward me, eyes sharp. They were forceful, humor gone. "Freak? Jenny, don't you realize how useful this talent of yours is?"

"Talent? How can something like this be a *talent?*" I was aware of my rise in volume, but I couldn't bring myself to care. "Now there's one more thing that sets me apart, one more reason for everyone else to want to kill me or use me or both."

"Jenny." Taylor took me by the shoulders, looking alarmed by my outburst. "In case you haven't noticed, we're *all* freaks. This *society* is mutated, not you." I looked away, but he put a hand under my chin and turned my face back to him. "And being different isn't some horrible curse. The things that make you different define you as a person. I know that sounds pretty lame, but it's true. Really."

Usually he just jokes around, I thought. *It's strange to know that he can be serious when he wants to be. That he can be wise.* "You say that as if..." I stopped. "You can do something, too, can't you? Something other Persuaders can't."

His hand dropped. He looked surprised. "How did you guess?" He didn't even attempt to deny it.

I tapped my head. "Persuader intuition, remember?"

He smiled. "Of course."

The balcony was a place I had come to think of as a sort of haven. It was still apart of the mansion, but somehow...not a part of it, and that seemed to make it the ideal location to clear one's head.

Still, the morning air was chilly. The sun hadn't even risen over the tops of the trees, only slipping through the breaks between the leaves in pieces. I wrapped my arms around myself.

"Haven't you ever asked yourself how I found you in the first place?"

I whirled toward the voice at my ear to see Taylor. I had almost forgotten he was with me. Almost. He was smiling crookedly, arms folded, smug about his little secret. I scowled. "No. I never wondered. I just always assumed you looked in the phone book," I replied, mockingly.

He moved around me with a brief chuckle, resting his hands on the banister, looking out at the dark pond. It reflected the patches of sunlight, its surface alive with rippling sparks. "It is not uncommon for a Persuader or Sentry of strong lineage—like you and me—to develop certain quirks. Unusual talents. You with your quick healing, me with my tracking."

"Tracking?"

Before he could expand on the word, there came a voice from behind us. "What he means to say is that he has potential to be a rather exceptional stalker."

Taylor turned. "And with your weak aura, *you* would be a fantastic one." He didn't look surprised by Vince's eavesdropping, just annoyed.

I found I was a little irritated, myself. "What are you doing up so early?"

"I sensed a disturbance in the force," he replied, shutting the heavy, black door behind him. "Literally, actually. And I could ask you the same, couldn't I?"

Taylor folded his arms, leaning back against the iron, vine-strangled handrail. "Talking." He sounded defensive.

"Hm." Vince looked unconvinced. "Well, you might as well explain your little stalker thing to Jenny. She's looking awfully befuddled."

"I am not!" I said, indignant, at the same time Taylor sighed, "It's not a stalker thing."

"Easy, easy. No need to get testy. *I'll* explain." Vince ran a hand through his dark curls, which looked oddly neat despite his just waking up. I suddenly felt self-conscious, and smoothed down my own disloyal tangles when he wasn't looking. "Tracking is a rare disorder—excuse me, *talent*— that allows someone to find where a specific person is by tapping into his aura."

"But only if I've felt the aura before," Taylor added. "I could find you two, but I couldn't find, for example, this Samuel guy because I've never met him."

"How fortunate," Vince muttered. I could only agree. Just the thought of those black, predatory eyes caused a shiver to run up my spine.

"So you found me," I reasoned, from what both boys were telling me, "by following my—what would you call it? Aura trail?"

"*Aura trail*," Vince scoffed. "How *sophisticated* that sounds."

I shot him a warning glare, but Taylor cleared his throat, drawing my attention back to him. "Yes, that's a way to put it. A *good description.*" He paused to look sharply at Vince, who was ignoring us both, preoccupied with Shifting apart the vegetation at his feet. Taylor continued with a shake of his head. "I've been around your aura for a long time. I know it pretty much like my own."

Vince heaved a sigh. "Why'd you even bother?"

Taylor turned, narrowing his eyes at the other boy. "What?"

"Well, it's not as if coming here changed anything. You just brought trouble down on all of us. I wouldn't have done the same, in your position. So she drives off with a big, bad Persuader." He shrugged. "Things happen."

I sucked in a sharp breath, Shifting Vince roughly against the door. He coughed once, the breath rapidly knocked out of him. "Not everyone has to be just like *you*."

There was a smile tugging at his mouth, despite being pinned against a door. I frowned at him with frustration. What did it take to bother this guy? "Alas," he sighed, regaining his breath. "Not everyone *can* be like me. I'm just one of a kind."

I dropped him, huffing. "That you are."

"Like you," he said, conscientiously brushing himself off so he was once again immaculate, as he almost always was. He stood. "You're quite different yourself, you know. That neat, little healing talent, your unfortunate knack for getting into trouble—" I took a step toward him, but he just laughed. "That temper of yours."

"I think you're trying to test that temper, Hallows," I accused.

"Doesn't take much, what with your habit of Shifting people at random and insulting powerful Persuaders willy-nilly."

"Well, it's not like the people I've insulted and Shifted didn't deserve it," I grumbled. "Especially you."

Vince smiled a little ruefully. "Perhaps, Jennifer." The sun had just broken the net of trees on the horizon and struck his eyes, turning them bronze-green. "Perhaps."

The door opened without his touching it, and yet I didn't even blink at it. How quickly I was becoming accustomed to the Persuader world, how inured to its ways and workings. I couldn't decide if this was a good thing or not.

The mansion was still gray with shadows when I returned. I guessed it was probably a quarter past seven now, and decided I would wander back to my room, where I could squeeze in a few more hours of sleep before someone decided it was a lovely day for more training.

My hand just brushed the door to my bedroom when I felt a presence strong enough to double me over. I whirled, expecting Taylor, but I only saw Laura coming down the hallway, hands nervously ringing a dishtowel as she seemed to always be doing.

Though when she approached, I only felt her usual aura. "Was there someone else with you before?" I asked, peering over her shoulder.

"No, miss." Her hands had stopped, her expression hardening into a very particular expression. A very careful one.

"I could've sworn..." I trailed off, deciding it wasn't important, and then tried again. "Is there something you wanted?"

The old woman huffed, melting back into her usual demeanor: frank and bitter. "Wanted? No. What I wanted was to work for a *respectable* Persuader, not a shut-in who spends almost every waking moment in that office of his. But you can see how *that* worked out." I fought back a grin. "In any case, your father sent me to fetch you, which is why I'm here. As if he doesn't have perfectly functional legs," she added, especially bitter.

I blinked. "Why would he want to see me?"

"That's something to take up with him, miss," she returned, wrapping the towel around her scraped knuckles. "I assume you know where to find him."

That merited a double blink on my part. Liam never allowed anyone to go into his office. I had never even seen Vince go in, in all the time I had been here. I cleared my throat. "Thank you, Laura."

The elderly maid was already bustling down the hall like a dark and thunderous cloud. I shook my head, abandoning the effort.

Liam's office was everything I'd expected it to be. Dark, dusty, secluded, and...boring. The only character the room possessed was within the messy stacks of paper and the framed photograph set carefully at the edge of his desk. I came closer to get a better view of it, eyebrows arching when I saw my mother's twenty-something face gazing back at me. I looked up at Liam quickly, partly to smother that twinge of pain I felt whenever I thought of my mom, and partly to discern what she ever saw in my father when she married him. I tried to imagine him younger, his face less severe, and his attitude less aloof and dark.

I gave up as he turned from the window to face me. In the dimness of the room, his face was only half illuminated, the other half a sharp-edged silhouette. When he noticed my interest in the picture, he gently set the frame facedown on the desk, motioning for me to sit in the chair across from his.

I sat, reluctantly, still not able to read exactly what was on his face. He looked tired, definitely. And very unenthusiastic about what he was about to say. "What is this about?"

Liam rubbed his eyes, and then threaded his fingers through his hair. "I've finally managed to contact Natalia, the Sentry leader closest to us."

My eyes widened, and I sat forward in the chair. "Isn't that good news? Did she say she wanted to talk to Taylor?"

"No," Liam said, looking away. "She...wanted to talk to *you.*"

I fell back into the hard, leather chair, clutching at the cracks in the brown material. "Me? But why?"

He made a sort of resentful laugh then. "You've known for some time that there would be people who would hope to convince you to come to their side. Well, I have a feeling Natalia is one of them."

I didn't have anything to say to that. Was it possible that this Natalia woman wanted me to join her ranks even without knowing me at all? There were plenty of Unavowed out there, weren't there? Why me?

I supposed I could attribute it in part to my parentage. I could develop a liking for my father's Persuader ways, or I could turn to my mother's Sentry lifestyle. I was the wild card that, for some reason, every Sentry leader and Persuader millionaire wanted in his hand. I imagined a noose resting against the hollow of my collarbone, beginning to tighten.

Both times I'd ridden in a car with a Persuader, it had been mostly quiet and...well, put frankly, extremely awkward. But wedged between two Persuaders and a rogue Sentry inside any tiny space was considerably less quiet. And a lot more awkward.

"I don't see why *he* has to come along," Taylor grumbled, jerking his chin in Vince's direction.

Sitting opposite him to my left, Vince responded with his usual caustic glare and self-important reply, "Vincent Hallows does *not* get left out of things." He sniffed, adding, "Besides, I'd be alone with Laura. Forcing small talk with her is like conversing with a brick wall."

Liam stifled a snicker at the mention of the old maid's less-than-friendly disposition, a disposition he was well accustomed to, I was sure.

"I think it would've been an excellent opportunity to build your blossoming relationship," I mused, to interrupt, raising my eyebrows at Vince. He made a noise that sounded both derisory and strangled.

"Well, still," Taylor continued, relentless. "Why can't he just sit in the front? His ego is practically crushing me to death against the door."

"Practically?" Vince frowned. "I'll have to work on that." He half-turned in his seat so he was angled toward Taylor. "And I don't see why *you're* going, either. Except the fact that Jenny is."

Taylor had long ago stopped responding to Vince's implications to some sort of brewing romance between us. It obviously wasn't true. "I wouldn't complain about me going, if I were you. Natalia might change her mind if I could manage to talk to her."

"Her mind was never made up," Liam said, looking a bit exasperated by this. "Direct answers aren't exactly her forte so much as direct *actions* are. Probably the moment she learned of Jennifer's arrival, she was resolved to meet her. No one else."

"You're famous!" Vince remarked, customarily adding something insignificant and mocking to the conversation.

"What's she like?" I asked, directing my question toward Liam, someone I knew for a fact had met Natalia in person.

Liam didn't answer for a moment, as if contemplating. He ran a hand through his short, thick hair, a nervous gesture. A habit Vince seemed to have picked up from him. "She's...she's very adamant, especially in her beliefs. She doesn't like taking commands, either, considering how hard she's worked to get where she is. You see, Natalia has a fractional amount of human blood from her father's side, and there are people who won't let her forget that."

"Outcrossed," Vince said, slouching in his seat. His face had grown serious. "She's outcrossed. Like me."

"What's the word for me?" I asked. Persuader culture seemed to have a vocabulary all its own. There had to be a word for what I was.

"You're an interbreed," he said, voice taut with something like unhappiness, which only posed a new question in my mind that I couldn't quite put into words. "Someone born with a Persuader parent and a Sentry parent. Only *slightly* less frowned upon by those bloody pretentious Purists than an outcross or rogue."

"Purists think they're superior because they belong to what they consider to be 'untainted' bloodlines," Taylor explained, before I could ask. "And any threat to the purity of the Persuader race is inexcusable."

My head was spinning. "Are only Persuaders Purists?"

Taylor nodded. "I think you'll learn that Sentries are a little busy to be concerning themselves with that business."

"Which is why I barely squeezed in this meeting with Natalia. She has mansions to storm. Plans to foil," Liam muttered.

"Persuaders to harass," Vince added, counting them off on his fingers. "Puppies to spit on. Flowers to stomp…"

"Is she really that bad?" I asked, beginning to feel more at unease than before. My insides were already writhing with anxiety as it was.

Liam met my eyes in the rearview mirror for just a moment, expression grim. "Worse."

The car came to a soft rumble in front of the Sentry stronghold, or what I thought was the stronghold, at least. "Are we in the right place?"

It was certainly huge, like I'd expected it to be, but I couldn't understand why it looked so…decrepit.

It was a simple rectangular building, like a warehouse, with most of the windows boarded up. The walls were a grayish brick, unpainted, and parts of it seemed to be crumbling. Vines of ivy formed a twisted net around the edifice, clawing their way into cracks in the brick and crevices between the boards across some of the windows. The clouds above us formed a thick, gray ceiling that looked ready to cave inward on us, only enhancing the general gloom and sense of foreboding.

"It looks deserted," I said, getting out as soon as we stopped. The feeling of dread didn't fade. If anything, it grew stronger as we made our way toward the building.

Taylor kept close to me as we reached the old warehouse. The front door was more of a wide sheet of rusted tin that probably slid upwards, like a garage door, though it didn't look inclined to move in its present condition. "Stay alert," Taylor murmured in my ear. I was more than alert. I could feel aura energy everywhere. "Chances are there are guards posted somewhere out here. We might be walking into an amb—"

Behind us, there came the light clearing of a throat, a deliberate, unfriendly sound.

We all turned to see a girl, trailed by two men, all of them with guns trained steadily on us. None of them appeared in either mien or conduct to have any misgivings about shooting us dead, I thought. Taylor, reflexively, grabbed my arm, pulling me a little behind him. The girl was looking right at me with the oddest expression on her face—a snarl turning the mouth but something a little more pitying in the eyes—and it struck me then that she looked...familiar.

"Gwen?" demanded Vince, in a hoarse voice. "What...what are *you* doing here?"

At the sound of her name, I realized why I recognized her. Vince and I had run into her at that Persuader party in Baltimore. I couldn't help but recall that she and Vince had dated once, and that she still had feelings for him. At least, it had *seemed* that way. Now I wasn't quite sure what to make of her—at one moment so miserable and listless, the next standing there with a gun comfortably in her hands and electricity in her every movement.

Gwen scoffed, tossing her pale, brown hair back as her eyes flicked to her ex. "Vincent. Fancy seeing you here. I see you've brought friends. Actually, I'm surprised you *have* friends." I didn't, however, recall her being so surly.

Taylor coughed into his hand something that sounded like "hardly" as Vince blanched a shade lighter than his usual pallor, looking ghostly. Still, he managed to recover some of his typical derision. "Well, you should know that I'm not here to pay you a visit or anything. Sorry to disappoint."

Gwen gave a short laugh. "My heart is just breaking over here." She said it evenly, sarcastically, but I could've sworn I'd heard something in her voice to contradict it.

I figured *I'd* have to be the first to say it. I stepped forward, pulling my arm out of Taylor's protective grasp. "I thought you were a Persuader."

Her eyes slid back to mine and there was that same look that made me wonder if she hated me or pitied me. I wasn't sure which I detested more. "That's certainly what I *tell* everyone I am," she said, smiling, perhaps a little too proud of having deceived everyone. "But my true allegiance is with the Sentries. I'm the stronghold's benefactor."

"Cool," Taylor approved, shoving his hands in his pockets. Seeing the confused look she tossed him, he shrugged and said, "You're, like, a double agent. I feel like I'm in a *Mission Impossible* movie, or something."

"Yeah, well, I'm sure it's not *half* as interesting as being a rogue, is it?" she returned, coolly, and Taylor and I both tensed. Seeing our reactions, she added, almost gloatingly, "My dad's kind of involved with the government. He's no David Ross or anything, but he's as familiar with the goings-on as any Senator is. So, yeah, don't look so shocked that I know who you are." Gwen looked back at her sullen ex-boyfriend, leaving Taylor no room to reply. "You keep interesting company, Hallows."

He scoffed, gesturing to me with a slight, mocking bow. "Well, Her Highness won't let us boot him onto the streets, so we're stuck with him."

I turned to him, glaring at him around an anxious looking Liam. "Just because you hate the world and everyone in it—" I began, sharply.

My father held up his hands, palms outward at both of us. "Enough of that," he said. He switched his attention to Gwen, composure once again drawn about him. "We'll keep your secret if you keep ours, simple as that. Natalia has requested an audience with Jenny, and that's why we're here. Nothing else, nothing violent. These two are simply..."

"A package deal," Taylor finished, putting a hand on my shoulder. I twisted around to look at him, and he smiled at me. Vince made no noise of disagreement, which I found surprising.

Gwen studied the four of us for a moment, and then sighed, ordering the two Sentries behind her to let us in. One of them called in on a dated walkie-talkie, growling a demand into it for the door to be lifted.

A moment later, it slid up into the ceiling with a long groan and several antique rattles and clanks. We were ushered roughly into the stronghold, Gwen in the front, Liam and Vince in behind her, and Taylor and I in the back. The other guards followed. "Move it," the bearded, leathery-faced one commanded, his voice deep and gruff. "We don't have all day."

The door squealed back down with a bang, kicking up pale dust as it shut us into hostile territory.

At least, it felt that way with the way they were looking at me.

Sentries were everywhere, huddled around blueprints, fervently and loudly discussing strategy with others, resting on military-style cots. The place was dimly lit, but I could see enough to realize that it wasn't just a stronghold. It was a shelter.

The whole bottom floor was sectioned off at each side by cubicle curtains and hole-riddled blankets, and there seemed to be a soup kitchen in the back, where gray-faced Sentries in tattered, thick clothing lined up, trays in hand.

I could feel it when they saw us, like dozens of nails hammered into the back of my neck. The looks shot at us ranged everywhere from confusion to suspicion to hostility as we made our way through. They could probably identify Liam as a Persuader by his elegant clothes, and Vince's conceited expression was evidence enough. "So," began the latter of the two, ignoring the acidic glares aimed his way, "when were you going to tell me that you were a renegade?"

Gwen's shoulders tensed in anger, but she didn't turn. "When were you going to ask?" she replied, bitingly. "You never exactly cared enough to take notice. Besides, I couldn't trust you to keep it a secret."

"Couldn't trust me?" he demanded, for a moment actually looking hurt, though it disappeared before she could see it. "I was under the impression that we were once a couple."

She whirled, jabbing a finger in his very surprised face. "You and I both know that you were never under that impression."

The rest of us fell silent as the two stared each other down. I held my breath, glancing back and forth from Gwen to Vince. No one else said anything, either, uncertain of what to do. They were likely dreading the outcome of the argument, as I was—especially considering the fact that one of the debating parties happened to be armed and lethal.

Then, Taylor cleared his throat, gracelessly breaking the silence. "Well," he said, clapping his hands together, "this is awkward."

Gwen, with a grunt, turned back around, motioning impatiently for us to follow her to the back corner of the warehouse where a rickety, metal elevator waited for us.

Posted in front of the doors was another Sentry, far younger than the other two behind us, maybe fifteen or sixteen. The blameless slant of his eyebrows and his gawky stature was at odds with the gun in his hands. When we approached, Gwen said, sharply, "Eli."

The boy stood at attention, rather clumsily jostling his gun to one side. "Ma'am," he replied, with a bit of a pubescent tremor in the address. I felt a flash of sympathy for the kid, so young to be already so a part of this austere and militant existence. He blinked at the four of us behind her. "Who are they?"

"Our lovely Persuader friends from down the road. And,

unfortunately, also my responsibility at the moment." I was thankful that she seemed to sense that Taylor being a rogue was something better left unmentioned. "So there's no need for you to worry about them."

Eli swallowed, his Adam's apple bobbing. His curious brown eyes found mine. "Down the road? As in the Cable mansion? So you must be Jennifer Cable."

I was well aware of the hush that went over the room in a short few moments. Eli apparently had a bit of carry to his voice. I risked a glance behind me, and I wished I hadn't turned. Dozens of eyes were turned on me, on Eli, on Liam. But mostly on me. I could hear several words rushing softly, yet venomously, through the crowd. Interbreed. Aberration. Menace. They all struck me like burning match tips to the skin. I distinctly caught the phrase "would've been better if she wasn't born."

Vince seemed to be just as affected, as if the insults were aimed at him, too. He grabbed my arm, pushing Eli out of the way as he hauled me inside the elevator. Everyone else, including Eli, shoved in after me, and Gwen slammed the metal door shut as the elevator started to carry us upwards.

Getting away from the chaos of accusations and outrage and disgust was a relief. I glanced at Vince, who was leaning against the far wall, away from everyone else. "Thank you," I said. He just nodded.

The gawky boy accompanying our group had turned bright scarlet, and he brushed his hair away from his face, looking faintly ill. "I-I'm so sorry, I—"

I held up a hand to stop his spluttering. "It's fine. I'm not mad, or anything. I'm okay."

"Good thing we escaped when we did," Vince muttered, kicking at the already scuffed floor. "They might've resorted to rope, a few matches, and a rather medieval idea."

I wanted to hit him for joking about it, but it really *had* felt like a sort of witch trial brewing down there. Also, I had come to recognize his form of humor (that is, anything he said purely for its lack of delicacy) simply functioned as a defense mechanism.

Liam released a troubled sigh, rubbing his temples. "We're going to need to make a quick getaway when this is all over."

"We're going to need a police escort," Taylor said, moving a little closer to me.

I wrapped my hand around his wrist, as if gripping a banister on a particularly steep ascent. "Wish me luck." He looked down at me with puzzled eyes. "I'll have to talk to her alone. I don't know what to expect. I don't know if I'm brave enough for this." Sweat prickled at the nape of my neck at the thought of confronting the Sentry leader, with all her alleged cruelty.

He turned his wrist in my grip and took my hand in both of his. "You're brave enough," he whispered back, full of conviction. I saw Gwen watching the two of us with an unreadable expression.

The elevator squealed to a stop at the top floor. This floor was exceptionally, if not exceedingly, cold, and despite my knowledge otherwise it seemed to have an almost *forgotten* air about it.

"Alright," Gwen said, prying open the door. "This is where you get off. She's in the room at the end of the hall."

I didn't move, glancing around at everyone in the elevator, then at Gwen, trying to see if she was joking. She wasn't. "Even *you* aren't going with me?"

"No." Her voice held a tone that made it clear the matter was nonnegotiable. "Natalia has requested an audience with you, and you won't dare waste her time by going back on your word now." I still didn't take any step toward the hall. Gwen sighed. "Eli," she barked. "Go with her. Make sure she doesn't try to cop out or anything."

"Gee, thanks for the vote of confidence," I mumbled, as Eli took my arm to lead me out of the elevator. I pulled myself free of his grasp. "I can walk," I said to him. He nodded, looking kind of sheepish.

I turned to watch the elevator sink back below us, catching Taylor's eyes. He gave me a small smile before he disappeared from sight.

"Come on," Eli said, not nearly as gruffly as his older fellow guards. "We shouldn't keep Natalia waiting."

"Whatever." I paced ahead of him.

I heard his gun rattling as he jogged to catch up. He fell into step beside me, coughing into his hand. "So," he said, drawing it out. He sounded hesitant, more than before. "Was that guy back there your, you know, your boyfr—"

"If you say boyfriend," I warned, glaring straight ahead, "I will shove that gun down your throat."

"Right," he said, flushing again. "He's not. Got it. Sorry."

I sighed. Why did everyone *think* that? "I don't see how it's any of your business, anyway," I added, more because I was stressed than because I was cross with Eli.

"I know. I was just curious, is all." He stopped suddenly, aware he was continuing on a very treacherous path. He cleared his throat. "I could...show you around the stronghold, sometime."

I raised my eyebrows at him. "Are you serious?" Oh, come on, not this guy, too.

"Well, I...I mean, in case you ever decide—"

I shuddered. God, even this person I'd just met was trying to convince me of the all the *virtues* of Sentry life. "I'd rather we didn't talk about that," I said, quickly.

"Oh, right. Right." He scratched his head, lapsing into silence. I suppressed a noise of irritation.

He started whistling something classical. Loudly.

I shot him a look, but he seemed to interpret it as one more inquisitive than annoyed. "It's Bach," he said, cheerfully. "You know what they say. If it ain't Baroque, don't fix it."

Some small, lame part of my sense of humor wanted to laugh at his stupid pun. I was quickly discovering that it was hard to really be mad at him. He had a certain child-like quality about him that was difficult to dislike. "I thought it was a Persuader thing to like pretentious music."

He laughed, relaxing a bit. "It's a Persuader thing to *be* pretentious, actually." His eyes slid to the side to meet mine. "No offense."

I shrugged. "I can't decide if that offends me or not."

"So that means you can't decide whether or not to hit me for it, hopefully?" He grinned in a boyish way.

"No, it means I'll hit you anyway, but I may or may not feel bad about it later."

Eli laughed again. "Remind me to keep on your good side, Jenny." Suddenly, his gaze snapped straight ahead, his expression sobering. "We're here."

I, too, looked in front of me, at the door at the end of the hall. There wasn't much light spilling in through the cracks in the boards of the windows, and neither was there much illumination from the lanterns that hung from the ceiling. I wondered if it was just as dark in Natalia's office.

"I'll be here when you two are finished," he said, all business, posture straight and soldierly beside me.

I took a deep breath, and opened the door. What struck me first was the brightness. All the windows were uncovered and, well, *glass* and there were even a few candles lit on the tables in the corners of the room. This office space looked less rundown than the rest of the warehouse, and the air smelled vaguely of cinnamon. The woman at the chair before me cleared her throat, and I jumped, not from the noise, but because of how she looked. She wasn't a huge, menacing creature with horns growing out of her head and scales and claws, after all. She was a middle-aged woman with white-blonde hair and calm eyes the color of copper. She didn't look particularly friendly, but she didn't look ready to bite my head off, either. "Hello, Jennifer," she spoke, her voice crisp and detached. She gestured gracefully to the chair in front of her desk. "Please sit."

I obeyed quickly, not wanting to tick her off in the first five seconds of meeting her. The seat was uncomfortable, plastic, but I didn't dare complain. "Thank you," I said, not knowing what else to say.

"No, thank *you*," she returned, raising her head in a decidedly regal manner. She seemed queen-like, almost. "For seeing me on such short notice, that is. I wanted to talk to you as soon as I could."

I swallowed. Thickly. "What for?" Of course, I already had an idea, if Liam was correct.

Natalia smiled, but it wasn't a pleasant smile. It was a cold, impersonal smile that only held polite interest. Maybe that was the way with all important, powerful leaders. "Why, to discuss the unique opportunity presented to you, of course."

I eyed her closely, feigning ignorance. "Opportunity, ma'am?"

"Your parentage, Jennifer. You do know of the unusual choice that is at your disposal, correct? You know of the expectations for an interbreed—or lack thereof, I should say. You know that you are free from the social conventions and familial bonds that commit most to where they've originated."

"And I've come from nowhere," I said, suddenly finding my nerve. "Is that what you're saying? I hate to be the one to break this to you, but if you think being an interbreed makes me 'free' from anything, you're mistaken. So, if we're done—"

"I'm afraid not," she said, something pointed and impatient finding its way into her tone. "I assume Liam has told you all about me, yes? How

I'm such a bad person and I only want to manipulate you, et cetera, and so on…" She waved her hand in the air, rolling her eyes at the mention of Liam. "He really has a *gift* for deception, you know."

"What are you saying?" My fingernails rapped on the armrests, and I began to feel agitated. "That my own father lied to me about you? Who do you expect me to believe?"

"You know you never considered him a real father, not for a long time, anyway," she said, her voice softening. I froze, caught by surprise. "Don't think I'm unaware of your parents' separation, how *indifferently* he left you. At such a young age, too. It's quite a shame, to be denied your own identity for so long."

"You don't know anything about me."

"Maybe not," she amended. "But I know Liam. And he rarely tells the whole truth."

"And you think *I* don't know that?" I asked, irritably, sitting up straighter in the chair. "It took him almost eighteen years to tell me that I had superpowers. Don't lecture me about my father. I *know* what he is."

She smirked. "You're a little firecracker, aren't you? I'd monitor that temper of yours, Jennifer. When a Persuader lets his emotions get the better of him, often times his control is forfeited." Her bronze eyes darkened with something unreadable, maybe a memory. "I have no way of knowing what exactly he said to you, but I do know he obviously convinced you that I was some sort of demon, waiting to lure you here to my lair and convince you to sell your soul to me, yes?"

"Something to that effect, yeah," I said, though I didn't add the part about how Vince had suggested she spit on puppies. "He told me that you were powerful. And stubborn. And that you worked hard to get where you are because—"

She waved her hand. "Enough. And he told you about how there are some who would wish to convince you to join one side or the other."

"Yes." I folded my hands in my lap.

"You think I am one of those people."

I *knew* she was. "Yes."

"Well." Natalia looked down at her own hands. "I don't know how, exactly, to convince you that I am not a bad person."

With her face downturned like that, I suddenly remembered the photograph Taylor and I had found in the west wing, the one of the girl crouched over the pond. "It's you," I whispered, more to myself, really.

She glanced up, her pale brow knitting. "Pardon?"

"I was rummaging through some boxes when I found an old photograph of a girl," I explained. "I'm *sure* it was you. But why…why would my father have a picture of you?"

Natalia looked caught off guard. Her fingers twitched nervously before she curled them into her palms. "You must be mistaken. Your father is hardly the sentimental type—"

"So you knew each other back then?" I asked, leaning forward.

The Sentry leader looked flustered, two spots of color appearing on her fine cheekbones. "Yes, but…I don't see how it's important."

"Did you know my mom?" I asked, quietly.

At that, Natalia rubbed at her temple, looking very tired. She paused before she said, "Yes. I knew Heather. But I wish…sometimes I wish I hadn't ever known her."

I fell back, as if she'd pushed me. "Why would you—?"

"If we could get back to the matter at hand," she interrupted, solidifying back into her original demeanor.

"Which would be?" I wasn't entirely sure what we were talking about, anymore.

Natalia stared at me for a moment, seemingly in meditative silence. "You've been told that there are people out there who want to manipulate you, and that is certainly true. But there are *also* people who just want to wipe you clean from this world. People who hate who you are, what you are, and what you represent."

I felt cold from the inside out, as if ice was rushing into my veins. "Why are you telling me this? To scare me?"

"No," she returned, standing. Her eyes were very severe, deep-set in her face. "I'm telling you this to warn you. I am not one of those people who would destroy you, but someone close to you might be. Someone who might not even realize it." On my way out, she called to me, "Keep that in mind."

11
DEADLY SECRET

Vince had told me of the translation of the word "Cavea", a word seemingly indicative of a place that was enclosed, a place that was restricted, though to me Cavea felt like a world of absolute and limitless freedom. If anything was *restricted*, it was the outside world, the Persuader world. There were all these rules I had to follow, customs I had to learn, people I had to socialize with—people I would much rather avoid, honestly.

But in my mind there was no Samuel out to get me, no Natalia requesting I speak with her immediately, no Liam reminding me every second of every day who I was and what I had to do and what other people wanted me to do. I had finally found the kind of world I had once only dreamed about as a child, where nothing would happen that I didn't *will* to happen, a world I had begun to think didn't even exist at all.

"You seem distracted."

Taylor's voice reached me like an echo in the quiet, empty mountainside. My only requirement had been that we would go somewhere peaceful and remote to train, and Taylor had been more than willing to oblige. The rocks and peaks below were shrouded in a layer of fog, the taller formations stabbing up through the thickness like pointed, gray teeth. I felt like I was sitting on the summit of the world, or at least this world, high up in the cliffs of the tallest mountain, surrounded by only stillness and forest. Our intertwined sky burned hazily above it all. I stared up into it. "You think it's possible to imagine ourselves up *there?*"

Taylor walked up slowly, Shifting a couple pebbles in his hand so they floated around like tiny planets. He sat down next to me in the dirt and pine needles. "I suppose anything's possible, right? At least, while we're in here it is."

I felt a tiny, wistful smile play at my mouth. "Right." I met his steady, watchful gaze. "Sometimes I wish Cavea was reality, and reality was only a really long, bad dream. You know?"

"I know," he said, something heavy in the words. "Me, too." He stood, brushing clinging needles and dust from himself, offering a hand to me. I took it, letting him pull me to my feet. "Only problem is, spend too much time in your head and you forget to look around at the people close to you."

Cavea melted around us, changing and morphing until we were once more standing in the attic of Liam's mansion. Taylor shrugged apologetically, seeing the disappointment on my face.

I went back over what he'd just said, not knowing why it sat so heavily on my mind. Maybe something about it had struck me as being loaded with something else he wasn't saying, and—more to the point— maybe it struck me that way because *I* was the one who had forgotten to look around. "Taylor…can I ask you something?"

His smile faded. "By the tone of your voice, it doesn't sound like a good question." He tried for lightness, but in the end it failed him.

I hesitated, but only for a moment. "Do you think I'm a selfish person for wanting you to stay?" He began to speak, but I stopped him. "Taylor, if you don't want to be here, I wouldn't blame you for it. I think if we managed to arrange another meeting with Natalia, or if we—"

"Jenny, what it this about? Why are you telling me this all of a sudden?" There was a flush across his cheekbones and his tone was almost accusatory. "Is this really about what I *want*, or is this about what I *am?*" He snapped his mouth shut as if he hadn't meant to say that. His eyes were a wide and vulnerable blue as he began to run his hand almost manically through his hair.

"What?" I demanded, grabbing his wrist to make him stop. "What are you talking about?"

He tore out of my grasp, grimacing as if he had just bitten into something bitter. "Try to tell yourself otherwise, but we both know you won't be joining the Sentries when you turn eighteen, not after what you just saw today." He barked out a humorless laugh. "I can see why you would want me out as soon as possible. A clean break, right? No new enemies to worry about in the bedroom next door."

I had no idea what had possessed him all of a sudden to say these things, and I didn't know how he could've convinced himself that they were true. "You actually believe...you think *that's* the reason?" My voice was low in my throat, tinged with exasperation. There was incredulity in my voice, too, and affection, but mostly it was exasperation. "You idiot, I'm *trying* to keep you *safe*. I don't want to lose anyone else I care about, and there's no one I care about more than you." It was the truth, but it still felt strange to say it, as if I was brushing the surface of some bizarre and untraveled territory between us.

It seemed my words, quiet as they were, had surprised him. "I guess I just thought that..." He looked at the ground. It was odd, seeing him like this, so closed off and insecure. "Don't think I didn't see the expression on your face after we left the Sentry stronghold. I thought, 'That's it, then. She's decided. She'll become a Persuader, become one of *them* and maybe even start hating me.' I was...I was terrified, just thinking about losing you. And I—"

I kissed him. Abruptly. Inexpertly. On the mouth.

I didn't know why, but I did. He'd been fumbling around for words, looking lost and hurt and uncertain—actually thinking that I could ever possibly *hate* him—and it had seemed almost reflexive, leaning forward to stop him, as if I was proving something by doing so. Though, when he kissed me back, it didn't feel that way. It didn't feel reflexive.

I felt his palms flat against my back and the line of his shoulders beneath my fingertips and everything else was pulverized to dust under the weight of something like *this*, this deep and acute sense of being surrounded by an entity that somehow blocked out all the nagging outside threats and worries. It was madness, madness that I was doing this, madness that I wasn't stopping myself even after realizing what I was doing.

And, in the midst of this madness, suddenly and out of nowhere a thought occurred to me, a thought I really didn't want to think at all.

What would happen after this?

The thought stuck deep inside my brain, no matter how much I tried to force it out, festering until new thoughts stemmed from it.

Taylor, recognizing the change that had washed over me, drew back, breathing hard. The light in his eyes went out, like a snuffed candle flame.

"What's wrong?"

The thoughts ricocheted around and lodged themselves into unreachable crevices, static where they were. How would I hide this from Liam? From Vince? How could I possibly deny what Vince was saying about us now that I knew it might be true? What would happen to Taylor if Liam found out? Would he be kicked out onto the streets for—oh, God— for Samuel to find him and *kill him?* The questions injected a cold and poisonous feeling into my system, leaving me shaking where I stood, looking at Taylor, wondering if this seemingly innocuous thing between us was actually something that could take his life.

"Jenny?" Taylor took me by the shoulders, jolting me. "Are you okay?"

"No." The word was just a rasping exhalation.

Taylor looked startled. "Is it something I did? *You* kissed *me.* I thought you—Look, I'm sorry if I—"

"It's not something you did," I said, flatly, feeling numb. "It's something I did. Kissing you was a mistake."

Alarmingly, I could see his brow lower darkly over his eyes, and I realized he looked not only shocked, but injured, as well.

"No!" I said, quickly, when I realized what it was that I had just said, how it might've sounded. "No, not like that. It's...I didn't mean it like that."

His gaze softened, worn down at the edges into something that appeared, more than anything, drained of animation. "How *did* you mean it, Jenny?"

"Just...just listen. I-I could get you in serious trouble, and I'm sorry. I shouldn't have done that. Please just pretend it never happened."

Something rose, slowly, in his eyes, like an object rising to the surface of water. It took me a moment to realize that the expression was a glint of dissatisfaction. "Pretend it never happened, after you kissed me like that?"

"It's not like we really have much of a *choice,* Taylor." Even to my own ears, the words sounded frustrated and miserable, childishly so. "If Liam ever found out about...about whatever *this* is,"—I gestured between us—"he wouldn't hesitate to turn you out for Samuel to find you. Even if you could avoid him somehow, you'd be alone. You'd be homeless."

"You could run away with me," he mumbled, half-heartedly, but we both unwillingly began to recognize the situation for what it was: hopeless.

"We could make it work. We could find a way to survive."

"Where would we go?" I reached up to brush my fingertips across his cheek. He covered over my hand with his, keeping it there. "Where *could* we go?"

"You're right." He pulled away from me, slowly, a tide withdrawing from the shore. "It's best if we just…go back to normal."

He walked out, and I sank to the floor and closed my eyes, willing myself together as I always did. It seemed there was always something else. Just when I thought I had set everything in its place there was always something else to upend it all again.

VINCE

Taylor burst into the hallway, barreling straight into me.

I stumbled a few steps back before regaining my footing. "Watch where you're—" Seeing his face, I caught myself. He looked like a man possessed. The violet-blue eyes staring back at me were flashing, like lightning, and his expression seemed to be on the verge of breaking apart and spilling whatever was inside. "What happened to you? Training not go well? Color me surprised."

"It went fine," he snapped. His eyes narrowed. "If you'd excuse me."

Taylor stalked past and I watched him go, puzzled at his change in demeanor. Usually training with Jenny caused him to be in rather high spirits. Not today. I went to find her.

She was sitting on the floor when I opened the hatch to the attic, and I walked over and dropped down heavily beside her, peering into her face when she didn't look at me. That same expression as Taylor's was in place, the same pain, the same uncertainty.

"Go away, Vince." She looked at me from the corner of her vision before closing her eyes. I decided she was definitely more put-off by my presence than usual.

"Did you two…have a fight?"

"Something like that," she sighed, after a moment. She pulled her knees up to her chest, leaning her chin against them.

"Do you want to talk about it?" The words felt unnatural and foreign on my tongue. It wasn't every day I played the Good Listener game. I wasn't sure I even knew the rules.

"No." The word frustrated me. Why couldn't she give me a hint, or something? A sign? A clue? A vague suggestion?

I tried again. "Well…then do you mind if I talk, instead?"

She looked skeptical, suspecting either deception or ridicule, no doubt. Then she shrugged, a weak half-lift of one shoulder. "I suppose it would distract me."

"Okay. Well, I guess you already know about my parents, but I used to have a brother, you know. James. He was a lot like me in some ways, but he was…gentler. More sensitive to other people and their situations, even though he was only a child not even in school, yet." My mouth had gone dry the moment I'd said his name, as it always did, but I continued. "I see him…*everywhere*, and in everyone. Sometimes I imagine what he would look like if he were alive today. Anyway, I know it's not much of a distraction, but that's all I have."

Her face softened. "You shouldn't be afraid to talk about him, Vince. If you don't talk about these kinds of things, you'll drive yourself crazy. Trust me." I didn't answer. My throat was constricting. "His name was James?" Her voice was gentle, understanding. I reminded myself that she had also lost someone. Only her loss was more recent. I wondered how she kept it together so well, especially after all that had happened on top of it during the past week or so. I decided she belonged to an unprecedented species, a rare class of people who could take things in no matter how those things seemed to stack up, leaving nothing uncategorized, leaving nothing forgotten or neglected. I knew from experience that neglect led to decay, and that decay led to an inability to sort out one feeling from the next.

"What? Oh. Yes. James." The word stung on the way out. "He would be sixteen this year."

"I'm sorry about your family," she said, and something in her voice made me believe she really was.

"So am I." I could feel that door inside me, a door only Jenny seemed able to occasionally pry open, beginning to shut again.

"Vince." Her forehead creased as she detected the sudden change in me. "Do you mind if I ask what happened—?"

I stood, quickly, pretending to not hear her. Pretending to not see the question that was on her lips. "Sorry I wasn't much help." I didn't look at her. "I guess you've come to expect that everything that comes out of my mouth is either going to be completely ridiculous or depressing. Again, sorry about that."

"Not everything." She gave a ghost of a smile as my gaze flashed back to hers and caught.

In that moment I felt, strangely, as if I Jenny—of all people—had given me at least a small ounce of her faith. I hoped I wouldn't make her regret it. I tended to do that to people.

Liam had decided that we would all eat in the dining hall, an arrangement I found to be almost *unreasonably* annoying. I couldn't recall the last time I'd actually eaten dinner at this table, and the fact that I had to sit across from the rogue—who had no more right to be at the table than a stray dog from the street—put me into a mood like no other. I glared down at my green beans as if they were the cause of all the misfortune in my life, and running them through with a fork would make it disappear. I looked up to see Taylor still across from me. Obviously, it hadn't worked.

To only make things *more* awkward, not even Jenny and Taylor talked to each other, I noticed. Which was odd. Were they still not over their little disagreement? Jenny sat next to me, avoiding looking him in the eye. I could tell by the way she glanced down every time he glanced up. As if that didn't stretch the air thin enough, Liam was busy trying to coax Jenny into telling us exactly what Natalia had said to her when they'd met earlier at the stronghold.

She didn't look ready to disclose anything, let alone any details of her meeting with Her Royal Highness, Queen Intimidation. "She told me what you said she would." Jenny sounded perhaps a little too disinterested. "All she wanted me to know was that my options were open."

Liam's fork dropped with a clatter, and he wiped at his mouth with his sleeve, a habit I had always found odd for a man brought up in the traditional Persuader fashion. "That can't be *everything* she said," he disagreed, shaking his head. The candlelight glanced off of his fair hair as he did and deepened the hollows under his cheekbones. "Natalia is a schemer. She finds out what she wants from you, and plans accordingly."

"She didn't seem like that," Jenny murmured, softly. Three pairs of eyes found her face at that, searching for signs of joking. She sighed, winding a drifting curl back behind her ear. "Natalia seemed...like she thought she had to defend herself from everyone. She's distrustful, but that's only because she's had to be in order to survive. But what's strange is that she's especially distrustful of *you*. It made me wonder if...if you two know each other better than you've led me to believe." Her stare turned on Liam, who seemed to drain of color. He coughed into his hand, sitting up straighter. I realized that he looked nervous. *Liam* looked nervous.

"Liam? *Is* there something you haven't been telling us about her?" I asked, almost losing my courage to say it as his gaze met mine, a line appearing at the side of his mouth. Taylor leaned forward onto his elbows, pushing his plate aside.

Liam cleared his throat, his eyes wandering across the room until they fixed on one spot, a smudge of pale red on the floor, cast from the glow of the moon through the stained-glass ceiling. "Well, we knew one another, back when we were children. You see, we grew up together. Most people forget this, but Natalia was born a Persuader, and brought up in a Persuader household as I was." It seemed to me that for Liam it was easier to confess his story without looking at any of us. "I saved her life, once. Natalia was eight. I was ten. There was...there was this pond near her house, and it was late January so it was completely frozen over. A couple of boys had been tormenting her, and they chased her out onto the ice. It was in the middle of the pond, where it was thin..." His voice caught, but he tried to hide it with another cough. "She fell through. If I hadn't gotten her out and carried her home, she would've died. I believe *that* was the moment we became friends. And we remained rather close until...well, until her Embracement, I suppose. To say that it came as a *shock* to everyone would be an understatement. I felt betrayed by her, and she felt disappointed in me."

After a pause, and a glance about the room, he reluctantly continued. "Long story short, we were very, very different people who turned out to have very different views on the world. So we severed our ties and never spoke directly again."

"That's it, then?" I demanded, feeling a bit underwhelmed. "Bit of a lackluster tale. The ending definitely needs work."

"While it wasn't exactly a nail-biter," Liam said, "it's the truth."

"But you left something out." Jenny had her hand wrapped around the stem of her glass so tightly I thought I might shatter. "You left out the part about my mother."

Liam froze, no nervous movements, no change in expression. It seemed every time Jenny's mother was mentioned, there was a particularly vacant look in his face. "She wasn't really involved in any of that..."

"That's a lie," Jenny said. "Natalia told me that she knew her when she was my age. That's also when Natalia knew you. Correct me if I'm wrong, but I think that means my mom is involved in *some way* with your story."

He swallowed. "Heather was...Heather was never supposed to *be* involved." Liam's hand shook almost imperceptibly as he pulled it through his hair. "You see, before I ever met her, Natalia and I were in a...romantic sort of situation..."

Jenny choked. "You mean to say, you *dated?*" Taylor coughed his food into a napkin. Even I was shocked, and it took something truly significant to surprise me.

Liam rubbed the back of his neck. "If you wish to call it that, yes. We dated."

"And how was my mother involved?" she asked, her bottom lip beginning to tremble.

"She unintentionally came between us." He frowned, looking grim. "I fell in love with her. And Natalia wasn't exactly oblivious to how I felt, either."

Jenny's mouth was in the shape of an O. "Did you ever *cheat* on Natalia? I mean, did you ever—"

"Excuse me," he interrupted, flushed with color. "But I need to...get some air." He swept out of the room, unable to hide the shaken expression on his face as he did. I stood, tossing my napkin on my plate, moving to do the same.

I had just slipped through the doorway when I heard Taylor speak, his tone low. "Jenny, wait."

I paused, deliberating. Feeling particularly low and ridiculous, I leaned against the doorframe, listening.

"What is it?" She sounded hesitant.

A sigh, probably from Taylor. Then: "I didn't intend for...what happened earlier to drive a wedge between us."

What *had* happened earlier? And perhaps more pressingly, why did I care? I leaned in closer, my ear to the wall as I strained to hear the rest. "I didn't either."

"I don't think I would be able to stand it if we stopped being friends, Jenny," Taylor said, after a moment.

"Yeah, I know," she said, humor finding its way into her tone.

"I know you know." At that, Taylor laughed. It was strange to me, strange that two people could dissolve the things between them with a few words, with a smile, with a laugh. Then again, maybe it *wasn't* strange. Maybe it was only strange to me. "Does that mean…we're okay?"

"Of course." She sounded so sure. "We always are."

I moved away from the door.

NATALIA

Something at the back of my mind had cracked open when I'd laid eyes on Jennifer Cable, releasing recollections of love and loss, of friendship and enmity, things that had been bottled up and out of mind for decades. Memories of Liam surfaced like the flotsam of a shipwreck, memories from when he went by a different name. Liam Cable was my enemy, but *Michael* had been my friend. My best friend, as it happened.

I was rummaging through some boxes when I found an old photograph of a girl. I'm sure it was you. But why…why would my father have a picture of you?

That little piece of information had rattled me the most. What it meant, I could only guess at. Of course, the picture had been taken years ago, too many to count, and it had been tucked away and out of sight. I supposed he had simply forgotten to throw it out and it was just left abandoned there. The worst part was that I knew what photo she was referring to, the only picture I knew of that Michael could own of me at that age. I was sixteen, and Michael was nearly eighteen. We were sitting on the little pier over "our" pond, and he had caught me by surprise with his parents' Polaroid, the one he'd brought along for photographing elusive snapping turtles and geese.

I heard a click and looked up to see Michael, the camera held in one hand, a picture in the other, staring at the image that was forming from the glossy black background. When he finally saw it, he smiled, looking up at me with those striking green eyes. "Your soul," he announced, "is now mine."

I gasped, feigning alarm. "Oh, the horror." Maybe other girls would've swooned at the sight of him smiling like that—blond and handsome, with perfect teeth—but not me. I figured nearly eight years of friendship had made me immune to his looks.

He laughed, scooting closer. I was surprised by the flush that I felt creeping into my face when our knees touched. I was always this close to Michael, so it shouldn't have made me feel embarrassed at all. That's what I told myself, but inside my bones had suddenly turned the consistency of jelly.

He sighed, looking back down at the photo. "Beautiful," he said, softly, which only made me blush harder.

"Th-thanks," I stammered, staring at my shoes. I had been told that I was beautiful before, but none of those people had been Michael, and it was strange to be complimented by him. I'd always thought that he merely tolerated me for our parents' sakes, and that I was the only one who had feelings for him.

Now I didn't know what to think.

I opened my eyes, catching myself in a memory I had thought to be just a blur of shapes and sounds, if not long forgotten. It had been as clear as if I'd been looking through a window.

I wondered what other memories might surface, and not if they *would* be painful, but which ones would hurt the most.

12
RESURFACING

JENNY

That next morning, Liam looked particularly in a mood, especially as he announced that he would be visiting Natalia again. "Prior arrangement be damned," as he'd put it. And he was taking Taylor with him. I sagged against the half-open door, watching the car as it backed slowly out onto the road, passing through the shadows of the trees that lined the driveway.

With a sigh, I threw myself down into a high-backed chair. What would happen to Taylor? Part of me wanted Natalia to accept him as one of her own, to prevent any harm that would come to him for being a rogue. But the other part of me, the more selfish part, wanted him to stay. The thought of him leaving me caused a pang of loneliness to echo throughout my chest, but with it there was also a tight knot of confliction. I wasn't exactly sure how I felt about him now or what it was that I wanted or expected from him, but I knew it wouldn't be exactly easy—even after our talk the other night—being so close to one another and trying to hide what had happened.

"Now that's an anxious face if I ever saw one."

Vince came over to lean against back of the chair, resting his chin in the palm of his hand. I ignored him. Or I tried to.

"I can't imagine why you would waste your time worrying." He gave a dramatic sigh, crossing his ankles as he did. "I'm actually glad. I thought they'd *never* leave."

I halfway turned my head to look at him, questioningly. "What?"

He leaned in close to me, moving my hair aside, his fingertips brushing my jaw. From the corner of my eye, I caught the curl of his lips as he whispered, practically against my ear, "I've been waiting for some time alone with you."

My spine prickled. "Vince, I don't—"

He pulled back, grinning still, his hand falling from my face. "My, my, Jennifer, are you *blushing?*"

My hand flew to my cheek. "Get over yourself."

"I did mean training, you know. It's easier to teach you properly without your little lapdog following you around."

I scowled. I may not have been entirely sure how I felt about Taylor, but that didn't mean I would tolerate his insulting my friend. "What's your problem with him, anyway? He hasn't done anything to you."

"My problem?" he asked, coming around the chair to brace his hands on either side of me. "Wouldn't *you* like to know? But I guess you wouldn't believe me. Couldn't believe anything bad about your Boy Scout Sentry, could you?" I found it hard to avoid his gaze. Everywhere I looked, it seemed I was still looking right at Vince. He was an overwhelming presence.

I could feel my teeth begin to grind together. "Yeah, he's a Sentry and you're a Persuader. I *get* that. But so what? What does any of it really matter?"

"What does it *matter?*" Vince's eyes were wide with anger. "Taylor *has* a home. He *has* a family. But he willingly gave it up, as if it meant nothing to him. You can't imagine what it's like, losing everything and then seeing someone throw the same thing away, and by his own choice—"

"Can you blame him? He loved them but they wanted him to be something he wasn't. It was *strength* that made him choose what he did, not selfishness." I folded my arms. "And if I can't imagine what it's like then just *tell me*. I want to understand, Vince, so why won't you let me?"

His face had gone blank for a moment as he stood there, hands loose at his sides. Then he frowned, turning away, starting for the staircase.

"Wait." I grabbed his arm, but he didn't turn. I sighed. "Please."

After a moment of hesitation, Vince bowed his head, and then faced me again. This close, I could see signs of sleeplessness on his face, how hollow his eyes looked under the curtain of his hair. "What?" He'd intended for the word to sound sharp, but to me it only seemed brittle, as if on the verge of breaking.

"Tell me what happened." He was about to refuse when I spoke again, more forcefully. "I know it's hard. I don't like talking about the past, either. But it made me feel better when I talked to Taylor about my mom. I think telling me about your own family would help you."

He glanced down at my hand still gripping his arm. "Why should I tell *you?*"

I took a deep breath. "Because you have no one else to tell."

"I was only eight when it happened, but…I guess you know how clear a Persuader's memory can be, how far back it can go without any of the details getting lost," Vince began, moving over to stand by the window. He moved the thin curtain aside, peering out but in a way that made it seem like he wasn't really seeing anything. "My father was a very wealthy, very *social* Persuader. And a powerful one, I suppose. My mother was half human, but that didn't discourage her from getting into all the Persuader affairs. They were rarely home. The earliest I could expect them to be back was some time after midnight. My brother and I stopped waiting after a while." His jaw clenched and unclenched before he said, "I remember waking up to this…*wall* of fire. The whole place had gone up in flames, like the tip of a match. I could hardly breathe because the smoke was so thick, so impermeable. By the time the firefighters arrived, half of it had already collapsed into rubble. I don't know how I even survived. I *still wish* that…that I would've just never woken up at all. That I would've just died in my sleep like I was *supposed* to." His eyes remained closed, and he leaned his head against the window, his face creased with pain.

"I don't." Vince glanced up, mouth twisting doubtfully.

"You couldn't mean that," he said, shaking his head. His expression was closed off. "Not after how I've treated you. Not after everyone I've stolen from and everyone I've taken advantage of, all my crimes. I don't think you realize how much I *hate* being a Persuader. But I don't know how else to be." He turned to me, suddenly all intensity and vulnerability. "Do you hate me for that, Jenny? Do you think I'm weak?"

"No." The word surprised him, and—in truth—it surprised me, as well. "I only hate that you feel like you have to live up to this…this *persona* in your mind, this concept of what you think a Persuader is supposed to look like. I hate that you think you have to be cruel for no reason or that you have to pretend like you don't feel something when you do."

He gave a small smile. Not an unkind smile or an arrogant smile or a forced smile. This smile was real. Real and sad. "Perhaps this alleged 'persona' is just another existent part of me, the other half."

"Maybe," I amended, capturing both his hands. "But I just think that it's because you're confused. You act like you're a bad person, and being a Persuader seems to imply in itself that you are, and sometimes you even *believe* that you're a bad person. But I know you can be kind and good if you tried."

"How could you know that?" he whispered, staring down at our hands, his weak smile already fading.

A wave of sympathy washed through me at the sight of him. He felt so much, and so deeply, and it was his greatest source of pain. "Because," I said, with absolute conviction, "you just aren't giving yourself enough of a chance. I've seen goodness in you. Your parents gave so little and yet you still loved them so much, and the way you talk about James…Vince, bad people don't love or feel or care like you do."

Vince's face looked something it hadn't looked in all the time I'd known him: Hopeful. "You make it sound so easy." He sighed. "I wish I could be as strong as you, Jenny. I look at you and I don't see that shadow of grief that I see in myself, even though I know it must be there. It *has* to be there, but somehow it doesn't show on you. I…I don't know how you do it."

I leaned into him, our joined hands trapped between us as I rested my cheek on his shoulder. His breathing caught in astonishment. "I'm sorry," I murmured. "I know you feel like you're beyond comfort or anyone's sympathy, but you should know—"

Vince pulled his hands away to grip the tops of my arms, so tightly it almost hurt. I blinked, looking up into his face, all at once so serious. "You're right," he said. "I am beyond sympathy."

He pressed his lips against mine, surprisingly gentle, as if he thought I was made of paper and was afraid to crinkle me.

I was too stunned to move for a moment, too stunned to do anything but hold myself perfectly still and yield to the kiss as sand yielded to pressure. But when I realized what Vince was doing—what *I* was doing—I moved away from the window, backing away from him until I could feel the doorjamb digging in between my shoulder blades.

Vince started for me, looking bewildered and hurt. "Jenny—"

"I-I need to be alone." My fingers reached behind me for the door handle, and I couldn't help but think, as the door clicked shut behind me, that maybe it was better if I was alone. I couldn't hurt people if I was alone.

TAYLOR

The road became rough and uneven as we slipped into Sentry territory, the kind of middle of nowhere that advertised boarded up gas stations and antique shops sagging against liquor stores. One always saw evidence of neglect in the bowling ball-sized potholes in the pavement and the yellow weeds growing up through the cracks.

Head resting in my hand against the door, I had just begun to drift off into my own unsettled thoughts when Liam spoke, the deep timbre of his voice drawing me back. "You're not as predictable as I once believed, you know."

I blinked, shifting upright in the stiff, leather seat. "Thank you?" I tried, not sure what else to say.

To my surprise, he laughed. "I think I should be the one thanking *you,*" he confessed, bowing his head as if ashamed.

"Why?" I was baffled by his sudden openness.

"You saved her life," he said, unusually quiet, "but, what's more, at her request you remained. Despite the danger, you remained. I try to understand you but, in all honesty, I don't." He looked at me and then back at the road. "Of course, that doesn't mean I don't appreciate what you've done for her."

I swallowed thickly, watching his face, his troubled green eyes, for any changes, any hint to what he really meant. "I'm not sure I understand why you're suddenly telling me this." Feeling braver, I added, "It's not like you've expressed your *gratitude* in the past."

Liam frowned, a crease appearing in his sharp profile from cheekbone to downturned mouth. "You're right," he said. "You're absolutely right. You *don't* understand." He sighed, rubbing the half-circles under his eyes, clearly trying for a lighter tone. "I'm telling you this to let you know, even though I am grateful, that I can't stand by and watch you continue on this path that you're on."

"What path?" I asked, hearing the edge in my tone, the hint of anger I couldn't help but let seep into my words. What right did he have to tell me what to do and where to go?

"You think because I'm old and cynical that I don't see as clearly as I used to." Liam's broad hands tightened on the steering wheel, his fingers whitening. "But I see what's going on between you and Jennifer perfectly." The blood drained from my face at that, my nerves ringing with panic. I tried to form a denial to his accusation, but he continued, his tone resonating with something darker, something ominous. "Because it happened to me, years ago. I don't know how far your feelings for each other have progressed, and I don't want to know. But let me give you a piece of advice: Leave it where it is. Better yet, leave it at nothing."

My teeth clenched and unclenched, grinding together at each word he uttered. "Maybe I don't want your advice."

Liam slammed his hand against the steering wheel, causing me to start. "You still don't get it, do you? I've been through this. I *know* what will happen if a Persuader and a Sentry go down that road, and it's *not pretty.*"

"You can't ask me to do that," I said, surprised at the almost inaudible tremor in my voice. "Pretend to be the perfect, caring father all you want, but I'm all she has. And, sorry to be the one to break this to you, but there's no guarantee she'll be a Persuader, either."

We fell into silence, and this silence was as taut as piano wire, stretched over our heads tighter and tighter until it seemed almost tangible—as if one could just reach up and snap it. I looked back to the road, folding my arms across my chest.

It seemed we had made it to the stronghold, though someone had beaten us there. Or rather, *several* someones had beaten us there, evident in the line of cars parked just outside the building. The man at the front of the blockade was tall and thin with eyes that looked like specks of coal from where I was. He rubbed his chin perplexedly when we didn't move, his scowl visible even from a distance away.

Liam put on a scowl of his own, going very still. "What is Locke doing here?"

Locke. That name sounded familiar to me. I studied the man, his sharp jaw, his even sharper eyes. "Locke? You couldn't mean—"

"The psychotic Persuader who threatened my daughter and sent his henchmen out to kill her? Yes, I mean him. But what I can't figure out is why he's here, or what he thinks he's doing."

Liam threw open the door. "Get down," he said, before slamming it back shut.

I slid low in my seat, ducking under the dashboard, trying to keep myself calm. Samuel. I remembered Vince had said that I was fortunate I had never met him. I could feel his aura radiating off of him like the heat from the sun, stronger than Jenny's, stronger than my own, and I could feel my pulse quicken. Samuel was just one of several Persuaders itching for the chance to kill me, one among dozens, but I got the sense that he was by far the most dangerous of them all, the most lethal. But, then again, who could say for certain what his intentions for me were? There were worse things than death. I'd heard of some Persuaders who were said to be able to administer a form of torture from within the mind, from within Cavea, and to able to do this until the victim snapped and became as unresponsive as a lobotomized patient. I shuddered, feeling cold, as if Samuel's black eyes were looking right at me, as if he could feel me there.

Despite my rogue status and the general uncertainty of my situation, I had never really been afraid for *myself,* only for the people closest to me— for Jenny and my parents, chiefly. But now I felt afraid. Now I was terrified.

SAMUEL

"What do you think you're doing?"

I smiled pleasantly as Michael Cable approached, stalking toward me with a glint of danger in his look. In that glare, I saw the angry, volatile teenager people had claimed he'd been in the past, the angry teenager who had managed to hurt everyone who'd ever been close to him. *Do it, Liam,* I thought, still smiling. *Go ahead. Hit me.*

Seeming to check himself, his pace slowed, and he brought himself up short. I sighed. Well, that wasn't very exciting, now was it? It was always the same with Persuaders—being at all times too reserved, too civil, too genteel. If there was anything to be said of the lesser faction, it was that they never lacked in bellicosity, and thus never failed to provide me with an ample source of entertainment. Persuaders, superior as they were in every conceivable aspect, had a habit of being rather...*uninspiring.*

"It's good to see you, too." My grin stretched up at one corner into a smirk. "And what else would I be doing but looking after the security of my fellow Persuaders and investigating a lead?"

Liam looked baffled. "A *lead?* Since when are you a detective, Samuel? And we both know you couldn't care less about your 'fellow

Persuaders.'"

I folded my arms, leaning against the side of my car. "That coming from a bitter recluse who's afraid to confront the consequences of his actions even decades later. *Speaking* of..." I looked off toward the stronghold, where Natalia was talking with—or, rather, talking *at*—two of my men before she abruptly broke off from them and started in our direction. "I suppose she's learned of my intentions and must now deign to mingle with us crooks, eh? Should be fun for you, catching up. Reminiscing about the days of your youth..."

Natalia's aura reached my senses like the feeling one felt before a storm. She jabbed a finger in my face. "You have no right to search my stronghold, Locke. I've told you this before and I'm telling you now: Give up your *vanity project*. Taylor Ross is a ghost, and he's a clever one to have evaded capture for so long. To take refuge in a stronghold would be a careless move on his part, and he's proven to be anything but careless."

Liam's face creased with shock. "That's what this is about? Even for you, this whole *investigation* seems a bit drastic."

I turned my gaze on Liam, detaching myself from the car, noticing a sheen of sweat across his forehead. "You look nervous," I said.

"Do I? Maybe I'm just angry."

"Oh?"

His lip curled. "Don't think I wouldn't report what you've been doing in an *instant* to the Adjudication if you didn't happen to have such pull with them. You're a criminal, Locke, no better than any other criminal. And you'll get what's coming to you, whether the government has anything to do with it or not."

I stepped closer to him, clasping my hands behind my back. "As you do, I very much doubt the Adjudication will step in to intervene," I said, drawing out the words. "You see, what you might not be aware of is that I was *hired* to find the boy, by none other than his father, Senator David Ross. Rest assured, I have my own reasons in pursuing him, but it doesn't hurt to have government sanction, does it?"

Liam moved away, but his expression hadn't changed. No, that was wrong. It had changed. There was a new defiance in it. *This is what I always hated about you, Michael Liam Cable,* I thought. *Your refusal to heed the rules of the game.* He was hiding something. I knew that. And as I watched him go, I couldn't help but feel as if finding out what that was would bring me ever-closer to the conclusion of this all.

Natalia still stood where she was after he had gone, arms folded, the set of her face as stubborn as ever, and I frowned. "Step aside, Sentry. Reasonable suspicion warrants a search of the premises."

She returned my expression, not moving a muscle otherwise. "You have no privileges here, Persuader. You may have all of the nation's capital under your thumb, but here you're outside of your jurisdiction."

"That may be so," I said. "But this is official Persuader business. I have a right to search your stronghold for evidence that could lead us to the rogue."

"Taylor Ross," she began, through clenched teeth, "hasn't stepped foot in my stronghold or anywhere near it."

I stared at her. Her face didn't appear to be withholding anything from me. But I knew she was an expert at keeping her emotions tucked neatly under that rigid exterior. "If I find out you're lying," I said, gravely, "you can expect another visit."

She didn't appear fazed on the outside, but her eyes—those eyes that always had the look of being made of some immalleable metal—faltered, quivering with no small amount of hatred, though it was a hatred diluted by something more akin to fear. "Get out," she said.

I backed away, letting my expression slip back into one of neutrality as I raised my hands in front of me. "I plan to. Thank you for your time." She just shook her head, and when she left there lingered the impression of a storm just passed. Such a *difficult* woman.

"Sir!"

I turned my head to see Thom, loping toward me, panting like a dog. "I have some…things to…report."

He rested his palms against his knees, hunching over. His each breath was shallow and rasping, the sound like sand against metal. With a fascination that had been ingrained in me from years of studying my mentor's work over his shoulder, my mind grasped at the word *pneumothorax*. I could still hear his uninflected voice as he leaned over an operation table, could see his stern face, his Latex-gloved hands. Thom's skin had taken on a bluish, bruise-like tint, slicked over by sweat. To this my mentor would attribute the cause to a lack of oxygen.

I raised an eyebrow at him, my appraisal complete. It wasn't everyday his little missions were successful, to any degree. "Continue," I said.

Thom propped himself up with one arm braced against the car. "My reconnaissance of the estate was successful, though I, uh, ran into a bit of trouble with two of the occupants."

I ran a hand through my hair, sighing. "And you didn't wait for them to leave?"

"No, sir, that's not what I meant. Two of them left." He fought to take a deep breath. "But two of them stayed."

That caught my attention. "You mean to say you saw Liam, Vincent, Jennifer, and...someone else?" My brow drew low in contemplation. "You couldn't mean a domestic or a maid?"

Thom coughed loudly into the crook of his arm before replying, "He didn't look like a maid."

"He?" I demanded. "Who is *he?*"

"The dark-haired boy—the outcross—he said the other boy was a Persuader, but I...I didn't catch a name."

Without warning, I threw a frustrated fist into Thom's ribcage, with satisfaction hearing the sound of things breaking. Shifting to deal that extra bit of damage as one landed a blow—*Shift-boxing,* as it was called—had gone out of practice among most Persuaders in the early twentieth century in favor of Cavea duels and had in fact been declared illegal some time ago by the Adjudication, though despite its unpopularity something about its gratifying savageness appealed to me. Thom slid to the ground, clutching his stomach, groaning in pain. "Idiot. I ask you to scare a little girl, and you *completely* make a mess of it. And now *this.*"

He coughed again, this time even louder, his whole body shaking with the effort as he kneeled on the sun-bleached asphalt. The ground beneath him was spattered with red.

"What did he look like?" I kicked him roughly onto his back, the toe of my boot striking him with another dull crack.

His head lolled from one side to the other, his eyes closing. "He..."

There were gurgling sounds coming from the back of his throat as he struggled to draw in another breath. His face fell slack.

I struck the headlight of the car, smashing it into pieces, feeling a cold rage fill me all throughout as the glass rained down onto the asphalt. The men I had brought with me to search the stronghold stood staring at me, and then at the body at my feet.

"What the hell are you all staring at?" I snarled, and each face turned

quickly away, every pair of eyes moving from mine. Except Thom's. His cloudy gaze still looked right at me, accusatory, taunting, locking away an answer I would never hear.

TAYLOR

"You've been awful focused lately."

Jenny looked up, her concentration slipping some. She had been practicing in Cavea more frequently since the morning of my short-lived expedition to the stronghold, and while I could flatter myself with the reasoning that she was contriving ways to spend more time with me, it seemed a somehow unlikely reason for the sudden surge of fervor.

She'd practically spent the day immersed only in mastering her inner mind, discovering the varying landscapes of her personalities and memories, finding a way to mold them to her use. I'd known Jenny was a fast learner, but I had never seen someone attain her level of control in so short a time.

My observation received only a shrug from her, and the world around us shifted into what could only be a memory. Black, metal tables lined the outside of the small café, birds strutting around underneath of them in search of stale bread. It was a bright January morning and frost still clung to everything. I knew this place because I had been here *with* her, what seemed like decades ago. "I want to be prepared in case Samuel decides to pay us a visit. We have to be more careful now that he's growing bolder. The first time he sent his hired thugs here it was only *me* he was after, but the second time was different…and what scares me the most about it is that we have no *clue* what that guy's mission was. We don't know what information he has on you at this point."

A sharp chill scraped my spine, not just from the cold and wind. "Even if you trained all your life, you would be no match for him."

Jenny didn't answer with anything but the downward twitch of her mouth, and I sighed. "Is that really what has you so on edge? Or is it something else? You can tell me." When I thought about it, I'd noticed other things that were, as of late, *also* notably odd. Namely, it was the fact that Vince had been somewhat quiet these last few days, especially around Jenny. And Jenny had been acting strangely around *him*, as well. "Is it Vince? Did he say something to you?"

Her eyes widened, the pulse at her throat jumping visibly. "What would give you that idea?" she demanded, too defensively, I thought.

"Well you've been weird around him, lately—"

"Just drop it, okay?" Her tone was sharp, her green eyes unyielding.

"Jenny—" I cut myself off. Any wise man knew that when a woman could send him flying out of a window with a wave of her hand, he ought to stop talking. "Fine, fine. Okay. Dropping it."

She stepped closer to me, her voice softening. "I'm sorry. It's just…I don't want to talk about Vince. I want to talk about something else."

"Like what?" I asked.

"Like…if you remember this place." There was something almost self-conscious in her look as she asked, "Do you?"

"How could I forget? You ran right into me!"

I saw her face twist, as if about to express irritation, but she couldn't manage it in the end. "The sidewalk was irregular."

My grin turned into a smirk. "You mean…like *this?*"

The ground under our feet tilted dramatically, sending birds fluttering away. She lurched forward, laughing, into my arms—and then she peered up into my face just like she had a year ago. I remembered thinking then that she was possibly the most beautiful girl I had ever seen. Now I was certain she was. I could see, this close, the flecks of brown in her eyes, the streaks in her hair, as fair as her father's and turned gold in the sun. "Maybe not *exactly* like that," she murmured. I began to notice that the trees that lined the opposite side of the street had begun to regain their leaves rapidly, and that the air had begun to likewise lose much of its chill. Jenny noticed this as well, with alarm on her face. "Oh. Sorry about that. The illusion's shattered, now, I guess."

"'Losing an illusion makes you wiser than finding a truth,'" I replied, smiling a little.

"That was always a favorite quote of my mom's."

"She sounds like a smart woman."

"Yeah, she was."

Something in her voice—some hitch or change of tone—made me release her, and I noticed how feverishly she worried her lip between her teeth, how she looked to be alarmingly on the verge of tears.

"Jenny?" I asked, quietly, trying to catch her eye. Her gaze remained stubbornly cast downward at the uneven ground. I took a deep breath, then slowly exhaled, looking off toward the wavering afternoon sun planted firmly between the blue and violet folds of the sky. Clouds drifted around it, not quite touching it, as if afraid they might burn at the contact. "It's about your mom, isn't it?"

No response. I laid a hesitant hand on her arm. "Look, no one expects you to be okay. *I* don't expect you to be okay, not after barely a month has passed since it happened. I know you're trying to be strong, but I just don't think keeping it all bottled inside will help any."

She wiped furiously at her eyes with the back of her hand. "Maybe it would've been better if I'd never lost any illusions in the first place." Her voice was hoarse with the effort of trapping everything within her. I was reminded of the humid, Virginian summers of my childhood, when I would catch fireflies in a mason jar from the cupboard and was always reluctant to release them. "Ever since realizing that I wasn't just a normal person, and that the world I lived in wasn't anything at all like I'd thought it was, all I seem to do is mess everything up. I don't feel *wiser* at all, I just feel...changed somehow. Made less human."

It began to snow as she spoke. Tiny, fast, stinging snowflakes fell in sheets, covering every surface in a powdery blanket in mere moments. The green leaves of the trees promptly browned and were swept away, leaving only the gray skeletons of branches. I stared at her through the almost impenetrable snowfall, blinking flakes from my lashes as I moved toward her.

"Jenny, you don't look any less human to me," I said. The second my fingers made contact with her cold cheek, the blizzard subsided, Cavea tumbling back into reality like the flick of a switch.

She looked at me, her face pale in the dimness of the attic, trembling silently for a moment with wide eyes. Then, for the first time that I'd seen since her mother's funeral, tears began to form in her eyes and slip freely over her cheeks. And I held her, as I had then. At least that was one thing that hadn't changed.

13
IDENTITY

LIAM

The knock on the door resounded all throughout the mansion, startling me from my thoughts.

I leapt up from my chair, setting Heather's picture down on the edge of the desk. Emerging from my office, I craned my neck to see Taylor and Jenny at the top of the stairs, both looking as puzzled as I was. She whispered something to him—presumably telling him to make himself invisible—and he nodded briefly before ducking into one of the spare rooms, shutting the door behind him softly.

She took the stairs two at a time, barefoot and bed-mussed, reaching for the door.

"Jennifer," I said, quickly. "Let me answer it." Had she forgotten so soon the target painted on her back? I hoped not.

Jenny made a face so characteristic of her mother right then—slight annoyance, as if she was offended that I doubted her ability to take care of herself—I was brought up short a few paces from the door.

After a moment the face disappeared and with a long sigh she took a step backwards, twisting a lock of her hair around her finger. As I turned the knob, I tried not to think about how Heather used to do that.

"Hello, Michael."

An unfamiliar woman stood in the doorway, arms crossed over her chest. Her voice held something of an accent—a certain Latin American lilt—and her dark, lipsticked lips turned up at the corners as she continued.

ERIN CAINE

"Nice place you got here. Must be hell to clean, huh?"

At the sound of her voice, I saw Jenny stiffen from beside me. Though she wasn't in the woman's line of sight in her position just behind the door, recognition had dawned on her face. I scrutinized our visitor with heightened wariness. "Who are you?"

"Cira Torres." The name was really less of a name and more of a continuous rolling of the 'r's. "I'm here at Samuel's request, really," she sighed in a listless tone, reaching in her back pocket for a slightly crumpled slip of paper.

She thrust it out to me, flicking her dark hair out of her face, and I unfolded it, smoothing out the crease. Feeling something in the middle of dread and resentment, I read the sharp, elegant words written on the inside.

Slowly, I refolded the paper and tucked it into my shirtfront pocket, glancing up to meet the messenger's indifferent eyes.

Swallowing hard, I said, "Tell Samuel...I would be delighted to attend."

Closing the door, I turned to my daughter, trying to read her expression, decode the hard glint in her eyes. "Jennifer, who was that woman?"

There was a pallor in her face as she said, "She's one of the Persuaders who tried to kill me."

JENNY

"The snake!"

Vince slammed his hand down on the table, upsetting a glass of water at his elbow. Its contents spilled onto the floor, the glass itself shattering on impact. Everyone ignored the mess but Laura, who came bustling over with a surly scowl and a dustpan that seemed to have manifested itself out of thin air.

After Cira's unprecedented and unwelcomed visit, everyone had gathered into the dining hall to discuss our next course of action. Though it was less about what we *would* do next, and more about what we *could* do.

Taylor sat to my right, fists clenched on the table, leveling Vince with a heated look. "If you hadn't let him go in the first place—"

Vince rose from his chair to snap something back at the other boy, but the question was already out of my mouth. "Who?"

He sat back down, reluctantly, and I noticed that he still couldn't look me in the eye. "Oh, you remember. That hit-man of Samuel's who tried to sneak in here a few days ago. Incidentally, also the man who tried to shoot you. And who Taylor, so I hear, hit with—a crowbar, was it?"

"We get the point, Vincent," Liam interjected, quietly. He sighed, putting his forehead down into the cup of his palm.

Taylor still stared at Vince, drumming his fingers a little. Samuel's note had been a seemingly innocuous invitation to a Friday night ball, as Liam had revealed, but it was an invitation extended to a certain "special guest", as well, and *that* was what had been the deeply troubling part of the message. Ever since learning of Samuel's knowledge of his being here— well, in someone being here who wasn't supposed to be—Taylor had begun fidgeting, getting little nervous tics every now and then. "If I didn't know any better, I'd think you had sympathy for the lowlife, Hallows."

Vince's mouth moved slowly, the sneer digging into his face like a shovel into frozen ground. "If you're suggesting that I *support* what's been going on, as if I actually *wanted* this to happen to Jenny—"

"No, I'm suggesting that *maybe* you start thinking about everyone else's safety aside from your own—"

"I have been! Look at you on your high horse. Becoming a Sentry doesn't make you automatically selfless, Ross—"

"How can you just sit there while that sadist is leveling a gun at her forehead?"

"Enough."

Three pairs of eyes turned on me, the mouths beneath them stunned into silence. I cleared my throat, looking from Vince, to Taylor, to Liam, and back again. "Look, we may not agree on everything, and we may never agree on anything, but we still have a huge problem on our hands. And I think we should discuss it in a civil manner, okay?" I leaned forward in my chair, slamming both hands down. "So *shut up*, and listen to what the other has to say."

Laura, straightening her uniform, grinned a toothy smile at Liam. "Fiery, little thing, isn't she?" Winking at me, she disappeared through the doorway with a dustpan full of glass.

Liam, likewise, nodded in my direction before addressing the other two. "Jenny's right. Put your differences aside for just a moment and try to think clearly about our next move."

"Our next move should be to go on the offensive," Taylor replied immediately, the hardness in his face making him appear older than he was. "It's clearly a trap. We should be the ones to strike first."

"As if that'd solve anything!" Vince prepared to launch into another argument but, catching himself mid-rant, took a deep breath and continued in a calmer tone. "It doesn't seem practical. What would that accomplish? It's four against...I don't know. Ten or fifteen. Who knows how many of Samuel's men will be swarming the party? It's suicide."

"Natalia," I said, at last. "She's the answer."

Liam blanched at his ex-girlfriend's name. "Come again?"

Vince put his fist under his chin. "Hm. If Natalia Blair's the solution to our problems, we must *really* be desperate."

Taylor merely watched me expectantly as I stood. "Natalia's stronghold is filled to the brim with experienced, battle-ready soldiers. They'd *leap* at the chance to make a move against Samuel."

"Yes, but they're not just *soldiers*, Jenny. They're Sentries. They would never cooperate, not even for something important." Taylor bristled silently, scowling down at his hands. I had never really thought about it before, but it was sort of ironic that he would say things like that about Sentries, considering he had once been *married* to one of them. Maybe, after all the years apart, he'd forgotten about the things that had made him love her to begin with, Sentry aspects included. "And also—"

"Also," Vince cut in, sweeping black curls from his forehead, "Samuel will be more on his guard than ever, which makes him at his most dangerous. I know you mean well, Jennifer, trying to organize this little alliance project between us, but it would never work."

Taylor straightened, looking steadily at me for a moment. Then he said, very carefully, "Say you could manage to get the Sentries on board. What then?"

A slow, calculating smile began to spread across my face, an expression that seemed to belong to the Persuaders as much as it belonged to the Sentries. "What else? We go on the offensive."

Vince and Liam were jolted by this proclamation, but Taylor was smiling precisely how I was. "Now we're talking."

My father held up his hands to object. "Wait a moment, now. We still have a few things to sort out before we dive into this plan of yours." His eyes slid to mine. "First, is the issue of getting ahold of Natalia. As you know, she hasn't exactly been amenable to my requests for an audience in the past..."

"Ring, ring." Vince pantomimed picking up a phone, pressing his knuckles to his ear, pinky and thumb extended. "Oh, hello Natalia. Yes, I'm calling on behalf of your ex-boyfriend, whom you have hated passionately for decades... Yes, *that* one. Here's the short of it: we need your help taking down Samuel Locke. Yes, it would be *very* dangerous. Possibly fatal! Mm-hm. Yes, and we have a fugitive here, too. Okay, thanks, see you there!"

I kicked Vince from under the table.

Liam, speaking over his adopted son's pain-filled howls, sighed, "Hm. I suppose it would be difficult, but...possible. The party is in a few days. Perhaps something will open up before then. This time I think I'll make the journey alone, though."

Taylor scratched the back of his neck. "But we're still not addressing the real problem here. Because of Thom's tip-off,"—no one missed the look he tossed Vince—"Samuel's expecting *four* of us, remember? And something tells me bringing Laura wouldn't suffice."

"And anyone else he would recognize," Liam interjected. "At least anyone else we could get to agree to this. He's always kept tabs on those close to him."

"There's a simple solution for that," I said, once again bringing about the quick swiveling of glances my way. They looked like bobble heads, the three of them. "A little hair dye and no one would know he's Taylor Ross. And didn't you guys read the invitation? Masquerade ball. He'll just wear a mask and his face will be covered enough for him to pass as someone else. It's perfect."

"Too perfect," Liam remarked. "If Samuel was looking for Taylor at this event, what would be the purpose of his making it a masquerade ball? And I don't think it's because they've recently become extremely fashionable."

"You know him," Vince muttered, bitterly. "Always one for dramatic effect. At the moment of his discovery, he would march across the room and unmask Taylor, just to put on a good show for the other Persuaders."

"But that won't happen. We'll be ready for him," I said quickly, unnerved by Vince's talk of "discovery".

Taylor reached under the table to grab my hand, ducking his head to whisper to me, "I really hope you're right."

LIAM

"This better be important, Liam. I am a very busy woman and I don't have time for petty Persuader affairs."

I tossed the last sliver of bread crust to the ducks waiting below. The speckled brown one snagged a piece before her green-capped companion gobbled down the rest. When they were convinced that I had no other morsel of food to throw at them, they wiggled their tails and dispersed, without a backward glance of gratitude. Greedy ingrate waterfowl.

I glanced up from the water to see Natalia standing over me, her impatience concentrated mostly in the arch of her brow. Her shoulders were set wide and her mouth was narrow, and from experience I knew these to be things that disguised an underlying discomfort. I sighed. How strange it was, the nature of love. When it fell through, the hate that filled the spaces could be just as potent.

"It is not," I replied, leaning back in the park bench, "petty. It affects all of us." I motioned for her to sit beside me.

Natalia sat, but not before giving me that dignified and reproachful kind of look she always did. She was perched at the very edge of the bench, as far away from me as possible. "Is that so?" The impatient brow grew even more arched. "If I'm not mistaken, *you're* the one who called and asked for *my* help, correct? So is this not about *you?*"

"Samuel's actions don't just concern me." I couldn't quite manage to sand down the hard edge to my tone. "He could upset the whole balance of things."

"Balance?" Natalia demanded, with a sharp laugh. "You think this world of ours is *balanced?* Open your eyes, Liam. Persuaders live in luxury, doing as they please, while Sentries are subjected to the dark corners of this society, working without rest, forced to resort to violence while clinging to the very edge of life."

"You made your choice," I said, through clenched teeth. "We all did. You chose to live this life—"

"Yes, but I've had to fight every step of the way. Fighting has been my whole life. Fighting and working and tearing my heart out for this cause while my enemies go to dinner parties and drink fine wine." She was staring at me with eyes like stone, and I couldn't help but remember when she had looked at me differently, looked at me with a smile, even with love. Any trace of that smile was gone now from her face, lines in the sand erased by the lapping waves of time. "But I learned from a young age that Persuaders are incapable of seeing how their actions affect others, incapable of seeing that the things they do are wrong. *That* is why I chose what I did."

"Look," I exhaled, lifting my hands, palms outward as a gesture of surrender. "I didn't want to meet with you to exchange thoughts about society. I hoped that you could look past our...our differences and lend me the support of your stronghold. I want to launch an attack against Samuel."

One pale brow shot up to meet the other, and she clasped her hands tightly in front of her. "An attack? Are you serious?"

I took a deep breath, awaiting her refusal. "Yes."

Natalia sat there, very still for a moment, lips pursed. Then she spoke, drawing out her words. "This couldn't have been *your* plan, Cable. You lack the backbone."

I ignored the insult. "It was Jennifer's plan."

Now Natalia smiled, but it was a smug one. "How interesting. Thinks just like a Sentry, that girl. Are you surprised?"

I tilted my head, considering. "No," I said, finally. "She's very much like her mother."

The smugness faltered into an expression that looked as if she had bitten into an orange peel. "Hm," was all she said.

"This Friday," I told her, backpedaling quickly. "Samuel's hosting a masquerade ball. Jenny suggested that it would be a good opportunity for an ambush. We just need a handful of soldiers as part of the equation."

Natalia glanced away, her gaze sliding over the glistening surface of the water. "This plan is insane, you do realize that?"

I nodded.

She sighed and looked at me. There was less hostility in the glance, less reserve. "Alright," she said. "I'll organize an attack. It'll be tricky, but it's not something my Sentries can't handle. If we want to be rid of Samuel Locke, we need to seize any opportunity we can. We need to take risks."

We both stood with a quick handshake.

"Thank you, Natalia."

Her lips twisted into a lop-sided smirk. "I'd say 'anytime', but I think it would be an unlikely statement in our case."

My throat moved around a sudden knot. "Yes. Yes, it would be."

JENNY

"Jenny, could you give me a hand?"

Warily, I uncurled from my favorite reading place by the window to discover what odd and seemingly purposeless job my mother was requesting of me this time. The tattered, red loveseat squeaked and groaned like the antique piece of furniture it was. I only liked it so much because it was one of the few furnishings we owned from before my father left. The others were a mismatched heap in some junkyard nearby, decomposing like my parents' discontinued marriage. Behold, the grandeur of The Rebuilding Phase.

It wasn't as if I was sentimental about the chair's history; it was just that the old, ruined thing—however old, however ruined—felt familiar. Very few things had felt familiar lately, especially my mother's ever-worsening condition. I *worried* about becoming familiar with it, though. I worried about the cancer becoming and consuming my whole life as it had consumed hers.

I could hear a ripping noise from the kitchen, clueing me in to my new task before I even saw the yellow wallpaper, curling in strips from the wall like withered flower petals.

My mom stood on a wobbly stepladder, garden trowel in hand, attacking the offending entity that still clung for dear life to our kitchen wall with the vigor of an artist at the canvas. Her dark, bright eyes were set like lasers on her work, and she only nodded in my direction. "Would you come over here? I'm feeling a little dizzy."

I held out my hand to help her down, swallowing the sour taste at the back of my tongue. She always felt dizzy. At first we hadn't understood why, but that was months ago. Now, we understood that and something else: Every moment had become precious, however trivial. During every conversation post-diagnosis, I was always cognizant of the fact that I would remember the words forever, as if they hung suspended somewhere, immovable and untouchable.

She leaned against the counter, pressing a hand to her forehead. Probably another headache, I thought.

I took the trowel from her, taking her place on the stepladder to pluck the rest of the yellow petals of wallpaper from the plaster.

"Because I value your opinion above all others and can think of no other viable candidate for this great and urgent task," she began, gravely, "what color would you like the kitchen to be, Jenny?"

I shrugged at her question, twirling the trowel loosely in my hand. "Purple?"

My mother laughed. "I figured." She sighed, almost sadly. "I was going to say blue." Of course she was. Blue had always been her favorite color.

"Bluish purple it is, then," I said, compromising. "You know, like a cornflower color."

"Cornflowers?" She laughed again, bracing her thin hands behind her, as if propping herself up. "As in...the color of Taylor's eyes?" she inquired innocently, batting her eyelashes at me.

The trowel hit the linoleum with a clatter, and I cursed myself under my breath. It was just a question; I wasn't sure why I was so embarrassed. "Well, I wasn't thinking of him when I...I mean—"

"Yeah, yeah," she said, blithely cutting me off. When I climbed down from the stepladder and looked back at her she winked.

I picked the trowel up, placing it on the chipped counter with exaggerated care, feigning nonchalance. "Speaking of Taylor. Can he come over today?" Taylor came over to my house more than I went over to his. Admittedly, this was mostly due to the fact that Tarek was inexplicably terrified of me, but it was also because I didn't really want to spend a lot of time away from my mom. It was a horrible, terrifying thing, not knowing which moment would be the last, which moment would be *it*. Not knowing if I would walk out the door one day without saying "I love you" and then never having the chance to say it again.

For what it was worth, at least I *had* someone to say that to. Taylor, as far as I knew, didn't even have parents—at least not any he could talk to. For this reason, I looked to him habitually for advice, for consolation. He was my anchor in a sea of uncertainty, and both my mother and I were grateful for it.

She smiled. "Of course he can."

She rarely said no to that sort of question unless her headaches were especially bad. My mother was quite a fan of Taylor and had been ever since she'd first laid eyes on him, standing there at the front door with his goofy smile and his well-bred manners. The moment he had addressed her as "ma'am" had been the real selling point, and he was a particular favorite from then on.

I smiled back at her. "Thanks." I reached for the phone on the wall.

My mom leaned back on her elbows. "I can't quite place it, but there's something I like about that boy. He's a good one, I hope you remember that."

"I'll try," I said, though it wasn't strictly the truth. At a later time, I would make no effort to remember this conversation at all.

But somehow I'd still remember.

GWEN

I had hated Persuader society for as long as I could remember.

As a child, I would approach my father after one of his many "business trips" and ask about the kinds of things he had done, and what was at first only a naïve and childish curiosity eventually grew into a profound feeling of disgust. As I got older, I learned how to hold my tongue, how to hide my discomfort. It wasn't easy suppressing my feelings in front of the other Persuaders, in front of my own parents, but to speak my mind would mean to be cast out from my home and stripped of everything I owned. Under normal circumstances, it would hardly be a problem, but I was the main supplier to Natalia's stronghold. Without me, the stronghold would suffer, as the Adjudication had for years consistently failed in apportioning a proper ration of food and supplies at the end of each month simply because it deemed Natalia less-than-fit to be a leader. The government was supposed to be *just* to Sentry kind and attribute to it the things necessary to survive, but it had become more and more frequent a practice to withhold these goods on false or discriminatory grounds. As I had come to learn, quite a few strongholds had been forced to seek out Persuader benefactors these days. I could only hope that the sudden high demand of such individuals wouldn't one day lead to our discovery.

"Gwen?"

Eli's thin, staccato voice yanked me sharply back into focus. I was glad; sometimes it felt like there was something gnawing at the back of my mind, eating away at my convictions. It was stressful, having one foot firmly planted in the earth while the other was still rooted inside the marble vestibule of a mansion.

Eli's Adam's apple rolled up and back down once, an annoying habit. "Are you ready to go?"

I blinked, looking down at myself. There was a pistol holstered to my hip, a knife tucked into my boot, and, underneath my thick jacket, more clips of ammunition than I probably needed—things procured through no small amount of haggling with crooked dealers and dodging packs of armed rogue Sentries hanging around the Lower Market. I was about as ready as I could be.

I nodded. "Let's go." I signaled the twins with a quick gesture. Natalia had made me third in command about a year ago, and only she and a rugged, leathery man named Silas held rank over me. Eli and the other two who'd volunteered to come along—dynamic duo, Darren and Sasha—all looked to me as the leader of this mission, which was both gratifying and nerve-wracking.

I sighed. Eli. The stronghold's biggest pain in the neck. The only reason I'd let him come along was because I kind of felt sorry for the kid. He held his gun awkwardly in front of his narrow chest, his eyebrows doing that uneasy slant they always did. He attempted a smile at me, which I ignored as I made my way around the side of the building to the truck that had been recently recovered from the neighboring scrapyard and nursed back to life by some phenomenon or another. Cars were one thing not sold on the black market, a fact that was both annoying and inconvenient. It spluttered a few times and gave a final hacking cough, signaling the always violent start of its engine. Huh. Usually it faltered twice. Maybe today was a day for triumph after all.

The others piled in after me, Eli snagging shotgun. Darren spoke up from the backseat as we lurched forward onto the beaten road. "We should go over a quick briefing, in case some of us are a little fuzzy on the details." By "some of us", we all knew he'd meant Eli, who didn't exactly possess a particular affinity for strategy.

"Okay," I said, tightening my grip on the steering wheel. "Here's the plan: We leave this clunker at the base of the bridge and proceed on foot until we can signal down another car, one that's quiet and unremarkable enough to follow the convoy. We're going to need the car later on to buy us some time. Eli will drive it into the head of the group and cause an accident, halting the procession and allowing the rest of us to slip into the back of the last truck unnoticed."

I saw Sasha's grin from the cracked rearview mirror, a white slash set into her narrow, dark face. "I assume you'll be the one to...*acquire* us the transportation, Farrier?"

"Given that he's male," Darren muttered, not so good-naturedly.

I scowled. "Unless you two have a better idea."

They both shook their heads at the same time, only emphasizing their resemblance to each other. Unlike me, they had been born under the stronghold's gray roof and lived and breathed a Sentry existence under Sentry parents. The day of their respective Embracements, the decision had been easy. Mine had been nothing but a lie to pacify those around me. For this reason, I envied them and would envy them forever, as strongly as they pitied me.

Eli sighed. "A necessary evil, I suppose. You know, stealing someone's car. And totaling it, too. That's also...unfortunate."

"Every time one of us does something a Persuader would do, we seem to think it's necessary," Darren said, in a quiet, grave tone. "But when Persuaders do it, we call it evil."

"Oh, both of you knock off the melodrama," Sasha snapped, dissolving whatever mirage of likeness I had seen between her and Darren before. "On paper, Gwen may be a Persuader, but we all know she's just as much a Sentry as the rest of us. I mean, it is *Gwen Farrier* we're talking about here. She's one of our best. This can slide."

I smiled gratefully back at her, though I knew it wasn't completely true what she'd said, that I was just as much a Sentry as they were. I knew better than to think that the entirety of my childhood and upbringing hadn't had any effect on me. But it was still a nice gesture.

"After that," Darren continued, resuming the plan from where I'd left off, "the delivery will go right to whatever hide-out it's en route to and—"

"And we destroy 'em from the inside," Sasha finished, gleefully. "I heard a few of those trucks are carrying barrels of gasoline. A couple shots and..." She pantomimed a gun with her left hand, dropping her thumb to signify the drop of a hammer. "Boom! Ka-blooey!"

Darren looked prepared to launch into another lengthy reprimand toward his sister—undoubtedly preaching about the dangers of using firearms against Persuaders unless in the presence of a Deadlock—when Eli spoke. "What would they need it for? I've heard of Persuaders transporting weapons, even drugs, but gasoline?" His fine brows crumpled together. "It seems pointless."

I shrugged. "Can't say I understand it, either, but when have Persuaders ever been governed by reason?"

138

"Anyway, they're armored trucks, Sasha," Darren cut in, his words as calm as his sister's were not. "The diversion isn't for sabotage, it's for infiltration."

She huffed, sinking low in the cracked seat. "That's not nearly as much fun."

Darren leveled his sister with a disapproving look. "We're on a dangerous and important mission. Not on holiday."

I had to fight to suppress a smile when Sasha stuck her tongue out at her brother. They were a mismatched pair, those two, but their loyalties to each other were unbreakable. I thought about our earlier discussion, the things they'd said that had momentarily suggested a wariness or even a distrust toward me. My fellow Sentries, my friends, were *suspicious* of me. And nothing I ever did, it seemed, could prove myself worthy of their trust. They could not be dissuaded from their doubts, not Natalia's instating me into a position of high rank, not my taking on dangerous missions, and *certainly* not my benefactor status—no matter how generous my donations. I wondered if something so drastic as heroic martyrdom would be enough to eliminate the doubt completely.

"We're here."

The truck swerved off of the road, into the muddy ditch at the base of the bridge. The other three were jostled by the sudden movement, but otherwise didn't complain. One sidelong glance to me and I knew exactly what I had to do next. What I really hated doing.

The car that stopped for us was small, tan, compact. Perfect. It slid to a halt next to the truck, and the man inside looked young, probably in his twenties still, yet his hairline seemed to be prematurely receding from his tawny brow. He looked from me to the truck to the others and back again. "Having car trouble?" he said, at length.

Swallowing the bitter taste of shame at the back of my mouth, I put on a relieved, slightly embarrassed expression and said, "Oh, thank God! I thought *no one* would stop for us."

The man smiled a little, obviously pleased with himself. "Well, I try to help anyone I can."

"Of course," I crooned, leaning casually on the door. "You have that sort of look to you."

He flushed. "Really? Oh, well I..." He was flustered now, lining up my opportunity.

My eyes prickled, and I could get a feel for the contents of his thoughts and emotions. He wasn't really the type of person who usually stopped to help strangers, despite what he had told me, which only barely lessened the guilt I felt. I grimaced when I detected that he'd only stopped because he found Sasha and myself to be attractive. As if to emphasize my point, his gaze flickered to over my shoulder, where I knew Sasha was standing, doubtless also grimacing. She didn't need to read his mind to know what he was thinking, I was sure.

If only the poor guy knew exactly how *slim his chances are with Sasha, in particular,* I thought. What was more, even *if* her tastes extended to men (which I knew for a fact they didn't) there was something about him that screamed "skeezeball."

His gaze moved back to mine and caught. Within the next two seconds, his eyes glazed over—looking like marbles in his skull—which left me feeling as gutted as it usually did. When I took control of someone like that, it always left me with a dirty feeling, like blood that wouldn't wash off the skin no matter how hard I scrubbed it with good intentions.

Obediently, he slid out of his car, nearly tumbling out into the dirt. He moved as if on stilts, his eyes facing forward, focused on nothing. Eli was the only one looking at me. The twins had their eyes studiously trained on the ground, and I didn't blame them for it. The man reached out to open the door of the truck, hesitating only when it stuck momentarily, clambering into the backseat and laying down without a word of protest. The up-and-down movement of his chest stopped as I fed him thoughts that went against the most basic and essential human instinct of respiration. How easy it was, I thought, to override someone's control so effectively as to make him dissociated even from a *reflex.* When I was sure he was unconscious, I finally dropped my hold over him. His breathing resumed.

I rubbed the back of my neck, feeling all at once unfathomably tired, seeing Eli step toward me out of the corner of my eye. "Gwen, are you—?"

I cut him off, sharply. "We shouldn't waste time. Let's go."

VINCE

It seemed any excuse to get out of the house I would've taken. I probably would've agreed to have tea with Samuel Locke if it meant Jenny wouldn't be coming.

Liam had looked somewhat shaken after his meeting with Natalia. It was apparent that everything that'd happened recently had started to take its toll on him, seen in the haggard lines of his face and the circles beneath his eyes, which was why I'd felt obligated to make the monthly trip to the city myself. A "business trip", as Persuaders preferred to euphemize it.

Some Persuaders—the insatiable ones, that was—made this sort of trip more frequently. But Liam preferred to fly well below the radar, not just edge by it. Besides, he had worked hard to not fall in among the more avaricious of his kind, and there was something to be admired in that. I wondered when he would start training Jenny to use her powers to do more than commit petty thievery, and I wondered (without admitting to myself that I was wondering it) how she would take to it. Some part of me wanted her to like it, or at the very least be able to resign herself to it, and yet some other part of me wanted her to be utterly repulsed.

My mind recoiled. *Don't think of her.*

It took some effort. My hands clenched and unclenched deep in the pockets of my coat as I skirted puddles in the road. I glanced behind me to ensure my steps were not being shadowed by another. I could see Nationals Park from here, in the distance, rising from the rubble of a construction site in the foreground. Weeds grew up around my feet, splitting gravel.

The place was sagging, old, its walls stained by age. The only outward indication that made me aware of its purpose was the sign above the door coinciding with the number written on my palm: 1107.

But there were other things to make me aware of the place. The aura of a Persuader—or maybe two—filtered through the rough, worn wood of the door, stronger as I walked up the stone set of stairs to knock. A man looking to be in his early thirties answered, a woman beside him of about the same age. The man smiled when he saw me, flicking his cigarette butt into the dirt, offering a hand. "Mr. Hallows? Name's Anthony Baker. This is Harper, my wife." I took it, nodding and noticing the bracelet of tattoos around his wrist as the cuff of his suit jacket pulled back, which was odd considering that most Persuaders had an aversion to anything deemed as "unsophisticated" as marking one's skin.

"Well, glad you could come. I'll be honest, I was actually expecting Liam. Not his apprentice."

I shrugged. "He wasn't feeling up to it."

Harper stepped back, nodding. "Come in. We have business to attend to." Her voice left little room for anything else, especially further small talk.

Inside, the sight of bulky black briefcases, stacked high enough to almost brush the ceiling, crowded my vision. Within the cases, I was sure, there could be any number of things, but most likely they were firearms. Persuaders would never use such weapons themselves; aside from the impracticality it really was sort of hypocritical to do so, sinking to the Sentries' level. And that was worse than being unarmed, worse than death.

The fact that we were selling weapons not to humans but to our own kind could only mean one thing: Whomever was buying needed to arm a large unit of Deadlocks.

As if reading my mind, Anthony scoffed, muttering, "Wonder what they could be doing with so many bodyguards. Can't stand Deadlocks, myself. They unnerve me, how they block out mental whatnot and all that."

It was hard to imagine what that was like, to be the offspring of Persuader parents, to have greatness expected of you, only to quickly discover that a flaw had emerged in your genes that made you automatically less significant. Though, being an outcross, it wasn't *so* hard to imagine. Deadlocks were at the bottom of Persuader social class, only because of their incapability to use the powers they should've inherited. The only thing that set them apart from regular human beings was their ability to block the psychological signals of others. *SERVUS* and *CUSTOS* were tattooed in small, bold letters along their foreheads, above each brow, at the age of eighteen—a sort of ritual that took the place of a proper Embracement. *Custos* meant something like "guardian", but *servus* meant "servant" or "slave", which was what they were more of than the former. Their servitude was not a choice. It was a requirement.

I shrugged, feigning indifference. "They get the job done."

Harper stood a little away from us, eyes set on the dingy window that faced the road. "They should be here by now," she murmured. Her already severe face pulled taut with anxiety.

Anthony, on the contrary, seemed unconcerned, waving his hand. "I'm sure they're coming. It's not the first time a convoy's been delayed." He turned a little, looking at me through hooded eyes. "Speaking of past mistakes. We've heard talk of Liam's little misadventure living at the Cable mansion now."

At his words, heat started to fill my veins. It burned in my head.

Harper's expression was one of warning at her husband, and her voice was equally reproachful. "Anthony."

He was undeterred. "Makes me *sick,* really." The heat had risen to a boil, sweltering in my throat. My clenched fists ached in their inaction. "How some people think they can just redraw the lines. That *girl* is part of what's ruining our society."

"Anthony." Harper's tone had changed, grown harsher.

"What?" he demanded. "It's the truth. You were there when she disrespected Samuel. You've heard the rumors, how she's been meeting with Natalia Blair. Probably negotiating living arrangements as we speak. And Liam sits back, as spineless and as *senseless* as he ever was."

I lunged at Anthony, slamming my forearm into his collarbone. He struck the wall, knocking a framed picture to the ground in the impact. I leaned close to his face. "Say one more word against my father or Jenny," I snarled, in a low voice, "and the deal's off."

Anthony's face screwed into one of scorn. *"Fine,"* he spat. "I'll take my chances. I only needed you as extra muscle, as security. Another eye to make sure nothing goes sour with the transaction. I can find someone else."

We both were acutely aware of the sound of thundering engines, a sound that rattled the small house to its foundation.

I smirked at him. "Looks like you're out of time."

I lugged the first of the cases outside, nodding my greeting at the group of men waiting before the front truck. The oldest of the three, the one with the scar running along the bridge of his hooked nose, ran a hand through his graying hair. "Good afternoon, gentlemen. Ma'am." He nodded at Harper, who stood in the doorway, pale and strained looking. He looked to me. "You have what we asked for?"

Anthony took the case from me, flipping the latches on the side before laying it on the ground.

The scarred man bent to open the case, withdrawing from the black felt lining a simple handgun, weighing it in his grip as if testing its legitimacy. He slipped the clip into the gun, aiming skyward. The blast echoed throughout the silent space as both Anthony and I tried in vain to mask the disconcerted looks that flitted across our faces. The old Persuader smiled like a shark. "Seems legitimate enough, Baker."

"Always has been, Anderson."

The younger man beside him barked commands at the trailing, solemn Deadlocks waiting silently in the background. As one, they flooded the house, returning just as swiftly with the black cases in their grip. Harper moved out of their way, blanching even more so than before.

A muscle in Anthony's jaw jumped, and he swallowed with visible effort. "And the payment?"

Anderson's hand twitched almost imperceptibly, motioning forward the holder of a padlocked briefcase. With an oily sort of smile, he unlocked the box, revealing its contents. Contents that were, in fact, also true to their word.

When Anthony had the money safely tucked under one arm, he seemed to relax some. "Always a pleasure. It took a little longer for you to get here, though. Stuck in traffic?"

Anderson rubbed his face. "No, it was some kid in a tan Lexus who rammed into us a few miles back. I couldn't get the whole tedious ordeal sorted out as soon as I would've liked to. Mostly because the boy wouldn't stop *apologizing.*" The two shared a laugh, though it was a mixture of sounds altogether too clipped to really be classified as laughter.

They continued to talk for a moment longer as I shut the case at my feet and delivered it over to the queue of armored trucks. Several Deadlocks flocked around the first three, but the last remained ignored. I lifted the handle, throwing open the back door, barely even glancing inside, at least not enough to notice anything above the fact that it was filled with at least a dozen barrels.

Then I heard a muffled cry, from behind one of the barrels, and my head snapped up.

Three figures crouched low in the very back, staring at me, keeping very still, to the effect that they seemed to not even be breathing. Two of them looked to be twins, with gleaming dark eyes set into narrow, almost identical faces. The third was Gwen.

Her gray eyes were wide, panicked, pleading, and our gazes were locked in a silent debate. But in truth, there really *was* no debate. Regardless of what had happened between us, there was some part of me that still cared for her, whether I would admit it aloud or not. There was some part of me that remembered the rare occasions she had let her clever disguise slip enough to show the *real* Gwen Farrier. Even before I'd discovered the true depths of her deceit (namely, how she had only dated me to make her ruse seem more convincing), I'd known that *something* was off about her. I'd ended it because I had felt that she was being untruthful to me. And yet…what was I doing now but keeping a secret of my own?

I shut the three stowaways back into darkness.

GWEN

First there was only nothingness, a great starless nightscape, and I was conscious only of the sharp sensation prickling at my temples.

Then a pulse of red swept across the backs of my eyelids, bringing with it a sensation much sharper and more painful than before. *Where am I?*

My eyes snapped open, threatening to slam back shut when met with the light from the naked bulb swinging pendulum-like above my head. I tried to shield them from the harsh glare, but found my wrists were strapped to the arms of a cold, metal chair.

"Look who's finally awake."

I started, glancing up from my hands to see a dark figure seated almost listlessly across from me, just outside the light's reach. Slowly, I recalled bits and pieces of what had happened. Vince, backlit by waning sunlight, his gaze meeting mine. The truck lurching forward and after a short time reaching its destination. No time to slip out unnoticed. No time to hide. Being discovered. Deadlocks swarming us like a hive of wasps, quickly incapacitating us. And then nothing but silent oblivion.

The figure leaned forward, a slight smile on his lips. He was most likely in his fifties, with silvery-brown hair buzzed short above watchful eyes and an unpleasant scar running along the top of his nose. "I would tell you to call me Anderson, but I know Sentries like you have no use for such formalities."

Ignoring the aching throb stabbing through my temples, I managed to compose my expression into one of disgust, one of defiance.

Anderson only smiled wider. "How contemptuous you look right now. How *dignified.*" He tsked. "It's rather out of character for your kind to look like that. If I didn't know any better, I'd say you were a—"

He stopped midsentence, sliding the chair forward so it squealed against the stone floor, peering intently into my face. "Wait just a moment. I recognize you. Your eyes are Farrier eyes." Anderson sat back, folding his arms, gratified by his discovery. "Well, I'll be damned. You look just like your mother, you know that?"

I jolted in my seat, as a current of electricity had been shot into me. "You're wrong," I protested, but even to me it sounded feeble. "What you're implying is *ridiculous*. It's—"

"The truth?" Anderson tilted his head at me, sly now with the information he held over my head. "My, how very scandalous. I'm sure Mommy and Daddy would be *delighted* to hear of this."

A cold wind cut through me at that, raising gooseflesh, elevating my heart rate. "You can't do that." My voice was a dry whisper, brittle enough to break.

The Persuader before me chuckled at that. "And why can't I?" Seeing my face, he contrived his own into one of sympathy. "Oh, now, I'm not as cruel as you think, lovely. I'll offer you a deal, to maintain your little charade. You just give me all that I require, and we'll forget about this whole ordeal."

I swallowed thickly. "What, exactly, do you *require?*"

"You know what I mean." He seemed impatient. "*Information*, stupid girl. Anti-aggression contracts. Weapons."

I lifted my chin at him. "If it's weapons you want, I'm sure any Sentry would be willing to oblige. How many knives, I wonder, can fit on your back?"

Anderson's hand was just a blur as it cracked across my cheek. It stung, and it bled, but my resolve was not broken by it.

"You're going to have to do better than that." I said this without thinking, without considering the fact that his aura suggested he had the power necessary to do *a lot* worse.

His eyes flashed, and before I knew what was happening, he had latched onto my forearm and we were in Cavea.

Most of the time Cavea could not be brought about unless by mutual agreement, but the blow had disoriented me, and I was left defenseless.

I lifted my head to find myself surrounded by mirrors. Anderson stood inside one of them. I started for him, but the image shifted and he was suddenly in every mirror.

"Gwendolyn," he purred, lingering over every syllable of my name. I started at the sound of it. He wasn't going to fight me. He was leeching the information from my head manually. I had heard stories of some Persuaders possessing uncanny abilities, but I had no idea that it could extend to *this*.

Anderson had vanished. In his place he left two other figures. My parents. Their faces were gone, but I could hear their voices everywhere.

Everywhere.

"Gwen, you disappoint us…you're an embarrassment to our family…a traitor…you have a name to uphold…think about the principles you were raised by…Gwen, Gwen, *Gwen…*"

"Stop it." I clamped my hands over my ears, sinking to my knees.

All was silent again.

I risked a glance back at the mirrors, only to see Vince glaring down at me, arms crossed. His eyes were completely black, even the white parts. "You lied to me." His head turned to the side, at an almost unnatural angle now. "You used me."

I started to say something, but the words were cut short by his sudden cry of agony. He dropped to his knees, reflecting my own pose, a slow stream of red pouring from his lips. He coughed, spitting up more blood.

I staggered toward him. "Vince!"

But he, too, disappeared. In his place were dozens of faces, warped ghoulishly, filling the circle of mirrors, chanting in hushed tones. "Not one of us…never be one of us…untrustworthy…liar…never be more than a Persuader…"

I could feel hot tears on my face. Though I knew instinctively that it was not within Anderson's capacities to be merciful, still I pleaded with him, pleaded in between gasps of air. "Enough, please, I'm begging you. *Enough.*"

Anderson reappeared in front of me, his smile fiendish, his demeanor sickly-sweet and saintly. I knew that his exterior, urbane as it was, masked a darkness within that he couldn't quite manage to conceal. "Does it bother you, Gwen? That I now know more about you than *you know* about *yourself?*"

I wondered what new demon he would unearth from my brain, what new instrument of torture he would discover within my private fears and anxieties, before I remembered—like something revelatory—that *I* had control over this world, as well.

The circle of mirrors constricted around us, and I lurched forward, dropping a shoulder into Anderson's gut, propelling both of us into the mirrors. They shattered and we hurtled into the blackness beyond the walls and straight into another room of my own design, the floor now littered with long shards of glass.

He shoved me off of him roughly and stood, scowling down at me in disgust as he slammed a boot into the center of my chest. "I *was* going to show pity on you. But now I think I'll have to put you in your place." He raised his hand, a jagged bit of mirror materializing in his grasp, glinting dangerously as his lip curled.

There was an explosion of light and sound, and Cavea crumbled, burning away into ash. With a jolt, I realized I was in reality.

I was in reality, and Anderson was dead.

He was in a heap on the floor, blood trickling from a gunshot to the back of the head. Eli stood over him, looking pale and as in shock as I was. He wiped the sweat from his forehead with a shaking hand, sliding the pistol back into the holster at his side.

I opened my mouth to say something ridiculous, something like: *You didn't need to kill him, Eli.* But I didn't, because I knew how it would sound. Weak, childish, and, not to mention, something a Persuader would say. The man had infringed upon the deepest corners of my mind, had tortured me. I had no reason to take issue with Eli's actions.

Yet somehow I did. Somehow, there was still that voice in the back of my head that questioned where the line was, that wondered where self-defense ended and where plain murder began, and if it even existed at all in this world where people were engaged in a constant and unseen war.

14

MASQUERADE

JENNY

"This is never going to work."

This was the first sentence Taylor uttered after sliding the mask down over the top half of his face, assessing himself in the mirror with a cynical lift of his shoulders. A black mop of hair peeked out from the edges of the mask, and it wasn't violet-blue eyes that I saw beneath the disguise but brown ones.

"Not with that attitude it's not," I replied, looking up at him over my still-drying nails, newly manicured in preparation for the night's approaching horrors. I couldn't decide which was worse: Being forced to attend Samuel's masquerade ball—most likely a catastrophe waiting to happen—or being forced to undergo yet another hours-long sprucing under the ministrations of Laura.

He glanced at me with suspicion from the corner of the enormous mirror before him. *"You* sound oddly optimistic."

I snorted. "Don't mistake optimism for something a little more resigned, my friend." Lowering my hands, I added, "I don't like this plan any more than you do."

Taylor sighed, carefully readjusting the mask again and brushing his hair from his face. "If you don't like it so much, why can't you have someone who's not, you know, *me* go in my place?"

"Aside from the fact that we have no idea how much Thom told Samuel of your appearance and therefore have no idea if this plan is even going to work in the first place?" Taylor tossed me a glare from over his shoulder. "You know why, Taylor. We all know *why*. My dad's a hopeless recluse. No one to call and ask for a favor. Besides, all the other Persuaders are too afraid of Samuel to do anything about it, anyway."

"Must be lonely," Taylor said, quietly. "Living here, being apart from his family for so many years."

That silenced me. I'd never really considered whether or not Liam was *lonely*. I figured Vince was company enough, and that Mom and I had not been enough, and that that was all. But I was starting to wonder if that was really the whole picture, if my perception of him had been a little shortsighted ever since he'd left. I had thought the world of him when I was younger.

Taylor turned and took hold of my wrists, pulling me to my feet. He removed his mask, pushing back damp black hair, and I sighed. "I miss your eyes," I said, without thinking. I really did, though. The blue of his eyes seemed like the only thing I had left of my old life, the only thing I could cling to that always reminded me of home. It was as if the contacts were little disguises of their own, concealing as much of Taylor's identity as any mask could.

He smiled a little. "It's only one night."

I reached up to ruffle his hair, feeling a little silly as I did it. I guessed a certain amount of levity had to be reached before there wasn't room for any at all. "I liked your hair brown, too."

He caught my hand, drawing it away from his face to intertwine his fingers with my own. On the contact, I suddenly had the acute realization that, not including Laura still putting things away in the bathroom cabinet, we were alone. "I can't win with you, can I?"

And he was standing so close to me, too close to be an accident. "Sorry, I…I just liked the way you looked." After a pause, I said, "I wish you didn't have to go through this. Any of this. Having to hide out here, brushing elbows with Persuaders. Being under the intense scrutiny of a dangerous Persuader who wants to kill you…"

Taylor's lips twisted into a smirk. "Kill me? How do you know he's not just planning to propose? It takes a devoted man to go to the lengths that he does."

Despite the gravity of the situation that Taylor was making light of, I laughed a little, leaning into his shoulder, breathing in the scent of some formal, expensive cologne Laura had undoubtedly insisted upon, underneath it the mint of toothpaste. I felt his chest move against my cheek with his own laughter.

There came the abrupt, deliberate sound of someone clearing her throat.

We broke apart to see Laura in the bathroom doorway gazing at us with an expression that seemed impatient, though there was something else there, as well. There seemed *always* to be something else there, and as she appraised the two of us, it became almost discernible. But before I even had the chance to study it more closely, the maid, rather ominously, dismissed Taylor with, "We'll see you downstairs, Taylor."

I blinked, not grasping the reason for her making him leave, at least not at first. Rather graciously, Taylor stifled a noise of laughter, sobering quickly—not quite quickly enough—when I glanced at him.

"Your turn," he said.

I turned a little in the mirror, gathering up the ruffles of the dress with both hands before letting it fall back to my knees.

"At least it's longer than the last one," I sighed at last. "But I still don't like the hair."

"That mess of curls on top of your head would never have been presentable at an event like this," Laura snapped, the words muffled around the row of garnet-laden hairclips stuck in her mouth. She moved the last few clips into place, sitting back. "There. That's more like it." At my rejoining huff of displeasure, she only spared me a look of warning.

"Wait here." She made her way to the door.

"Where are you going?" I craned my neck to see her retreating form disappear into the hall. She didn't answer.

I rotated back to inspect my reflection once more. Yes, this dress was better than the first, but that didn't mean I *liked* it. It was a sort of burgundy color, simpler in its artful rumples, blessedly designed with *sleeves*, even if they were only lace. I wondered if Taylor would like it. Some ridiculous part of me hoped he did, but the other part was afraid of that. True to his word, he had given not the slightest inkling of evidence to betray what had happened in the attic. Admittedly, I was a little torn by my feelings on *that*, too.

Laura returned, with a velvet black box clutched carefully in her hands. She set it down on the vanity. "Liam was originally hoping to surprise you with it at your Embracement, but…he thinks you'll need the extra luck tonight."

"Luck?" I opened the tiny box and gave a soft gasp. "Oh, my God."

I touched the delicate chain of the necklace, brushing my thumb over the amethyst stone in the center of a labyrinth of silver. It was breathtaking.

The maid smiled a little as she leaned over my shoulder, looking at the necklace with a peculiar fondness. "It was your mother's. She wore it at her wedding. Swore that it had special properties to bring good fortune to its wearer."

I struggled to speak around the sudden knot in my throat. "I guess she was wrong."

Laura's sharp eyes met mine in the mirror. "Is that a fact? Not a year after she received that from me as a wedding gift, you were born." She touched the purple stone. "*You* are a continuation of what this necklace meant to her, in a way. The fact that you're here, that you *exist*, means it wasn't all for nothing."

She tugged it from its place in the box, latching it around my throat. It dropped below the hollow of my collarbone, surprisingly heavy against my skin. I looked at my reflection again, and decided that the necklace suited me, in a way. Maybe not how it would've suited my mother. It suited me differently.

"You knew my parents back then?"

The maid snorted. "It's really a riveting tale of how we met, but I think Liam would be displeased with me if I told you it." Seeing my face, she laughed. "Maybe some other time. Tonight you just need to focus on not making a mess of things."

"If that's the case, someone better fetch her a cat's eye or two because the luck in that necklace may not be enough."

Vince leaned against the wall, tugging at his lapels almost self-consciously. But no—that wasn't correct. *Vince Hallows* didn't get self-conscious. At least, I'd thought that once. Now the statement was suspended above me, available for dismantling like so many other things I'd thought I had known for certain.

I made a face at him. "You could knock."

He batted his eyes at me. "Cute, knocking. I'd almost forgotten how very *human* you still are."

I smiled sweetly at him. "I could say the same to you, outcross."

Laura looked uncomfortable with our taut exchange, taking the opportunity to gather her supplies and leave the room.

Vince looked after her as she brushed by him. "Oh, my, we seem to have frightened her off." He glanced back at me with hooded eyes. "Best be careful with the names you toss about, interbreed."

I spared him only a frown and an "Excuse me" as I tried to skirt around him to get past the door. His arm shot out to hit the opposite side of the doorframe, in front of my face, blocking my exit. "Wait."

I stepped a little away, not looking at him. At least, not until his thumb moved under my chin, gently lifting my face to his own. And how *earnest* his face was. His smile wasn't as hard or as brittle as it usually was. Surprisingly, it was anxious, and it was also sincere. "You look nice."

GWEN

Pop. Pop. Pop.

Schnip. Schnip. Schnip.

The bullets struck at the heart of the target, leaving behind cleanly shaped, black punctures in the paper. With a tight, satisfied smile I moved to the next one and fired three more shots.

Pop. Pop. Pop.

Schnip. Schnip. Schnip.

As I paced sideways to take aim at the third target, I felt a familiar sensation at the nape of my neck. Over the years, I'd learned to identify the auras of certain people not just by the varying levels of intensity, but also by the impression that lingered afterward. Vince's often left a chill in the air, evidence of his detachment toward others. Lately, though, it had been thawing, as I suspected was Jenny Cable's doing. I fired a single bullet into the paper.

Pop. Schnip.

Samuel's aura made you feel as if it was taking something away from you. It was an oily aura, full of malice.

Pop. Schnip.

And Natalia's aura was an anomaly. She was a quarter human, an outcross, but through sheer strength of will it struck the senses as forcefully as any pureblooded Persuader's did. It was a determined aura. Maybe that was why I admired her so much and why she pitied me. We were both trying to become the very person everyone else was telling us we weren't, the person we could never be. The decision Natalia had made during her Embracement had caused quite the commotion, from what I had heard. Like me she'd been raised by Persuader parents, but that was where similarities stopped. Her decision to become a Sentry had been public, immeasurably dangerous for her. The only reason she hadn't been hunted down was because she'd had the initiative and force of character necessary to establish her own stronghold.

Pop.

Schnip.

I lowered the gun, finally turning to face her, but Natalia's eyes were looking past me. "That last one went a little wide."

I glanced at the third hole, well distanced from the other two, barely grazing the ear of the human outline. "I've been…distracted."

Natalia sighed. "I can tell. It's why I'm here to talk to you."

I swallowed, slowly holstering the weapon in my hands. "What is this about?"

"Tonight is an important night, you know that. This mission is going to require…focus." Her eyes searched my face, for signs of comprehension.

My lips twisted. "You mean to say that I lack the resilience to be a part of it." I recalled the occasion when Jenny Cable and company had paid a visit to the stronghold, remembered the Sentry rogue in the elevator murmuring to her, *You're brave enough.*

Before, I had only envied her, envied her of the choice that was being offered to her like it hadn't been to me. I resented her for not being grateful for it. But what I *hadn't* considered was how Jenny must've felt, being thrust into this world and told that she would have to make a life-changing decision in only a short time, and that, either way, there were lingering consequences and no small amount of danger involved in her choice. It was in that moment I decided I really didn't envy her at all, and that we were more alike than I'd wanted to believe. Jenny was indeed brave enough to have lasted this long. A weaker person would've run from it or resigned herself to the path of least resistance, and harboring a rogue didn't seem to be the way toward any such path.

The problem was, I didn't know what my *own* limits were, in terms of both the emotional and the psychological. We had trained to withstand torture under Natalia's watch, had trained for months, but when Anderson had put that training to the test, I'd failed completely in no time at all. I wondered if I would've eventually given in to his demands had Eli not found me when he did.

Afterwards, when Darren and Sasha had been liberated, as well, they'd asked me what had happened and the words had dried up on my tongue. I couldn't tell them. It would mean admitting to both my friends and to myself that I'd been afraid. It would mean admitting weakness, which was, to the Sentry soldier, an incurable illness.

As if reading my mind, Natalia said, "Gwen, you shouldn't blame yourself for what happened. The only way to move on from what you went through is to not dwell on it. It'll only fester."

I was about to say something else—an angry retort of some kind—but I stopped myself. My hands clenched and unclenched once, falling to my sides. "Yes, ma'am."

"You should get ready."

My head snapped up. "Ready?"

Natalia offered me a rare smile. "For the mission. You think I would leave one of my best Sentries here, sulking and taking her frustration out on something that's not Samuel Locke?"

I returned her smile. "Thank you, Natalia."

She waved my gratitude away, characteristically serious once more, turning to leave. "Now's not the time to thank me yet. See to it that the mission goes successfully first."

On her way out, she stopped, twisting slightly to look at me. "Oh, and by the way, your level of resilience isn't something determined by someone else. Bit of advice for you."

JENNY

Guests surged into the mansion in glittering twin streams, here and there the plume of a particularly over-adorned mask fluttering above the throng like some colorful leaf carried by the current. Vince, Liam, Taylor, and I traveled with the tide, and Taylor-who-was-not-Taylor peered at me sideways through his simple black mask, a furtive look I returned only for a moment before turning my attention back to the crowd. I tried to find Gwen among them; she would have no need to remain hidden, considering that in everyone else's eyes she appeared to be just as much of a Persuader as any other. Unsuccessful in my search, I studied Samuel's lavish abode—

the dazzling array of lights curling around the columns, the more modernized, sharpened design of the building. Where the Cable mansion was a worn-edged monument that displayed its signs of age like an old veteran would faded battle scars, Samuel's residence was upright and polished, much like its occupant.

The front doors were wide open, letting in the cold of October and the even colder elite of Persuader society. As we made our way through the congestion at the entrance, Samuel was quick to spot and greet us.

It was evident, by his expression, that he was unpleasantly surprised by our arrival. His eyes were like glass beads set into a face of stone. "Liam Cable." His anger was only superficially concealed by his silver-tongued civility. "How good it is to see you. Mr. Hallows, Miss Cable." He acknowledged Vince and me with polite detachment. But then his gaze locked onto Taylor, to my left. "And who might this be?" The words dripped from his mouth like venom.

Taylor was unwavering in his response. "Seth Sinclair, sir." I smothered a noise of surprise. We hadn't discussed fake names beforehand—a minor but fairly important oversight—yet Taylor had said the name as if it was his own. Even Vince couldn't help but look impressed.

"Ah, Mr. Sinclair, we meet at last. I've heard so much about you."

Taylor smiled a titanium smile, detecting his bluff. "Really?" he inquired, good-naturedly. "Nothing too condemnatory, I hope."

"Of course." To his evident disappointment, Samuel's close evaluation seemed to be nearly complete. "How did you happen to make the acquaintance of the Cable family?"

"My father conducted some business in D.C. some time ago." Taylor was really finding a rhythm, and his upbringing had rendered him more than capable of adopting the inflated manner of speaking characteristic of a Persuader. It was slightly disturbing how well he could lie, and how eloquently, though I suspected this was mostly because I'd never noticed a particular dishonesty about him before. "He happened to cross paths with Mr. Cable there. I'm only visiting for a few weeks, really, and then I ought to be heading back."

"Where did you say you were from again?" Samuel was quick to ask.

"I didn't." For a moment, I was afraid that Taylor had been stumped by the question, but he picked up effortlessly with, "My family's lived in Philadelphia for some time."

It was a wise location; Samuel wouldn't be familiar with anyone from there, but at the same time it wasn't an unreasonable distance away to be making business trips, especially to the capital. Samuel's jaw clenched once, signaling a rare defeat. "Please, enjoy the party."

Liam nodded tightly. "Thank you." He snatched a champagne glass from one of the silver serving platters passing by, holding it up to Samuel in an oddly brazen performance. "Cheers."

"Seth Sinclair?"

Taylor's—Seth's—eyes slid to mine. We both slouched unobtrusively at the edge of the gathering, not even feigning interest. I felt an odd mixture of resignation and anxiety, waiting for the moment when Sentries would storm the party, and dreading it. "That's my name," he replied, mildly. "Don't wear it out."

I suppressed an eye roll. "I mean, where did it come from?"

He shrugged. "Old childhood friend from Alexandria." He paused. "Really a bland sort of guy. But he was a Persuader, after all."

Without thinking, I said, "Vince isn't bland."

He didn't look at me. He didn't have to; the bitter tone to his voice revealed his irritation plainly enough. "Honestly, I would prefer him that way."

"Prefer me what way?"

Taylor and I whirled to see Vince, leaning forward a little, his hands politely clasped behind his back.

I frowned. "How do you know if we're even talking about *you?*"

"Most of the time I can tell by the envious tonality of one's voice." He unclasped his hands to thrust them into his pockets, tilting his head. "Also, I know how you two *love* to talk about me." With a wink, he dissolved back into the crowd.

"God, I think I might drown myself in the punch bowl." Taylor ran a hand through his hair, ruining Laura's careful combing as he returned it to its natural disorderly state.

"You'll miss all the excitement," I reminded him.

Taylor tossed me a half-amused look before melting into the party like Vince had done moments before.

And I was alone.

GWEN

I navigated through the tightly packed bodies, my head automatically swiveling to those who greeted me, a smile plastered on, a quick reply their way. I knew the drill with these sorts of events as well as I knew any Sentry training exercise.

Then I saw Vince, headed toward me, and I was glad for the mask; it hid the color that rushed into my face at the sight of him. He reached me, gripping my arm, pulling me away from the Persuaders with a look of unease.

"Gwen, we need to talk."

At his tone, the heat faded. Suddenly, I just felt cold all over. "I...what about?"

His eyes swept the room briefly before returning to mine. "Are they in position?"

"I don't think here is the best place to discuss—"

With an impatient noise, he took my arm again and dragged me off toward the doors at the end of the large room. No one loitered around here, and we slipped out into the pool yard unnoticed.

The water threw off stars of white and yellow from the lights that hung in a lattice above it. A biting wind cut through me and I looked at Vince, loathing him and yet still loathing myself more. I'd started dating him only for appearances and had acted how I imagined one in the position ought to, and I'd known from the *start* that nothing real or lasting could've come out of it. So why had I let myself *forget* that?

"Your people," he said, reiterating himself. "Are they ready?"

I considered making some dignified comment about the phrase "your people", but thought better of it. "Vince, I don't have time to stand out here. What is this about?"

He rubbed a hand down his face. "I'm sorry. It's just I'm...I'm getting this feeling. Something isn't right. It's feels too risky."

"Risky?" I asked, incredulous. "This is the only chance we have at getting close to Samuel without him spotting us a mile away. People are flooding through in torrents. I already have several of us in. I can't just ask them to leave now. *That* would be risky."

His hands flailed to his hair, pulling at it. "It just doesn't make sense! Why would this be a masquerade ball? Why aren't the doors being guarded? Samuel isn't careless. All his actions have motives."

I shook my head. "I have to get back to the party."

"Wait," he said, stopping me. "You're armed? You have a gun on you?"

"Of course I am. I'd be an idiot not to be."

He stared into my face, his own suddenly drawn and intent. "Ask yourself why." The words came through strained.

I blinked at him, perplexed. "Well, obviously in case of—"

I froze, realizing his meaning at last. He nodded when he saw my understanding. "Deadlocks," he said. "The masks. That's why the masks. I knew I felt *something* when I walked in, but there could be *dozens* of them and we wouldn't even know. There's no way to know."

I clasped a hand to my mouth, my next words muffled by it. "Oh my God. I have to tell Natalia."

"Are the others armed?" he asked.

I shook my head, numbly. "Not many of them. We have weapons, but ammo's in short supply. Not that it hasn't always been like that, but it wasn't exactly a big help to us when a man named Anderson bought most of what was available last week. He must've been working for Samuel." Only now did I realize it had been a calculated move. No Persuader went to the black market without a reason.

His eyes were wide. "We have to stop this."

I was poised to reply when the glass doors shattered, and with it came the shrieks of Samuel's unsuspecting guests.

JENNY

I saw Vince, Gwen in tow, disappear out into the pool yard and tried to convince myself that it was a harmless conversation about the weather, even though something told me it wasn't.

I sighed, turning back to the crowd, only to run headlong into a mountain of a man doing just the opposite. He scowled down at me, his mask casting a shadow across his eyes. "Watch it," he snarled.

I mumbled a quick apology before hurriedly moving around him. Some Persuaders could be nasty, not all of them as bland as Taylor had said. I studied the gigantic man as he crossed over to the refreshments table. He removed his mask, wiping his brow with a sleeve. His head turned to the side as he did, and I saw a mark across his forehead. I squinted at it, realizing it was a tattoo.

I found Taylor, leaning against the wall, looking unhappy and tense. I attempted at humor to ease his anxiety. "I was almost run over by that bulldozer over there in the corner."

His mouth quirked up at the corner. "Him? Geez, he has to be at least 6' 7"."

"*Custos* must mean 'look at me and I'll kill you.'"

Taylor straightened, surprising me, his grin slipping. "What?"

I pointed to the place above my eyebrow. "He had a tattoo right here; it said that." I paused. "Taylor, what's wrong?"

He had gone very still. "Jenny, you need to leave. Tell Liam we need to go right now. Go find Vince, too."

"I don't understand." I grabbed his arm. "What is it?"

He shook me off. "You don't *need* to, Jenny. Just get out of here—!"

His voice had risen to a shout, but it was lost in the shattering of glass and the ensuing screams of surprise and horror. Then came the gunshots, and all was bedlam. Holes were ripped into the wallpaper not even two feet from us. Taylor roughly seized me, pulling me behind an overturned table. Glass and dust and bullets littered the floor at our feet, and we could hear return fire from the Sentries just in front of us.

I thought I would be in hysterics at the prospect of facing death down the barrel of a gun once again, but instead a cold composure flooded me. "What's happening?" I asked.

Taylor was breathing heavily, looking at me with panicked brown eyes. He tore off his mask. "Deadlocks. Persuader bodyguards. Don't try to Shift; it won't work with them here." He cursed. "Samuel was one step ahead of us this whole time. He orchestrated the whole thing."

"How could he have?" I asked, more to myself. This sort of thing couldn't just be *arranged*, scheduled as if it was a piano lesson.

Taylor shook his head. "I don't know." He put his forehead to mine. "I don't know, Jenny."

VINCE

"Vince, we have to find Natalia."

I opened my eyes to see Gwen looking up at me from the circle of my arm, her expression calm and without fear, and realized that at the shattering of the door I'd dove for her, knocking us both into the grass. I barely got out an apology before Gwen shoved me off of her without ceremony, rolling to a crouch and grabbing my arm to pull us both upright. I brushed glass dust from my shoulders. "Find her, then. She needs *you* right now, not me. I have to get to Liam and Jenny."

She nodded. "Okay. No use going after Samuel. He would've fled by now, the coward." She turned and, with the toe of her boot, upset a potted plant along the edge of the pool, cursing.

I took her shoulder. "There's no way either of us could've been prepared for this. You did the best you could."

She didn't look at me. "Why is my best never enough?" she said, quietly. I didn't need to look into the question too deeply to know what she really meant by it—or, rather, the *many things* she meant by it.

I didn't, and couldn't, answer, and instead turned wordlessly to leave, already inspecting the property for ways inside that didn't involve the probability of getting shot several times before I even stepped foot inside the house. Already, stray bullets and glass had struck out several lights that hung above the pool. Gwen grabbed my sleeve, her gray eyes staring into my face. Looking at them, an odd thought struck me then that—after all those months we'd dated—I'd never even noticed the blue ring around the pupil. It was the blue of the sky just after the sun disappeared. "Be careful," was all she said before slipping around the side of the house. I went the opposite way, running for the far corner, hoping for at least a low window on the other side to get into. I never made it that far.

Samuel appeared in front of me like a shadow, palm outward. His fingers splayed apart, almost carelessly, and I found myself airborne, thrown like a discarded doll across Samuel's estate.

I hit the ground hard, what little air left in my lungs leaving in a way that made me feel as if my breath had been ripped out of me. Samuel was there, crouching over me with those dark eyes, still not a strand of coppery hair out of place. There was something tucked under his left arm, something red. I could barely choke out the words at him: "How...how can you...Shift?"

He smirked, clearly satisfied that he held even a greater amount of power over the rest of us. His lifted his arm, the sleeve slipping down his wrist, revealing a thin band of metal underneath. "Just testing my new toy, Mr. Hallows. You see, a few electrical signals and my mind is utterly free from Deadlock influence. Technology these days is truly fascinating, isn't it?"

My fingers curled. "I'm a bit old-fashioned, myself," I said, and struck him across the face.

He rocked back on his heels, and I lurched to my feet, lifting my blood-flecked fist to hit him again. Samuel, very calmly, lifted his own hand. My knuckles collided with an invisible wall, glancing off of the barrier as Samuel stood with a smirk. I could see that underneath his arm was a gallon gasoline container, and in his left hand he grasped a second one, and I froze at the sight of them.

"I think it's time you modernized, Vincent," Samuel said, taking a step back. Belatedly, I realized that he had taken a step back not onto solid ground, but onto the glistening surface of the pool. He unscrewed the cap of the first container, emptying its contents into the water as he went. Spirals of color swirling listlessly about, barely disturbed by his footfalls.

He took more steps backwards as he dabbed at his face with a handkerchief, wiping away the spots of blood. The water seemed to gather and solidify underneath of him, and I watched in part-horror, part-bewilderment as he performed a feat that was nothing short of blasphemous. "We are entering a new age," he said, his voice taking on the undertones of a seasoned orator giving a speech, except his only listeners were myself and the stars, who observed coldly from above us. "An age where the strong shall walk on water, while the weak drown beneath it." Unwillingly, my mind flashed to Jenny, and unwillingly I relived the horror of watching her disappear beneath the surface of the pond. "An age where the world is untainted by the lesser classes of our society. Free of the outcrossed, free of interbreeds, free of rogues and benefactors."

My throat had gone dry. "You're a Purist," I rasped. "That's why finding Taylor Ross and persecuting my family is so important to you. You're a sick lunatic who thinks himself better than those who are different from you."

"*Different?*" Samuel looked coolly amused. "My dear boy, you seem quite confused, blinded by the ridiculous principles instilled in you by Liam Cable. People like to pretend things are equal to each other by using the word 'different', when clearly they are not. Let me ask you something, is the value of stone *equal* to that of diamond? Is bronze *equal* to gold? Don't liken different to *inferior*, Vincent." He had made it all the way across the width of the pool by then, abandoning the now empty container and starting on the next without ceremony. When he at last drained and discarded it, he reached a hand into his inside jacket pocket. "Maybe this is an analogy you can understand. Can an outcross ever be *equal* to a full-blooded Persuader? I'll answer that for you. No. No, he cannot." He had produced a worn paper box, withdrawing a single match from it, not taking his eyes from mine. He lit it, holding it out to me. "The weak like to believe they're strong until that strength is put to the test. Once tested, that belief is proven to be nothing but a trick of the imagination. Here's one last comparison for you. Is it possible for something to be *equal* to a fire that consumes it?"

I looked away from Samuel now, entranced by the faint flicker of yellow at the end of the match. I could still hear the gunfire, the shouts of Sentries and Deadlocks, the high shrieks of the unarmed Persuaders trampling others to get out, but it all sounded distant, like a quiet conversation going on in another room.

He answered for me again. "No, it isn't. Do you know why?"

The words I wanted to say were lost in the memories of England spilling across my vision like ink across paper.

He smiled, his teeth glinting. "It is because the fire makes nothing of it. What was once there no longer exists as it existed before. Few things are invincible to it, really—oh, but you already know that, of course. Do you think, Vincent, that you're *stronger* than you were ten years ago? If you do, let me do you the kindness of saying that no amount of time can erase what you are by nature. Not ten years, not ten lifetimes."

Samuel tossed the match into the blackness of the water, and a wall of flame leapt from its surface.

TAYLOR

"Taylor, how are we going to get out of here?"

Her eyes were very green, her face very pale, yet to me she appeared at that moment utterly indestructible. Her question had not been some hopeless, empty plea, but rather something that demanded an immediate course of action.

"There's no easy way out. I saw Liam with Gwen and Natalia. They're trying to filter the Sentries out of the windows in the side rooms it looks like. We should follow suit." A bullet struck the top corner of the table we had taken cover behind, taking off a chunk of mahogany while it snipped by right over my head. "*Now* would be a good time."

Jenny pressed her fingers to the backs of her eyes. "This is all my fault."

"Jenny, no, it's not. You shouldn't think that—"

She grabbed my wrists. "*I* was the one who came up with the plan! *I* was the one who asked for the Sentries' help. I sentenced dozens of people to *die,* Taylor!"

"Samuel was the one who—"

"Pulled the trigger?" She gave a sharp laugh. "I might as well have put the gun in his hands."

I opened my mouth to argue further when I caught sight of Liam, leaning against the inside of a doorway, to one of the other rooms, pulling Sentries inside, ushering them to the windows. His gaze found mine, and he pointed at Jenny, jerking his thumb backward, signaling me to get her to safety. Whatever he thought of me, he knew I wouldn't let a bullet touch her, even if it meant shielding her with my own body.

"Come on," I said, taking her arm.

We sprang from behind the table low to the ground, and I moved so I was to her right. The space between Liam and us seemed to stretch out before me, a hundred feet instead of twenty. It was as if we were encased in glass, shouts blurring together and the golden glow of the room melting into a dark tunnel.

A shape blackened my peripheral vision, and turning I saw that I faced the end of a Deadlock's gun, so close I could've leaned forward and rested my forehead against the barrel. And yet…my experience with Wolves had afforded me the knowledge that, for all its bravado, a position like that was *too* close. His maneuverability had vanished, and so had his chances of killing me. Twisting to the side, I grabbed his wrist and pulled him off-balance, throwing a knee into his elbow to disarm him. However, in no time at all the Deadlock had somehow wrestled himself free of me and was coming at me again, this time with a knife in his hand.

Growing up, I'd had little hand-to-hand combat training—if any at all—though once I'd set myself on the path of a rogue, I'd been forced to learn very quickly how to defend myself. This was before I'd found safety under Tarek's roof, and the Wolves at night were always about, always on the lookout for sheep that'd strayed too a little too far from the flock.

The Deadlock was upon me, and I blocked his first swipe, dodged the second. My eyes caught thoughtlessly on Jenny for a moment, who stood tensed just behind me, when I felt pain explode from my midsection like a fireplace poker had been pressed flush to my skin. I kicked the man's legs out from underneath of him, seizing the knife that'd been knocked from his hand.

Don't look, Jenny, I thought. *Please don't look.*

I drove the knife into the Deadlock's heart.

When Liam's hand finally closed around Jenny's arm, I wasn't relieved as I thought I would be. I only felt numbness, an odd confusion as my hands moved reflexively to my stomach, clawing at the torn fabric of my shirt. They came away red.

Before I knew what was happening, Jenny and Liam had disappeared into the darkness of the next room, and I was being shoved into the doorway by an irregular stream of Sentries escaping from a fight they couldn't have hoped to win. Blood mixed with broken furniture and shattered champagne glasses across the floor. My head was swimming, my vision hazing around the edges. What was wrong with me? I had to get to her. I didn't have time to stumble around in the dark. I had to...

I collapsed to the floor.

VINCE

As if in a trance, I watched the blaze, the swirls of black and orange, breathing tapestries of gold and yellow and gray.

I curled in on myself, my arms wrapping tightly about my ribcage as if to keep all that lay beneath it inside. Cold sweat broke out across my forehead, and I was distinctly aware that I was shaking. *It's only fire*, I chanted to myself. *Only fire. Only fire.*

I fell onto the grass, slamming my eyes shut to keep out the stinging brightness of it. I could feel its heat on my skin, could feel the smoke get inside of me and fill my nose and my lungs and my head. I fought to get away, blinded and seized by wracking coughs, my shoulder smarting as it struck the side of the house.

Breathing hard, I glanced up, blinking smoke from my eyes, and could see Sentries scrambling out of the windows, in full retreat, but didn't see Jenny or Liam among them. I shoved around them, lifting myself through one of the windows, into the dim side room of the house.

Jenny wasn't here, either. She had to already be out. I prayed that her and Liam were all right, that they'd somehow escaped unscathed. I turned to leave when, through the tightly packed bodies, I caught sight of something in a heap on the floor.

Taylor laid very still, his hands circling his waist. A slow trickle of blood slipped between his fingers. I sucked in a breath, and for once I didn't think about how much I hated him. I didn't think about how he'd given up everything I wished I had, and I didn't think about how Jenny looked at him. Instead, I bent to slide my arms beneath his, and drag him to the window where another Sentry helped pull him out onto the grass.

Not that I would ever admit to it, but maybe Taylor Ross had more guts than I gave him credit for.

15
THE CONTENTS OF THE HEART

TAYLOR

"What do you mean there isn't anything that can be done?"

Jenny's face was only a faint smudge against a black backdrop, outlined by the harsh glow of the light above. Laura's face joined hers, creased with anxiety, her expression grim. "The wound is deep. He's suffered a lot of blood loss—"

"We have to get him to a hospital, then!" Her voice had risen alarmingly, and it struck me as strange that she was more distraught than I was—though I was really too weak to feel much beyond vague emotions, and for only brief amounts of time. "We can't just let him *die.*"

"Moving him will only worsen things, Jenny." Liam appeared at her shoulder, looking very tired. His fair hair was in disarray about his head. "We're doing all we can for him here."

"It's not enough." Her voice shook, her hands closing into pale, little fists. "There has to be something." She wiped at her face furiously. "If only he was like me. If only I could just...*give him* my healing ability..."

She went very still, then.

"You don't think—"

Laura made a sound from the back of her throat. "It's worth a try. He doesn't have long. Maybe a few hours."

Jenny surged forward, her hair hanging into her face, her hands moving under the blood-suffused bandages to cover my stomach, hesitant as her fingers found the edges of the wound. A fresh wave of pain rolled through me, almost knocking me unconscious again. I was distantly aware of my cry of agony. Her brows knitted together at the sound, her teeth gritting, as if the sound was a tangible thing that had struck her deep in the heart. Her hands were shaking, and perspiration had broken out across her forehead, pasting stray strands of hair to her skin. I drifted in and out of a limbo state between consciousness and oblivion during those outstretched minutes, aware of nothing but her face, her gentle touch, and the heated pain. But then a coldness started to spread from her hands, almost soothing in the relief it brought. It followed the map of veins under my skin, shooting throughout my entire body like a jolt of electricity. With it came a trailing sensation that conjured images of playing in the summer rain as a child, and the last remnants of the fire in my blood were extinguished.

I breathed a sigh and let my eyes slip closed.

"Is he...?" The voice belonged to Vince. I almost wanted to laugh at the thought of him hovering like an anxious mother beside the bed, but I barely had the strength to speak.

In a voice like gravel, I said, "Alas...not yet."

With a cry, Jenny threw her arms around me. It felt like my own arm was filled with lead, but I managed to lift it enough to wrap it around her trembling shoulders, whispering hoarsely in her ear. "It's okay, Jenny...I'll be fine...thanks to you, I'll be fine."

She laughed, her voice cracking. "How is it that *you're* the one comforting *me?*"

Laura unraveled the bandages from around my waist, tugging them away with a whistle. "Handy little talent, Jennifer. Appears as though you've stitched him back up."

I saw Liam standing apart from all of this, looking at Jenny as if she was a stranger to him. After a pause, he cleared his throat softly. "Let the two have a moment alone."

Jenny lay beside me on the bed when they were gone, our arms barely touching as if she was afraid any contact at all would hurt me, but after a while her head lolled to my bare shoulder and I could see she was as exhausted as I was. I reached to grip her hand, twining our fingers together. It felt as natural as breathing, as it always did.

"You have no idea how worried I was," she whispered.

"I have an idea," I murmured back. The memories from the night she'd been shot—how red my hands and her dress were, and how pale her face—distracted me, drawing me into only a half-consciousness.

"Taylor?"

I started slightly, blinking away the thoughts. Jenny was eyeing me curiously. "You must be tired."

"Yeah, I must be." I ran a hand through my hair, feeling the sticky coarseness of nearly dried blood and sweat, even bits of glass.

She was still looking at me, and I wanted to take her face in my hands and I wanted to kiss her, but I couldn't. And I didn't; instead, my teeth slammed together, biting back the words I really wanted to say. I was sick and tired of suppressing everything I felt, of hiding in the dark, constantly kept on edge by the threat of my discovery. I may not have been proud to have been born a Persuader, but I felt as if I'd truly made an effort to redefine myself over the past year. I would always be the son of David and Alice Ross, would always have generations of Persuader blood flowing through my veins, but it was almost like I'd managed to almost *rewrite* some aspects of who I used to be. I didn't feel that ache of loneliness anymore, like I had growing up, with feelings inside of me I couldn't put words to and no one to tell about it. I didn't feel guilty anymore, like I'd been whenever my parents took me to the city to exercise my abilities. I'd long stopped hating them for it after realizing that those outings were what had ultimately driven me to ensure that I would never in my life have to manipulate people again. And then I'd met Jenny, and she'd helped me come to terms with the fact that sometimes you had to let go of the people you loved. Not to stop loving them, exactly, but to stop making my duty as a son my excuse to not do what I thought was right.

I managed a smug smile at her. "And you thought your ability was some horrible curse."

She scoffed. "Even in poor health, I should've known that you would take the opportunity to gloat." After a moment, she sighed, her expression closing shut against me, her eyes darkening with a heavier guilt than should've been possible for a girl of only seventeen. "I should've never suggested anything so *stupid*. I put Natalia's whole stronghold at risk. I put *everyone* at risk."

"Jenny, it wasn't your fault. No one could've anticipated that Samuel would do something like this." Her hand was cold against mine. "We all knew there was a risk. I can even venture to say that the risk was worth it. We showed Samuel Locke that we weren't afraid to stand up to him. It may not have gone well for us, but that's *life*. You take shots in the dark, and you make leaps of faith, and sometimes you don't always hit your mark."

Her head came to rest again on my shoulder, under my chin. I could smell the tang of salt on her skin over the subtler, peculiar trace of smoke that clung to both of us. "When did you become so wise?"

"I didn't. Near-death experiences put me in a philosophical mood."

She laughed a little at this, but I remained silent. I could talk all I wanted about shots in the dark, but it wouldn't change the fact that I was still too afraid to take one and tell her the truth. Where a leap of faith was needed, I took only a step aside.

JENNY

I listened to his breathing, the soft lull of it as he slept. It was strange to think that one could memorize the way someone talked, and the way someone signed his name, and what his favorite color was, and what music he listened to, but could still so blindly choose to overlook all the dark spots and blank spaces about that same person. All those nights spent talking on the back porch of my house, all the times he'd made me laugh out loud and embarrass myself during one of those god-awful slashers at the movies, not *once* had he mentioned, "Hey, by the way, I'm telekinetic and, oh yeah, everyone's out to get me."

But maybe it would've been better if I'd never known the truth about him. It would've certainly been less *complicated,* because it was easier to ignore how you felt about someone who wouldn't even tell you who his parents were or where he'd grown up. Now that everything about him was on the table, it was harder to ignore those feelings, harder for me to admit that—close as we were—there was space between us, yet, to tread.

I breathed a small sigh, eliciting only a twitch from the corner of Taylor's mouth. It'd all happened so quickly, so quickly it hadn't even seemed real at all. There'd been blood and shouting and hectic urgency when Vince had carried Taylor to us, as Liam and I—already in a state of panic—had searched the Sentries for them both. Vince was almost translucent in how pale he looked, even after depositing Taylor into Liam's arms, his haunted gaze flitting away from mine every time I tried to catch it. But I didn't have time to wonder about Vince's latest odd behavior, becoming soon preoccupied, instead, with situating Taylor to be as comfortable as possible in the backseat of the car as Liam blasted through stoplights like a madman.

When we arrived, Laura was quick to grasp the situation, demanding he be brought upstairs to the first room available. I remembered nothing during that period but feelings of guilt, of horror, of panic. Landmines in the brain, detonated all at once.

The healing had surprised *me* more than anyone—how well it'd worked, and how quickly. *Appears as though you've stitched him back up,* Laura had said. I wondered if my lack of awareness of the ability back when I'd had the gunshot wound had caused the process to be slower or if it was just more difficult to use it on myself than others.

In my peripheral vision, I saw the glint of something under the lamplight. Turning my head to the side, I caught sight of a scalpel, gleaming from a silver tray on the table beside the bed.

My feet, almost involuntarily, hit the floor with a light thump, and I found myself in front of the nightstand, gripping the scalpel in one clammy palm as I swiftly drew its wicked edge across the other, curling my fingers over it. When I opened my hand, there was only a thin smear of blood. No cut. No sting. But I knew better than to think that my ability was as much of a blessing as Taylor said it was. I could heal all the little cuts I wanted without getting close to treating the real disease.

Taylor still slept peacefully enough, and I decided to let him rest. He didn't need me there beside him any more than I needed to be in the house another minute. Where I truly *needed* to be was somewhere else, somewhere hostile and in disorder. I had to go to the stronghold.

However, my attempts at sneaking out had never gone particularly well before, and I'd barely even touched the knob to the front door when I felt an aura drawing near and heard a voice at my back.

"I hope you aren't planning on leaving, Jenny."

My hand closed into a fist against the door. "And if I am?"

He was silent for a moment, so silent I eventually relented and turned toward him. He'd changed out of his formal attire, now in a loose shirt and drawstring pants. His hair stuck up on both sides, as if he had been tossing in bed, and there was a slight bruise-like color under his hazel eyes. He sighed, folding his arms. "Then I'd have to stop you." When he had said that the first time, he'd been so unfeeling and so daunting, but now there was a faint smile on his lips.

"Vince, please. I have to go."

He nodded as if to himself, passing a hand down the length of his face. At length he said, "I know you have to do this. And I know I can't stop you, not with my words or by force. Definitely not by force." A small smile lifted his mouth at one corner. "I just...I want you to be careful. I wish I could go with you, but I'm not sure the sight of me would put them at *ease*, exactly..."

"This is something I have to do alone, anyway," I said, more to convince myself than to console him.

"Remember not everything has to be...like that, of course." Vince cleared his throat, looking away. Something about his discomfort made him more approachable somehow—less enigmatic *greater being*, more awkward human boy. "I'm here, you know, if you need someone. I know we didn't exactly start off on the right foot, and things have been complicated lately, but I...well, I..." His neck flushed as he spoke, pooling into his cheeks.

"I understand," I said, softly. I found I couldn't look directly at him, either. "Thank you, Vince."

He tossed me a small, metallic object from his pocket. I caught it, unfolding my hand to see that he'd given me the keys to his car. Wordlessly, he turned and left, disappearing when he reached the top of the stairs.

"What are *you* doing here?"

Gwen stood in the entryway, arms crossed about her, her gray eyes flinty as she stared me down. Her hair was pulled back into a severe ponytail but a few strands were coming loose, hanging into a face that was on the surface only annoyed, but hiding what I knew to be no small amount of distress. I shifted my weight. "I...I wanted to help. I wanted to help you with the wounded, I mean. You see—"

"Do you have any medical experience?" she demanded, cutting me off. Her eyes narrowed when, reluctantly, I shook my head. "Then what good are you to us? Don't you think you've done enough?"

I flinched. "I'm sorry. I didn't mean to put everyone in danger—"

"Natalia was shot, you know." Her mouth tightened at the corners. She appeared to be on the verge of tears. *Gwen*, who carried a gun with utter confidence and could probably break a man's jaw with a glance, looked about to cry. "She's in critical condition, but she'll only let our own medics tend to her and refuses to let us take her to a hospital. She's never trusted human doctors." Gwen shook her head. "Won't let us move her an inch."

"Gwen, you have to take me to her." I reached for her arm, and she glanced down at my hand as if it was some sort of poisonous insect. "I can help."

"I don't have to do anything." The Sentry girl shook me off. *"You can help."* She echoed my words with disdain, and then added, "What could you *possibly* do for us?"

In my desperation to explain, I found myself stumbling over the words. "Look, I don't know *how* but I have this…this ability. I can *heal.* It worked for Taylor and I see no reason why it shouldn't work for Natalia. Just…let me help her. And anyone else who needs it. Please."

Gwen regarded me for a moment, deliberating. Her hand, almost unconsciously, moved to the knife at her belt. After a pause, it dropped to her side. "Fine," she said, at last. "But you better not be wasting my time."

I moved forward, toward the sliding metal door, but she held out a hand to stop me. "I wouldn't advise it, interbreed. The Sentries in there would love to tear you apart. And Daddy isn't here to save you this time."

"It was Vince who pulled me into the elevator."

The words were out before I could bite them back. At the mention of Vince, Gwen's expression had frozen into a careful and practiced disinterest. "So it was," she said, softly. After a moment, she seemed to remember what it was she had been saying before. "Anyway, we should use the fire escape around the side of the building. It's kind of unsteady, but it's safer than hurling ourselves headlong into a mob of people who think you're practically the antichrist."

"Do they really?" I stared at the ground, at the brown patches of grass that grew defiantly in the cracks of the pavement. "They don't even know me. They hated me before any of this happened, even."

"Don't take it personally. Persuaders hate you, too," Gwen offered.

"That makes me feel so much better."

She sighed, seeming to soften a little. "Interbreeds…they aren't common. People don't really know how to act around you. You're unpredictable by nature. They're afraid of associating themselves with someone who could turn out to be their enemy one day. I guess the Sentries here are so vocal about their dislike for you because…well, everyone assumes you'll be a Persuader because of your father."

"I just thought it was because Sentries are rarely ones to censor themselves." The side of Gwen's mouth screwed into a rueful half smile. "Besides…I'm starting to think I don't really belong anywhere."

She just shrugged. "Can't say I don't understand where you're coming from. The more you see of this world, the more you come to realize that no one really *does* fit the mold completely. I guess it's just that Persuaders and Sentries have both gotten so used to twisting themselves into different shapes to fit in the boxes they're given. Sometimes you have to make yourself bigger than you are, sometimes smaller."

Gwen led me around the side of the age-blackened warehouse, and we both stared up with mild horror at the warped tangle of metal that somehow still miraculously clung to the wall. "After you," she said.

I tossed her a look from over my shoulder before beginning my slow, rattling ascension toward the open window at the top of the fire escape. The black paint chipped away under my hands, and the whole structure seemed about to rip apart at the slightest of missteps. This wasn't helped by Gwen's added weight, as she began to climb behind me, her heavy, booted footfalls causing a tremor that made my teeth clatter together. I grabbed the sill of the window, hoisting myself through. Gwen whispered something from beneath me, but I didn't hear it. My feet had just struck the floor when a voice shot out of the darkness of the hallway.

"Hey, you there! Don't you dare move an inch. State your business."

Gwen cursed, swinging herself up over the sill in a single, fluid motion. "Silas, lower your weapon. She's with me."

I peered into the dim space, lit only by the faint light of the storm lanterns dangling above. A tall, lanky man stood in the middle of the hall, gun in hand, his leathery face creased at the mouth as his lips pursed. He was rather old, but his eyes were as clear as my own, and they shone with a sudden probing curiosity. I stared back, unable to repress the feeling that I *knew* him somehow. My throat felt dry, and I struggled to remember his question. "I…I'm here to offer you any assistance that I can. My name is Jennifer Cable. Liam Cable's father."

The man—Silas—took a few steps toward us, tilting his head. He holstered his gun. "Oh, I know who you are." He spoke in a deep growl, not particularly pleasant but, then again, neither was it unkind sounding. "You think I don't recognize my own granddaughter?"

The floor dropped out from under me. "Your *what?*" The question was barely audible, a croak. Even Gwen looked startled.

Silas's face didn't change, as if he didn't consider such news to be anything significant. "You look just like your mother, you know. Don't you recognize me from the funeral?"

Now that I thought about it, I recalled that I *had* seen him before, a tall, grim, soberly-dressed figure among dozens of people who looked much of the same. Only his face, I remembered, had struck me as more worn than the others', his gaze steady and unclouded by old age, and his presence one that drew attention. Now I realized that it was his aura, not his presence, that had captured my interest. "Why didn't my mom ever mention you?" Since I was little, I'd imagined what it was like to have grandparents, being doted on and baked for and pinched on the cheek at regular intervals. Though Silas did not seem the type of man who donned an apron and made apple pies "with love".

Silas bristled a little at this. His gruff voice grew even gruffer as he spoke. "Well, you see, Heather never really saw eye to eye with her mother and me after she married Michael. I regret not making an attempt to patch things up earlier..."

To my surprise, a bitter laugh sounded from the back of my throat. I realized I was slowly becoming jaded to these sorts of revelations, things that would've been earth-shattering to the Jenny who'd existed a little over a month ago. "Okay, so I find out two weeks ago that my father *didn't* drop off the face of the earth, after all, and that my parents and my best friend were actually telekinetic but never told me, and now—what? You're telling me you're my *grandfather?* What next?"

Silas jammed his rough hands into his pockets, looking abashed. "I suppose you want nothing to do with me."

I opened my mouth to say something—whether it was to comfort or criticize the old man, I couldn't be sure—but Gwen cut in before I could. "Silas, we don't have time to waste. We need to see Natalia immediately."

"Gwen, you can't—"

"The hell I can't," she snapped. "Silas, where is she?"

"They're keeping her in a room down the hall." He gestured in the direction. "Last door on the left."

Gwen grabbed my wrist, leading us in a half-jog toward the room. Her grip was tight, tight enough to nearly cut off the circulation to my hand. She didn't look at me, her gaze focused on the door, her jaw set. With a jolt, I realized that she felt the same about Natalia as Vince felt about

Liam. Natalia, though she didn't appear on the surface to be particularly warm or affectionate, was probably the closest thing Gwen had in her life to a real parent. If she died, Gwen would be alone. She would be alone, and I would practically be a murderer.

The room was dimly lit, as all the other rooms in the stronghold were, and just as cold. Three other Sentries milled about, tending to their leader, who lay very still in the narrow bed against the far wall. Her pale hair fanned out around a face that was paler, still. Her eyes, appearing almost sunken into her face, were closed, and the lids held a bluish tint.

When Gwen and I entered, the three Sentries turned to us, their faces betraying only astonishment at first. Then, almost uniformly, that astonishment boiled into hostility.

"Gwen?" said one of them. "Why is she here?"

Gwen went to him, taking his arm. He didn't take his dark eyes from me, and with each word of explanation Gwen uttered to him, his full-lipped scowl deepened.

He pushed past her, taking a few uncertain, careful steps toward me. "I want Jennifer Cable to explain it, herself."

"Darren—" Gwen started to say, looking uneasy, but I stopped her.

"No, it's fine. I'll tell him." I looked at the boy, taking note of the slight sheen of sweat coating his skin. He was worried for Natalia, too. Of course he was. I understood perfectly that he hated me for being the cause of her injury and wasn't willing to take risks when it came to her survival. "I know you don't trust me. But I need you to take the chance that I'm telling you the truth right now."

"We already took a chance on your word," he spat. "And *this* happened because of it."

I lowered my head. He was right. He was completely right. Why should they believe me now after everything that had gone wrong?

Another Sentry moved forward, her chin lifted. On a Persuader it would've only looked arrogant, but on a Sentry it looked highly critical and highly dangerous. Her face was the same shape as Darren's, I noticed, her eyes the exact same shade of brown. The two could be identical twins. Only, where there was ice in Darren, there was fire in this girl. "What, nothing to say?" she snapped. I lifted my head to look her in the eye, trying not to flinch away from her sharp words and even sharper gaze. "Yeah, I bet you don't. I never trusted you. For some reason Natalia did, so we went along with it. But I knew no good would come from trusting a Persuader."

My teeth ground together. "I'm not a Persuader."

The third Sentry stood, uncertain. I glanced over to see it was Eli, his face paler than ever in his alarm. "Please, stop fighting with her, Sasha...Natalia—"

"Was *shot*, Eli," Sasha said, bluntly. "If none of you will say it out loud, I will: Jennifer Cable may think she's something special, but we all know *exactly* what she'll become even if she won't admit it, herself." Her arms folded across her chest as she spoke, and she still hadn't taken her glare from me. I could only stare back at her, shocked into silence. "Only a Persuader could've done something like this."

Gwen took the opportunity to insert herself between us. "Sasha, that's not fair."

The other girl turned away, putting a hand to her forehead. All the fire seemed to have gone out of her. "You know what's not fair? *This.*" She gestured to Natalia's still form on the bed. "*Look* at her, Gwen. There's nothing to be done anymore."

Against my better instinct, I moved toward her from around Gwen, surprised when she didn't ward off my advance. I spoke softly now. The Sentries may have seemed cold or hostile at first, but now they just looked...lost. They *needed* Natalia, all of them. "Let me help."

Sasha didn't even look at me, but Darren peered into my face, skepticism in the hard lines of his mouth. "How?"

I looked around the room, desperate to prove my ability in the most convincing way I could think of. My eyes locked onto the knife tucked securely in Gwen's belt. I pointed to it, seeing her stiffen and look aghast when I said, "Your knife. I need to borrow it for a second."

"Absolutely not—" she started to say, but I cut her off, holding out my hand impatiently. "Gwen, come on. I can't prove it if I can't show it." I paused, fumbling to reassure the four very highly strung and highly trained soldiers in the room. "Besides, what harm could I possibly do with *that* to *anyone?* You guys are the ones with all the combat training, remember?"

Gwen muttered something under her breath, but handed me her knife without further complaint. I set the tip of it to my palm before deciding that the circumstance required a larger platform and pushed back the sleeve of my shirt, placing its cold edge to my bicep.

I saw their fascination and confusion turn to horror as I cut a shallow line of red across my skin. I let it run for a second, as if admiring my handiwork, and then placed my hand over the wound, feeling that cold tingle—a sensation becoming almost familiar by now—resonate throughout the length of my arm. When I drew away, there was nothing to suggest there had ever been a cut there, not even the ghost of a scar. The Sentries stood around me for a moment, mouths agape.

With nothing between us left to be said, Gwen led me to Natalia's bedside, nodding at me as if healing another person—a very gravely wounded person, no less—was just as easy. Was it? Healing Taylor hadn't exactly been easy, per se, and in fact it'd been rather exhausting. But the decision to do so had been simple. Was that the same thing? An ordinary human being couldn't will himself to fly if he lacked the faculties to do so. But being what I was, a *greater being* with capacities still yet unknown, where were the boundaries when it came to *choosing* to do something and physically *being able* to do something? I wondered if there were certain limitations to my power that prevented me from healing as many people just under my feet as I'd previously planned to. And I wondered if I would be able to forgive myself for it.

Natalia made a small, agonized sound like the whine of an injured animal, alerting me to her condition more than before. The wound was just as mine had been in the way the bullet had seemed to strike her at an angle. At least that's what it seemed like, a grazing blow. But what did I know? I wasn't a doctor. How was I even supposed to go about doing this? When I removed the towels and bandages, the blood would flow quickly, and I would have to *heal* quickly, more quickly than I technically could, possibly. Oh, God. Why did it have to be *me* that had to do this? Why couldn't this ability be entrusted with someone older, wiser, braver, more certain?

I peeled away the bandages, trying not to lose my nerve at the sight of all the blood flowing freely from her throat, and pressed my palms to the wound, the heels touching, forming a brace with my hands.

I could feel that it was working, but it wasn't working fast enough. Blood continued to pump through my fingers, spilling down my wrists. She was losing too much. I had to push myself, had to push my ability and possibly even my physical limits.

Okay, what would Mom say at a time like this? She had always been in the habit of straining to the very precipice of her mental, physical, and emotional boundaries. She had come to every soccer game, every school event, had agreed to go with Taylor and I to see local bands play when it was clear her illness was starting to get the better of her. But still, I thought I was missing something from that. A memory began to surface, an early one, when I was about nine or ten and I'd broken my arm playing street hockey with the older boys a few blocks down.

Badly shaken, my cheeks sticky with tears, I felt cocooned in her embrace as she set me gently on the kitchen counter. Her cool fingers felt along the length of my right arm, and my sudden cry clued her in to the break just above my wrist. She drew back.

"Well," she said, "it looks like we have to make a trip to the hospital."

My eyes flew wide and in my alarm I managed to speak clearly enough through the sobs. "No! Mommy, the boys will l-laugh at me. They'll call me a baby."

She folded her arms. "I saw the way you played out there. Down and dirty, just like a Halford. No one is going to call you a baby, Jenny."

I smiled a tiny smile, but my resolution was not so soon abandoned by flattery. "But I can't go to the hospital. I wanna be strong…like you…" I dragged the sleeve of my uninjured arm across my face.

"Jenny." She moved to sit beside me on the counter, gingerly wrapping her arm around my skinny shoulders. "Being strong isn't just holding back tears and suffering because you feel like you have to. Maybe that's part of it, sometimes. But it's also knowing your limitations. It's putting your foot down when people are demanding too much of you."

I nodded. "Like with you and Daddy."

Her gaze wavered for only a moment. She swallowed and smiled. "Yeah, like that. I know you might not understand why he had to leave, but think of it like breaking your arm." She lightly touched her fingertip to my wrist, careful not to press too hard. "Your dad and I were two sides of the bone, putting tension on each end, adding pressure and more pressure, until I decided I wasn't going to wait for it to snap."

I winced. "Don't say snap. It grosses me out."

She laughed, helping me down from the countertop.

I opened my eyes to see that the blood had stopped. Removing my shaking hands, I saw that there was only a scar where a gaping wound had been only moments before. This scar was more pronounced than Taylor's had been, an inelegant job on my part, but it was healed all the same. I glanced around to see the four Sentries still present, and noticed a fifth, Silas, standing equally silent as the rest in the doorway. They all looked relieved, incredulous, even wondrous. And there was gratitude, as well, something I hadn't expected to see in their expressions. I took a step toward them but stumbled.

Gwen said something, moving forward to attempt to steady me, but it was lost in the rushing sound in my ears. There was a black ring around my vision, constricting and constricting until there was only a pinhole of light.

Knowing your limitations.

My knees buckled, and I slid to the floor as the light vanished.

"Should we call Liam Cable?" This voice was deep, serious.

Gwen's voice was the one that answered him. "Are you insane? 'Hello, Mr. Cable? Yes. We have your daughter. Mhm, she's perfectly alright and *unconscious on the floor.*' Come on, Darren. Be reasonable."

"I am being reasonable. What do we do with her?"

"How am I supposed to know?"

"Well, you *are* third in command, Gwen. Silas is watching the elevator to make sure no one tries to come up here, and Natalia is...well...still resting. It's your call."

A new voice joined them, unsteady over the syllables. "No pressure. Just remember, if anyone sees her we're dead."

"Thanks, Eli. That really helps."

Sasha made an impatient noise. "Should we move her?"

"Go right ahead. I'm not touching her," grumbled Darren. "Not after all that crazy magical healing business."

My eyelids fluttered, heavier than I remembered them being. Their voices, sounding as if they were reaching me as I held my head underwater, became gradually more distinct. I let out a breath I hadn't known I'd been holding and the four went silent. I could hear them as they shuffled closer to me. When my eyes finally opened, I was met by only the blinding glare at first, which gradually softened and dimmed into its usual poor state as my vision adjusted. Gwen, Darren, Eli, and Sasha huddled around me, looking down, and I was faintly reminded of when Taylor used to tell me stories about zombies and ghosts and things that came from lagoons as I stared back up at their unblinking faces. A laugh sounded from me, sending a flicker of unease across Gwen's face. "Is she alright?" I heard Eli mutter.

I stopped laughing when a jolt of pain went through my skull, down my spine, until it dissipated in the soles of my feet. Gingerly, I sat up and, assisted by Gwen, finally stood.

I felt almost nauseous, tasting the tang of iron and salt in my mouth, which was as dry as paper. "How long was I out?"

"A couple hours," Eli said. Then, almost abashedly, he added, "You talk in your sleep, you know."

"What did I say?" I tried to sound less horrified than I felt.

He was silent, his nose twitching as if he was about to sneeze. Gwen cleared her throat. "You were...calling out for your mom, I think," she said, and I could tell it was a great effort on her part to speak gently, considering she probably hadn't much practice. There was little use of gentleness in a stronghold.

My heart constricted in my chest, and I found it was difficult to breathe all of a sudden. "Oh," was all I mumbled in response.

Out of the corner of my eye, I noticed something stir, with it a sound like rustling paper. Turning my gaze to the movement, I saw that it was Natalia, blinking into consciousness at last. Gwen looked overjoyed, and I realized that I was strangely glad to see her awake, as well.

The Sentry leader, even in her pale, slightly rumpled state, looked regal among the starchy sheets and pillows. She cleared her throat, looking from me to Gwen, from Gwen to the others and back again. "What have I missed?"

After a quick reunion and confirmation that Natalia was perfectly functional and mended without a fault, she sent the Sentries out to return to their duties and to assist the wounded downstairs. I turned to follow them, but she insisted I stay for a moment to have a word with her.

Her eyes searched my face as I pulled up a chair to the bed and sat. She was sitting upright now, leaning against the headboard with her hair neatly smoothed over her shoulders. "I'll be honest, I have no idea why you're here. Not that I am upset by your presence, or surprised, just..." She touched the scar on her neck. "Curious."

I folded my hands in my lap, trying to avoid her gaze. "What do you mean you're not surprised?"

She sighed. "Only that I know what kind of girl you are. Selfless, but often carelessly so. The kind of girl that would assume all guilt of the situation and wouldn't rest until that guilt was alleviated, even if that meant sneaking out and offering aid to people who detest her very existence."

"You don't seem to detest me too strongly," I said, pressing my thumbs together. "Is that because you want me to join your stronghold one day?"

"Hm. I should've assumed you would adopt Liam's general cynicism. I guess it's only logical, considering what you've been through, to believe kindness is only bestowed in the Persuader world when the person has something to gain from you." Natalia paused. "I have nothing I hope to gain from you, Jenny. Nothing except possibly your trust, and for you to trust me when I say that—for the moment—all I want is to thank you."

My eyes snapped to her face, which was unsmiling, but not altogether unfriendly. It appeared somehow softer than usual. "Thank me? For what?"

She motioned to her scar. "My recovery has something to do with you, does it not? I know of the things certain powerful Persuaders or Sentries can do. Often times it runs in a family. The Cable family has had a long history of extraordinary abilities. I always expected that you'd be no exception to this."

I meditated on her words. "Does my father have a...a gift?"

Natalia's gaze finally shifted away from mine. "I suppose an aptitude for deceit wouldn't count," she said, sharply. After a moment, she blew out a long sigh. "Well, he spent most of his life trying to hide what he could do, but I was one of the few people who knew about it."

"Why would he try to hide it?"

Natalia straightened the edge of the blanket so it lay unruffled. "Back then, when we were younger, the world we lived in was very different. Persuader society has always balked at social reform, despite its devotion to knowledge and innovation. They're all so stuck in their ways, so rooted in their traditions because they're afraid that any sweeping change will mean an end to their own reign. Many marriages in my youth were still arranged, and no women or minorities that I can remember were ever in positions of power or authority. As children, we were raised upon the notion that anyone who departed from the general Persuader mold was beneath us. As an outcross and a woman and a sympathizer with the Sentry cause, you could imagine my struggle to fit in. But Micha—Liam never stood out from the crowd, at least not until he married Heather, because he chose to suppress his feelings, and suppress even the ability that he possessed within him. I don't remember the last time I saw him use it, or the last time that he wanted to." She looked up at me, becoming aware of my anxiety. "Liam, himself, would hardly call it an 'ability' so much as he would call it a curse. But his touch, especially when he's angry, when he's beyond his capacity to keep it in check, can kill."

My hands constricted, fingers digging into my knees. "You couldn't possibly mean that *literally.*"

Natalia shook her head, slowly. "I started to suspect he had some sort of unique ability around the age of sixteen. We—"

"Dated?"

Natalia didn't blanch and try to shove the topic away as my father had, only frowned a little deeper and said, "I guess you could call it that. We were betrothed, arranged to be married when Liam was still a toddler and before *I* was even born."

"Arranged marriage?" I was dumbfounded. The term was so...*antiquated.*

"As I said, Persuader society has always balked at social reform."

I was horrified, and shocked, but also strangely fascinated by Natalia's history, the old ways of Persuaders, how they'd changed through the years. And how they hadn't changed. "What happened?"

The Sentry leader was silent for a moment, her gaze focused on the far wall, or maybe not on anything at all. Maybe someplace distant—some instance, perhaps, that had transpired some thirty years ago.

Finally, in a thoughtful voice, she said, "Liam fell in love with Heather." My pulse jumped at my mother's name. "I had thought that, in time, he would come to see me as more than a friend, as I had come to see him. Perhaps there was a time when he did, but that was before he saw her." She snapped her fingers. "The spark was instantaneous. He became *entranced* by the girl. He fell in love just as quickly as he turned around and broke my heart."

"What did you mean when you said there was a time when you thought he...returned your feelings?" The way she said it, the instance sounded like a dark smudge in her memory rather than a brief ray of hope. "Did he love you, too?"

"'Love' is hardly the word for it," she sighed. "There were small moments between us, delicate, tender moments, but they were quick to be smothered by his temper. I'm sure you've noticed how hard he works these days to suppress his anger."

I glanced away. "Sometimes it slips."

Natalia nodded as if she understood completely, and I was sure she understood much more than I did what kind of temper my father had. "When he was a teenager, it was practically impossible for him to reign in his anger. One moment we would be smiling and laughing with each other, as comfortable as you and that Sentry boy, Taylor, seem to be, and the next we would be shouting and I'd be left with bruises on my arms from where his fingers had touched. Sometimes just a slight contact would cause my nose to bleed, my lungs to constrict. His ability—his curse—was one of the reasons we ended any relations with each other. It was one of the reasons I decided to become a Sentry."

"To get away from him."

It was among the bitterest of ironies I'd heard. Her mouth thinned. "It seems I can't even escape him thirty years later, seeing as *you're* here and Liam and I live about twenty minutes apart." She rubbed her forehead tiredly. "The mansion used to sit abandoned by its former owner and almost hopelessly decrepit. About eight years ago, Liam moved into it. He wanted someplace remote, but also someplace...close."

"Close to you?" I was mystified. Why would he move close to his ex-best friend and ex-bride-to-be when he had the means to go someplace very, very far away?

"No," she said, lifting her chin. "Close to *you.*"

I frowned. "Sometimes, I think he looks at me and sees only a reminder of what he left behind."

Natalia closed her eyes, breathing deeply, as if she had drifted into unconsciousness again. But then she spoke, as if drawing from some reservoir of bottled emotion. "Liam has always had trouble coming to terms with his true feelings. He's always thought himself next to damned because of what he can do. But if I know anything, it's that—despite any reservations he may have about your being here—he loves *you* unreservedly. Go easy on him once in a while. Give him a chance."

Rain had begun to fall. I could hear it thrumming against the walls of the stronghold, against the thin boards that crisscrossed the windows. A chill had crept uninvited into the room, and I stood to find another blanket for Natalia. She took it with a small smile, and in the expression I could see how my father had once felt something for her. Kindness was so rare in this world; in some it was burned away by hatred, and in others it was hardly present at all. I felt a twinge of sadness that Natalia's kindness had been blackened by years of bitterness.

My fingers found a small slit uncovered by the wooden planks, and I could feel cool, damp air through it. "Natalia?" My voice was barely audible.

"Yes?"

My fingers curled inward, the skin of my knuckles scraping against the roughness of the boards. "My father's...curse. Could it...could it cause something like a long-term illness?"

Natalia paused. "You mean your mother's cancer."

I nodded, unable to respond verbally. Her voice was subdued as she responded with, "I don't know. I think you'll have to ask him, yourself."

I exhaled a long breath. I was afraid she would say that. My fingers reached for the necklace still at my throat, closing around it tightly.

VINCE

"Vince?"

I was leaned against my usual post, one leg hanging over the windowsill, watching the rain spatter against the glass and wondering where the hell Jenny was. I heard footsteps, but not before I sensed him coming.

"It's one in the morning," Taylor announced, as if this was some gargantuan revelation, barefoot as he made his way downstairs and over to me with a hard glint in his eyes.

"How observant." I didn't spare him half a glance as he approached. "Shouldn't you be resting?"

He scowled, running a hand through hair still wet from the shower. Laura had suggested as soon as he'd woken up that he ought to do what he could to get clean of the blood and grime still clinging to him from the party. "Where's Jenny?"

"Out." I gestured noncommittally to the front door.

"Out?" Taylor choked. "After all that's happened—I can't believe that—" He stopped himself, pointing a finger at me, so angry he was almost shaking. "And you let her?"

Boredom discarded, I whirled, hopping down from the sill. "As if I could've stopped her," I snapped. "Jenny's never listened to anyone before. Especially not when she's determined. You ought to know that."

His demeanor changed, and what had been anger just a moment before had become something dark and guarded. "What makes you an expert on what Jenny is and isn't, anyway?"

"I know her better than you think," I said, and immediately regretted it when I saw the look on his face. His brow was pulled low over his eyes, mouth twisting. *Careless words,* I thought. *Careless words from someone always so meticulously careful.*

"What's that supposed to mean?" His voice was taut with suspicion.

My mind flashed to Jenny and me on the windowsill, her head against my shoulder, our hands interlocked between us. I pulled myself upright, my expression a mask of apathy. "Well, it's not as if she's the sort of girl to *hide* her nature," I replied, coolly. "A hero complex like hers doesn't mix well with that added mile-wide streak of indiscretion."

"I'm going after her."

I stepped in between him and the door. "Taylor, she told me she needed to do this alone."

"She should've told *me.* Not you." He looked wounded, wounded and visibly agitated. "*I* would've gone with her, made sure she was safe. I would've..." His throat worked, and he looked away from me.

I sighed. Why did I actually feel sorry for him? "Look, she didn't come to me and say, 'I'm leaving. Don't tell Taylor', okay? She was *sneaking out* when I noticed her."

"You seem to do that a lot," he said, quietly, and yet the words were loaded with an implication that was impossible to brush aside. "'Notice' her."

I could feel my pulse quicken. "What?"

"I'm not an idiot."

"Apparently you are, because *I don't know what you're talking about.*"

"Like anyone has missed how you look at her." His laugh was short and derisive, but his eyes not so self-assured. "Streak of indiscretion or not, at least Jenny has the good sense to avoid spoiled *pricks* like you."

My hands curled into fists, and I could hear the knuckles pop individually. "Really?"

Taylor stepped closer, narrowing his eyes. "Yes, *really.*"

He was breathing too hard, the vein at his neck pulsing too quickly. I could taste the words before I said them, bitter with their potential to cut deep. "Then why," I demanded, "did she kiss me?"

He stiffened, his body going rigid with disbelief. "You're lying," he said at last.

The hateful, bitter words continued to tumble from my mouth

without my complete volition. "You only say that because you're too *in love* with her to realize that she *doesn't feel the same way.*"

Taylor struck me across the face, sending me crashing backwards into the door. Before he could hit me again, I drove an elbow into his side, and he folded in on himself.

"Is that all you've got, Ross?"

He glared up at me through a veil of disheveled hair and lunged for me again. I held my hands up to ward off his advance, fully prepared to teach him a lesson or two if need be.

I didn't get the chance.

Midway to me, arms outstretched to wrap his hands around my throat, he paused. No, rather, he *froze*. When I tried to move, I found I faced a similar dilemma. I couldn't even blink, couldn't breathe.

"Please. *Stop.*" Jenny's low voice came from the doorway, wavering over the last syllable.

She released us a moment later, and we both collapsed to the marble floor onto our hands and knees, drawing in heavy breaths. *Women*, I reflected, *were always more likely to kill you than any jealous lover.*

She was just a pale smudge against the storm at her back, her arms held out in front of her. She dropped them to her sides. "Why are you two—?"

Taylor stood, one arm wrapped about his ribcage, over the spot where my elbow had come down over. "Did you kiss him?" he asked, cutting her off.

She shut the door behind her, pushing damp hair out of her face. "Did *I...?*" Her eyes shot to me for the briefest of moments, filled only with anger and disbelief, before they moved back to Taylor. She appeared at a loss for words.

"It's late," he said, not giving her time to say anything else. "I'm going to bed."

He whirled around, starting determinedly for the staircase to retreat back into the solitude of his room. I started forward, in an attempt to explain or to at least make things not quite as bad as they were.

"Jenny."

She didn't look at me. "What...what did you tell him?" Her face turned from mine completely, and I thought that maybe this time there was nothing I could say to make things better.

TAYLOR

Generally, I wasn't one to overreact, wasn't one for melodrama—unlike Persuaders, whose very natures existed in a perpetual state of theatricality. Only, when it came to Jenny, each and every emotion became electrified, and everything suddenly became a lot more personal than it was.

Then why did she kiss me?

I could hear Vince's voice still at the back of my thoughts, overlapping in places so that everything else became half-consumed by it. I'd known for some time how Vince felt for Jenny, or at least had known that he was in his own way charmed by her. What I hadn't considered was how *she* felt for *him*. I leaned my forearm against the cold glass of the bedroom window, closing my eyes as I rested my head against it. What if Jenny had pushed me away after kissing me because of guilt? Because she knew how she felt about Vince and it was unfair to me for her to pretend? I remembered her saying that it'd been a "mistake", and I could feel something inside of me, something vital, shatter again. Stupid, *stupid* pride. The *arrogance* to think that she would ever look at me like that.

A knock came at the door.

I crossed the room, putting my ear to it. "Please," I said, fighting to keep my voice even. "Spare me the details."

Her voice was soft, rasping as if she'd been crying, but I knew she hadn't. Jenny didn't cry. "Taylor, let me in. Just *talk to me*. You at least owe me *that.*"

"I don't owe you anything." I was surprised at how harsh I sounded. "I thought we were friends, Jenny. I thought we could trust each other. And now I find out you're making out with some self-important Persuader psycho?" It was more than just petty jealousy. It was the fact that I'd assumed, naïvely, that she'd been *repulsed* by Persuader kind after seeing what they do, that she would eventually see that *anything* was better than controlling another person against his will, even a life of blood and poverty. The incident that had allegedly happened between her and Vince had put a swift end to those delusions.

The door trembled slightly as if she had hit it with the side of her fist. "It was none of your business, anyway!"

I threw open the door, causing Jenny to stumble inward slightly. She righted herself, staring up at me with dark green eyes. Her dress was ruined, torn at the sleeve and soaked through with rain. *"None of my business?"* I demanded. "In case you've forgotten, you kissed me—what? A week ago? Did this involvement with Vince happen earlier than that?"

She looked stunned. "What? Of course not! I didn't know he was going to do…what he did. It's not like I kissed him back."

"As if that excuses the fact that you kept the truth from me for all this time!" I strode away from her, back to the window, where I again braced my arm against it.

"Why are you so upset? I don't understand." Her voice shook ever so slightly. "You lied to me for almost a straight year about who you really were, what you really were. I was never as upset with you when I found out."

"That's different," I snapped. "I only didn't tell you because I thought I could protect you that way. Your mother did the same—"

"Don't you dare bring her into this," Jenny said, her voice dropping lower. "And you still haven't told me why."

I flinched, but I didn't turn around. "Why what?"

"Why are you so angry?"

Because I love you, I thought. *I love you and I hate the thought of Vince with his arms around you, and I hate even more the thought of you suddenly keeping things from me when before we told each other everything. Because it means that you don't even realize how these things affect me or why they do. Because I don't want you to forget me.*

But I didn't say any of that. Instead, I just bowed my head and whispered the very all-consuming fear I'd been too afraid to give a voice to in the past, the fear that all others in my mind ultimately came down to: "Because I don't want to be your enemy."

She began to ask what it was I had said, but I cut her off. "Good night, Jenny."

"Taylor—"

"Good night."

A moment later, the door shut with a barely audible click.

16
THAT WHICH IS HIDDEN

JENNY

It was scarcely daybreak when Liam found me on the balcony, shivering violently, my fingers slowly turning blue at the tips. But I didn't dare go back inside. Not to them. I would sooner freeze to death than have to see the look on their faces again. Vince's guilt, the coldness in Taylor's voice when he'd told me to leave. When I thought about it, his detachment was worse than anger. *Anger* I could've dealt with because the fire in his words always went out more quickly than the ice melted. The fact that he was acting so indifferent to me was…well, it was like standing outside for hours in a below-forties, late fall morning. Numbing.

My father's voice was somewhat resigned, though it wasn't completely without concern. "Why are you out here?"

I gave only a lift of the shoulders, eliciting a gusty sigh from him. He treaded carefully on the half-frozen remains of flowers beneath his feet, bracing his hands on the railing. "It's early."

"I couldn't sleep." My eyes flitted away from his. It was a partial truth, I supposed

"You couldn't or you didn't?"

I made an impatient noise. "What's the difference?"

"Conscious choice," he said, with tired eyes, just crescents of green from beneath his lowered lids and dark lashes. "You seem to be punishing yourself, seeing as you've been out here for awhile." I didn't respond. He shook his head, and I noticed his hair was, for once, not perfectly arranged and rendered immobile by gel. "You shouldn't blame yourself for what happened. Our kind likes to imagine we can control everything around ourselves, yet there are still things that occur *outside* of that control."

My gaze flashed to his. "You sound like Mom," I said, surprised.

"Well,"—his head bowed—"I suppose we weren't as different as we once believed."

In the light of oncoming dawn, I couldn't help but notice the lines in his face, around his eyes and mouth particularly, the silver streaks in his hair shining white in the sun. He looked...aged. Maybe he always had, and I'd just never noticed until now, when I was willing to really look at him. "I miss her."

Unexpectedly, Liam's arm wrapped around my shoulders. I moved to pull away, unaccustomed as I was to his paternal gestures, but for some reason I stopped myself.

"Come on," he said. "You need a change of scenery."

"No one's out here," I observed.

"Mm?" Liam seemed distracted, tugging at the sleeves of his coat as he sat next to me on the bench. I'd seen these cherry trees a hundred times before, sometimes in bloom, sometimes not. Naked as they were now, there was still a sad, simple kind of beauty about them, their delicate limbs darkened by the rain and dripping condensation.

"No one's here," I repeated, gesturing to the emptiness around us. "What's the point of bringing me here? There's no one to—"

"Steal from?" he finished, lifting a brow at me.

"I was going to say 'practice on', but if you want to be blunt with it, then yes."

I could've sworn there was a rare glimmer of humor in his eyes. "You've been learning quickly. I thought it time for a little break from it. You didn't seem inclined to stay in the house, either. So here we are."

My gloved hands curled together in my lap. "Can I...ask you something?"

He looked at me, all seriousness, nodding once.

I could feel the question rise to the surface of my mind, just dancing at the edge of my mouth. *Did your ability, your power to kill, have anything to do with—?*

But I couldn't say it, couldn't bring myself to ponder the possibility more than I already had. So, instead, I asked him, "Can you tell me more about Persuaders?"

Liam looked a little taken aback, as if it was the last thing he had expected me to say. "Of course," he said, after a pause. "What is it that you want to know?"

I considered this, and found I really *was* filled with questions on the subject. "Where do Persuaders come from?" I felt like I was eight years old again, dangerously approaching the subject matter contained within The Talk through my over-curiosity.

Liam leaned back on his hands, regarding the pale sky. "Well…historically, there have almost always been people with special psychological abilities, people who have even been persecuted for it, even. Like New England, in the late 17th century. Persuaders were discovered for what they could do and were branded as evil for it, consequently hanged as witches." His tone had taken on a scholarly lilt to it. "Others realized their potential and became conmen, street performers, thieves. No one knows precisely when the first Persuaders came into being, when one branch of human beings separated from the rest, or what caused it. Some think it was a mutation, like the mutation that occurred to give us different eye colors. It varies for different people, with its own characteristics and quirks, much like one human brain differs from another. However, the first time our kind began to put a name to what they were, to form a society governed by its own principles and leaders, was sometime around the early 1900s. It wasn't long before Sentries branched off into their own division, some twenty or thirty years later, I believe."

I fidgeted with my necklace, mulling this over. "Can new Persuader lines be created?"

"It's rare, but sometimes there are cases of someone developing Persuader abilities without having Persuader parents, without being raised in the Persuader world, the gene for it having laid dormant in the ancestry until conception."

"What then?"

"It's difficult to trace, and often times unnecessary, but if this person is viewed as a threat to our general safety—if he's cognizant of his powers and is irresponsible with them—then he would be tracked down by the Wardens."

The word had a particularly threatening sound to it, or maybe it was a particular inflection of the voice. "Wardens?"

Liam's face had blanched a few shades at the mere mention of them. "They belong to a rather covert branch of our society, specially trained and disseminated all throughout the world."

"They sound tough."

"A better word would be dangerous," he said, grimly. "They ensure that our secrecy is upheld, by any means possible."

"Any means possible?" I couldn't help but think that the noncommittal expression, his vagueness, was completely purposeful. "When they find this person—the Persuader who's using his powers recklessly—what do they do to him?"

"They don't kill him. Not immediately, anyway," Liam said. "But they do sentence him to trial, before the most powerful Persuader official in the country: The Adjudicator. She's the first woman ever to be instated into the position, and if you think Natalia is intimidating, you should see *her*. Where their characters diverge, however, is the fact that she's as raging as Natalia is composed, and moreover, she descends from one of the purest Persuader bloodlines in the world. There have been rumors about her, how odd it is that the notoriously misogynistic Senators of the Adjudication board were willing to not just *accept* a woman into their ranks, but make her their leader. It leaves one to wonder just how powerful she is." He paused, as if deliberating whether or not to continue. "If the Persuader in question is found to be a threat to our way of life, he is then...he is sentenced to die."

I started, unable to help the small gasp that escaped me. "That's not *justice*. That's...that's murder!"

Liam's expression looked bleak as he took my hand, patting it in an attempt to comfort me. "There's nothing to be done about it, Jenny. You shouldn't concern yourself with the matter. It isn't an often incidence, believe me. Most of the time the Persuader agrees to the terms of secrecy and pledges himself to a faction without much argument. *If,* that is, he needs even to be dealt with in the first place. Recall that you had no idea you even had powers before you were told you did, and couldn't tap into them until the situation demanded their use."

"Is secrecy the reason you live so far from the city?" Images of the Cable mansion, with its countless empty rooms and the ever-present chill in the air, flashed across my mind.

"Ah, no, not really," Liam admitted, somewhat reluctantly. "The majority of Persuader kind finds it simpler to live in densely populated areas, existing among ordinary people to better detract suspicion from themselves. I suppose I just needed the seclusion to...find a clear head. I'd lived for too long in and around the city. I needed a change."

I couldn't stop the words that came next, not even if I wanted to. "Natalia told me that you wanted someplace nearby. To Mom and me, I mean."

He looked alarmed at first, and then suspicious. "When did she tell you that?"

"I can't remember," I lied. "A while ago."

"She's right," he said, after a pause. "I never wanted to lose touch with you."

"You did."

"I'm sorry."

The conversation lapsed into silence as we both studiously focused our gazes elsewhere.

"Can I ever go back to school?" I asked, if only to mend the break in dialogue.

Liam laughed the softest, briefest of laughs, but it was an unmistakable sound. "You *want* to go back to school?"

"Not particularly," I said, shrugging. "But I want an education."

"My father homeschooled me until I was eighteen," Liam began, hesitant. "I would be glad to further your studies if you would be a willing pupil."

I nodded my consent. "Sure."

"Good...good," He nodded, as well, though more times than necessary, as if unsure what else to do. "And your training. It seems your teachers have been somewhat lax in their instruction, lately. I could certainly spare time for those subjects, as well."

Well, since Taylor and Vince probably wouldn't speak to me ever again, the offer seemed more tempting than it would've otherwise. "That's fine." I attempted a smile at him.

Liam returned the expression, though it held a saddened quality to it. "I have faith you'll go on to do great things in your lifetime. You have...your mother's drive, her passion to make things better for everyone."

Again, the question surfaced, the question I had originally set out to ask him, but it was, again, suppressed. This time, I didn't know the reason why. "Did you love her? I mean, even after the divorce?"

Liam crossed his ankles, thoughtful. "Yes." He scratched at the light stubble at his chin that wasn't usually there before continuing, "I did love her. I still do. Love—genuine, artless love—isn't something that can be easily broken, or lessened by any mortal condition."

"You seem to be able to keep it together." I couldn't look at him. Instead, I reverted back to fidgeting with the necklace, trying to find the words I wanted. "Aren't you...I mean, don't you—?"

Liam made a noise of disbelief. "If you think I wasn't destroyed by the news of Heather's passing, then I must have been hiding it better than I thought." He stopped, as if checking himself. "Don't think I'm not aware of the fact that I tend to keep my thoughts and emotions to myself. I worry, sometimes, that maybe you've inherited some of that reserve. I have concerns for your health, Jenny, and the state of your mind."

I looked down at the ground, still generously saturated from last night's rainfall. "I try not to break, not when I can help it. If that affects the *state of my mind*, then so be it." My voice cracked, and I stopped talking.

"It's hard," Liam observed, looking straight ahead. His eyes moved to me and softened. "To let yourself feel. But I hear it's better to do so, even if it's painful, even if it fills you with anger and grief and longing, because at least you're full of *something.*"

We were both silent again, but this time it was comfortable, introspective. The leaves brushed against the walkway, the only sound to ruffle the delicate, precious, rare moment of our mutual understanding. Perhaps my father was a wise man.

"You're right," I said, at last. "But—but don't think I'm going to spontaneously burst into tears, now, or anything."

Liam cracked a small, crooked smile. "I wouldn't dare expect it of you."

VINCE

"Vincent, come down here,"

I was ten, which meant I was undergoing a natural stage of defiance toward anyone who assumed his authority over me. But I was also newly bereaved, which left me angry and lonely and unreasonable. I turned my face away from the finely dressed man, who stared up at me with a look of disapproval from fifteen feet below.

"No!" I shouted, the words muffled from around my arm. "You can't make me."

Liam Cable sighed. "Technically, I can." I didn't answer. He extended his hand to me, as if I could just reach out and take it. "Vince, please."

The word rang in my ears. Vince. I had never been called by a nickname before. Neither Malcolm nor Amelia Hallows seemed inclined to alter my given name to something more personalized and affectionate when I lived in England. I blinked at how strange the word sounded, strange in that it meant Liam cared for me to some degree, despite the fact that I had experienced difficulty in returning those feelings from the very first moment I'd stepped foot inside the Cable mansion.

Michael Liam Cable did not resemble my father in any way. This was the first observation to make me hesitant. He was too tall. Malcolm Hallows had been of an average height, with a dark beard and dark hair. Liam was both clean-shaven and fair-headed, his peculiar green eyes too unlike my father's brown ones for me to look into for long periods of time. And his demeanor. I almost convinced myself that they were at least similar in this way, but then I recalled all the nights my father had not come home. All the nights James and I waited for him only to wake up the next morning with our faces to the glass and our spirits crushed. When he finally arrived, disoriented, as he was undoubtedly hung-over, he simply spared me a half-glance, ignored James completely, and proceeded to his room.

But Liam...Liam was different. He seemed to never venture far from his office. In fact, one could without much argument call him a recluse. And while this would seem just as bad as my former arrangement, there were also the times when he was not absorbed in his work. There were times when he would smile and put a hand on my shoulder when I showed him a new skill I learned, or how he would endure the coldest winter nights without lighting the fireplace because he knew I wouldn't be able to stand the sight of it.

I peeked through the branches of the tree, tilting my head a little with my newfound regard for him.

After a moment, I began to make the unsteady descension from my hideout, trying to find footholds but also debating with myself whether or not to look down in order to do so. The edge of my sneaker hit a loose limb, and I couldn't find purchase with my scrabbling hands before I fell from the tree.

I shut my eyes, wondering if the ground rising up to meet me would kill me on impact or break my spine or if I would crack my skull open or—

I stopped falling, just a foot from the ground. All backward momentum dissipated as Liam gently released his Shifting hold on me and lowered me to the ground.

I scrambled upright, eyes wide, breathing hard. Liam was as calm as he ever was, his eyelids slightly lowered. "Are you all right?" he inquired, in an oddly gentle voice.

I looked down at myself. Aside from a few scrapes on my knees and hands, I was perfectly fine. "Yes," I answered, faintly.

Liam nodded, offering his hand once again. "Come on, then."

The phone rang.

I snapped out of my reverie, wondering for a moment what it was that had brought it about in the first place.

Maybe it had been the sight of Jenny and Liam in the driveway, his arm around her shoulders, her allowing it, that'd caused something inside of me to twist. If we were to share him, now, to share in his affections—which were scarce enough as it was—then I would have to get used to the idea of Jenny being family.

My hand shook as I picked up the phone, as I tried to force down the wave of nausea that came with the thought.

Jenny, a girl I'd kissed once upon a time on the windowsill, *family*. The idea tied itself into knots when I tried to straighten it out. I sighed, abandoning the effort. "Hello?"

"Vincent, it's Liam." So we were back to *Vincent* now, it seemed. Well, he'd been calling me that more recently, anyway, considering my age, but all the same it still stung to hear it. "I need you to take Jenny home."

My agreement was automatic—as it usually was when Liam asked something of me—and he began rattling off directions. I even supplied him with a half-hearted "I'll be right there" before hanging up.

In the foyer, I found Taylor at the bottom of the staircase, his look as he stared up at the ceiling somehow all at once both listless and livid. When he saw me, he only scowled and stood, turning to go back upstairs.

I couldn't have said why, but I called out to him. He stopped, but he didn't turn. "Taylor, I'm sorry. What I did...I had no right to do that."

His shoulders tensed in surprise. Slowly, he spun back around, his forehead furrowed. "Vince Hallows is *apologizing*? Really?" I nodded, which only made him look more baffled. "I...don't know what to say, honestly."

I could see more clearly than ever how much he cared for her; on his face there were occasional unchecked expressions of wounded pride and anxiety and devotion. Before, I had only wanted to throw the words at him out of anger, but now I could see just how much it was *true*. It was right there in his eyes, almost unrecognizable from beneath the bitterness, stars covered over by black clouds. *You don't need to say anything*, I thought.

He turned and started up the stairs again, but not before calling over his shoulder, "Touch Jenny again, Hallows, you better pray she's there to save you like before."

I scoffed, shaking my head with a smile. "Your memory must be failing you. As I recall, *you* were the one who needed saving."

JENNY

After punching the end call button, Liam turned to me and explained that he had a bit of "business" to take care of downtown and that he was sorry to cut our little outing short and et cetera and et cetera. I'd been given this speech on plenty of other occasions as a younger child, when he would disappear to God-knows-where and Mom would pick me up in her arms and not say anything about it. Only now did I get to know the reason for those disappearances. Only now did it occur to me that, while my mother had given up her old life to raise a child in the safety of the human world, my father had never been able to completely abandon his ways. Not then, and certainly not now.

With a rueful duck of his head, he left me, and I sat on the bench alone, waiting for Vince. As a kid, I'd always thought that a plain disinterest was to blame for Liam's faults and absences, but now I began to realize that for all of his life, the only thing that had separated my father from the people close to him was his *obsession* with living in the way he felt he ought to live. It was that obsession alone, and not his indifference, that had been the cause of everything. Against all reason, some things stayed exactly the same, even when everything else seemed to change completely.

Just behind me, I heard a car whine to a halt at the curb and, turning, I saw Vince through the window fiddling with the radio and not glancing up at me once. As I climbed into the passenger seat, he continued to ignore me as he reached over to turn the radio up. He was listening to some obscure classical station, which I guessed shouldn't have surprised me.

The song changed, and as I looked out at the brick buildings and trees passing through the window, I imagined that it sounded almost familiar. I turned to him. "Vince?"

In my head I went through all the possible—though tricky to navigate—topics of conversation. We could start with how he'd made me look like some hopelessly infatuated girl who couldn't help but throw herself at him, or how he had so gracelessly let it slip that he had kissed me when he *knew* that it would injure the trust Taylor had in me.

That impassive gaze forward never wavered, but I continued anyway, with an entirely different conversation in mind. *"Quasi una fantasia."* The words jolted him slightly. His eyes darted to me briefly before they shifted back just as quickly. "What does it mean?"

Vince was silent for a moment, his mouth opening and closing as if he didn't know quite how to respond. "It…well, I didn't think you would remember something like that." He cleared his throat. "It's Italian. 'Almost a fantasy.'"

I found my face flush slightly at the way he said it and wasn't entirely sure why. Maybe it was in the way his eyes again slid to mine when he spoke, the way the music seemed to cocoon the two of us within it. I couldn't help but remember when he had first said the words, his arms on either side of me, his face so close to mine.

He cleared his throat, looking uncomfortable. "That's the literal translation, anyway. What Beethoven actually intended to mean was 'in the manner of a *fantasia*', *fantasia* being a type of free-form composition—I'm sorry. I seem to be rambling on about boring classical music facts…"

"I like it when you talk about boring classical music facts. You actually looked interested in something for once." I looked at his hands, long-fingered and delicate, perfectly crafted for the purpose of pressing keys with skill and precision. "I've never heard you play. Not really."

"Lately, I haven't felt inclined to," was his answer.

"Why?"

Monosyllabic as it was, he seemed unreasonably frustrated by the question. "I just haven't," he replied, tersely. "I usually only play when I need to ground myself. When I need to feel…*peaceful* again."

I observed the high color in his face, the tautness to his shoulders. "Hm. It seems as if you're not very peaceful right now."

Vince pinched the bridge of his nose. "So it does."

I paused, listening to the song as it drew to a tragic close. "Do I…irritate you, Vince?"

He didn't even need to consider it for a moment. "All the time." Seeing my face, he amended slightly, "But that's just because we're opposites."

"I thought opposites attracted?"

Vince flushed deeper. "Well, whoever said that obviously had no idea what he was talking about. It's not the same with people as it is with scientific forces, Jenny. Take someone like me, for example. Embittered and sarcastic and overall exceptionally unpleasant." For someone who seemed so arrogant, he could be at times rather self-effacing. "And then there's you. You just...*captivate* everyone you meet, and you don't even have to try. You don't even have to pretend." Before I could form any kind of response to something like that, he continued. "You don't need anyone to tell you who you are, Jenny, and yours isn't the sort of character to bend just so you'd fall in among the rest. I've spent most of my life pretending to be the same, when the reality is...I'm too weak *not* to bend. And I'm too weak because I'm desperate. I'm just...sick of being pitied and patronized and treated like some damn *charity case* all the time. All I want, really, is..." The words seemed to be beyond his reach, burning away into ash on his tongue before he could put a voice to them. "I don't know. Forget it, just forget it."

"Vince..." I put a hand on his shoulder, trying to catch his gaze. "I know things are confusing between us, but I want you to know I really do care about you. And I don't think you're weak, and I *don't* think you're a charity case." In one sense, at least, I felt I understood him perfectly.

He swallowed thickly, his hands tightening on the wheel until the knuckles turned bone-white. He opened his mouth to respond, but he never got the words out.

A fist-sized piece of asphalt struck the windshield, a million tiny cracks radiating out from where it hit as Vince slammed on the brakes.

My face came within an inch of the damaged glass.

Vince shut off the radio, and I glanced around to discern from where the object could've originated and saw a crowd gathered in mob-fashion in a wide alleyway between a brick warehouse and a squat, gray building. There were a dozen or so people I could distinguish, seven or eight of them roiling in a tight circle around something I couldn't see. The others paced the streets like restless animals, and one of them was looking at us and calling to his friends, drawing attention to the black car stopped on the opposite side of the road. Two of them broke away from the rest of the crowd, heading for us.

"Vince." My voice sounded far away. "Vince, drive. *Vince—*"

But they were already upon us, the taller one having taken up a metal bar in his hands. He wound up, the bar over his shoulder like a baseball bat, and swung it toward my window, shattering it.

I let out a strangled sound as his hand reached in and grabbed my wrist. He leaned in close, his breath reeking of tobacco and alcohol, and said with a smile, "What do we have here? Looks like a couple of Reds passing through. You're just in time to join the fun."

Vince's fist was a blur as it passed inches from my face and slammed into the man's already crooked nose.

He howled in pain, releasing me to cup a rough hand to his badly bleeding face. Vince didn't hesitate to hit the pedal hard, propelling us far away from the danger.

It was only until we were a certain distance away from the scene that I looked back to see what it was the others had been amassed around.

Only it wasn't a what...but a *who*.

He appeared to be badly beaten, bloodied and writhing on the concrete as they took turns driving kicks into his face and ribs and stomach without mercy or pause. His red tie was torn from his throat, lying in an even redder pool around him. When they lifted him to his feet, I saw the knife that was in his captor's other hand and I looked away, feeling hot anger fill my face.

"He looks like a Persuader," I said, feebly.

Vince's face was grim as he stared into the rearview mirror. "He was."

"Why are they doing that to him? We have to go back."

He shook his head. "There's nothing we can do. There's too many of them."

"Who are they?" I asked, but somehow deep down I already knew the answer. I just didn't want it to be true.

Vince looked at me, frowning. "They're Sentries."

TAYLOR

The door slammed hard downstairs and, with a sigh, I cast the book on my knee aside and made my way down into the main foyer. The first thing that struck me was the sight of Jenny's hands, shaking visibly, so visibly that she laced them together when Vince glanced over at her. Her eyes were wide and haunted, and looking at them, I felt my throat constrict and the ends of my fingers go cold.

He was attempting to calm her the best he could. "Jenny, it's alright. You just…you just need to lie down, get your mind off of it—"

He trailed off when he saw me, his mouth opening and shutting twice before he called to me. "Taylor. Jenny seems to be…unsteady at the moment. If you could help her to her room…I'll-I'll go get Liam."

Before I could object, he was gone, and Jenny and I were alone, staring at each other as if we were unrelated species interacting for the first time. She looked prepared to ward off my assistance, but I descended the last couple stairs and took her arm without hearing it, without saying a word in return. That was how it usually was between us, right? I would grin and bear it without objection. She at least owed me the same service.

Either she was too dazed to fight with me or at a loss for words, but somehow I managed to help her up the stairs, down the hall, and into her room with no protest at all. Hm. Jenny. *Silent.* This I found unsettling.

She didn't even take off her shoes or coat before lying down on the bed, staring up at the ceiling, still without comment or explanation.

I supposed that *I* would have to be the one to broach the subject. "What happened?" I stayed at a distance from her, my arms folded.

Her head turned away to the window. Jenny didn't answer me at first, and when she spoke, it didn't do much to clarify the situation. "At Samuel's masquerade, you stabbed a Deadlock in the chest. Do you remember?"

I cringed, bile rising up to burn the back of my throat. It wasn't a memory I wanted to bring to mind. "Yes," I said. "I remember."

She turned back. In a softer voice: "Have you done it before?"

I sat in the chair across from her, maintaining a sense of calm, though I had to struggle to do so. "Done what before?"

"Killed someone."

"What is this about, anyway? I had no choice, you know that." I narrowed my eyes, and she seemed jolted by my sudden anger. "Throwing myself in between you and a knife, by the way, would feel a little more worth it if you would stop staring at me like that. Like I'm some sort of monster for protecting you."

She sat bolt upright. "Taylor!"

I stood. "Nothing I do is ever enough for you, is it?"

"I'm sorry," she whispered, dropping her face into her hands. "I sound like a broken record, but I am. I *am,* Taylor. It's just…today I saw something…something horrible."

I found myself back in the chair without realizing it, gripping her wrists to pull them gently away from her face. "What happened?" Maybe I had no right to blame her for asking me the questions that she had asked. After all, what did the word "monster" even mean anymore in this world where murder and manipulation were no longer the acts of a criminal, but the acts of a productive member of society?

Her breath shuddered through her. "We were attacked by Sentries." My eyes flew wide, but she continued before I could say anything. "Not the kind of Sentries like you or Natalia. They were…coldblooded. They all stood over the man, k-kicking him over and over without stopping…" Her hands began to shake again. "And then they killed him. I didn't watch, but I know they killed him. I've never seen anything so…disturbing."

"I'm not like them," I said, after a pause. I wasn't sure why I felt the need to convince her of it, and yet to be classed in with the Wolves— people my father had once called "the *personae non gratae* of the Sentry faction"—seemed utterly unendurable. There was too much at stake for me to have become indistinguishable from them, especially in the eyes of the person whose opinion I valued the most. It would mean everything I'd done, everything I had given up… It would all have been for nothing. "You know I wouldn't do what they did."

"You don't have to tell me that," Jenny said, passing a hand over her face. "I understand that. It's just…I've never witnessed anything like it." She looked up at me suddenly, through her fingers. "Why are you comforting me? You're not still angry?"

"No, I am," I said. "But I hate seeing you cry."

Her hand dropped into her lap. "I'm not crying."

I unsuccessfully tried to hide a smile, my mouth crinkling on one side. "I know you aren't. Just trying to get your goat, is all."

"My goat is not to be easily gotten, for your information," she shot back. "It's very secure."

"I'm sure it is."

"*It is.*" She tried to look at me severely, but of course she couldn't manage it. Vince had been correct when he said Jenny was never one to hide her nature.

It was a well-known fact between us that Jenny dropped straight faces almost as quickly as my resolve to act unfeelingly toward her did, and suddenly we were friends again. Just like that. We didn't even need to say it aloud to each other, such was the profundity of our relationship. But, of course, just because I was glad didn't mean I necessarily had to be totally *satisfied* with it.

It was so easy to be friends with her and nearly as easy to sustain it through the bumps and rough patches, and yet, it was so *hard* to change how things were between us. When it came to Jenny, I didn't want to be "near" her. I didn't want to be "around". What I really wanted to be was *beside* her, and both of us seemed to be taking great pains to ensure the futility of that desire. On my part it was only cowardice, and on hers I couldn't be sure if it was reluctance or indifference or something else.

"Jenny?" My voice sounded low and feeble to my ears, certainly not the voice of a boy who could convince a girl like Jenny Cable of his merits.

"Yeah?" She ran a hand through her hair, pushing it out of her eyes, something I really, really wished she wouldn't do when I was trying to focus. Gold-red curls spilled down her back, revealing beneath them eyes that shone as bright as a cat's, equal parts bronze and jade. I was aware of too many things about her, sensitive to each minute movement she made. How her slim fingers twisted together as she waited for me to say something, how her teeth came down lightly on her bottom lip. I had to tell her. If my feelings weren't reciprocated, then at least I wouldn't be burdened by the weight of the secret...

I floundered for words to grasp onto, to make my declaration seem less sudden, somehow. "Remember...in the attic—?"

Her face flushed slightly in alarm, and she was quick to interrupt. "We were probably just both a little on edge because of what happened in the stronghold. I don't think we should worry about it getting in the way of us being friends, if that's what you're worried about."

I imagined planes shot from the sky did not plummet as hard as my romantic aspirations did when she said that.

I could only nod, numbly staring at the floor. "Good," I choked out. "I wouldn't want to ruin what we have."

17
ARRANGEMENTS

JENNY

I found that Shifting came quite easily to me when my instructor was a bit more obliging, or, in other words, not Vince. But Shifting many things at once while under the intense, quick-to-correct scrutiny of said instructor... Well, at least we were indoors and the likelihood of ending up in the pond again was considerably lessened.

"Jenny, the book to your left appears to be dipping a tad," Liam called to me, gesturing vaguely to the object in question.

We were in the dining hall, the floor painted with banners of light from the stained glass dome above us. A green one here, a red one there. It was a pretty sight, but not so pretty as to be the source of my lack of attention. I glanced over at the offending article, suspended significantly lower than the rest of the objects floating above me, and corrected myself. Liam nodded his approval, but unsmilingly so, which was to be expected.

No matter how much I pushed myself to use my mind to do something other than *think*, there were still recollections and thoughts that wouldn't leave me a moment's peace.

We were probably just both a little on edge, I could hear myself saying, and again I cursed myself for it.

God, what a lame excuse. Taylor couldn't know, of course. Couldn't know that I had kissed him not because of any irrelevant lingering nerves from my experiences within Natalia's stronghold, but because I had *wanted* to.

But it was a selfish desire, imagining, *hoping* that we could be anything more than what we were presently. If I were to in any way let on that I had feelings for him...I was sure Liam wouldn't hesitate to send him on his way. Despite the fact that I was slowly—reluctantly—beginning to see my father as more than just an estranged villain, I knew he wouldn't listen to me if I tried to convince him out of it. The man could exist for eternity set in his own convictions, and as a consequence was unable to separate his own life from mine enough to realize that things wouldn't be the same for Taylor and me as they'd been for my own parents. Besides, he operated on the assumption that I would become a Persuader and made his parallels accordingly. It was infuriating.

It was because of this that I had to cut one wire and hope I didn't unknowingly cut another, had to tolerate being near and around the person I most wanted to stand shoulder to shoulder with.

"Jenny, focus." Liam snapped his fingers twice, pointing toward the large rotating globe slowly lowering to the floor without my realizing it. I adjusted once more.

My father sighed, slipping his long-fingered hands into the pockets of his slacks, which, paired with only a long-sleeved shirt, must've been his version of "casual". "What has you so preoccupied today?"

I shrugged, for fear that words would betray me if I opened my mouth, and that was when I felt the nape of my neck tingle. On cue, someone cleared his throat, lightly, from across the room.

Liam and I glanced over at the same time to see Taylor in the doorway. Only, where Liam was only mildly interested in what he could be doing there, the mere sight of him so soon after I'd lied to his face was enough to sidetrack me completely.

A glass paperweight slipped from the ring of items leisurely circumnavigating the room, shattering with an abrupt sound that sent Liam into a state of exasperation.

He threw his hands into the air. "I give up!" he exclaimed to no one in particular. It could possibly have been some sort of plea to the heavens for a more attentive pupil.

Taylor's gaze darted to everywhere but my own. "There's someone at the door. Should I...make myself scarce?"

"Please do," called another familiar voice from behind him. Vince strode past Taylor into the dining hall, glancing from me to the miniature solar system above my head and back to the doorway. "And feel free to ask to do so more often, while you're at it."

Taylor only frowned at him, inured to his unpleasant nature by now. "Well?"

He looked to Liam, who only shrugged. "It's just the organizer I hired to make certain…arrangements. The dye in your hair hasn't faded, yet. You should be fine. Mr. Monroe has little interest in politics, I believe."

It was Vince's turn to frown. "Well, great," he muttered. "Always glad to be in your company, Ross."

Taylor gave a slight bow, which I couldn't help but smile at when I was sure neither of them were looking. "I am equally elated, Hallows."

The doorbell sounded throughout the mansion, and we all looked toward the entryway in surprise. "We have a doorbell?" Vince asked, one eyebrow lifted. Liam shook his head, straightening out his shirt and walking out of the room.

Taylor smiled at me, the sort of smile that affected the entire face, the sort of smile that made it difficult to return in kind. He looked up at the objects still making their rounds and nodded in my direction. "Not bad."

I spared a glance at the remains of the paperweight in shards on the floor. "Would've been better if you hadn't distracted me," I pointed out.

"Your usual lack of concentration is hardly my problem, Jenny," he countered, grinning wider.

Vince gave a dramatic sigh. "Oh, God, I think I'm going to be sick from all of this."

The globe dipped again in the air. "All of what?" I demanded, maybe too defensively. He lifted his eyebrows, backing out into the hall.

Not even five seconds after he had departed did I hear an abrupt and cultured voice from just outside the door. "Ah, hello. Pleased to make your acquaintance, young man." Vince didn't manage to get a word in edge-wise before the voice started up again. "So where is Miss Cable?" Without taking a breath, he interrupted whatever Vince was about to say. "Never mind that, I am certain I detect a strong aura in this direction…"

A sharp-edged man possibly in his late twenties or early thirties stepped into the room, his movements full of purpose. His blond hair was trimmed short and gelled into a rigid peak just above the forehead, and he was dressed (even down to his shoes) completely in red, not a trace of Persuader black visible upon him. When he saw me, he made a gesture of the head like a predator locking in on its prey, striding over to shake my hand far too vigorously.

"It is a delight to finally meet you, Miss Cable." Despite his words, his voice didn't betray any feeling of the kind. He released my hand and bent sharply at the waist. Unlike Taylor's, it was done in utter seriousness, and that coupled with an exaggerated movement of his hand was almost enough to make me laugh aloud. "I am Charles Monroe and I shall be organizing your little event and making everything absolutely immaculate."

Taylor scoffed, drawing Charles' attention. "'Little event'?" he repeated, incredulous. "You mean her Embracement?"

Charles straightened his jacket with a crisp twitch of his hand. "And who might you be, young man?"

Taylor, again, remained visibly unfazed by the question. "Seth Sinclair," he said.

Charles narrowed his eyes. "There is a certain Seth Sinclair in Virginia who hired me some time ago. His mother had some kind of job in government, if I remember correctly, though personally I'm not interested enough in politics to know what it was." He folded his arms behind his back. "I cannot say the two of you bear too similar an appearance. You're taller. Different build."

Taylor's mouth twitched, barely perceptible. Charles was keener than we'd assumed. "I grew up in Philadelphia. The Seth Sinclair you're thinking of must be a different one."

"Uncanny." Charles looked at him for just a moment longer before returning to me. "Miss Cable, if you would come with me." He glanced up at the floating objects in mild distaste. "Perhaps it would be best if you just set those down before joining me."

I had no idea why I was even present, with Charles commandeering all of the responsibilities and decisions of the event.

The three of us were gathered in Liam's office and, while my father and Charles were poring over details of both the aesthetic and the processional components of my Embracement, the only thing left for me to do, really, was the tedious task of writing out the invitations to people I barely knew or didn't know at all. I blinked at the name in front of me, wondering if I was beginning to hallucinate after composing about thirty or so invitations already. "Natalia Blair?"

Liam barely looked up, his shoulders still hunched over the piles of paperwork before him. "Yes. Though the Embracement itself is to be attended by mostly Persuaders—considering that I, the parent, am a Persuader—at least one Sentry is required by law to be in attendance, should you decide to become one. However, there's no law that says a Sentry *has* to take you in. You should be glad for her partiality toward you."

Now he did look up at me, and I saw a strange emotion flash across his face. It was gone too quickly for me to discern what it was.

"Laughable, really," Charles remarked. "As if she has any inclination to join the ranks of those...those shameless guerrilla *saboteurs.*"

The pencil Liam had been writing with broke in two, and I looked up sharply at the organizer. "My mother was a Sentry." There was an edge in my tone that caught him by surprise. "And what do *you* know about my *inclinations?*"

Charles had blanched slightly, pulling a handkerchief from his breast pocket to dab at his brow. "I meant no disrespect, Miss Cable. I just naturally assumed—"

"*Assumed?* As if you even know me!"

"Jenny," Liam said, calmly. "That's enough. Mr. Monroe is unused to the sensitive subject matter that concerns an interbreed."

Charles nodded vehemently. "You'll have to forgive me," he said, as I fell back into the chair. "I've only ever worked with Persuaders. In truth, I can count the number of Sentries I know by name on one hand."

"And yet you don't seem to have any reservations about classing them all together as guerilla terrorists."

"Saboteurs. I believe I said saboteurs." He coughed uncomfortably in his hand, squirming a little. "When one lives as they do, kills as they do—I mean, I'm sure your mother was an exception—"

I opened my mouth—most likely about to unleash the insult of the millennium—but Liam spoke first, to my surprise. "I would thank you *not* to speak of Heather." He rose from his seat. "I'm almost inclined to ask you to leave my house immediately, Mr. Monroe, but I don't want to go through the trouble of hiring another organizer undoubtedly just as imbecilic as you are. So I must say to you now that any more comments like that and I'll gladly permit my daughter to Shift you through a window. Am I making myself understood?"

Charles Monroe swallowed thickly and nodded again, this time so fervently the immobile peak above his forehead bobbed with him.

VINCE

Jenny had been navigating the room in a strictly circular pattern for about ten minutes, and *I* was growing anxious just by watching her.

"What are you doing?" I demanded, withdrawing my hands from the piano. Nothing seemed to be sounding right, anyway.

She stopped, but only for a moment, glancing at me briefly with a look of vexation before she continued her pacing. "Do you know when my birthday is, Vince?"

The question caught me by surprise, as I realized that, in fact, she had never mentioned the precise date of her birth, only that it was soon. "No. Is it next month or—?"

"This month," she said, cutting me off. Her fingers pulled at each other, as if she was ticking numbers off of them. "Oh, God. *This* month. It's on the seventh."

I spun around on the piano bench. "That's in a week."

"I *know* that," she snapped, flinging her arms out to her sides. "Jesus, I'm not even ready. I have no idea what I'm going to say."

"You'll know," I said. "When the time comes, you'll know. I'm sure of it."

"How can you be sure?" She switched direction, moving in a counter-clockwise fashion throughout the foyer. "This decision that I have to make…either way, I'll be miserable."

"At least you'll have other people around you to be miserable with."

"You're making it worse."

"Come here." I patted the space next to me. She sat down—albeit unenthusiastically—folding her arms.

"If I become a Persuader," she began, after a pause, "would it change me? Would I become some altered, self-indulgent version of myself?"

"Jenny—"

"Or if I become a Sentry," she continued. "What would that make me, then? How could I possibly stay totally like myself, totally human? I'd like to believe that it wouldn't transform me into a monster like the kind we saw yesterday, but…" Her voice hitched softly. "The truth is…I'm not certain of anything, anymore."

"I had my doubts," I said, after a moment's hesitation. "About what I wanted to be. I'd seen what decadence had done to my parents, how those urges and impulses had overtaken them completely."

Jenny looked surprised, astonished that I'd ever had any doubts that Persuader life was what was best suited to me. "But you decided to become a Persuader, anyway. Why?"

I sighed. "Well...I felt like I had an obligation to set it right, somehow. To prove that I could be a better person than my parents were even though the same opportunities were presented to me."

"Do you think you have?" she asked, turning to me with an elbow rested on the piano. "Proven yourself better, I mean."

I shrugged. "My parents tended to reject any emotional tie with someone else that wasn't superficial or self-seeking. You said you cared for me, and so I must hold you to it." Her lips twitched into a half-smile. "In a way, it's *you* who's proven me better."

A light coloring spilled across her cheeks. "Well, I don't know about *that...*"

Seeing her blush like that, looking away from me with that small smile, I couldn't help but turn back around to face the piano, couldn't help but ask her, "Can I play something for you?"

Mild disbelief flickered across her face at the question, but she nodded and I set my hands to the keys. A song started to unfold, quiet at first, but with growing tension. I remembered Taylor, standing in the foyer, telling me he couldn't forgive me.

And I wondered what it was like, feeling for someone as he did, so much that the most painful thing imaginable couldn't possibly come from anywhere but from within.

Jenny seemed to understand me—how I thought and how I felt and how I hurt—when no one else did. What was *that* called? I didn't have names for these things, never having much in the way of context for them. I knew what it felt like to love a brother, as I'd loved James. I knew what it felt like to love a mentor and a father, because I had Liam. But the love amongst people without blood or obligation between them puzzled me. As a child, my parents had never once said to each other the words, "I love you." From what I'd observed from *them,* alone, love was vain. It meant treating each other like prizes to be gloated over and, when I'd started dating Gwen, that was exactly how *I'd* treated her. Liam, on the other hand, had taught me that love was painful, and so I'd kept myself reserved and distant, giving away none of myself at all. My fingers accordingly glided into the lower region of the piano, churning out deep, ominous tones that spoke of my confusion, my confliction, of how much I didn't understand.

I became suddenly and acutely conscious of the weight of her steady, green eyes on me, and the song flowed into a paper-thin melody, soft and gentle, like how it felt when she took my hands in hers and told me that I was a good person. Only then did the song drift to a close, until the only sound was the resonance held by the sustaining pedal. I lifted my foot and turned to her.

Her face was delighted, enchanted. "It's beautiful," she said, softly, as if speaking loudly would ruin something important and fragile.

I slammed the cover down over the keys, shutting them away from sight. I couldn't be sure why, but more than anything at that moment I felt *agitated*. My skin itched, and my thoughts grasped for something like fingers clawing at air. I'd read so many books. I knew so many words. But the words I wanted just weren't there.

I stood and left her, ignoring the sounds of her protests.

JENNY

The next morning, the very last person I expected (aside from maybe Samuel Locke or the president) called as I rooted through the kitchen cupboards in search of a tolerable and unwholesome breakfast.

His voice was audibly uncomfortable as he spoke in his low, gruff drawl. "Morning, Jennifer. I, uh, well…" I could picture him scratching his head in his discomfiture before continuing. "It's Silas. Silas Halford?"

"Yes, I remember your voice," I said, mostly to find something to say. I opened the fridge, examining its contents with an elbow leaned up against the countertop.

"Hm," he replied, sounding slightly amused. "I suppose you weren't expecting this call."

"Why did you? Call, I mean. Did something happen?"

"Ah, well, no. I just…" He cleared his throat, the sound like gravel tumbling down a sheet of sandpaper. Liam entered the kitchen, probably looking for coffee, and saw me. He tossed me a puzzled look, mouthing, *Who is it?*

Silas Halford, I mouthed back, the fact that Liam wasn't aware that I knew him slipping my mind entirely. His forehead creased in an expression that was probably meant to be severe, but his overall look of panic overpowered it.

Hang up, he commanded, silently. I shot back, *No,* equally soundless. He mouthed something else, but I ignored it as Silas spoke again, "I would like to see you more often, Jenny. I want to get to know you. The opportunity to repair my relationship with my own daughter is long gone and I feel like...like I owe it to her, to myself, to have a simple conversation with you."

I decided against telling him that we were actually already holding a conversation. "Sure. I'd like that very much. Why don't you come over and have lunch with us?" I paused, considering. "I promise none of it will be canned."

His deep chuckle caught me by surprise. It was a kind sound, and genuine. "That's very considerate of you. I don't think I could stand to eat another bowl of canned peaches."

Before I hung up, I assured him that I would make sure that Laura was aware of his aversion to the fruit.

Turning back, my smile quickly faded when I saw Liam's face. It was a difficult one to read. Anger, of course. Alarm, maybe. And something else mixed into it. "What?"

"You know *what,*" he snapped. "How is it that you know Silas Halford?"

"You mean *my grandfather?*" I demanded, returning his anger. The pan hanging on the rack above us rattled slightly. "Which, by the way, was a fact you *kept* from me?"

His eyes narrowed, and he jabbed a finger in my direction. The pan shook again. "Don't you dare stand there and pretend that it wasn't for your own good. You snuck out, didn't you? The night after the masquerade? Do you have *any* idea what could've happened? How much danger you put yourself in?"

"In case you haven't noticed," I began, in a tone as cold as his was heated, "I'm already in danger as it is, and I have been from the first moment I stepped foot in this house. And I snuck out because I wanted to do the right thing, Dad. Doesn't that mean anything to you?" His stance did not waver, and neither did his expression. I let out a humorless laugh. "Of course it doesn't. All right, how about this: Natalia was *seriously injured* at that masquerade. She could've *died.* And you know why she didn't? Because I was there. I was there to save her *life.*"

Liam looked stunned now. "She was...?" The muscles in his throat moved as he swallowed. "I didn't ask how you healed Taylor before because I didn't want to know, but now I *do*. Do you have an...an ability? An aptitude for it?"

I folded my arms. "Wouldn't it just figure that I'm your opposite?"

I hadn't meant to say it like that, to shock him with my knowledge of his most buried secret. His face went absolutely white, and the pan rattled off of its hook, banging against the floor.

"How did you find out about that?" he asked, in a voice not entirely his own.

"Natalia," I said, softly, trying not to cringe away from him like a guilty child. "She told me that when you get angry your touch c-can hurt people or even...*kill*. That's something else you neglected to mention. What other things are you hiding from me, Dad? Why can't you just trust me with the *truth* for once? I'm not a child, anymore. I can take it."

Liam sat down in the chair by the counter, lowering his head into his hands. "It's not something I'd gladly admit. I didn't want you flinching away from me every time I reached out to you." His shoulders shook, barely noticeably. "I wouldn't call it an ability. It's more like a—a curse."

"Is it how Mom got sick?" The question that had been scratching at the door for all this time somehow escaped, causing Liam's head to snap up so quickly it was a wonder he didn't get whiplash from it.

"You're actually asking me that?" he whispered. The corner of his mouth trembled. "I never laid a hand on your mother. I swore to myself I would never again hurt someone I loved. I swore that—"

He stopped talking abruptly, breathing hard, breaking eye contact.

"Is that why Natalia hates you so much?" I asked, trying for a gentler tone that before.

"One of many reasons," he sighed, his head dropping back down into the crook of his arm.

I didn't ask him about the other reasons. Those were the secrets I would just have to learn to deal with until he—rather, *if he ever*—decided to share them.

"I'll be honest," Silas said at last, setting his glass down with a glance around the table. "I expected this to be a little more..."

"Exclusive?" I supplied, noting how his eyes darted around from Taylor to Liam to Vince and back again. "Sorry. They insisted."

"I was just hungry," Taylor mumbled, in between bites. In each hand was a biscuit, individually slathered with sizable pools of honey and butter that dripped onto the tablecloth.

Vince only shrugged. "I was curious."

While the three of us had pretended not to be gawking at our guest for the last ten minutes, Liam sat at the head of the table, his eyes never leaving Silas. "I was not," he said, folding his hands in front of him. "But that doesn't mean I won't be making sure you don't say something to Jenny you shouldn't."

"Dad—" I started, but Silas only chuckled, overlapping whatever complaint I was about to make.

"What? You think I would try to convince her to join the Sentries? You're wrong if you do. Too dangerous, for one. If she were to get hurt, there's no way I would have that on my hands." I opened my mouth to protest his babying of me, but he seemed to already know what I was going to say. "Of course, if she's anything like her mother, there's no stopping her kind of determination if she's set on becoming one. Her decision is her own."

I found I suddenly liked Silas a lot more than I thought I would. I smiled at him from across the table.

Liam rubbed his chin, which was starting to look less clean-shaven than usual. "Of course it is. I know that. Forgive me, but I just don't think that *you're* the best influence on her—"

"Why?" I demanded, cutting him off.

Liam looked at me with an intensity that caught me by surprise. "Jenny," he said, between his teeth. "Don't push this."

Silas sighed, spreading his napkin out before him and refolding it. The edges were crisp, perfect. "My sentiments on your parents' marriage, of course, are what he's referring to. Don't think this means I'm against *you* or anything like that. You're my granddaughter, even if just a few days ago you didn't know it. But my stance remains intact, and it's that Persuaders and Sentries should remain just what they are: Separate and in conflict. The balance needs to be upheld no matter what."

Taylor's fork slipped from his hand and clattered against his plate. He had the strangest expression, but my attention was diverted elsewhere by

Liam's bark of a laugh. "Hypocritical! Absolutely hypocritical! You say you love her as a granddaughter, and yet all the same you can't stand the fact that she was even *born.*"

Silas's leathery face creased at the mouth and forehead. "Michael," he snapped, irritated enough to forget that my father no longer went by that name. Or maybe he was using it as a reminder of things lost. "You know it's true. You've seen it for yourself. You've *experienced* it." He pointed a knobby finger at Liam. "I *warned* you that day you came to me to ask for my blessing. I *warned* you to stay away from her. But you wouldn't hear it."

Liam stood, almost knocking over his chair. "I *loved* her." I blinked in astonishment. It wasn't often that Liam admitted to his feelings for my mother, and never so loudly, so straightforwardly. "How could you not see that to *not* marry her would be impossible?"

Silas stood, as well, red-faced. "You should have stayed away from her," he growled. "You knew you would never be able to make it work. It was only a matter of time."

"Because of people like you," Taylor said, quietly.

Silas looked taken aback. He blinked twice at the unfamiliar boy across from him, and his face returned to its normal color. "*What* did you say?"

He brushed his hair back from his face, looking at the old man unflinchingly. "If our society would stop propagating hatred and ignorance and calling it 'balance'," Taylor said, a flush creeping into his neck, possibly out of anger, "then maybe there wouldn't even be a problem."

Silas didn't respond with fire in his words, only sadness. "Unfortunately, your 'let's-just-all-get-along' idealism is just that. Reserved for the idealists. I'm a realist, son, and if there's one thing I know, it's this: *Our society* isn't changing its mind any time soon. You ought to know that it's always had a hard time outgrowing things." Silas picked his hat off of the chair beside him, pulling the brim low over his eyes. "I think it's time for me to take my leave, now." He nodded to me. "Another time, Jennifer."

TAYLOR

Persuaders and Sentries should remain just what they are.

Maybe the old man was right, to some degree. Or maybe the correct thing to say was that they *had* to remain just what they were. A system like the one we perpetuated and nurtured every day couldn't be pushed against without pushing back. If, or when, Jenny became a Persuader, where would that leave us? If she took Silas' warning to heart...would she forget about me? Even worse, would she reject me? I didn't think I would be able to handle that. I could remember our conversation in the attic perfectly. She'd told me there was no one she cared about more than me, but had she even meant it? If she had, was it in the way one cared about a brother or a best friend, or was it more than that? She'd kissed me, after all. But then my mind conjured something else she had said.

I don't think we should worry about it getting in the way of us being friends, if that's *what you're worried about.*

It was a dismissal, of course. A dismissal of everything she had said in the attic. Everything she had done. She *regretted* it. Jenny regretted a moment that, for me, was absolutely precious, something I wouldn't take back for the world. I just felt...used. I knew it was selfish—presumptuous, even—of me to feel that, but I did. It stung to know one was deluding oneself.

But I could never resent her for it. I couldn't even bring myself to *mind* too much, being kept on her leash, kept closer or farther away on her command. At least it meant that I could still be near her, like how a moth could still be within the heat and glow of a porch light for a short time before burning out against the bulb.

VINCE

I glanced out my window, setting down a book, peering through the foggy twilight to see someone at the door. Again. The Cable mansion had suddenly become quite popular.

When I made my way downstairs and into the foyer, I was surprised to see no one else there to answer it. Perhaps they were all holed up in their respective rooms, Liam and Jenny most likely fretting over the details of the upcoming Embracement, and Taylor...well, he had to be *somewhere*, that pest. Probably where Jenny was.

I opened the door to see Gwen, the hood of her coat up, her pale brown hair curling around eyes that were the precise color of the overcast sky above her. "Can I come in?" she asked. I moved aside, nodding, too surprised to speak as she drew back her hood and stepped into the foyer. She sighed and turned back to me. "I was hoping to talk to you."

I attempted to mask my astonishment and failed. "Me? Why?"

"Well...there was no one else I could ask. Darren and Sasha are helping Natalia tend to the injured, and Eli is…well, he's not, per se, the right person for the job." She fidgeted ceaselessly with her sleeve.

I grabbed her wrist to stop her before she managed to somehow make me as anxious as she was. "What is it you're asking of me, exactly?"

She took a deep breath. "You know of the Lower Market?"

"The Sentry black market, you mean?" Reluctantly, Gwen nodded. "Yeah, I've heard of it. Some dismal harbor in Annapolis. What of it?"

"It isn't somewhere you go alone," she continued, looking almost ghostly pale against the gray rectangle of the doorway at her back.

"From what I've heard, I could only agree…" At that point, my mind had finally caught up with her words. I started again. "Hold on just a minute. You're asking me to go with you?"

"Yes," she said, her lip catching between her teeth for a moment in her apprehension. "To survive in a place like that, you need to smooth-talk some people, you know? You need…a certain amount of charm, I guess, but without seeming weak."

I peered at her through lowered lids. "Gwendolyn Farrier, are you calling me charming?"

She blanched at my question. "No need to inflate your ego even more over it. I was only saying that you…well, people tend to like you when they meet you."

"Do *you*?" I inquired, innocently. "Like me, I mean."

"Of course not," she snapped, finally yanking her wrist from my grasp. "I know better than to trust that pretty exterior."

"'Pretty exterior?'" I echoed, enjoying the look of annoyance and discomfort that flashed across her face. "So I'm charming *and* good-looking?"

With only a glare, she turned and walked out into the rain, calling over her shoulder, "I'll be back tomorrow. Be ready before noon."

Unable to resist, I called back, "It's a date, then. You'll have me home by nine o'clock, of course. Wouldn't want Liam to worry, would we?"

I couldn't be sure through the fog, but I thought I saw her gesture to me in a very unladylike manner. Hmph. So be it. Not that I would admit it to her, but I rather liked *this* Gwen better than the last. Better to be genuinely surly than superficially well-mannered.

18
RHYME OR REASON

Gwen slouched against the wall, reluctance in every line of her body. How this had happened to me I was still not entirely sure. "You should know, the Lower Market is no place for someone like you," she said.

"Someone like me?" I fidgeted with the scratchy, wool cuffs of the hooded jacket Gwen had tossed at me when I'd first arrived. "Meaning?"

"Meaning someone who can't keep his mouth shut even when his life literally depends on it," she clarified, not even looking at me. She seemed to be preoccupied with concealing knives in various locations and hidden sheaths, preparing herself for a "just-in-case" scenario.

I decided once and for all that Sentry women were by far the most baffling of creatures I had ever encountered. "Ah. Well, then, why did you say yesterday that I was the only one you could ask?"

Gwen had switched her focus over to me, pulling a packet of what I hoped was fake blood from the inside pocket of her coat and meticulously applying it to my clothes in a way that looked entirely accidental and authentic. She smeared dirt from the ground across my cheek, which I suffered without much complaint. I stooped and dug my fingernails into the muck, wiggling the black crescents at her with a smile. She nodded her approval and I added, "I think we both know you only arranged this so you could see how I looked in this...this Sentry get-up. I bet the thought alone was all the reason you needed."

She attempted to hide a smile as she reached to draw my hood up. Our eyes met for a moment. "Among other things," she said, quietly. Then she stepped back.

"Oh." I blinked, reassessing. "Wait, what other reasons are there?"

Gwen shrugged, thoroughly seeming to enjoy being the one who was vague and mysterious this time.

"I always knew it would come to this." My lips pursed—an expression half-impressed, half-disturbed. "That my teachings would take root, eventually."

She turned her eyes skyward before gesturing me to follow her through the parking lot, toward a gray collection of shops along the waterfront.

The Lower Market was a bleak place. The sky was still fairly overcast, which only seemed to throw an added layer of gray onto the scene before us. From what I knew, the market was a system of different services, a place comprised of seemingly abandoned storefronts set up along a gray harbor, gray water churning below, gray men's gray faces appearing in the windows. I looked over at Gwen and her flint-like gray eyes that seemed just at home.

There was too much silence that surrounded us, too much stillness. The only sound was the distant cry of a seagull every now and then or the chime of a door as some stooped figure walked in or out. Gwen warned me to look out for rogue Sentries in the alleyways, the ones who traveled in packs and tore apart any Persuader they saw without hesitation. A rogue by himself was a nuisance and a wild card, but a rogue in a pack was something else entirely. I whispered back to her that I was grateful for the sense of absolute security she had instilled in me by saying that.

I peered sideways at my companion. "I never see any children at the stronghold," I began, catching her a bit by surprise. "Or anyone much older than sixty, either. Why is that?"

Gwen looked at me with a puzzled expression. "Natalia is an outcross and a woman in a society that's just starting to break away from its chauvinist ideals. She's had to work harder than most to secure a place for Sentries in the area to gather. But our stronghold is smaller than most. And less accommodating. Many of our Sentries with young children or elderly parents live a few miles from the rest, mostly self-sufficient and only called into duty during the hours they're off from their paying jobs."

I could almost picture how my face looked, how my eyebrows had shot into my hairline in my surprise. "So they're forced to be separate from the others because the Adjudication deems Natalia too under-qualified to have charge of a larger facility?"

Gwen sighed, her face trying to work itself into something less frustrated and failing. "Yeah."

"That's *rubbish*," I said, and in my usage of the word I suddenly reminded myself of my father.

Her hand moved to cover her mouth as she coughed or possibly smothered a laugh. "Well, if the Adjudicator we have currently had been instated at the time Natalia had requested a stronghold, maybe they would've been more sympathetic. And did you really just say 'rubbish?'"

I declined responding to the question and pursued another path of conversation. "So this…Lower Market. Is it strictly Sentry-operated or is it faction-neutral like the Adjudication? Well, I mean, like the Adjudication is *supposed* to be, rather."

"Its main purpose has always been to be of service to Sentry benefactors, but that doesn't mean the occasional Persuader doesn't drop by to arm his Deadlocks from time to time."

This didn't make me feel any better about the black market. Something about it felt…hostile. Dangerous in its still bleakness. Places that were still and bleak typically were also unpredictable.

"One more thing," she said, stopping finally in front of a red door with a small and faded medical cross carved into it. "See if you can do anything about your accent. You need to make yourself as unremarkable as possible, and being a foreigner might make them suspicious."

"With my excellent cheekbones and impressive physique, being *unremarkable* may be a problem, but the Yank voice I can do just fine." I sighed. "So that means no 'Gov'na' this or 'Shall I' that, to be clear?"

One gray eye winked quickly in my direction before she turned away with, "And no referring to anything as 'rubbish', either."

Inside it was cold, of course. And quite dim. A stocky woman with missing teeth and possibly a glass right eye waited patiently for us from behind a counter, her long nails clacking against the counter.

She nodded at Gwen. "Farrier." Her one good eye swiveled to me, narrowing with suspicion. "What can I do you for?"

"Always a pleasure, Shirley," Gwen returned, her tone polite yet still rather reserved, with just a hint of sarcasm. "Alex, here, has the money for you."

I cleared my throat, shooting her a quick glance. *Alexander* was my middle name. I wondered if it wasn't a coincidence that it was the alias she'd chosen for me. That thought of her *remembering* it, after all this time, was unexpectedly pleasing. "Good afternoon, ma'am," I said, my voice sounding strange in its unnatural inflection.

Shirley pointed to the water cooler over in the corner of the room. "Why don't you get yourself a drink, Gwen?" Seeing nothing better to do, she wandered over to the nearly empty container and churned yellowish brown liquid from it into a paper cup. She cringed, but didn't complain. Shirley turned back to me. "Take a seat, kid, right in that chair."

Her tone did not suggest she took kindly to refusal, so I obliged, glancing quickly back at Gwen, who appeared to be studying her untouched beverage for signs of life. When I glanced back, the almost toothless woman was looking at me with a certain glint in her eyes. For the right one, maybe it was just the light reflecting off of the glass, but the left one was decidedly fascinated by what it saw. "Gwen Farrier, we've done business for years and you never mentioned a boyfriend." The woman tsked, as if admonishing her.

Gwen lost her grip on the cup for a moment, discolored water sloshing over her boots. "Oh, he's not...I mean, he *was,* but that was a while ago. We're just..." She trailed off, her gaze finding mine as she fumbled for the correct word for our relationship as it stood.

"Friends," I finished, seeing my own surprise reflected back at me in her expression.

After a tense silence, Shirley, seemingly oblivious to our exchange, scribbled something down in a notebook in front of her without even glancing at it. "Well, everything seems to be in order, I suppose, though there is still the matter of payment."

I slid a black backpack from my shoulders, throwing it down with little ceremony onto the counter before the glass-eyed woman.

As she jammed the bills into the slot of a counting machine, Gwen leaned in close to me, murmuring, "That went strangely well. Usually Shirley likes to hassle me a little more than that. We didn't even run into trouble with any Sentry pack around the harbor."

"It's all that charm and good looks," I replied, smugly.

Her lips parted angrily as if to make a response, but Shirley had finished sorting the stacks of bills, grinning her piano key grin at us.

"Expect delivery in two days."

"I'll have to tell Natalia about the early shipment," Gwen said, as we ducked back outside into the gray afternoon. "She might be able to attend the Embracement if we can treat and medicate everyone who still needs it."

When she felt something, strongly, I couldn't help but feel it, too. I smiled widely down at her. "That's great. It really is. You were brilliant."

"You, too." She sighed, fanning herself dramatically as she leaned her head against my shoulder. "Brilliant, eh? Oh, how I missed that accent of yours. No girl can resist it, trust me on this."

"Have you...missed *me?*" The question came unexpectedly, causing us both to pause for a moment. She detached her head from my shoulder, pulling herself abruptly upright. "I mean...I've been thinking that maybe we should spend more time together. We could be friends, you know. I don't see any reason why not."

"I'd like that, Vince," Gwen said, softly. "I really would. I've been thinking, too. About you, admittedly." A blush bloomed across her face, a surprisingly lovely sight.

"Do you ever regret anything?" I asked, unsure what was compelling me to do so. "You've always been the type of girl who knows exactly what she wants out of life. Someone who doesn't look back."

This seemed to visibly affect her, make the blush fade, cause her hands to jam into her jacket pockets almost reflexively. "I look back occasionally, but you're right in saying that I don't *regret* a lot of things. At least, I try not to. I don't regret joining Natalia's ranks. I don't regret anything I've done for the sake of the stronghold."

I opened the car door for her, jumping into the passenger seat as she continued her thought with a nervous bounce to her leg. "Maybe I regret having to manipulate people or using my powers on the defenseless, but...the only thing I *truly* regret is—" As she was speaking, she turned the key in the ignition, looking surprised when the engine didn't purr to life.

She gave the key another, sharp twist and still there was nothing.

And that was when the car exploded, in a single, abrupt blast of heat, fire, and the smell of things burning. With this was the ear-scraping, teeth-gritting sound of things wrenching apart.

Surrounded by an inferno in a warped cage of metal, I threw myself over Gwen instinctively, as if that would make a difference. We were both going to die. I couldn't help but think it, over and over. *I'm dead. I'm dead. Why?* Why *did it have to be like this? Why like this?*

I opened my eyes when the world was still again, perplexed. There was the sky of Heaven, I supposed, though it was the precise gray of the sky above the harbor. Maybe that meant I was in Hell. And then there was the matter of everything else that looked the same: The boats waiting at the docks, swaying slightly in the breeze, the gulls resting atop the masts, the low, ramshackle buildings of the black market, the burning skeleton of a car just behind me, and...Gwen.

She lifted her head, her nose nearly touching mine, her eyes holding the same confusion I felt. "Vince?" Her voice was faint. "Vince, we're not...how did...how did you do that?"

"Do what?" I moved away from her, to get a better look at us both. She appeared only slightly singed, her sleeves and shoes blackened, the tips of her hair much of the same. My hands searched my own clothes and face and body for any injury, any sort of irregularity at all, and found nothing.

"You..." Her brows furrowed, as if she was still trying to understand what had happened, herself, piecing the details together to make sense of them. "You saved my life, I think. The car it... How did we get here? How did we get *out?*"

I looked down at my hands, as if the answer was written there. "I...I don't know. A miracle, I suppose."

"No, not a miracle," Gwen said, untangling herself from me. "I think you have a gift, Vince. Some sort of ability you never realized you had."

"A gift?" I scoffed. "I'm an outcross. I couldn't possibly have a gift."

"Well, how else can you explain it?" she demanded. "It's possible that you underestimate yourself."

I could hear an ambulance's wail as it grew closer, and just beneath it the sound of something else. The sound of maybe a motorcycle engine, becoming increasingly farther away.

I walked over to the ruined car, studying it, Gwen trailing behind me. "Someone was trying to kill us," she observed.

"Not just someone," I said, with a shake of my head. "Samuel Locke. I know it."

"Well, that's just fantastic." She scratched at her ear. "What should we do now?"

"We have to get back to Liam to tell him about this. Natalia, too. I'm not sure which of us Samuel wanted dead. And, regardless of who he was targeting…I have no idea what his motive could be."

Gwen examined a lock of her slightly singed hair. It struck me that she was oddly nonchalant considering what had just happened, but I realized it was probably just her reasoning that if she *acted* calm, she might be able to make herself believe she *was* calm. "It could just be because he's a psycho," she offered.

"That's not good enough, and you know it," I said, and she nodded after a moment, reluctant to admit it.

I glanced off toward the skyline, where the dark curtain of clouds met the darker waves. "Something is going on here. Something that's more complicated than we realize. Something more involved."

Gwen put a hand on my shoulder. "Come on. We shouldn't waste any more time."

JENNY

"A truly arresting sight." Charles turned to my father. "I *told* you lavender was her color, did I not?"

Liam smiled faintly in my direction, amused by the fact that our *illustrious coordinator* had actually campaigned at first for the dress to be burgundy before my father had suggested something more befitting to an interbreed such as myself, a fact about me Charles seemed to be conveniently forgetting. I was grateful for Liam's intervening. There was no reason to make it seem as if I was decided quite yet, no reason to hurt anyone until I absolutely had to. "Oh, you did," he confirmed, coughing in his hand to cover up a laugh. "It's very nice."

"Very," Taylor added, from the corner of the room. Before he had been slouched backward, his chair balancing on its back two legs, but when I had walked in he leaned forward sharply, the legs slamming back down to the floor. When our gazes met he smiled, and I returned it with a slight, satirical curtsy, which made him laugh.

He stopped when he noticed Liam watching us. My father cleared his throat, softly. "The necklace adds an especially nice touch."

I looked down at it, realizing I had forgotten it was even there. I'd hardly even taken it off since receiving it except to sleep or shower. Something about it comforted me, made me feel like I had a small piece of my mother with me, resting close to my heart. "Yeah, it does, doesn't it?"

I caught sight of myself in the mirror next to Charles, once again surprised by my own reflection, as I had been when changing into the dress in my room. The first time I'd barely even spared myself a moment's admiration, feeling both vain and a little silly. But now I realized that was the whole *point*, wasn't it? I was *supposed* to feel vain and silly because that was how someone felt when she actually liked her own appearance, for once.

As much as I loathed Charles Monroe, I had to admit that he was a brilliant designer. On paper, the dress had been beautiful, but tangibly it was even better. It was predominantly a lavender color, per Liam's suggestion, but the material was lustrous, like satin or taffeta, and artfully layered, falling asymmetrically in overlapping layers of blue and red silk underneath. My back was a bit more exposed than it'd been the last two times I was forced to comply with wearing a dress but, even so, my mind formulated fewer complaints than usual.

I opened my mouth to grudgingly express my gratitude to Charles, but right at that moment Vince and Gwen burst into the room, looking for all the world like a pair of ghosts.

Liam stood, his gaze going back and forth between the two, undoubtedly noting how pale and out of breath they both looked, the spots of black on their clothes and skin, how Vince's hands were shaking. "What happened?" he demanded.

"Samuel," Vince choked out. "He tried to kill us."

"What?" Liam strode forward, gripping Vince's shoulders. "Are you hurt? Is Gwen?" They glanced at each other briefly before both shaking their heads no. Liam released a sigh, his alarm only partly relieved. "Why were you at the stronghold?"

"He—" Gwen began to say, but Vince interrupted, his eyes unable to meet his adoptive father's.

"I wasn't at the stronghold. We went to the Lower Market."

"The Lower Market?" Liam's face had gone scarlet, his voice rising in volume to the point to where even Charles seemed visibly uncomfortable. "Do you even realize how dangerous that place is? Especially for a Persuader. You should've known better."

"I'm sorry," Vince said, his head lowering. "But I had an obligation to help."

"*Obligation?*" Liam was incredulous. "Where is this coming from?

You've never been indebted to any Sentry before. You should've stayed home and let Gwen—"

"What?" Vince snapped, cutting him off. His head lifted, his shoulders squaring. I had never seen him defy Liam in such a way. "Die? Because she would've if I wasn't there. Is that what you want? For other people to get hurt because they aren't like you?"

"You know that's not what I meant."

Charles cleared his throat, recognizing his cue to leave the room. He began shoving papers into a briefcase. "Perhaps it's best if I go now…"

When the door shut behind him, Gwen started again, attempting to smooth things over. "Look, we didn't come here to argue with you, Mr. Cable. We came to tell you that we think Samuel has some sort of a…a *plan*. A plan for all of us. One that goes deeper than we'd like to believe it does."

My father's green eyes narrowed, his hand going to his chin in contemplation. I looked at the other girl. "What do you mean? This isn't just about getting to Taylor?"

"It's about getting to everyone," she said. "He was trying to kill either me or Vince, which means his endgame is about ultimately affecting either the stronghold or…or *you*, Mr. Cable." Liam dropped his hand, his eyes flying wide again with the revelation.

"Or both," Vince added. His eyes swept the whole room as he spoke, yet oddly seemed to skip over me entirely. "Like she said, it's about getting to everyone. Each of us represents everything Samuel despises. That's what we all have in common. Jenny's an interbreed. You married a Sentry. Natalia and I are outcrossed. Taylor's a rogue. Gwen's a benefactor. What I'm trying to say is…he might not stop after just a single attack. There's a pattern."

Taylor seemed to reason with what Vince was telling us, leaning forward onto his elbows. "Samuel's a Purist?" he asked at last. His hair fell into his face.

"Yes." Vince's hands almost imperceptibly curled inward at his sides. "He made that much clear at the masquerade. I was outside when the fighting broke out. He attacked me and I…I tried to fight him but he had some kind of…device on his wrist that gave him the ability to Shift even when we were still within range of the Deadlocks. I had no idea technology like that even existed."

"The point is," Gwen cut in, taking a deep breath, "there's nothing standing between *him* and *us*. Any of us could be next. The only defense we have is our awareness. If we want to prevent any more casualties amongst us—"

"We have to cooperate," I finished, and she nodded shortly in my direction.

Liam reached for the phone on the wall, dialing a number and not saying a word until a sharp, unfriendly voice was audible on the other side of the receiver. "Natalia. It's Liam." I could hear her snappish reply even from where I stood. "Look, it's an urgent matter. One of your own and my son were almost killed today. I'll give you one guess who was behind it. They think Samuel may be plotting something more involved than he's letting on." Liam paused to hear her response. For a moment, there was nothing.

Then, we all leaned forward to hear her less antagonistically say to him, "I want the details. Put Gwen on."

Liam handed the phone to her, and in the succinct manner of a Sentry she began telling Natalia everything she deemed essential to the situation. When she was done, Natalia ordered her to return directly to the stronghold to discuss the matter further.

Gwen hung up, pinching the bridge of her nose. Vince gripped her arm, turning her toward him. "It's going to be okay. We'll sort this out."

"By the time we do, it might be too late," she replied, wearily.

I stepped toward her, saying quickly, "I'm going with you." This announcement received several raised eyebrows. "I have to speak to Natalia, as well."

Gwen sighed, giving an indifferent wave of her hand. "Okay, fine. Whatever. I'll be waiting for you outside."

I started for the door, but she stopped me, casting me a sidelong glance. "You might want to change out of that."

"Nice car," I remarked, as Gwen shattered the speed limit like a criminal evading arrest. Rolling down the window, I added, "But there is that *wet dog* smell that's hard to get around. Wouldn't have pegged you for an animal-lover."

"I guess it's not much of a shock to hear that this one is, er, *borrowed*. Not proud of it, but as a benefactor I find it easier than most Sentries to steal out of necessity. *My* car is currently in little burning pieces across a parking lot," she replied, her fingers curling tighter around the wheel. "It was rigged to detonate when I turned the key."

"What?" I sat bolt upright in the seat. "How did you get out of there?"

Her gaze seemed unfocused. "I'm still not sure. All I know is that Samuel must've hired one of those Techies to do the job while Vince and I were gone. Rumor is those guys are trained to telekinetically assemble and dismantle a bomb in under ten minutes. Blindfolded."

"What do you think is happening here?" I asked, and then added, quietly, "I don't think it was meant for Vince. I don't know *why* I think that, but that's what this *feels* like."

The corner of Gwen's mouth slid down. "You think all of this is about Samuel targeting the stronghold?"

"Possibly," I amended, biting my lip in meditation. "But even *that* could be part of some chain of events we're not seeing."

"Everything he does seems to be connected to something else," she replied, bitterly. "We just have to find out what the big picture is."

"Maybe there is no big picture," I murmured, seeing the stronghold rise up from the fog just ahead. "Maybe his type of insanity has no real reason."

Natalia was waiting for us outside the building, her hands braced on her hips, the wind tugging at her near-colorless hair. Gwen glanced back at me as I followed her to the entrance, mouthing, *Don't antagonize anyone.*

I pretended not to be insulted.

"Jennifer Cable, what in God's name are you doing here?" Natalia demanded, seeming to forget that just the other day we had shared a sort of heart-to-heart.

"Wow," I said, twisting the cuffs of my sweater. "I'm always so warmly welcomed."

Natalia sighed. "Well, things have been a little tense around here." She turned to Gwen. "I don't suppose you have any good news to share about the supply shipment?"

"In two days," she answered, allowing for the smallest of smiles. "That's when we should expect it."

"Good," the Sentry leader breathed, nodding to herself. She appeared relaxed some, but only barely. "Good. But what is Jenny doing here?"

"I need to talk to you," I said, even though the question was technically aimed at Gwen. "I think Samuel may be trying to weaken your stronghold, make it vulnerable, somehow."

Her arms folded, her look narrowing in contemplation. "I'm listening."

"The bomb rigged to the car, I think, was meant to kill Gwen. *Gwen,* who's your stronghold's benefactor, your third in command."

"Samuel couldn't know that," Natalia said, dismissively. "She's too careful, and her family is one of the elite. A Farrier would never be suspected."

"He knows more about what goes on here than you might realize," I insisted, trying desperately not to lose her attention. "It's that sort of overconfidence you have in the stronghold and your Sentries that he's playing off of." Her look of detachment turned instantly to annoyance at my slighting of her character. I sighed. "Look, I know how you've worked *so hard* just to get where you are. You have every right to have confidence in this place and in your position as a leader. But I'm just telling you to be careful."

Her lips twisted in reluctance, which I could also understand.

"I've been wrong about him before," I admitted. "I underestimated him. But now I think we all know better than to make that mistake again."

After a moment's hesitation, she nodded, unfolding her arms. "Alright. Well, since you're here, I suppose I do still have some use for you." She turned and walked through the entrance, gesturing over her shoulder for me to follow.

Inside, the stronghold was more chaotic than I remembered, filled with the sweet-sour reek of blood and sweat and people in need of medical attention, the walls echoing the cries and moans of those worse-off than others. Resources were spread thin, as well as able hands. While some were being treated, others were left having to be wrapped in blankets rather than bandages, with belts or scraps of fabric as tourniquets and, from what I could see, nothing on hand to kill the pain.

"Why aren't these people being treated at a hospital?" I murmured to Gwen, who walked beside me.

"Well, a few of the more severe cases are there as we speak, but we don't really have the money for *everyone* to be given the attention they need, especially not on a regular basis. No one ever said being a Sentry came with health insurance, you know. It may come as a shock to hear this, Jenny, but we Sentries have come to terms with the likelihood of an early death, and we're consoled by the knowledge that there's always someone behind you who can fill your shoes once you're gone."

I was silent, glancing back and forth between the rows of people, and a few eyes swiveled to me as I passed. They seemed too preoccupied with illness and injury to pay me much mind.

Natalia stopped in the middle of them all, turning to me. "See what you can do about the ones who are critically wounded. You don't have to heal them completely; I wouldn't ask that. Just...see what you can do," she repeated, wandering off in the opposite direction before I could respond. Gwen followed her.

And suddenly I was alone, along amongst dozens upon dozens of unfamiliar people, quite of few of them probably imagining me dead.

I glanced around, looking for someone who met the usual criteria of "critically wounded", and my gaze fell on a woman just to my left, lying very still and pale on a cot. Up close, she looked worse. Her skin was slicked over with sweat and—as I reached out to her—cold to the touch, her hair fanned around a face that appeared almost colorless. Her arms rested over her torso, a plastic bag filled with water clasped in one hand. It had probably been an ice bag at some point, I figured.

"Ma'am? How are you hurt?" I asked, as gently as I could manage. "And where?"

The woman's eyes snapped open, her mouth working in surprise. Her lips were so cracked they bled. "Jenny Cable?"

"I'm a healer," I explained. "I'm here to help. I need you to tell me what your injury is."

After a pause, the Sentry released a rattling cough and said, "Broken ribs. Maybe a punctured lung. Been unable to move around much for days."

It was worse than I'd thought. There was no way I could heal one of her injuries and leave the other unattended. I would have to make an exception with this one. And the worse part was, I'd never healed bone before.

Fighting the wave of apprehension that tugged at me, I placed my fingertips lightly over her, feeling for the break. At her sudden sharp intake of breath, I closed my eyes, telling her to be very still. I could hear footsteps behind me, vaguely, Darren's voice demanding to know what it was I thought I was doing.

I could see the injury in my mind, could see the tissue of the punctured lung begin to knit back together at my will, the bone righting itself and slowly, but surely, forming back into one piece rather than two.

When I opened my eyes again, I had to brace myself against the edge of the cot, my head spinning a little. It had been easier to do, I supposed, when the patient wasn't near death, as Taylor and Natalia had been. But that didn't mean it still wasn't incredibly taxing.

Darren had made his way over to us, and his hand shot out to take my arm roughly in his grasp. "Jenny, you shouldn't be here—"

The woman I had just helped began to sit upright, swinging her legs over the side of the bed, and he stopped talking, his mouth hanging open.

I pulled my arm from his. "If you'll excuse me, I have work to do."

It was Silas who found me slouched against the wall in my exhaustion, late in the night. He stood beside me, leaning against it, himself. "You did well today, Jenny. Real well."

"Thanks," I said, with a heavy sigh. "But it doesn't feel like I did. There are still more people waiting for medical attention here. A dozen or so was all I could manage."

My grandfather looked at me with a stern glint in his eye. "You did everything you could've done without killing yourself in the process. You've made amends with these people. You've gained their respect. That's what matters at the end of the day: Hard-earned trust."

"I guess."

Silas pulled his hat low over his eyes. "Make sure you get yourself home safely, Jenny. I'm off to do a little patrol with Eli." I leaned around the old man to see Eli headed toward the rusted Chevy parked outside, his bright smile visible even from where I stood.

"Alright, you be safe, too. And be on your guard. You never know what Samuel might do—" My breath caught. I could hear Gwen clearly in my mind, as clearly as if she was standing right next to me. I could hear her saying, *Any of us could be next.*

Silas looked at me oddly, confused about my sudden change in demeanor. "Is something the matter?"

"Who here is second in command?" I demanded, without answering his question.

He frowned, looking even more puzzled. *"I am. What has you so uneasy, Jenny?"*

My thoughts froze in place when everything finally clicked together. "Oh no. *No.* Eli! Eli, stop!" I shoved past Silas, running for the entrance, weaving around Sentries, my eyes locked onto his retreating form as he disappeared around the corner. *"Eli!"*

My footfalls echoed throughout the stronghold, and startled faces turned to look at me as I sprinted past. I felt too slow, my voice too soft, unable to reach him through the other voices surrounding it. When I at last reached the entrance, Eli was already in the driver's seat, turning the key in the ignition without a second thought.

It might be too late. That was something else Gwen had said, and it echoed around inside my head over and over.

All I had time to do was cry out his name again before the truck detonated with a tremendous sound, louder than anything I'd ever heard, chased by plumes of fire and smoke and bits of metal flying as the blast threw me to the ground.

I braced my scraped palms on the pavement, and my ears were ringing as I stood again, stood only to see a burning mass of metal and rubber occupying the lot. The truck's roof was completely gone, as well as its driver.

19
THE SOLUTION

We all gathered around his pyre, as was tradition for fallen Sentries. Like ancient Celtic warriors, I thought.

But Eli had not been ancient and was certainly not a warrior as his fellow Sentries were. He had just been a fifteen-year-old boy, awkward yet charmingly so, sweet-tempered and never unkind to me as some of the other Sentries had been. And now he was dead. He was dead because of me. He was dead because I failed to see it coming soon enough. He was dead because of the trouble I had stirred by coming here in the first place.

I glanced from face to face, trying to detect any antagonistic looks tossed my way, because I certainly deserved them. None came. Every set of eyes was on the flame, which consumed not a body—considering the fact that Eli had already been incinerated in the explosion—but his belongings. A knife had been plunged into the meager pile, its blade turning bright orange as flames flickered around it.

Vince stood off at a distance, looking into the night sky with his hands thrust deep into his pockets. Gwen continued to glance back at him with a worried look in her eyes, probably deliberating whether or not she should go over there. Taylor sat next to me, and I leaned into the warm circle of his arm. Liam spoke softly with Natalia on the other side of the fire, and I was surprised to see them behave so civilly toward each other. It was strange, I thought, that the one thing that would finally bring Persuaders and Sentries together would be the death of an innocent, though I suspected Liam, Vince, and Taylor were here mostly for my benefit. I had insisted on staying for the ceremony.

"Brothers, sisters," spoke Silas in a resonating voice, standing slowly. "We have gathered to commemorate a fallen comrade, and to remember fallen brothers and sisters of the past." A woman—the woman I'd healed earlier—nodded a little, her eyes bright with tears. "Elijah Todd was young, yes, but he was honorable. He never confronted his responsibilities with anything less than unsurpassed enthusiasm and ever-constant bravery. For this reason, among many others, you will be missed, Eli."

A unified whoop of agreement rose from the crowd, voices that shot straight into the stars, including my own, including Vince's and Taylor's and, perhaps most surprisingly, my father's.

GWEN

"Well, I don't like it," Richard Farrier remarked into his cup of coffee, undoubtedly cold with neglect by now.

In his hands he held the latest issue of *The Persuader Post,* and this morning the front page did not feature the current debates amongst the senators of the Adjudication as it usually did, and neither did it quibble on the shortcomings of the inferior and impotent human government with whom the Adjudication shared a city. Rather, it decided to focus on a twin set of occurrences in the middle of nowhere.

CAR BOMBINGS OCCUR WITHIN HOURS OF EACH OTHER, the bold print read. Beneath it, in smaller text, it continued with: *The Adjudication suspects a relatively new and highly dangerous subdivision of the Sentry organization—known as Sentry "Wolves", due to their pack-like tendencies—may be behind the incidents. Adjudicator Khan has this to say regarding the bombings ...*

"The Adjudication has been so damn biased, lately," I muttered, sliding low in my chair.

"Gwendolyn, you shouldn't mumble," my mother said from across the table, her face creased with disapproval, as it often was. She turned her attention back to her husband. "What is it you were saying, Richard?"

"Oh, nothing, Isabel." He cracked his knuckles absently, setting the paper down with contempt. "I just don't like the idea of all of this Sentry nonsense and violence happening so close to where we live. Never really know what those people are planning. I just thank God for Kaia Khan, and her sensibility in a time like this. It's time the Adjudication stops brushing incidents like this off its shoulders."

"Shame what happened with the Adjudicator's son," Isabel sighed. "That whole, messy Renouncement process. Oh, what was his name?"

Richard looked scornful. "Who cares? He became a nameless nobody after he Renounced. Those people who throw away all the ease and comfort and sophistication of the Persuader world to live like mindless sheep in the human world are beneath *my* sympathy."

"And so young, too, to be making decisions like that," my mother added, with a mournful pucker of her lips, as if she hadn't heard him. "Which reminds me, I read in the paper the other day that most benefactors are younger than *twenty*. Alarming, really, that some parents don't even know their own children."

My father cleared his throat, picking up a fork and knife and cutting into a sausage link on his plate. After a pause, he said, "I believe the Cable girl's Embracement is in just two days."

Isabel's mouth, still puckered as if she'd bitten into a lime, turned down at the corners in dismay. "And we're going?"

"Of course we are!" Richard was not to be discouraged by his wife's reluctance. "It's practically all anyone talks about, lately."

"Well,"—she tapped her dainty chin in contemplation—"I know how much you love to go to these scandalous types of things…"

"Gwen," he said, fishing for direct consent elsewhere, "wouldn't you like to go? I mean, seeing as a certain old flame is going to be there—"

My fork dropped onto my untouched breakfast with a clatter. I felt my face begin to burn. "Dad!"

"Well, you've been miserable about it for months. I just thought—"

"Oh my God," I groaned, pressing my palms into my eyes. "Please stop talking."

I excused myself from the table, feigning a lack of appetite, knowing I would have to fake another sort of condition if I wanted to avoid going to the Embracement.

Alarming, really, that some parents don't even know their own children, my mother had said. I could only agree. Truly, truly alarming.

JENNY

A sort of gloom had passed over the mansion since the day of Eli's death, an added layer of melancholy trembling ominously throughout the house like a winter draft slipping under doors.

It wasn't as if anyone in the Cable mansion was overly mournful of the incident—we had barely known him. I had the feeling it was more about the significance of such an incident. It meant that no one, not even some blameless boy within the secure walls of Natalia's stronghold, was out of Samuel's reach. It meant that no one was safe.

I supposed that we had known all along, anyway, that our lives were at the precipice of destruction, but now the evidence became more concrete, driven home by the fact that the person who'd died hadn't just been some faceless casualty of an everyday conflict. We'd *known* him.

My eighteenth birthday was in two days. I had to be as prepared as I could possibly be. I had to be ready to face Samuel Locke.

I took in the scene before me. I was outside, away from the distractions of the mansion and those who dwelled within it, my back to the pond. Propped up on tables of varying heights at varying distances were long-forgotten things I had found in the unoccupied rooms in the west wing. Ever since I'd figured out how to pick locks with a certain concentrated amount of Shifting, getting into those rooms had become much easier. Liam had waved me away when I requested permission to break the objects within them into tiny little pieces, as he was absorbed with the final details of the Embracement and, in truth, too rich to care much about knickknacks.

And so there they were, waiting like mismatched soldiers, and my fingers curled twice at my sides. I lifted my hands and imagined invisible forces, unseen masses flying into the plates lining the first table.

One by one, they shattered, fine china scattering into the shin-high grass beneath the tables.

"Impressive," someone remarked at my shoulder. I had been so focused on what I was doing, I hadn't sensed Taylor's aura until he was just behind me. I turned to him, taken aback some.

"Oh. Hey, I didn't..." His eyes shone with amusement, and his hair—beginning to fade back to brown—shone like tarnished gold at the tips. Almost instantly, I forgot what it was I had been about to say. After a moment, though, I decided it didn't really matter. "Never mind. Was it really?"

"What?" he inquired, smiling that toothy grin of his. "Impressive? Of course. You always impress me."

My breath caught a little at that, though I wasn't sure why. I spun back around to face the motley assortment of targets, raising my hands again. "Shall I go on?"

He took a step back, bowing a little. "By all means." He studied the objects. "Aim for the vase."

In that same moment, the intricately designed vase on the second table shattered just as the plates had. My gaze never strayed from Taylor's.

His lips twitched into a smirk. "Okay, now you're just showing off."

I reassessed what lay before me among the wreckage. On the second table, still, were two lamps, an old Polaroid camera that no longer worked, and a collection of dusty champagne glasses. Several paces away waited the third table patiently, a simple coffee table with a glass top and stacks upon stacks of yellowed documents that were, according to Liam, useless and cluttering up the place.

"Watch this," I said, refocusing my attention completely on my father's banished possessions.

In my mind I imagined complete and utter destruction, as I could well picture being an image that made frequent appearances in Samuel's mind. To fight a monster, I had to *think* like a monster. I had to take those dark thoughts into my head, all without letting those thoughts *turn* me dark.

The air began to tremble and waver around us, like heat waves from a hot summer afternoon. Taylor made an anxious sound from behind me. "Jenny, I don't think...whatever it is you're doing...*stop.*"

But I couldn't. I couldn't tear my eyes away from what was in front of me, and I couldn't force my hands back down to my sides. "Taylor, I...*I can't.*"

In a single, abrupt motion everything—from the lamps to the stacks of paper to the camera to the tables and even the grass beneath it—split apart into fragments, suspended in the air. Taylor gasped, calling out my name again, but I was silent, observing the destruction I had caused without laying a hand on a single thing. I liked how it felt, how using my abilities like this made me feel...powerful. I recalled my father's voice, telling me that I was a *greater being.*

The shards and fragments of glass and wood and plastic undulated almost lazily in the cool November air, turning point-first toward us and glinted wickedly in the yellow morning sun for a moment.

Then, without a thought on my part toward anything in particular, they shot toward Taylor and me like discolored, misshapen bullets.

"Jenny, look out!" Taylor shouted, with a trill of panic in his voice.

He sprinted toward me, tackling me to the ground as sharpened pieces of once-whole objects zipped by over our heads, cutting into the air where just a moment before we had been standing.

"Jesus, Cable, I told you to *stop.*" His voice sounded furious but when I looked up into his face I only saw relief there, surfacing from an initial panic. "What were you *thinking?*"

I realized that I was shaking, and my head was spinning fast, too fast to form a proper sentence. "I…I wasn't…I don't know…it just happened."

"*Just happened?*" he demanded, repeating my words with anger. "You could've gotten yourself killed! Don't do that again. Please, if you even value your life at all, don't do that again."

My voice was a dry croak. "Okay."

At that Taylor's eyes softened a little. He stood, offering a hand to help me up, which he then used to draw me into a lung-crushing embrace. He was shaking, too. "I'm sorry. I shouldn't have yelled at you. It's just…I always feel like this kind of life we've found ourselves in is going to tear us apart one way or another."

My arms encircled his waist just as tightly, my head resting in the hollow of his shoulder. "It won't. I promise."

"Well, that little stunt may have been reckless and dangerous," he muttered into my hair, "but I guess I have to admit that it was pretty amazing, too. Kind of like you. Reckless, dangerous, and amazing."

"Hm. Thanks." I considered for a moment each adjective individually. "I think."

"You're welcome." He released me finally. "And, hey, look on the bright side. At least we don't have any cleaning up to do." His gaze moved past me, to the circular patch of brown where the tables had been before, now devoid of any item or, for that matter, green. "Though maybe there's room for a bit of an explanation as to why the yard appears to have been marked by extraterrestrial life."

"And our extremities remain attached to our bodies, not to mention," I added, shoving him a little.

His smile was immediate. "*That's* the spirit."

Of course, the second I stepped foot in the house, the light mood Taylor had put me in dissipated when I noticed Charles and my father engaged in a heated argument, and my blood ran cold when I gathered what it was about.

"I *knew* there was something off about the boy!" the organizer was shouting, while my father watched him with a quiet look. "The second I looked into those violet eyes I knew who he was. Taylor Ross. Look at his hair, even. *Horrible* dye-job! Imagine! I was in the midst of a wanted criminal this whole time!" He threw up his hands, turning away.

Liam swallowed hard. "Now, Charles, we mustn't be unreasonable."

"Unreasonable?" the other man demanded, matching composure with fury. "No, no, *unreasonable* is harboring a Sentry rogue in your home underneath *everyone else's* noses. Unreasonable would be *not* notifying the authorities right this second. You know the law, Liam. No Persuader or Sentry may harbor any individual of the opposite faction, *especially* a rogue. Wardens could swarm this place in an instant."

Liam considered for a moment. "Mr. Monroe, you have never been driven solely by civil duty. You know that. I know that. How about I double the payment for your services. And for you to keep your mouth shut about this."

"Triple," Charles said, without pause. There was a tick in his jaw. Apparently Liam had assumed correct about what truly governed his actions. "Make it triple and I swear to keep it a secret."

"Fine, then," Liam said, at last.

After shaking hands on the agreement, Charles turned to Taylor with a tilt to his head. "Hm. Little wonder I couldn't tell you were a Sentry, at first. You were born and bred to be a Persuader, brought up upon decent principles—though all that time with a murderer's heart in you that your parents failed to recognize."

Taylor stared at him, silent, his back perfectly straight. I glared at Charles. "Taylor isn't a murderer."

"Really?" he shot back, smiling a little. "Tell me he's never killed a single person in his life and I'll believe you."

I was silent now, as well. I couldn't help but remember the haze and confusion of the masquerade, Taylor driving the knife into the Deadlock's chest.

"That's what I thought." Charles seemed satisfied. "Oh, but don't look so upset, Jennifer. I'm sure that karma will catch up to him, eventually, as it catches up to us all. You see, I don't even have to run to Samuel Locke and inform him that his suspicions have been right all along. It's only a matter of time."

With a flash of his teeth, he departed, the door slamming behind him.

CIRA

"Again," Samuel barked at the bruised and bloodied men that surrounded him.

They surged forward, some wielding weapons, some unarmed, as Samuel, himself, was. His black eyes quickly assessed the situation, discerning weakness and vulnerability from the pack of assailants.

I watched from the corner of the room as he Shift-boxed one with a long metal pipe in his hands, swinging it in a wide arc toward Samuel. He was on his back, sputtering in surprise, in the blink of an eye. A memory flashed to the surface of my mind in that instant, of Thom, his lungs crushed, his eyes staring vacantly up into the sky. *Muerto.* My hands clenched into fists, and I willed myself not to let any sign of my grief show on my face. Thom and I had always been so very alike, I thought, though some might never have guessed it. We both were outcrossed, of course, as ironically most of Samuel's underlings were, but it went deeper than that. I knew Thom had held no respect for Samuel Locke, and neither did I. We were simply too terrified to act on any impulse to refuse his demands; any stray thought about deserting his employment or of defiance was always smothered by his silent authority, the hunger in his bottomless gaze.

Hand to hand combat for a Persuader was a peculiar sight, not just because it was decidedly a Sentry practice, but also because of the way Samuel was moving. Silently, with the grace of a *leopardo,* using his Shifting like a third, extended arm. He was a born fighter, I realized with a jolt. A warrior. Which made me wonder…

I shook myself free of the thought. No. It wasn't possible. He was a Persuader through and through, and a Purist at that, with all the arrogance and scorn and refinement of one.

I heard the click of a gun being cocked somewhere in the tangle of limbs, followed by the sound of three shots in quick succession. The space around the two—shooter and shootee—was cleared in an instant, and I saw Samuel, his hand up, three bullets suspended in the air, almost touching his fingertips. His hand clenched into a fist, and the bullets collapsed in on themselves and blew away into silvery dust. The gun followed suit, much to the shooter's alarm. He stepped back, thrusting out, rather feebly, his other hand in an attempt to Shift Samuel off of his feet.

Samuel's other hand shot forward to join the first, and the air between them rippled with the mounting pressure. The outcross swallowed thickly, his Adam's apple sliding up and down once. He didn't stand a chance.

And then the decidedly unlucky man was sent flying, into the wall at his back, which was less of a wall and more of a floor to ceiling window that spanned the entirety of the room. He crashed through it with a tremendous sound, causing all the others to turn and gawk at what had happened. Samuel did not gawk. Instead, he simply looked on very calmly at the jagged edges of the hole he had just opened in his once-impressive glass wall and said, "Someone go fish him out of the koi pond. And then have that glass replaced. It's rather an eye sore now when moments before it was somewhat dramatic."

When the bleeding, breathing punching bags had dispersed, I was left alone in the room with Samuel as he strode across the room to examine the damage he had caused but was undoubtedly not going to assume any responsibility for.

I cleared my throat, hesitant. "Should I get the broom?"

He was silent, his profile gilded by sunlight, though his eyes remained the color of deep shadow.

Steeling myself, I skittered forward a little, toward him. His face was drawn. "If you don't mind me asking, *señor*, what exactly are you thinking about?"

Samuel's hands were clasped neatly behind his back as he watched the hazy sunrise. "Tomorrow is young Jennifer's Embracement, as I recall. Just think for a moment what this could bring about, Cira." His gaze turned to me, thoughtful and deadly. "If she chooses to become a Sentry, then she will undoubtedly join Natalia's ranks and her pathetic stronghold will continue to vex me further. If she decides to become a Persuader like her dearest father, then she will be in a position of power. Too much power. *Don't you understand?*" he snapped, suddenly livid. He grabbed my shoulders and I had to bite my tongue to not cry out at the pain. "*She's strong.* She'll grow stronger. I haven't met another Unavowed yet with her kind of potential. Her father was able to *kill* with only a simple touch at her age. Rumors have spread about her own gift, a gift that would render her practically immortal with practice. I can't allow her to become any more powerful than she is."

When he finally released me, I cleared my throat and said, "There's something I have to tell you—"

"I suspected as much," he said, softly, his hand taking mine in one swift movement. He held my wrist lightly between his forefinger and thumb, turning it so my palm faced the floor. "Your hands have been shaking all morning."

Nothing was beyond his notice. If he wasn't so perceptive, then I would've certainly kept my mouth shut about the matter. But I *had* to tell the truth now that his watchful, unblinking stare was on me, as if the look alone could reach in and drag it right out of my mouth. "My mission was unsuccessful," I blurted, watching as his face went from blandly confident to something much darker.

His voice was as calm as ever, but resonating something colder than that, much like how icebergs drifting in the arctic seas were hiding a far greater mass under the waves. "Cira, Cira," he chided me, as if I was a child. "It seems the one person I thought I could count on has disappointed me at last. Tell me, tell me how you could've *possibly* messed this up. I thought you were reliable. Quick. Efficient."

He gripped my chin in one hand, and I could feel something at the base of my skull, like a metal clamp squeezing down on my neck with bone-crushing force. I gasped in agony as the pain bloomed across my vision, tingeing everything red.

"What—what's happening to me?" I choked out, and would've slid to the floor had Samuel not have been holding me upright against him.

"If you're really so curious, your cerebral arteries are constricting and depriving the brain of oxygen." He shrugged, and said in a voice without inflection, "In a word? You're dying."

"You're...a sociopath." I reached out to grab his shirtfront. "The second explosion killed an innocent. A boy not even sixteen."

"Innocent?" Samuel crooned. "Oh, but no Sentry is *innocent*. If he hadn't killed already, he would've. Eventually there would be blood on his hands just like the rest of them."

"And yours...are so...*clean*," I managed to get out, my lungs feeling as if they were about to burst. But it was more than just my lungs. It was as if my whole body was shutting down, as if I was dying from the inside out.

Samuel smiled wickedly. "The lives I've taken were for a greater cause, but what of the lives *they've* taken? What cause do *they* serve? The Sentries claim all that they do is for the protection of human beings, the lesser species, but I know better. It is because they crave the slaughter of their enemies, and nothing else." He scowled. "But I'm getting away from the topic at hand. You still haven't told me about the first one. The one meant to destroy the Farrier girl. The benefactor."

My hands encircled his wrist, feebly trying to wrench it from my face. "I don't—I don't know! *Suéltame. Suéltame, monstruo—*"

"Answer the question!" he roared, all traces of serenity gone from his voice. "How did the girl survive?"

"Vincent Hallows," I wheezed, feeling the cold glass against my back and shuddering at the thought of being thrown through it as the other outcross had been. "He...I don't know what he did. He saved them both, somehow."

Samuel leaned in close, his eyes narrowing into slits, giving the impression of having no eyes at all within the sockets. "You seem to be forgetting something: Vincent is an outcross. Contaminated."

I bit back a reply that surely would have sent me flying into the decorative pond below and whispered, hoarsely, "It's what I saw."

Finally, the throbbing agony subsided, and I fell back against the wall, Samuel gripping my shoulders again, though this time much lighter, more possessively. My legs were unsteady beneath me, my hands resuming their shaking.

"Cira," he whispered, against my ear. His breath hit the side of my face and I couldn't help but wince. He felt my reaction and laughed, savoring my terror. "Now, we don't want another slip-up like this, do we?" When I didn't answer, his voice took on a more menacing edge, the words driven into my eardrums like nails. *"Do we?"*

"No," I gasped, turning my face away.

"You should feel thankful for that pretty face, *querida*. That and the fact that I still need you may be the only things keeping you alive."

He released me, and I slumped to the floor, my breath scraping through my lungs, my vision swimming with spots.

Samuel turned to go, and then thought better of it for a moment, whirling back to me. "But if you wear out your value, remember that I can always do to you what I did to poor Thom." He tapped the side of his head.

"Tenlo en cuenta."

JENNY

At first there was nothing. I was reminded of the first time I had ever seen Cavea, with its infinite blackness and its infinite possibilities. I realized that in this place I came to a reversed conclusion.

The world around me was bleak and dark and seemed as if it was closing in around me, its boundaries sliding closer and closer together until I would soon be crushed between them.

I slammed my eyes shut, trying to take a deep breath and finding I could not. When my eyes flew open again, there was not blankness and nothingness but gold and silver, red and blue. Persuaders. Sentries. On one side of the room stood Liam, Vincent, and a few faces I half-recognized, many more I did not. This side was much adorned, glittering like a jewel. The fallen angel statue dominated the center of the room, though it seemed to be alive, Lucifer's eyes glowing red, the snakes slithering and hissing around him like living chains. On the other side of the room, which was simple and dimly lit, stood Taylor, and, next to him, Natalia with the members of her stronghold. But there were also, just behind them, the Sentries I had seen attack and kill someone in the street. One of them looked up at me, smiling, his teeth as pointed as a shark's.

"You don't *really* have to choose, you know," whispered a voice at my ear. I whirled to face Samuel, his eyes glowing as red as the eyes of the statue. His hands were folded behind his back, as he pretended to be civil. As he pretended to be human. "I can take all of this away," he said, his burning eyes taking on a hypnotic edge, like a cobra's. "Why tear yourself in half, Jennifer? You care for Taylor, yet you care also for your father and Vincent, and you hate the thought of choosing between them, no? It's painful, this life. You're so young and already you've been through so much. Why bring more suffering on yourself? How much of it can you take before it's too much?"

I set my jaw, determined to not let myself buy into his game, though—game or not—I couldn't deny that what he was saying was the simple truth. "I don't need your advice. And I don't want it."

Samuel sighed, pacing around me to glance from Persuader to Sentry, side to side, as if assessing. "Hm. It rather seems as if you *do* need me."

"To do what?" I shot at him. "You've done enough."

"Have I?" he replied, turning back to me with something in his hands. It was a knife, gleaming like the surface of polluted water. He held it out to me.

"I don't understand," I said, after a startled pause. "Why are you handing the knife to *me?*"

"Oh, but it's not a knife." His words were spoken softly, yet I couldn't help but notice the weight beneath them, the poison within them. His eyes blazed like hellfire. "Suffering has made you close yourself off. Now's your chance to open yourself *up.*"

He took my wrist and pushed up my sleeve to reveal the map of veins along the pale inside of my arm, and to my horror I saw that they were beginning to change color. The blue lines underneath the skin had begun to turn as black as ink.

"It's not a knife," he repeated. "It's a solution."

I awoke with a scream, my legs tangled into the bed sheets, my t-shirt sticking to my back with sweat despite the chill of the house.

My chest heaved as I glanced about the large, dark room, searching for movement within shadows, for the gleam of red eyes or the edge of a knife. The dim, bluish light of early morning trickled in through the window on the far side of the room, and, satisfied that it had all been just a dream, I laid back against the pillows.

I felt Taylor's aura prickling at the nape of my neck before the door opened. He slipped inside, his brow creased with concern. "Jenny?" he whispered. "Are you alright? Your scream woke me. I thought…" His eyes scanned the darkness, just as mine had a moment before.

I sat up. "I'm fine. It was just a bad dream."

This only seemed to alleviate his concern marginally, and he crossed the room to sit at the foot of my bed. "What was it about?"

I could still hear the echo of the words, *It's a solution.* A tremor pulsed through me. "I don't want to talk about it."

Taylor was quiet for a moment. "Do you remember when I told you about my tracking ability?"

I nodded. "I threw Vince at a door."

He smiled a little at that and continued, quietly. "You never asked me why. Why I came to your room that morning."

My breathing slowed, and I forced myself to stay very still. "Okayyy."

What a weird thing to fixate on, I couldn't help but think. "Why, then?"

His hand tugged through his hair self-consciously. "I…I couldn't sleep. I was lying awake for hours, thinking about…well, thinking about you." At this declaration my breathing stopped entirely. "After everything that happened, I couldn't get the thought of you in actual danger out of my mind; I was driven crazy by it. What was almost worse was when you came back with Liam and for a moment you looked *happy*. Like you *enjoyed* being one of them. Like you…"

"Taylor," I said, softly, trying to catch his eye. He seemed so insecure lately, so afraid that I would turn on him in a heartbeat. "I don't enjoy manipulating people. The part I liked was spending time with my dad, for once. He's been absent from my life for so long. I just…I missed him so much, it hurt sometimes. You understand, don't you?"

Of course, he had separated himself from his parents by his own decision. But that didn't change the fact that he still sometimes wished things had been different, as he'd once told me. He nodded. "I understand." His eyes held something in them, something searching and hopeful. "You said you didn't like taking from people, didn't like controlling them. Does that mean you—?"

"Taylor!" I snapped, and immediately regretted it when I saw the hurt in his face. I sighed, softening. "Please, don't say it. Please. Just for five minutes, I don't want to talk about it, okay?"

He nodded again. "Sure, whatever you want."

His gaze fell downward, and I couldn't stop the wave of sympathy that rushed through me at the sight of him like that. "It's just…" I began, in a voice that was barely audible, "I don't think I could ever really *kill* someone. Even if it was the right thing to do."

Taylor looked up at me, sliding closer so that he could really look at me. "I hope you never have to, and I'm sorry I tried to convince you otherwise," he said at last, looking resigned. "But I do hope that you would choose what you *want to choose*. Not because of me. Not because of Vince or your father or Natalia, but because it's what you think is best for *you.*"

I leaned forward, planting a light kiss on his cheek. I laughed a little when I saw the blush bloom across his neck, spilling quickly into his face. "Thanks," I murmured.

He stood, smiling crookedly. "Any time." His tone was much more serious than the goofy grin suggested. I remembered the two of us alone in

St. Ambrose, back before any of this had happened, watching the sunset. And Taylor had looked at me and said, with the same gravity, that he would do anything for me. Even after all the time that had passed, I realized I still didn't deserve him.

Taylor walked across the room, whistling to himself out of tune, leaving me to wonder what I meant to him, and what he meant to me, and if he was right when he said this world would tear us apart.

I sat upright, unable to bear the sight of him leaving after the thought. "Wait."

He turned, and there was something unidentifiable in his eyes. "Yeah?"

I smoothed the covers, feeling a little selfish when I asked him, "Can you stay? Just for a little while? I don't think I can handle being alone. Not after…"

"The nightmare," he finished.

I nodded, unable to look at him. "But you don't have to if you don't want to," I mumbled, picking at a loose thread. "You know what? Forget I even asked. It was stupid."

But he was already back across the room, his arms folded as he leaned against the bedpost. "Jenny, come on," he said, rolling his eyes. "When have I ever said no to you? Besides, you talk in your sleep, and it's hilarious. I definitely don't want to miss *that.*"

He came around to the other side of the bed, throwing himself down unceremoniously next to me, his shoulder knocking against mine. My face began to burn, but whether it was from the shame I felt because of what he had said or something else I couldn't be sure. "I suck, don't I?" I asked, abruptly, eliciting a laugh from him.

"A little," he allowed, his gaze swinging sideways to look at me. "But you make up for it, occasionally."

I was somewhat surprised by this. "How?"

He reached over to tuck an escapist curl behind my ear, and I was suddenly aware of how I must've looked to him, disheveled and still ghostly pale from the shock of the nightmare. His smile was saintly as he replied, "Not telling."

I made a noise of frustration. "Jerk."

"Hey," Taylor said, in defense of his infuriating secrecy, "I have to keep that air of mystery about me, remember?"

I sighed, my hand finding his in the dark as easily as I would've found my own. "I like you better when you're genuine."

"What if I'm genuinely mysterious?"

"I don't believe you," I said, my voice dropping lower, my fingers squeezing tighter around his.

"Then I guess that makes me genuinely a liar," he whispered back, making me snicker. Taylor turned onto his side to look at me, our hands still intertwined. "Jenny?"

"Yeah?"

"Good night."

"It's already morning," I pointed out, gesturing vaguely to where a rectangle of faded light painted the floor.

"In that case," he said, flopping onto his back again, "good luck."

Bright daylight spilled into my room by the time I opened my eyes again. For a moment, I was struck by how rested I felt, how it felt as if I'd slept better than I had in years, despite the nightmare.

Then I glanced to my right and saw Taylor, still asleep, his face peaceful and his hair as messy as ever. Our hands were still touching.

And then Laura burst in, disrupting any sort of peace I had felt seconds before. She picked up rogue articles of clothing strewn across the room and threw them into a basket tucked under one arm, not even looking at me as she spoke. "Up and at 'em, lazy girl. Busy day today. Busy day *tomorrow*, too, but I'm sure you're already—"

She stopped babbling about my ever-demanding schedule when she saw Taylor, who was now also wide awake thanks to Laura's grand entrance, blinking rapidly as if he had suddenly found himself before a firing squad. He attempted to put his feet on the floor but only succeeded in tumbling out of the bed completely. He struck the ground with a loud, "Oomph!"

Her eyes swept from me to Taylor and back again, probably probing our thoughts for any indication of a secret love affair, I supposed. I tried my best to clear my mind of attics and window ledges, as to not give her the wrong idea. After a moment, she only laughed a little to herself and bustled out of the room, basket in tow. I thought I heard her mutter something like, "The poor boy" before she left, but I couldn't be sure.

"What was that about?" Taylor asked, when she'd gone.

I stood up, running my fingers through my hair, looking down at his sprawled form on the floor for a moment before glancing back at the empty doorway. "I don't know."

As we made our way down the stairs for breakfast, I couldn't help but notice the fading black in Taylor's hair, the way his eyes found the front door, as if he was thinking about Charles's discovery of his identity like I was. *I'm sure that karma will catch up to him, eventually.*

"Taylor?"

"Mm?" He seemed distracted, almost, looking distant as we crossed the foyer and headed for the dining hall.

"You aren't...I mean, are you okay? The whole thing with Charles yesterday—"

He held up his hand, shaking his head. "I don't want to talk about Charles Monroe. It was only a matter of time. Anyway, I don't think we have anything to fear from him. He's greedy, and what he does he does to the orders of the hand that fills his pocket."

"So you aren't bothered by it?" I asked, unconvinced by the way his voice sounded. Strained, slightly angered.

"No," he said, too sharply.

I wanted to press him further about it, but we had already walked into the dining area, and both Vince and Liam were already seated, Vince doing what teenage boys did and stuffing his face, Liam doing what middle-aged recluses did and reading a thick novel while a plate of pancakes stood by, uneaten.

"Mornun, J'ny" Vince called to me cheerfully, his words muffled around a large bite of pancake, drowned in syrup. Taylor looked positively envious. Vince swallowed, casting a bored look over at him as if he would rather forget Taylor was even there at all. "And bedraggled friend."

Taylor sighed, taking a seat next to me, resigned to the fact that it was probably the most flattering of titles he could hope to receive from Vince. "I just hope to God there are chocolate chips in those pancakes," he muttered, and I couldn't help but smile despite his sour mood. He never stayed in them for long, anyway.

"Today's the sixth," Liam noted, without looking up from his book.

"Profound," Vincent remarked. "What staggering announcement will you think of next?"

Now he did look up, albeit to cast a withering glare at his adopted son. "Here's one: Tomorrow is the seventh. Jenny's Embracement. And I expect you to at least make an effort to suppress the sarcasm, Vincent."

He crinkled his brow, looking aghast. "If I can't subtly let people know just how absolutely ridiculous they are, then you *cannot* expect me to put up with them for any extended amount of time. Simple as that."

"Well, then, just be direct. Observe." I cleared my throat. "Vince, you're being ridiculous."

"Absolutely ridiculous, actually," Taylor added, still glancing over his shoulder for Laura.

"In any case," Liam said, "I'd like a moment after breakfast to discuss things with Jenny. That means no interruptions or distractions. Do I make myself clear?"

"Oh, yes, crystal," Vince consented. "I need to practice my waltz, anyway. I just might use Taylor as my partner."

Taylor made a choking sound next to me. "Like hell."

Before Vince could arrange any other romantic activity for them to pass the time with, Laura came and set down a fresh plate of pancakes for Taylor and me. Taylor dug in like a rabid dog that hadn't eaten in days, making the occasional noise of contentment as he ate. He was especially delighted to discover chocolate chips within their fluffy depths.

"It was almost as if she *knew,"* he pronounced, dousing his breakfast generously with syrup.

I twisted to look at her as she retreated back toward the kitchen. Her face was turned a little to the side, and she smiled ever so slightly when she caught me looking.

I turned back. "Weird, huh?"

I made a mental note to see if I could one way or another get her to confess her clairvoyance, after I was finished my talk with Liam. At least that would be *one* thing in my life resolved, if nothing else.

Liam waited patiently for me in his office, reclined back in his chair, staring vacantly toward the window. He wasn't exactly looking *out* of it, or even *at* it. No, it was apparent from the glassiness of his gaze that he wasn't really seeing anything at all.

"Liam?" I asked. When he did not respond, I moved toward him, shutting the door quietly behind me. "Dad?"

I laid a tentative hand on his shoulder, causing him to start. "What?

Oh, sorry. I was…I'm feeling a bit preoccupied."

"I can tell," was my reply as I settled into a chair across from him. "What is it you wanted to talk to me about?"

He sighed, and once again I couldn't help but notice the lines in his weary face and, silhouetted by the window, the gray in his hair. "The Persuader mind is capable of remembering many things, even from early childhood," he said, taking a seat, his eyes darting to the picture that still rested on his desk. "Am I correct to assume the same of yours?"

I nodded. Whenever I needed to be reminded of her, I could always remember my mother's words verbatim, though I'd always just assumed it was because she consistently said things worth remembering.

"Do you remember when…?" Liam paused, rubbing his chin and taking a deep breath. His hand shook. He tried again, repeating himself. "Do you remember when you were six years old and we went on that camping trip, how you got lost in the woods?"

My mind churned, overturning things, things I didn't even know I could recall, with ease. I found the memory, tucked and filed away with the rest of the darker childhood experiences that were better left untouched. "I was terrified," I murmured. "I was trying to chase a rabbit and ended up in the middle of the forest, and I couldn't see the cabin anymore."

Liam's face was grim. "I was terrified, too." Our gazes met, and I saw that he meant it. "When we found you, you were curled up under a tree crying your eyes out and your face was streaked with dirt. But the important thing was, you were safe."

Safe. When I tried to imagine what that felt like, I was surprised when I came up empty-handed. Even prior to learning about the Persuader world, my life before hadn't exactly been safe. It was hard to feel safe when the person you depended on most in the world sat you down when you were thirteen and told you she had cancer. It was hard to feel safe when at sixteen she told you that the cancer might not go away. "Why are you telling me this?" I asked.

"Because, since that day—since the day you were born, even—my greatest fear has been the thought of you losing your way. And of me losing *you.*" I knew what was coming next, but somehow his words still came as a shock when he said, "Which is why I must urge you, *beg* you, to become a Persuader."

I stood. "Dad, that's not fair of you to ask and you know it."

"I am only trying to keep you from living a life that puts you in constant danger." Now he stood, as well. "I'm not blaming the Sentries for how they are, how they live, but you've seen for yourself. A boy's life was claimed in the blink of an eye, and there was nothing anyone could've done to save him. There's no way I can keep you from getting hurt if you throw yourself in among those—those contentious people! Conflict is unavoidable when you're a Sentry. Samuel will make an easy target of you."

"'Contentious people?'" I gaped at him. "You mean Mom? You mean the woman you *married?*"

Liam blanched as if he had just realized fully what it was he had said. Clumsily, he reached out to me but I flinched away from him, and he dropped his hand.

Without another word, I left the room and didn't look back at him, not even when I heard my mother's picture knocked from the desk by an angry swipe of his hand. It struck the floor with a dull crack, the sound almost lost in the dull crack of the slamming door.

For the better part of the day, which probably should've been spent preparing for the unavoidable, I was in my room staring up at the ceiling, sulking about things I couldn't change.

My father had always been opinionated; it was one of the reasons he'd left, I was pretty sure. But that didn't absolve him of his prejudice, his hypocrisy. Obviously, he hadn't cared much about the lines of division between the two circles when he'd married my mom, so why would he— *how could he*—try to convince me now that one was more desirable an option than the other? As if either side could rightfully call itself *better.* I should've anticipated this. Change was hard; it was easier to stay entrenched in a single way of living. Why had I ever thought my father would be any different from anyone else? How could I have believed that he'd truly *transformed himself* into a better man just because I had dreamed of it happening ever since I was nine years old? The people around you did not metamorphosize on a whim, and to go on the rest of my life hoping otherwise wouldn't benefit anyone.

"Losing an illusion, are we? Or is it that you're finding a truth?"

I spun around to see Laura standing in the doorway, her eyes bright with the unfathomable sadness of an old woman who'd felt much of it in her life.

I blinked, smothering the initial shock I always felt after one of the inscrutable maid's strangely clairvoyant suggestions. "It's funny," I said, finding my voice. "I've never really been able to tell the difference."

"You're a clever girl, you know. Not even Vince had any inkling of suspicion about me until Liam finally told him the truth. It's good that you can distinguish between what's real and what isn't, even when others can't." She sighed, taking a step into the room. "The gift of clairvoyance is not one that is particularly...welcomed. Imagine what it would be like if I'd allowed myself to become all that I could've been, instead of resigning myself to a life of safety. I could've secured a place in the Adjudication, even, if I wanted it." She shook her head firmly, straightening her uniform with a crisp twitch of her hand. "No, that would've caused trouble for me. That would've put the people I loved into danger. *Myself* I could've protected, but my family...they would've been at the mercy of my enemies. When someone has power, it's only human nature for others to seek to eliminate it, or to seize it for themselves. Any way to tip the scales back into place. No one likes to feel like his way of life is at stake, after all."

I fixed my gaze carefully on her face. "Why are you telling me these things, Laura?"

The old woman stared off into the nothingness just over my right shoulder, two deep grooves forming along the sides of her mouth as her lips pursed. "I've wasted my life living in constant worry, hiding my abilities, seeing opportunities pass me by..." Her steady gaze found mine. "Don't live like that. Don't let yourself live as I have."

After she left, I stayed awake for some time, well after midnight, mulling over those words. My Embracement was in less than twenty-four hours, and on the subject of which faction I would pledge my permanent allegiance to I found it was not unlike tossing a bucket down into a well and pulling back only air. Again and again, I threw the bucket down into the well, and again and again it returned as dry as bone.

Half of me wanted to stay at the mansion, to stay with my father and rebuild the relationship between us, to stay with Vince, who was dark and brooding and sarcastic, but also someone I saw great good in. He needed someone to understand him, to patch up his old wounds, and I almost felt as if I would be abandoning him if I were to leave. The Persuader life, at first, had seemed horrible to me, a society that glorified self-importance and decadence, encouraged unrestricted kleptomania and taking advantage of the weak. But I had come to recognize it as misguided, a gifted people who truly believed in their rightness and felt a passion for knowing all they could about the world and for testing their limits. I thought, maybe, if I decided to stay, that I could help at least *some* of these people see the difference between ambition and corruption, as I had the rare advantage of coming from humble human roots.

But then the other half of me wanted to venture out, to run away with Taylor and find a far away Sentry stronghold to blend into, safe from Samuel and any other Persuader who wanted to kill us or use us. We would build a new life there. The second I had first stepped foot inside Natalia's stronghold, I had been shocked not just by the impoverished state in which all the Sentries lived in, but also by the burning hostility of their glares, the intensity of their animosity. How anyone could have so much hatred, I just couldn't bring myself to understand at all. But now I knew better. Now I knew that they had just as much a passion for righteousness as Persuaders had for knowledge, and that there were times when they felt something *above* hatred. There were times when they felt only a pure sense of justice, and an all-consuming intent to deliver it.

The question was, which faction was I willing to sacrifice the most for? Choosing the Persuaders would mean giving up Taylor, and maybe even a piece of my morality. Choosing the Sentries would mean bloodying my hands, leaving my father, one of the only members of my family I had left, and leaving—

I heard a soft chiming noise through the floorboards, piano notes being struck with deft precision. The sound was like heartbreak and moonlight interweaved.

Vince.

Without consciously realizing it, I was already making my way down the dimly lit hallway, to the sweeping curl of the staircase, the steps cold on my bare feet.

As I quietly inched down the stairs, I caught a glimpse of Vince's dark head, bent over the keys, his shoulders tense in concentration. The glossy black of the piano was at odds with his fair-skinned neck, his long, pale hands as they glided back and forth, barely making contact with the instrument before him. The sight, and the sound, was achingly beautiful, enough to make me hesitate on the last step.

"It's awful late, isn't it?" Vince murmured, just loud enough to be heard over the music. His voice was low and velvety, thick with exhaustion.

"I could say the same to you," I returned, moving to a place just behind him. I peered over his shoulder. "What are you playing? It's beautiful."

"Is it?" he inquired, only half-focused on what I was saying. "It doesn't have a name yet."

"You wrote it?" I was speechless, but I supposed that was mostly because I hadn't had formal music lessons of any kind, myself.

"The term 'wrote' would imply that I have recorded each note down on paper, which,"—he turned his head to the side to raise a fine eyebrow at me—"I have not."

"Oh," I said, somewhat lamely, looking down at the waxy mahogany floorboards.

His focus shifted back to his hands, and he continued playing. "Anyway, what are you doing up? Big day tomorrow, you know. Well, I suppose it's *today*, now, isn't it?"

"I…I couldn't sleep. I've been thinking too much, I guess."

"And to ward off insomnia you decided to bedevil me, of course," he snapped, unreasonably bad-tempered. "What, is the boyfriend not around for you to complain to? If you think I'm going to sit here and listen to you talk about your problems all night, you're quite mistaken."

I ground my teeth together. God, I hated when he acted like this. "Sorry for interrupting your sulk-fest, then, Your Highness." He didn't respond, which only fueled my irritation. "You really don't have to be so cruel and unpleasant *all the time*. You may *act* like you can't stand me, but I think we both know that's not true. Need I remind you that, not too long ago, *you* kissed *me*—"

The song cut off in a clamor of sour notes. "You're one to talk of *cruelty*, Jenny."

"What's that supposed to mean?" I demanded.

Vince spun around on the piano bench, so he faced me. His hazel eyes were molten. "Hm, let me think—Oh, yes! That funny little tête-à-tête of ours when you all but spat in my face. I know I pretended not to care, but guess what? I did. You treated that moment as if it meant nothing. You treated *me* like I was nothing."

"You're not nothing to me, Vince—"

He grabbed my hand, holding it to his chest. I could feel his pulse in my fingertips, as deeply resonating as his music. "Then *what* am I? What is so wrong with the idea of *us*? I thought…" He swallowed, with visible difficulty. I knew I'd done something wrong in pushing him away that morning he'd kissed me on the window sill, ruined one of the only times he'd ever been perfectly honest with me. With effort, he continued, "Well, I don't know what I thought. But I could make you happy. If I'm not *nothing* to you, then at least I'm *something*. Please don't tell me you can't see it."

Of course I could see it. I could see it perfectly, the two of us together. I could see my decision to become a Persuader. I could see my whole life with him, and, admittedly, it seemed like a good life. But I was just a confused and self-centered and indecisive seventeen-year-old girl trapped between two walls that were slowly sliding together. And I didn't want to think about what was *beyond* those walls; I just wanted to figure out how to not get crushed.

"Vince…" I began, haltingly.

His eyes darkened, as if he could read the uncertainty on my face. He turned away, idly pressing keys again, the tempo much slower, the octave much deeper. "I understand," he said, quietly, his eyes closed. "I just wanted to make you aware of the possibilities, is all."

"You didn't have to," I said, leaning against the side of the instrument.

We both were silent for a while, the only sound flowing delicately from the piano, a sound like water at night, like early winter, like twilight approaching. All beautiful things, though beautiful things that elicited peculiar feelings of sadness.

"It's for you, you know. This song. Every song. All of them have been for you." The final notes hung suspended in the air around us, reminding me strangely of the silver tinsel my mother used to hang on the walls during Christmas time.

I looked down at him, starting to reach toward him but stopping myself, my hand frozen in the air for a moment before retracting back to my side. "Then why does it sound so sad?"

Vince pushed himself up from the piano, sliding the cover closed slowly so that it didn't make a sound. "You tell me."

He wandered off toward the stairs, leaving me alone with the oncoming dawn bleeding through the windows.

I hardly registered the significance of opening my eyes and seeing the morning light creep across the ceiling; for a single, precious moment I was unable to fully grasp onto any memory from the day before.

And then, with heart-stopping clarity, I remembered, and it felt as if a trap door had given way beneath me, and I was falling into an emotional cellar where no one feeling was distinguishable from the next. It was like groping around in a dark, crowded room for a lightswitch, the only reward for one's efforts being a sharp elbow to the stomach.

Everything had been leading up to this day.

And, somehow, everyone seemed to have the solution for my problems but me.

20

STRANGER

Despite the occasion, Liam and Vince (both probably still furious with me, I supposed, though in decidedly differing ways) were careful to ignore me while everything was being arranged for the Embracement. Phone calls had to be made, Charles had to be grudgingly reimbursed for his efforts, and I had nothing to do the whole half of the day but mope around and let the anxiety pick away at me little by little like a carrion bird until nothing was left of my conviction but the fragile bones—that is, if I even had anything so fanciful as *conviction* in the first place.

It was in this state that Taylor found me, as he was in the habit of showing up, genie-like almost, when I needed him most.

"Uh, Happy Birthday, Jenny," he said, leaning against the railing as I was. "I guess."

I pulled my jacket closer about me, plucking a petal from one of the purplish flowers growing up the side of the wrought iron balustrade and twirling it between my fingers. "You know, it's the *strangest thing*, but it doesn't feel happy at all."

He sighed, his breath curling away in a white cloud. "That's what's so unfair about this whole thing. The Adjudication forgets, I think, that we're human beings. All it's worried about is corralling people into these…these *pens*—as if we're livestock, or something, and not people."

"It's not just the Adjudication. It seems like everyone around me wants me to be the version of myself that suits him best. I mean…I know that didn't make any sense—"

"Makes perfect sense," Taylor disagreed. "When I was preparing for my Embracement, my parents were *so certain* that I was their perfect son, that I would become a Persuader and marry a nice Persuader girl and have nice Persuader children. But I wasn't that son. I couldn't be."

"You might be the bravest person I know," I said, and his eyes found my own, widening in surprise. "I mean it. It couldn't have been easy, making the kind of decision that you did."

"If you're half as brave as I think you are," he returned, wrapping a long arm around my shoulders, "tonight will be momentous."

I smiled up at him, turning so that we faced each other. His arm still circled around me, his hand dropping to press into my back, urging me even closer. "You really think that?"

Taylor looked down at me, his hair falling into his eyes. Unable to help myself, I reached up to push it back. His other hand caught mine before I could return it to my side. "Jenny," he murmured, "you make everything momentous."

Unexpectedly, he dipped his head so that his lips grazed mine, causing a million jolts of electricity to fire underneath my skin at once. I pulled away, more abruptly than I'd planned. He seemed more hurt by this than surprised.

"Taylor," I said, fighting to keep my voice even. "We can't keep playing this game with each other. We can't keep saying we're friends and then...and then contradict that a second later. I have to know *exactly* how you feel, Taylor. With everything that's at stake right now, I have to know it's not for nothing that we keep doing this."

His shock dissipated in that same instant, leaving behind only an intensity that, for a moment, made my breath catch in my throat. After a pause, he just sighed, once again narrowing the distance between us as he bent to rest his forehead against mine. "Why do you think I've stuck around for so long, Jenny? I've always been *right here*, even when I knew you didn't feel the same way as I did. You still don't, but I can accept that." I opened my mouth to say something, anything, but he continued, fervently, "Do you even realize how much it kills me to constantly feel as if I'm putting you in unnecessary danger by just being *near* you? But you asked me to stay, and that's what I'm doing, because sometimes you need me almost as much as I need you, even if you won't admit it."

His confession left me reeling. For so long, I had envisioned Taylor as safety, Taylor as solace, never realizing that he didn't want to be either of those things. "All this time?" I asked.

"All this time," he said. "And I never minded a second of it. I love you too much for that."

He had said it. Right there, he had said the words "I love you". My heart swelled and twisted inside my chest at the same time, the sensation somehow more painful than I expected it would be. Maybe because I already knew—knew instinctually, somehow—how this would end. I knew the casualty report before the battle, and it made me sick to my stomach to understand that all the sacrifice would yield no discernible victory for anyone. Further loss of ground could be avoided, certainly, but to gain anything, to advance a single step forward, would be impossible.

"Taylor, I just wish that…" The passionate violet in his eyes began to fracture into a colder blue, his throat working as if he was dry-swallowing an exceptionally large pill. "Everything has been so confusing and I never know if…if what I'm feeling is genuine or if it's just what I think I'm *supposed* to feel."

He looked at me steadily, but his true feelings were given away by the hard set of his jaw. "I see."

I felt acutely desperate, desperate to curb the casualties even when I knew the situation was hopeless. "What do you want me to say?" I whispered, my voice rough. "I'm so tangled up in all of this insanity, Taylor. I don't know what it is you want me to say right now."

With a shake of his head, he touched my cheek and murmured back, "Nothing. Don't say anything at all."

He kissed me hard this time, the pressure of his palm against the back of my head making it clear he wasn't about to let me go any time soon.

The black door banged open, and Liam was visible in the doorway, his green eyes still lifting toward us as he spoke. "Jenny, it's time to—" He stopped talking when he saw us, knowing the truth even as we quickly sprung apart. He could probably see it written all over our faces, bleeding into our expressions like spilled ink. "…leave."

"Dad, I—"

He held up a hand to silence me, slowly walking toward Taylor. "I told you to stay away from her."

I looked between the two. "Taylor, what is he talking about?"

Taylor stood perfectly straight, his face betraying nothing, drawn like a soldier's. Without looking away from my father, he said, "And I told you that I couldn't."

"Get out of my house," Liam barked. The discarded pots lying around the balcony shattered all at once, dirt and fragments of terracotta spilling out onto the bed of white flowers.

"What did you say?" I demanded, causing Liam to finally turn and look at me.

Liam's hands clenched so tightly his knuckles whitened. "You heard me. He can't stay here."

"Then I'm going with him," I said, frightening myself with the knowledge that I was completely and unreservedly serious.

Liam took a step back, looking betrayed. "You can't just *run away* and think it will solve anything."

"And why not?" I asked. *"You* did." Some cruel part of me almost enjoyed watching the startled anger flash across his face.

Before he could shoot something back at me, Taylor spoke, in a voice that was worse than my father's anger. It was cold, uncompromising. "He's right. You can't come with me, Jenny."

Even Liam looked surprised now. I paused for a moment, trying to reason with what he had said. Suddenly, the smiling Taylor who had confessed his love to me was gone, replaced by a stranger. "What do you mean I can't go with you? You're being ridiculous—"

He took me by the shoulders, his violet eyes boring into mine. "I'm not." His grip tightened. "I'm trying to protect you."

"I don't need any protecting!" I burst out, losing my temper. I tore away from his hands, glancing between Taylor to Liam as I spoke, not sure who, exactly, I was addressing. "When will you realize that I'm not some helpless little girl? I can make decisions for myself without anyone else telling me what I *should* do and what I *shouldn't* do or what I *ought* to do."

Taylor frowned. "Maybe someone *should* make your decisions for you," he said, without emotion, not even registering the look I gave him. "Because you never seem to make the right one."

Furious, I threw out my hand at him, Shifting him into the balcony railing, for a second not even caring if he dropped twenty or so feet toward the ground. The ancient banister groaned and warped backwards, bending him back with it, before it finally gave way and he fell to the pavement below. Before he made contact, and to my slight disappointment, he Shifted and landed lightly on his feet, in a crouch. He looked up at me for only a moment with something like astonishment—which I found to be ridiculous, given the circumstance—before he started off toward the line of woods on the far end of the yard.

Cursing, I followed suit, leaving Liam standing there, silent and rigid. I landed much less gracefully, pitching forward onto my elbows. Ignoring the scrapes, I scrambled after his quickly retreating form, now just a silhouette against the dark trees.

I threw out my hand, causing him to stumble slightly. He turned, but, still unsatisfied, I threw out my hand again, knocking him back two steps.

"You're such a *liar,* Taylor!" I shouted, still charging toward him.

"A liar?" he demanded, livid now, as I was. "What are you talking about?"

He stumbled back three more steps. "You know *what.*" I could feel my face grow hot with anger and humiliation. "You told me that you would be here for as long as I needed you. I *still need you,* Taylor!"

"Well, sorry to disappoint!" he shouted back, with a sneering animosity so unlike him I wondered if this was a dream, and that any moment now and I would just wake up. "But you and I both know I don't belong here. I never did. *Look* at me, Jenny. Really look. I'm a murderer, like Charles Monroe said. A Sentry. A rogue."

"You're supposed to be my friend!" I accused. "I never cared about any of that. I never cared if you belonged here or not. I thought you belonged *with me.*"

A chunk of grass and dirt tore itself away from the ground and flew at Taylor's head. He ducked away from it, turning back to look at me with disbelief and something else beneath it. After a moment, his face cleared, frozen into an expression I couldn't read. "I belonged *to* you," he corrected.

Spinning on his heel, he disappeared into the tree line, leaving me alone in the cold.

Laura was as silent as she ever was, which I was glad for.

Getting ready was a somber affair, and when I looked in the mirror, the only thing I could see was a miserable, selfish girl with eyes like quarried tunnels, so vacant as to betray just how truly isolated she was.

Laura had taken care of the circles under my eyes with a little make-up, and the scrapes on my elbows had healed before I'd even walked back inside. I wish it was in my power to do something about the hollowness reverberating in my chest, where there resided a mutilation that no one could see—one that no longer bled yet at the same time refused to heal.

The dress was still beautiful, I supposed. But the girl inside did not rightfully belong in it. She had always been damaged, but before all of her problems had come from a reluctance to say, "I'm not okay", and now…now she found that the words "I *will* be okay" were the ones sticking in her throat, unspoken.

Laura reached for the opal pins on the dresser and paused. She returned her hands to my hair, leaving the pins where they were.

I managed to register a small degree of surprise. "You're not putting it up?"

Her eyes met mine in the mirror. "It's time for a change, maybe."

When I stepped out into the hall, Vince was waiting for me, but I ignored him, brushing past him without a pause.

"Jenny," he said, quietly. "Please. I need to talk to you for a second."

"Then talk," I replied, not looking at him as he caught up with me. "But I'm not going to listen."

"Just wait for a second, will you?" He grabbed my arm and spun me around to face him. "Look, I'm sorry about Taylor—"

"You're *sorry?*" I let out a humorless laugh. "Before he even stepped foot in this house, you hated him. What could've changed since then?"

"A lot of things have changed since then," he said, releasing me. "Even you've changed. Maybe it was time to let him go. Maybe…it was for the best."

"For the best? *Who* was it best for? You?" I was well aware how cruel I was being, but at that moment I didn't mind being the one who was dealing out the damage this time. Maybe I'd *always* been the one dealing it. If that was the case, then I supposed I was only demonstrating a consistency of character. "Because he's finally gone, just like *you* wanted?"

Vince rocked back on his heels. "That…that's not what I meant."

"Of course it is!" I tried to move around him, but he wouldn't budge. "Get out of my way," I said, through clenched teeth.

"I…Jenny, I know how you must be feeling right now, but—"

"You don't know how I feel, Vince," I snapped. "You've never had—or even *wanted*—anything resembling friendship, and you've never lost it."

He swallowed, looking injured. "I thought *we* were—"

"What?" I demanded. "Friends? Please, don't deceive yourself, Vincent."

Vince paled as he realized they were his own words being thrown back at him. "I never meant that when I said it..." he rasped, barely audible. "Is that really how you feel?"

I was too exhausted, too angry, too heartless to care how much I was hurting him. "Yes," I whispered, knowing full well it was a lie. His face fell, and I felt myself wince at his stricken expression, but the words continued. "Don't pretend you weren't always jealous of Taylor. You said yourself that you hated him because—"

"I hated him," Vince interrupted, his amber eyes burning, "because he had *you.*"

Finally, he stepped aside, not looking at me.

"Don't want to be late, do we?"

Unable to come up with a response, I gathered the front of my dress in my hands and continued down the hall, out through the front door into a groggy, overcast afternoon, and finally to the Audi idling in the driveway. Liam didn't speak to me as I got in on the passenger side, and Vince didn't speak to me as he slid into the backseat behind me.

It seemed to me that the solution all along had been to make the people I cared about hate me. This way, I could decide to become either a Sentry or a Persuader and it wouldn't matter. None of it would matter because I would no longer hurt anyone with my decision, and I wouldn't benefit anyone, either.

It was the most important day of my life and it didn't matter.

I wasn't sure what I was expecting. Maybe something more akin to the small gatherings that usually marked the date of my birth, where my mother snapped a few pictures and a few semi-friends from school came over and sat with me on the back porch as I opened gifts and laughed about how concerned my mom was that I was "growing up too fast". Looking back, I suppose she had more to worry about on that subject than other mothers did, of course.

The place that had been rented for the occasion rested at the top of an exceptionally ornate and well-manicured lawn, a small queue of expensive cars already curled around the circular drive before the manor. There was a fountain in the center, nothing so dramatic as the fallen angel at the Cable estate, but upon closer inspection it *did* appear to be spouting two different colors of water from opposite ends. From the gaping maw of one of the lion heads spewed a dyed red stream, while the other lion released a steady current of blue. Tacky. Absolutely, unrelentingly, unabashedly tacky. Approaching the wide-faced building, I noticed the glittering lights wrapped around each cylinder. Violet. It seemed they were determined to stick to a color scheme even before the guests stepped foot inside, and would cling to their tackiness as a shipwrecked sailor would to a buoy rocking in the waves.

And inside, the determination really bloomed, and in the Persuader world I supposed it was only natural for the event to be nothing short of blindingly elaborate and completely over-the-top.

The walls were what particularly caught my interest, at first. On one side, the wall was a bright crimson, while on the other, of course, was a deep, Prussian blue, the colors separated by the gold, silver, and white in between. Two chandeliers hung from the high ceiling, intricate in design, the first swaying slightly above us at the front door, the second hovering possessively over a raised section of the floor at the opposite end of the room. Alarmingly, the section looked somewhat like a stage, and I could only assume I would be standing up there in front of everyone, presented to the crowd like a painting on auction.

Charles stood in the center of the floor, directing people where to go, what to do, where to move a sculpture or how to hang the banners of gold silk just right against the backdrop of the red wall, while the silver swaths were to be hung on the blue. Tables with immaculate white tablecloths were set with gold edged china and sparkling silverware, glasses of champagne bubbling excitedly on trays, waiting to be served. Gold and red. Blue and silver. All the colors seemed to blur together, and I stood there for a moment, my head spinning, before I found myself being dragged into another room by some wide-eyed woman who gestured dangerously as she spoke. From what little I could gather from her unbroken line of speech, she was to rehearse with me before the guests arrived. Apparently, there was a specific way I had to approach the platform and a certain way I had to answer the Warden who would be in the center of it. It was as if I was getting married, but not to a person, but a decision.

Taylor would've laughed at it all, and I would've joined him. I knew he couldn't have been here, anyway, but the thought of his absence being prolonged even after everything was said and done painfully wrenched something within me.

"Alright, then, watch me very closely, Jennifer," the woman was saying, lifting her chin haughtily.

She stood at the front of the large room, beginning to make her way forward. "Shoulders back, spine straight. Watch my steps. One must have poise."

She approached the platform and stepped up onto it, leveling her eyes on an invisible person before her. "The Warden will begin to speak now, remind you that your choice is binding, and then ask you for your decision. It's very concise, not to worry. Brief."

Yes, I was definitely not worrying *now*, when the heaviest decision I've ever made was *concise*. "Okay."

"Remember: It's all about poise."

"Oh, I remember." She *had* demonstrated it to me, after all, and had even said the word aloud not two seconds before.

Her eyes cut to me, narrowing. "Is that impudence I hear?"

I sighed. "No, ma'am."

"Good." The woman obviously seemed satisfied in her skills as an instructor, and appeased concerning my respect toward her, though in actuality both were significantly lacking. "If you'll excuse me, I have to go see what Charles is going on about."

She departed, scurrying to Charles Monroe's side to meet his strident demands, leaving me by myself again in the center of the room.

I felt Natalia's aura before she spoke, so the surprise I felt at her sudden appearance was less of a disturbance. "Look at them all. They're like circus oddities, running around vomiting color onto everything."

I turned toward her, noting the sophisticated twist of her hair, the sleek dress she wore that fell around her in ripples of slate blue. I supposed even Sentries could be elegant when they wanted to be. "Has anyone else arrived, yet?"

"Mostly the members of my stronghold who came with me," she said. "A few for security, Silas, and—well, Gwen insisted I go in her place. She wanted to be at the stronghold with the rest, to lead it in my absence. She seemed...uneasy. In any case, I'm here. And you know I would welcome you into my home with open arms."

"Yes, I know that," I answered, looking away. "Thank you, Natalia."

The Warden was exactly what I had expected.

He was old, and sour-tempered, and his face spoke of years of dirty work and bloodshed and living in the harsh shadow of the law.

It took a few minutes to coax conversation out of him, and even then he had little words to spare toward an eighteen-year-old girl. "I didn't know Wardens officiated these sorts of things. Like priests."

"I am not a holy man. There is little room for religion under the harness of the Adjudication." His deep-set eyes, embraced by two or three folds of skin underneath, swiveled to me with scorn. "There seems to be *much* you're ignorant of, child," he added, as a contemptuous afterthought.

I frowned. "I'm eighteen. I'm not a child."

He made a noise at the back of his throat that suggested he still thought otherwise, but made no other sound.

"How did you become a Warden?" I asked, attempting at friendly conversation if only to keep myself from getting too much on his nerves before the ceremony even began.

Without looking at me, he said, "Through many years of hard work and sacrifice."

"You were a Sentry before you became a Warden?" I guessed.

This seemed to surprise him. "How did you know that?" He rubbed his bearded chin as if mildly impressed.

I shrugged, and I was a little surprised, myself, that I had caught this statue of a man off-guard. "Intuition, maybe. Something about your face reminds me of a Sentry I know." I was referring to Silas, of course, but I wasn't about to tell this surly man he reminded me of my grandfather.

The Warden coughed into his hand twice before saying, "I was a Sentry. A decent one, at that."

"What made you give it up?" I asked, somewhat intrigued now by his story, where he'd been in life and what he had done.

"I didn't," he growled, but it was more defensive than anything else. "I moved up the ladder. I had a higher purpose to protect not just regular people from us, but to, in turn, protect *us* from *regular people*. And to save us from ourselves, on occasion."

"Sounds demanding," I observed.

"It is," he said, gruffly. "But it is also rewarding. Many former Sentry brothers and sisters of mine now work alongside me."

"Only Sentries can become Wardens?"

"No," he said. "But that is often the case, as it is a somewhat militant lifestyle. Persuaders who wish to make more of themselves typically apply for government jobs with the Adjudication."

"One more question," I said, much to the Warden's dismay. He heaved a sigh, but nodded for me to go on. "The Embracement...is it...inescapably required?"

Smirking, the Warden released a bark of a laugh. "Indecisive, are we? Unfortunately, under the laws of the Adjudication, if you decide nothing at all you are no longer under the protection of our government and therefore no longer our problem. If someone wanted you dead—and I'm almost certain several people do—they could do it and there would be no consequences at all."

A shiver pulsed down my spine. "That's kind of sick."

"I don't make the laws, kid," he grumbled, turning away. "I just enforce them."

After my conversation with the Warden, I felt as if I had been prodded even closer to the edge, and that I would eventually look down into the ravine and see something I wished I hadn't.

I had no time to be concerned about it, though, not while guests poured into the room like the torrents spilling from the fountain. Red seeped in through one door, while blue came in through the other. The two colors did not intermingle, but instead remained on their respective sides, talking amongst themselves and occasionally throwing venomous glares over to the opposite faction when the mood suited them.

"I haven't seen this many Sentries and Persuaders in the same room together since—well, since the masquerade, I suppose. One can only hope the end result will be less...heated."

"You just find yourself hysterical," I said, not even turning to look into those magnetic amber eyes. "Don't you?"

"And I'm afraid *you* find me pathetic, at best," he returned, and this time I did look at him. His face was not guarded as it almost always was. It was broken down into its baser components: A creased brow here and clear, fracturing eyes there above a tightly pursed mouth. *You've never had*

anything resembling friendship, and you've never lost it, I had said to him. But his expression claimed otherwise. It spoke of much more lost than friendship. "Don't you?"

Before I could respond, Vince spun around and melted into the crowd. Taking in the room again, I recognized hardly anyone, Sentry or Persuader. They were all strangers to me.

21
TOO LATE

GWEN

My parents had believed that a sudden illness had befallen me more easily than I was entirely comfortable with, as they were eager to go to the Embracement regardless of my presence—as they were eager to do *most* things regardless of my presence.

I walked among the cots, trying not to let my disappointment in them show on my face, and eventually Darren came over and fell into step beside me. "You don't have to be here, Gwen."

"Yeah, we all know where she *really* wants to be," Sasha whispered, just behind Darren, winking at me when I turned my gaze to her. By her look, I could only assume she meant Vince. With an indignant scoff, I whirled back around, flushing angrily.

"Even if that was true—*which it's not*—my obligation is to this stronghold. I'm not about to leave it when it's most vulnerable. It needs leadership." I straightened my back, trying my best to look like a convincing third in command.

Darren sighed. "What makes you so sure something is going to happen, anyway? We've got everything under control here."

"I thought that once," I replied, quietly. "Until the masquerade. Until the night Eli was murdered. That can't happen again. I can't have anyone else die."

Darren and Sasha looked at each other worriedly before leaving me alone again at the elevator. I punched the button and waited as it groaned and slowly began to move with an ancient reluctance.

The hallway was as silent and as lifeless as it always was. The only one who ever really came up here was Natalia.

Inside her office, I felt like an intruder and in an odd fit of absurdity wondered, for a moment, if the Sentry leader didn't rig the place with alarms before she left it each afternoon.

I closed the door behind me and sat at the desk. It was quiet here, as it wasn't anywhere else in the stronghold. One could think here. One could reflect on the ephemerality of life and all that, the frailty of mortality, though for Persuaders it was a dangerous business to get lost in one's head. When someone thought too deeply, too feelingly, he could warp himself into an entirely different shape than before. For people, the word for that was "overthinking", innocuous enough in most cases. But for Persuaders, the word was more like "insanity". It was a wonder Natalia could sit at this desk every day, could sit in this chair, could file paperwork, could cross names out in thick, black ink and still keep her sanity about her like a well-worn shawl. I doubted that I would be able to one day fill this chair as she had, not without losing my mind. Without Natalia, without that indomitable way about her that defied all convention and all reason, this place would surely crumble away, revert back into the empty, gray warehouse it had been before she'd found it.

I stood, too quickly, knocking the chair over.

It all seemed so obvious to me now. The explosions may not have eliminated their intended targets, but that wouldn't stop Samuel from following through with his plan. It couldn't.

He was going to attack the stronghold.

I raced toward the elevator, bouncing up and down on my heels as I jammed my thumb into the elevator button over and over to no effect. Shrieking in frustration, I gave up on the endeavor, throwing my shoulder into the stubborn, swollen door that led to the staircase before I realized, past the haze of panic, that I could've just Shifted it open.

My shoulder smarted as I leapt whole flights of stairs to where the rest of the stronghold waited, oblivious to my newfound knowledge.

"Darren!" I called, into the mass of feverish groans and pain-stricken expressions. "Sasha!"

As soldiers did, they reported at once, though the time in between still felt as if it dragged on too slow, their movements not hurried enough for what I would prefer. Before they were barely in earshot, I was shouting orders. "Transfer the sick and wounded upstairs. Everyone who is able is to be armed immediately. Do you hear me? I want to be prepared. And someone needs to call Natalia right now and warn her."

The twins shared looks of bewilderment. "About what?" demanded Sasha. "What the hell is going on?"

"We're about to be attacked," I said, loud enough so that other Sentries close to us turned to stare at me with pallid, glistening faces.

Darren looked dubious, but utterly attentive, his dark eyes fixed on me. "How do you know?"

"The bombings were meant to kill two people. Silas and myself. The second and third command. Darren, tell me what would happen to this stronghold without leadership? A stronghold still licking its wounds, especially?"

He swallowed hard, looking even more confused, but answered anyway. "It would fall into disorder, most likely."

"Natalia is our leader, the queen on the chessboard. And she's at the Embracement of an interbreed, with her father present, along with her grandfather, our second in command. Vince once said that everyone connected to Jennifer Cable represented something Samuel despised. And most of them are in the same room, at the same time. Defenseless as we are, if not more so."

Sasha gasped, putting her hand to her mouth, and Darren's eyebrows shot into his hairline. "But…" he started, haltingly. "But we have to warn them! We need to get over there right now."

I shook my head. "But Samuel's more careful than that. We'll be surrounded by the entirety of his Deadlock legion in just a moment, I'm sure. That's why we need to prepare for it. To prepare for a likely massacre or the surrender of our stronghold. Even *if* we win, he'll have delayed us long enough to keep us from going to Natalia's aid."

Sasha took my shoulder. "But we still have leadership. We still have you. We can't just stand aside while they take our home—"

"I'm holding a vote," I said. "A vote to either lay down our arms or fight, even if it ends in a slaughter. I won't take away your choice. Not now."

Darren shook his head. "But why would he still go through with it if his plan fell apart?"

"It didn't," I replied, grimly. "I'm just a child to him. Weak-willed. He knew Natalia would never go down without a fight, would never give up this place, not after all she's done to obtain it. It's simpler this way for him, to lose less of his men. To secure the stronghold without much resistance. He anticipates a surrender from someone like me, someone born a Persuader. He expects nothing more."

"*We* do," someone from behind me said, and I turned to see a woman in her thirties, a jagged scar running from her upper lip down to her chin. Her name was Juniper, I remembered. She and I had never been as close as I was with Natalia or the twins, so I was surprised by her next words. Her voice rose as she addressed the whole stronghold. "When you first joined our ranks I had my doubts, because you were a Farrier. Because, as you said, your were born a Persuader. But what you were born as has nothing to do with what you *are*. You've always been a Sentry, one of us. I think I speak for everyone when I say that you've earned your rank. And we know what you would have us do if you felt the decision were up to you: You would have us fight. I'm casting my vote. I want a gun in my hands."

A noise rose up from everyone else around me, a wordless endorsement after so many months of self-doubt, wondering if I was unworthy in their eyes.

"All right." I looked from face to face, seeing no apprehension or doubt or disapproval. "I guess it's settled then."

TAYLOR

The trees around me seemed to be whispering. I zipped my jacket to my throat, shivering violently, possibly not just from the cold. God, what had I *done*? I hadn't meant to hurt Jenny. I'd only wanted her to be safe. And "safe" at that time had meant only "far away from me."

I remembered saying to her, as if in a nightmare, *Maybe someone should make your decisions for you, because you never seem to make the right one.*

In a way, it was the worst thing I'd said to her during our argument. It was worse than anything else I could've said and I knew that. I knew it because everything she had ever fought for had been centered on the concept she kept in her mind of "free will", around choice and instinct and trying to do the right thing or the best thing. She continually made the right decisions, every day, even if she didn't know it, but I had dared say otherwise.

274

Her only bad decision had been me. If she truly had meant it when she said she cared for me, I was sure she didn't now.

I thought, surprisingly, of my parents, how much love they had given me for so many years, only for me to throw it back at them. I couldn't imagine they had any love left for me, either. Not even in dreams could I imagine I deserved anything more than to be alone.

Though perhaps I weighed my own love above others', made theirs seem fickle and conditional while mine remained perfectly irrevocable. I still loved Jenny more than I'd thought was possible, and though she'd changed in the weeks that had passed, the change was similar to that of a tree growing, becoming stronger, blooming in the spring. My own change had occurred a long time ago, when I'd left home, and then another change had happened the day a Sentry Wolf—seeing my Persuader clothes, and in his drunken rage unable to see the two weeks-worth of wear and grime on them—came at me with a knife. That was the day someone else's blood had spilled onto my hands for the very first time in my life, and though it wasn't done in cold blood, it could not be overlooked that murder was murder. *My* change had been the inverse of Jenny's, the decay of the same tree.

I remembered how desperate I'd felt, how alone, how broken. Tarek had found me sleeping on his back porch, trying to escape the freezing rain under his eave, and had reached for my shoulder, his brown eyes searching mine. "Rogue?" he asked, sensing my aura, seeing my clothes and the state they (and the wearer) were in. I nodded. "Sentry?" he asked, because, as I learned, he had grown to hate Persuaders, and wouldn't have had them in his home even if they'd begged. I nodded again. From that moment, we were friends, utterly dependent upon each other; he was my keeper and I his companion, after so many years he'd spent with only himself. But my loneliness and emptiness and brokenness continued. I'd almost grown resigned to the feeling, but then, of course, I'd met Jenny.

It wasn't how she'd looked that had captivated me at first. It was how her aura had seemed to burst from her like a blinding light, seemed to be as much a part of her as her green eyes or her clever mouth. It'd sent a shot of warmth into my veins, and suddenly I'd felt...intact.

When her foot had caught on that raised lip of sidewalk and she'd stumbled into my arms, I'd felt as if I would melt at the contact, candle wax to her flame. She'd looked up at me, the clever mouth twisting ruefully, the green eyes sparkling, her cheeks darkening. "Sorry," she murmured. Her voice had been like a good dream.

It had taken me a moment to compose myself. "That's...that's alright. It was an accident." I scolded myself immediately after the words had left my mouth for not saying something that sounded more intelligent.

She'd only smiled, and my stomach had jumped into my throat. "My mom always tells me if I paid half as much attention to my surroundings as I did in class, I'd be smart *and* graceful." I had laughed at that, but then her head tilted suddenly, her smile vanishing. "You know, it's at a moment like this one I vaguely recall something *else* she said, something about not talking to strangers? I think that extends to hugging them, too."

I'd released her quickly, flushing from my neck to my forehead. "My bad. Uh...I'm Taylor. I swear I'm not a weirdo."

Her smile had returned, albeit slightly amused. "You really shouldn't make false promises, Taylor," she'd teased. I had been too caught up in the fact that she'd said my name to process her words as anything insulting.

"Okay," I said. "Fair enough. How about this: I swear to you that I'll have bruises from where you hit me."

Her laugh had been more perfect than anything else. "Again, sorry about that." She'd held out her hand to me then. "I'm Jenny. Jenny Cable."

I had, almost involuntarily, started at the name. Cable. But...but she *couldn't* be. Could she? Without realizing it, I'd started looking at her in a sudden new light, one tinged by the elitist ideals and Adjudication propaganda that had been funneled into my head during my childhood. It didn't matter that I didn't believe in them and had never believed in them. She was an interbreed, and she was someone to be wary of, someone not to be trusted, someone to avoid. Right?

I'd looked at her again and saw only a sixteen or seventeen year old girl with soulful eyes and a quick humor. It was a funny thing, but I'd found then that I didn't particularly care, anymore. I wasn't my father or my mother or a Purist. And then...then I wasn't even a rogue. I wasn't a Sentry. I wasn't anything but a boy who really, really liked this girl.

"Nice to meet you," I returned, taking her hand in mine.

And now, as I trudged through twilit woods, I couldn't help but feel the pull, the pull that would always be present no matter what, ever since that day. The further I got from Jenny, emotionally and physically, the more painful that pull would become, like a string around my chest, growing taut, compressing my lungs and heart and soul.

Eventually that string—tugging at me incessantly yet holding me together at the same time—would snap, and I would slide apart. It would snap, and I would be all alone again.

GWEN

I waited in front of the door, my hand resting on the butt of the gun, fingers curling in anticipation. Darren and Sasha were silent beside me, mirroring my pose.

We were guardians to the injured upstairs, warning to the wounded so that they had time to escape when the first shots were fired. I considered the possibility of us being mowed down on sight. And then, reluctantly, I accepted the probability.

I glanced from Darren to Sasha, seeing no sign of apprehension, no trace of weak will.

When I glanced back toward the horizon, I saw black shapes gathering, and the gun was out of its holster on impulse. Darren and Sasha did the same.

"Hold," I commanded.

They drew nearer, and I could see that there were about two-dozen of them, all heavily armed and muscled except for a slim, slinking shape at the front of the crowd.

"Hold." My hand lifted, palm outward, arm bent at a ninety-degree angle. My fingers curled into a fist.

I could see that they were not tightly packed like a Deadlock unit, but rather loosely organized, if one could even call them *organized* at all. Their whoops and howls reached me next, and I felt my fingers go numb.

"What the hell?" Darren murmured, shifting restlessly.

"Hold," I snapped, noticing his discomfort. I glanced at Sasha and she looked even less at ease than her brother.

Finally, the group stopped, just twenty feet before us. A woman—a woman I recognized as one of Samuel's subordinates—smirked at me, the crowd trailing behind her looking like nothing even remotely similar to the silent, orderly Deadlocks I was familiar with. Their grins were poisonous, their movements resembling something more akin to a pack of animals.

And then I understood. "Samuel didn't send his bodyguards," I said, my voice wavering. "He sent his attack dogs."

The woman laughed. "Oh, very good. Aren't you a clever one? What was your first clue?"

Darren made a noise at the back of his throat, striding forward to place a hand on my shoulder. "We're not surrendering. Not even to our own kind."

She flicked a piece of her hair over her shoulder, and I noticed something metallic around her wrist like a bracelet. "Oh, that's precious. *El amor lo conquista todo,* no?"

Love conquers all. I didn't understand what she meant by it, but surprisingly Darren's hand dropped from my shoulder, and again he shifted his weight to the other foot in agitation. I turned back to the woman, moving forward a few steps with caution. The Sentry Wolf pack roiled like a sea at storm with the eagerness to spill blood. "We're not leaving," I said, with a quiet weight, one I had heard in Natalia's voice many times.

She cracked her knuckles. "I was hoping you would say that."

Her hand flashed toward me in a blur of silver, and I arched backwards to avoid it, nearly toppling over onto the pavement.

Darren slid his gun back into its holster, switching it for a machete strapped to his back. Guns had no place in this kind of a battle, as they were easy to disarm and more of a danger to the holder than to the intended target. Natalia once remarked that, once Shifted so that they were rendered unable to be fired, their only use was as very inconvenient clubs. Sasha started to bounce on the balls of her feet, a pair of wickedly curved knives in each of her hands.

I straightened, returning the woman's smile, reaching to my belt and feeling the familiar weight of the tomahawk's handle.

"Likewise."

Chaos erupted.

The pack surged forward, toward the stronghold entrance, and a tide of able-bodied Sentries crashed against it, creating a wake of cries and growls and metallic *shings* as blade met blade. I swung the tomahawk at the woman in a sweeping arc, and she barely escaped the sharp, curved edge of it as she rolled to the side, popping back to her feet. Her hand lifted to her ear, and I enjoyed the look of rage on her face as it came away red.

"You're going to regret that, Farrier," she hissed.

"I already do," I shot back, twirling the axe in my hand. "I was aiming for your throat."

Her arm blurred toward me again, and I rolled forward, hooking her ankle with the inside curve of the weapon and yanking upwards. Her elbows made a thwacking sound as they hit, and I whirled and swung, just missing her back as she scrambled out from underneath me. The blade made sparks against the asphalt.

She stood and kicked the weapon out of my hands, sending it flying into the din, lost amongst entangled limbs and blood.

The woman smirked down at me. "Oops."

I fumbled for the hidden blade in my boot. My fingers found the small hilt easily, and I slashed out toward her, the knife embedding itself deep in her thigh. I backed away several steps, avoiding a blind stroke of her knife as she tried to dislodge my own.

With an enraged shriek, she threw out her hand, trying to Shift me off of my feet. But she wasn't a soldier. And she wasn't pure-blooded. And she certainly wasn't prepared for the attack to be countered.

I could hear Natalia in the back of my head. *Redirecting a frontal attack is the same in nearly any form. When someone takes a swing at you, you would simply use his weight against him. Shifting is no different. The mind of a Sentry can be used to fight just as any other limb or part of the body, arguably more so. You just need proper training, airtight technique.*

Time moved sluggishly in that moment, and I could feel my body begin to sway backwards.

When you feel yourself rock back on your heels, that's *when you have to throw it back at them, understand? Fight against the weight of it, and make it your own. Plant your feet. Yes, just like that. And direct it right back.*

I flung my arms out before me, as if physically shoving something away, and the woman barely had time to brace herself before she was knocked into the air.

She hit the asphalt hard on her side. I could almost hear the bone of her forearm shatter, and she cried out through her teeth. Shakily, she gathered herself underneath of her, standing with an unsteady tilt. She was tough, I'd give her that.

Distracted by the woman, I didn't sense the Wolf behind me until it was too late. Something blunt struck me in the back of the head, and I dropped to the ground, ears ringing, my vision swimming with dark spots. I rolled onto my back to see him standing over me with a long, bone-hilted dagger in his hand, probably homemade, the handle most likely crafted, if the stories I'd heard had any truth to them, from a portion of the human femur. Sentry Wolves liked to be grotesque, liked to use fear tactics. He smiled a crooked, rotten smile, his eyes glinting like shards of glass. The blade shone in the fading sunlight as he raised it over his head.

He drove it downward, the point slicing through the air with pinpoint deadliness, but it never reached its intended.

Darren moved in like a shadow between the blade and me, and the bloodied point came within an inch of my nose as it drove right through his chest as easily as it would've gone through butter.

I cried out his name, scrambling to my knees to catch him as he slid off the dagger and slumped to the ground.

Sasha turned, staring wide-eyed at her brother, and charged straight at the Sentry Wolf with a rage like fire in her expression, a fire that burned away any remorse at all as she slit his throat with a single, neat swipe. He didn't even have time to raise his hands.

I cradled Darren in my lap, holding my hand to the hole in his chest. "Darren! Darren, stay with me, dammit! Just hold on…w-we'll get help or…or *something.*" Sasha dropped to her knees beside me, tears streaking their way down her face as she stroked Darren's cheek. "That was a stupid thing to do," I snapped, but my anger wasn't at him. It was at myself.

He managed a smile at me. His skin was slicked with sweat, and he was shaking uncontrollably. "I know," he whispered, hoarsely. "But I would do it again."

I looked at the dead Wolf, and glanced behind me, in search of the woman. But I didn't need to worry about her. She was gone.

I turned back to Darren, making a pained sound when I saw that a pool of blood was steadily pouring out underneath of him, dark and thick and mirror-like. He reached up to touch my face with bloodstained fingers, wiping away the angry tears there. "D-don't do that. Please don't cry, Gwen."

His hand dropped from my face, leaving a smear of red across my cheekbone.

Sasha sobbed against me, her slim hands curling painfully around my shoulders. But I didn't mind the pain. It didn't hurt as much as the ache inside my chest, not nearly as much. In fact, I hardly felt her touch at all.

I reached down with a trembling hand, pressing two fingers into the place just below his chin, waiting.

Sasha's head lifted suddenly. "Gwen," she said, roughly, through the thickness in her throat. *"Gwen, he's breathing."*

Almost on cue, his pulse leapt under my touch, albeit nearly too faint to register. "Someone help! Please, he needs help!"

My head snapped up to find someone in the crowd, but too late I noticed that all had gone silent. Bodies lay strewn out before me, lying across a parking lot that seemed painted in red. A quiet, tower of a man named Victor came to lift Darren out of my arms.

Numbly, I stood and asked him, in a voice that was surprisingly unwavering, "Casualty report."

Victor did not smile or frown, but his eyes seemed to glow with triumph and darken with cold anger simultaneously. "Some got away, disappeared into the trees." He gestured with a jerk of his chin to the distant belt of brown and gray on the other side of the road. "The others were eliminated. Twelve injured, though most of them are minor. Nine casualties of our own." He swallowed, thickly, and his face registered a new emotion. Grief. "One of them was Juniper."

I remembered vaguely that Juniper and Victor had been particularly close. I looked down at Darren, barely breathing, and my burst of pride vanished, replaced by only a gripping coldness in my chest. "Get Darren to the stronghold and make sure the count isn't ten," I murmured, not looking at him. My eyes fixated on the setting sun as it rested against the horizon, wrapped in swaths of amber and gold. "We can't afford to lose any more good Sentries."

He looked down at the bleeding boy in his arms. There was a dark stain beginning to spread across the big man's shirtfront from the spill of blood that was not his own. "Yes, ma'am," he said, solemnly. "I apologize. He'll be treated immediately."

"Don't apologize," I replied, turning away from him. "It wasn't your fault."

It was mine.

Victor, without another word, spun on his heel and carried Darren away. The rest set to work constructing pyres for the deceased, digging shallow graves for the Wolves.

Sasha put a hand on my shoulder, but still I didn't turn. I felt as if I could never turn back to face the stronghold again. I didn't deserve this rank. I didn't deserve leadership or camaraderie or their trust. I had failed them so many times…and for what? So that I could prove myself? Was I really so desperate to escape the Persuader title over my head that I had become nearly as selfish as one?

"He got hurt because of me, you know. I understand if you hate me."

Sasha made an irritated sound. *"Hate* you? I could never hate you. You're my friend. You have to stop doing this to yourself, Gwen, really. Stop *blaming yourself* for something that...well, it's a natural part of our existence. Fighting, bleeding, dying. Even if Darren dies from this, he wouldn't want us to be sulking around. He would want us to endure for his sake, to...to—"

Her words, unexpectedly, cut off. Now I did turn, to see that silent tears were streaking their way down a face that was stubbornly turned away, and I pulled her into my arms. "I'm so sorry," I whispered. "You're right. I know you're right. It's just..." I drew away, my arms falling back to my sides. "Sometimes I don't know what all of it is *for*. It never seems to change anything. Tomorrow we'll *still* fight, we'll *still* bleed, and we'll *still* die. It doesn't have an ending."

Sasha shook her head. "It doesn't need an ending. Only a purpose. Sometimes purpose is all you have."

"What's Darren's purpose?" I asked, looking off toward the stronghold entrance, which he had long ago disappeared through.

"Like he said, to protect you." Her brown-gray eyes rippled with some profound sadness. "He...he loves you, you know."

"I love him, too."

She shook her head again, that strange sadness lingering in her gaze. "No, you love him like you love me. Like you love Natalia and this stronghold. Darren...Darren's *in love* with you."

I was silent for a moment. Then, squeezing my eyes shut, I said, "I am such an idiot."

"He's good at hiding it, keeping what he feels buried," Sasha said, in my defense. "He knows you don't feel the same way."

I walked over to where most of the bodies had fallen, flipping one on its stomach with the toe of my boot to reclaim my bloodied tomahawk from underneath of him.

My fingers flexed on the handle. "Don't let anyone follow me, understand?"

"You're going to the Embracement alone." It wasn't a question.

I nodded, slipping the axe into its belt loop. I looked down to see the band of metal that had fallen from the woman's wrist lying at my feet, picking it up and slipping it into my pocket for safekeeping. "I can't ask any of you to put your lives on the line for the sake of a couple Persuaders."

"But Natalia's there," Sasha protested, her hands fluttering to her twin knives. "You need back-up."

"She had bodyguards with her. It should be enough to hold off the Deadlocks until we can get everyone out of there." Her face fell. "Sorry, Sasha. I need you here to lead in my stead, just in case they come back."

I slammed the door of the car—the *stolen* car, as I unwillingly reminded myself—trying not to think about it detonating horrifyingly and graphically as I Shifted the ignition switch hard to the right. I would return it at some point, maybe. That is, if I lived through what was to come.

I also tried without success not to look in the rearview mirror at the figure becoming more and more distant as I drove away, Sasha's restless expression becoming harder and harder to discern.

JENNY

I took a deep breath in, and considered not ever letting it out.

When my lungs started to itch with their inaction, I finally exhaled. It hurt more than I thought it would.

I should have told Taylor I loved him back, even if I wasn't entirely sure if I meant it, even if the reality was we loved each other in two completely different ways. At least it would've convinced him to stay, maybe.

Or maybe not. He had always been good at telling my lies from my truths. I wished *I* could tell my lies from my truths. Strange how some people could know you better than you knew yourself.

But alas—as was typical for me, I couldn't seem to distinguish one emotion from the other as it was. All of my thoughts and fears and hopes ran together, and I learned that the color of confliction was red and blue. It was gold and silver, black and white, cornflower blue and gilded amber. All of them, mixed into one.

When the time came, Vince had said, I would know. I wasn't exactly calling him a liar, but…I had a strange feeling that when he'd said that, it had only been to comfort me.

I had asked myself what faction I was willing to sacrifice the most for, but what if the price for either was too much to pay?

I glanced about the room, for a sign, maybe, but my gaze locked onto only one thing.

A knife, with its intricate hilt laden with amethyst, lay atop swaths of blue and red satin. It was stiletto thin, the blade as black as pitch, with a point meant to prick the finger to draw blood for the ceremony. This was a detail the woman had neglected to mention, unsurprisingly.

Natalia had told me about it, which was fitting, considering the grittier details were best saved to be revealed by Sentry lips. The swaths would be laid across an altar-type slab of marble, the blue on the left and the red on the right. The Warden would prick my finger with the knife, and I would press it to a particular swath to represent the faction of my choosing.

Then the Warden would take my forearm, and I his, and Cavea would be reached between us. If my decision were one that I truly believed in, in my heart, then the color of my inner mind would coincide noticeably. The rituals involved with the Embracement were important; the mind needed something concrete to cling to in order to change. Natalia shook her head and told me that her aura had started to display what her parents called "troubling signs" when she was just eleven years old, rather abnormal when it came to a child so young. Rather unusual for a child yet to be exposed to anything that could influence her mind's natural hue. Her parents had consulted a doctor immediately, and she had undergone several excruciating months of "therapy" before her aura was deemed to be in a normal and healthy state. She would never forgive them for it.

Seeing the look of confusion on my face, she then informed me that the sky of Cavea was the color of someone's aura. Violet was what naturally came to someone with exceptional psychological abilities. It meant we were more in touch with our truer potential than normal human beings. Blue indicated someone who endured, a survivor, someone intelligent and able to lead others with ease. Red spoke of a certain uncontainable energy, a drive to endeavor toward success and to come out on top. It surprised me to learn that everything that made a Persuader was ingrained into his nature, and that the same was true for a Sentry.

Natalia smiled grimly at me. "But, you see, human nature takes those qualities and turns them into something…less. Something corrupted." She shrugged. "It's an inevitable truth. Persuaders are supposed to be people motivated toward achievement, but instead they are individuals who manipulate others to gain power. Sentries are supposed use their gifts to aid others, but look where that's gotten us."

Look where that's gotten everyone, I'd wanted to tell her.

I couldn't tear my eyes away from the knife, couldn't stop my mind from erasing all the thoughts in my head except: *Maybe I was never meant to choose either. Maybe I'm just an in-between freak-of-nature that exists nowhere at all.*

I felt powerless. I felt like a tool to be used, not a person who was considered and valued. Like Taylor had said, we were livestock being corralled into one side or the other. I could almost feel the bodies packing in close around me, could almost hear the crack of the whip. My nightmare flashed in front of my eyes, and I remembered Samuel, holding a knife out to me, his glowing red eyes reflected by its silver blade. I remembered the exposed skin of my wrist, the veins beneath it turning black.

It's a solution, he had whispered.

I wrapped my fingers around the hilt, turning the point of the knife with a shaking hand toward myself. My hand seemed somehow disembodied, as separate from the rest of me as my racing mind. Powerless. That was the word in my head, now. I wouldn't be powerless. I refused. Everything anyone had ever said to me tumbled into my thoughts in a wave that nearly drove me to my knees.

Maybe someone should *make your decisions for you, because you never seem to make the right one,* Taylor had said.

Vince, telling me, in a heated voice, *You're one to talk of* cruelty, *Jenny.*

Liam's voice overlapped them, with more volume still. *You can't just* run away *and think it will solve anything.*

I'm not running, my mind replied, the words drowning everything else out. I felt cold, like marble, numb to everything but the pressure of the blade's point against my chest, not hard enough to draw blood, but not light enough for me to deny the fact that I could very well do it. Easily. I could plunge the knife straight into my heart, and no amount of healing ability could save me then. I wouldn't have to choose anything but to do this, right now. That was what my subconscious was telling me, through my nightmare. That was the sign I had been looking for.

I added pressure, just a little; my other hand moved to grip the handle of the knife, as well. A bead of red appeared at the spot just above my collarbone, streaking down my chest, leaving a stain—barely noticeable—on the neckline of the dress.

And then my mother's voice entered my mind. *If someone couldn't give anything up for the ones he loves…Jenny, it wouldn't be love.*

My grip loosened on the knife, and it clattered to the floor, me along with it. The dress pooled around me, as if I was nothing more than a candle melted down into a puddle of wax.

With a strangled, frustrated sound, I threw a swipe at the dresser, not caring when my knuckles smarted as I pulled my hand away and cradled it to my chest.

I had been wrong. I had been wrong to think I was doing something brave. My mother had always been the brave one. *I* had only been the one who was too afraid, too afraid to make the necessary sacrifices. I'd been too afraid to make any decisions to hurt anyone, and so I'd ended up hurting *everyone.* There was a wetness at my eyes, a tightness in my throat, but I knew there would be nothing more of it. That emotional reservoir—dry as bone even after all this time, it seemed.

I looked down at my hands, still shaking. I wouldn't have done it. The thought struck me later than it ought to have struck me, but there it was: I wouldn't have done it. After my mother had died, I'd thought about it. Dreamt about it. But my mother had lived for my sake, while she could—even when it was painful, even when getting out of bed every morning must have seemed impossible—and it was only right of her to expect the same from me. I owed her at least that much.

I took long breaths in and out, trying to calm myself, to think rationally for *once in my life,* especially now that it actually mattered. Rationally, like my mother used to think.

I picked the blade up off of the dusty floor, returning it to its place among the satin swaths.

I had to go out there and make a decision. I had to make a *real* decision and not one I knew I didn't mean, one I would regret.

What would my mother say, was my first thought. Then I shook my head. What would *I* say?

After a moment, I rubbed my thumb across my collarbone, wiping away the blood. It occurred to me, then, that there were no words left to say, not now. The time for words was approaching, but right now all I could do was brush the dust from my dress, square my shoulders, and walk into that room.

"Jenny?" Vince stood in the doorway, his hands folded behind his back. His tone was flat, inexpressive. "Everything is ready. They're waiting for you."

Before I could say anything to him, he left.

I sighed, gathering my resolve about me, or trying to. It seemed to be one of the many things I lacked at that moment. Straightening my dress with sweaty palms, I marched out the door, crossing a threshold into the room where the ceremony was taking place. I tried to look dignified, tried to hold my head high, my back perfectly straight. *Poise*.

Somehow it felt wrong, holding myself that way. It felt unnatural, as if I wasn't even me, anymore. Of course, it could be said that I hadn't been *me* for weeks, now.

The chairs before the section of floor where I would stand were split in two, a sort of matrimonial aisle down the center. I knew better than to think this was for *my* benefit, alone. They were simply arranged in that fashion to separate the two factions.

It was easy to distinguish the Persuaders from the Sentries enough as it was. On my left, I could pick out Natalia—or the back of her head, that was—by the ramrod set of her spine and shoulders, and by the intimidatingly muscled Sentry bodyguards on either side of her and in the chairs just behind her. I couldn't imagine any one of the Persuaders challenging them, just as I imagined she hardly needed them at all. She was more than capable if it came down to a fight. The rest of the Sentries I didn't recognize, aside from Silas. They had probably been acquainted with my mother when she was younger. All were very simply dressed. Some had made an attempt to look nice, but most of them were in dark, uncomplicated clothing, clothing that was for the most part unadorned.

The same could not be said of the Persuaders, who shone as brightly as stars in their rubies and diamonds and precious metals and perfect, white smiles set into perfect faces. They lacked any of the ruggedness of their enemy faction, any edges smoothed over, any imperfection altered by expensive means. I recognized Vince and Liam, of course, by their plain, black suits, and then there was Charles, whom I recognized by those ridiculous red pants he was wearing, and I recognized even some of the Persuaders I'd seen at the party in Baltimore. My disgust toward them had not lessened since then, just as I was still unbelievably terrified of some of the Sentries who were looking at me, swiveled in their chairs just as the Persuaders were. I noticed two middle-aged Persuaders in the last row who looked particularly contemptuous through their curiosity. They looked like Gwen, I noted, distractedly, especially the man, with his storm gray eyes. Silas gave me a half smile as I passed, but I was too anxious to return it.

My eyes lifted to take in the Warden, standing very still like a statue. As I approached, they fell to land on the knife, and the memory of its wicked point pressed to my skin sent a chill through me.

"Jennifer Leigh Cable,"

My head lifted to meet the elderly man's cold, unfriendly eyes. Several lines of age crisscrossed his leathery face, though none around the eyes and mouth seemed to indicate that they were the kind of lines formed through laughing or smiling. "Daughter of Michael Cable and Heather Halford, pledge yourself to a faction. Remember: Your choice is binding." His sharp gaze rested on me with indifference, as if he didn't care. But I knew everyone in the glittering, silent room was hanging on each syllable I uttered, nearly as anxious as I felt. I could feel the weight of their gazes like massive cathedral bells on my shoulders.

I risked a glance behind me, at my father. His olive green eyes, the unusual, trademark eyes of the Cable family, stared back at me. They were carefully blank, neutral. I had expected him to be trying to communicate some message of how he wanted me to respond, but his face was partial to nothing. I saw Vince, to his right, not even meeting my gaze, his handsome face drawn and pained. Remembering the things I had spat at him earlier— horrible, selfish, frustrated words—I felt a pang of guilt in my chest. I wished I could say something to take it back, somehow, but I knew there was nothing.

The only thing I could say was one word…or the other. Persuader or Sentry. Decadence or poverty. A life of greed or an existence in hatred. There was no in between. There was no avoiding it.

Lastly, I thought of Taylor, his face before he turned away from me, cold and resentful. He hadn't even spared me a final glance, as if I was a stranger. No, an enemy. Maybe I would be his enemy. Maybe I already was.

"Jennifer Cable," the old man prompted, a tinge of impatience creeping into his tone. "Have you made your decision?"

I turned back to face him, setting my shoulders. "Yes," I said, with a lift of my chin. "I have."

The Warden laid the swaths of blue and red out before me, gripping the knife tightly in one hand, holding out the other to take my wrist with the same iron grip.

"Just as your words are binding, so, too, is the seal of your blood. Choose wisely, Jennifer Cable, for this decision cannot be revoked."

Cannot be revoked. When he said this, something within me tried to scratch its way to the surface. I *knew* that it was irreversible, so why was I so unnerved by the words?

I looked down at the knife, as it pressed into my finger and, with a tiny jolt of pain, drew blood.

It was unfair. *That* was the thing that'd been clawing away at me for all this time, stripping the skin from my bones and leaving me exposed: The *unfairness* of it all. Here I was, making this decision, this decision that would affect me for the rest of my life. Here I was, barely eighteen years old, meeting a fork in the road, the path falling away behind me, forced to choose left or choose right. I was too young to know which path would lead me astray, and too old to turn around and head back to the place from which I'd come.

I pulled my hand from his, and his face, though it was an unexpressive face, registered the barest hint of surprise.

"Wait."

A murmur rose from the crowd, startled whispers edged with mistrust and confusion.

The Warden looked particularly displeased. "Jennifer Cable, if you do not choose, you are left only with a final option of Renouncement."

The murmur rose in volume at this.

Sweat prickled at my brow. "I—I just need a moment to think."

"You have not decided already, Miss Cable? I seem to recall you saying you had, in fact, chosen."

My lips turned downward at this new note of dry condescension. "Please, I just need to—"

But my words were cut short by the sudden movement of the knife between us.

It levitated, suspended for a single, fragile moment, spinning almost lazily in the air. But then it stopped, just as suddenly as it had risen, its point frozen in the direction of the Warden.

His mouth moved angrily, as if to demand what was going on, but he never managed to say anything at all, only release a startled gurgling as the knife shot forward, burrowing itself to the hilt in his chest.

He pitched forward, folding over the marble altar before tumbling to the floor, in a heap at my feet. I stumbled away from the dark blood pooling around him, my face frozen in horror and my arms lashed to my sides in shock.

Screams began to tear from the throats of Persuaders, shouts of confusion rippling from the Sentries. Natalia's guards launched themselves to their feet, looking around with sharp eyes for danger while Vince and Liam stood staring at the front doors, now thrown wide open to let in sharp, autumn air.

Samuel was just a silhouette against the indigo sky, his profile sharp, his eyes as he took a step into the room even sharper. He smiled like the Cheshire cat as he said, "My apologies for the interruption, Jennifer."

The doorway blackened as more human shapes moved in to fill it. Deadlocks. I could feel my mind close like a steel trap, but somehow I knew Samuel's hadn't. When he stepped closer toward me, the band of metal around his wrist caught the light. Of course. Vince had told us about the device, how it allowed him to Shift even in the presence of Deadlocks. I supposed when you were as powerful and as rich as Samuel Locke, there wasn't any technology you couldn't get your hands on.

"Of course, it seems that you've already interrupted it, yourself. Bravo. It was very dramatic. Suspenseful." He spread his arms out wide. "In that way, I suppose we are alike."

My hands curled at my sides, and I scowled at him, trying to ignore the sweat beading across my brow. "I'm afraid I don't see the resemblance."

His eyes flashed, like the quick motion of sea creatures under black water. "There's more of it than you think. For instance, we're both rather *practiced* liars, wouldn't you agree? But you already know that, of course, because you lie more to yourself than to anyone else."

"*You're* the liar, here," Vince snapped, catching me by surprise when he moved to stand at my shoulder. "Not Jenny."

Samuel chuckled a little at this, clearly amused. "Is that so? Well, then I guess you knew what she was about to say, then." He gestured grandly to me, enjoying himself thoroughly, I was sure. "That she was about to say the word 'Sentry' so she could run off and find her degenerate friend, Taylor Ross. Like some goddamned fairy tale ending. Happily ever after."

I fought to keep my expression from betraying anything. "I've told you before, I've never even met—"

"Ah, yes," he gracefully interrupted, "that would've been a very convincing *lie,* as you are very good at it. However, I have *evidence* of your crime now, my dear Jennifer." He jerked his chin toward a Deadlock to his right, who moved silently into the room, holding a slimmer figure by the shoulders. Without ceremony, he threw the man down at Samuel's feet.

I was unable to smother the small cry of astonishment and horror that escaped my lips when I saw that it was Tarek, his face bloodied, his legs dragging on the floor as he pulled himself upright onto his elbows to stare at me with a mixture of shame and fear and pain. "I-I'm sorry, Jenny. I had no choice. I c-couldn't..." He coughed blood onto the carpet.

"Tarek!" I started forward. Vince grabbed my arm, pulling me back.

"No." His grip tightened as he spoke into my ear. "Keep away from him. Samuel's baiting you."

"I don't care," I snapped back at him. "Let me go, Vince, he's hurt."

Samuel moved forward, practically sauntering, kicking Tarek onto his back. "You see, I've been very suspicious of you, Miss Cable. Ever since that fateful night in Baltimore, I've known that you were hiding something from me. I paid a little visit to your charming little suburban home, did you know? Very quaint." I strained against Vince's arms, but his hold did not let up. "I happened to come across this young man, and I found it not entirely just a matter of coincidence that someone with his aura—and his *history,* which I'm sure he never divulged to you—would be living right next door. I've never believed in coincidences, myself, of course. So, with a little *urging,* he told us everything. *Everything,* you understand. So you see, lying will get you nowhere now, Jennifer."

For a moment, I couldn't even breathe. Everything I had feared suddenly had sprung forth into focus, into actuality. Everyone in the room was equally still, most unable to piece together exactly what was going on. "Okay, you've found me out." I said, swallowing hard. "You *win,* what more do you want? Taylor isn't here. He's long gone by now."

Samuel slid his hands into his pockets, his chin tilting to the side. "Rest assured, I'll deal with him, eventually. But harboring a Sentry rogue isn't the only crime you're guilty of, Jennifer. In fact, everyone here is guilty of it, as well."

"And what is that?" I shouldn't have asked, because I knew the answer to the question already, but for some reason I wanted to hear him say it out loud. I wanted him to say it without shame or remorse or hesitation so I could know just how far he had managed to drag himself away from humanity and compassion, so I could know *for certain* that inside of him there was more rot than soul.

"Impurity," Samuel replied, not taking his black eyes from me as Deadlocks poured in around him.

22
WHEAT FROM THE CHAFF

JENNY

They descended on the crowd in a great, silent wave, meeting resistance with brutality, outraged shouts with unwavering taciturnity.

At a careless wave of Samuel's hand, the folding chairs in their neat, orderly rows collapsed in on themselves and scattered across the floor into pieces. Samuel's sleeve rode up some as he made the gesture and the bracelet around his wrist glinted in the light, almost mockingly. From across the room he smirked at Natalia like a wily fox that had escaped the hands of a hunter. "This must be rather embarrassing for you," he crooned, holding a hand to his heart as if he cared about anyone's feelings above his own, as if he had the *capacity*. "The indomitable Sentry leader half-breed, vanquished, at last."

She only looked at him with a steady gaze and said, coolly, "As it will be equally embarrassing for *you*, after all your righteous claims of virtue and purity, when you eventually find yourself making pretty speeches in Hell."

"I can assure you there will be no shortage of listeners." His face didn't change, but there was something in his aura that changed, then, something that made it sharper to the senses, made it burn. "Though I suppose that begs the question of who will be the one to send me there?" When no one would meet his gaze he scoffed. "Just as I thought. It saddens me to see my fellow Persuaders resigned to attending this...this *aberration's* Embracement against all tenets of morality."

"How dare you," Liam growled, taking a step toward him, quickly restrained from taking any further steps by an expressionless Deadlock guard. *"How dare you* stand there and call my daughter an aberration when you, yourself, murder innocent people and intimidate others into following your selfish demands."

Samuel's fine brow lifted into his hairline, though his expression bore little other signs of surprise. "Well, well. If it isn't Michael Cable, coming to his daughter's rescue. Interesting. Where were you nine years ago, Michael?" My father's mouth twitched at the remark, and he said nothing.

Encouraged by his silence, Samuel turned to me. "Does she forgive you? Does she forgive the father who lied to her for all those years? Who abandoned her when she was still a child?"

Liam's green eyes were wide and bewildered, and he moved away from the Deadlock to stare at me. He didn't look pleading, exactly, just...searching. I looked from him to Vince, still standing beside me, to Samuel, who appeared as if he knew exactly what I would say. I swallowed hard, tasting my own desperation. I wanted to say *yes*, that I'd forgiven him for what he had done, but...but I didn't know if I really had. My mind conjured all the loneliness and heartache his departure had caused, all the nights I'd gone without sleep, waiting for him to come back, and then realizing that he wasn't. How my heart had dropped like a stone into my stomach when I'd realized that. "I..." Seeing the uncertainty in my face, Liam's posture seemed to deflate, the hard lines around his mouth and the one between his eyes deepening as it dawned on him that I couldn't say anything at all, not a word more.

Samuel smiled a wide, self-satisfied grin. "Oh, how tragic." He snapped his fingers, and the Deadlocks moved closer, standing shoulder to shoulder, forming a barrier between himself and everyone else. "In any case, you must know that I cannot allow anyone here to leave. Not alive."

He had said it so simply, so nonchalantly, in a way that was almost conversational. When the words finally processed in everyone's minds, that was when true chaos began.

Shrieks and shouts were coupled with elbows and knees and flashes of color, Persuaders and Sentries straining against the arms of Deadlocks and Natalia's guards flinging themselves against the silent, human wall in an ultimately futile attempt.

One man used this diversion to break free through a gap in Samuel's buffer, making a blind run for the exit.

Without pause or ceremony, Samuel pulled a pistol from his waistband, aimed, and fired, all in one motion. A plume of red burst from the side of the man's skull, and he collapsed onto the floor in a heap. A woman screamed.

"Now that I have your attention," he said in a low, calm tone to the suddenly silent throng, "I should inform you of the *perils* just beneath your feet. At this moment, the basement below is filled nearly to capacity with around two dozen or so drums of gasoline, rigged to a detonation device that is set to go off when the twelfth hour of this night is *struck.*" There were several tense whispers among the guests, while others remained silently bewildered. "Doesn't that sound exciting?"

Liam looked aghast. "You would murder dozens of your own kind?"

"Wheat from the chaff, old friend," he replied, splaying his hands as if to assume none of the guilt for his actions. "Persuaders who associate themselves with interbreed kind are better off not among the living." He looked from face to face, his eyes heavily lidded, displaying a deep and falsified contemplation. "But I am not ungenerous. As John Milton says, 'Why should all mankind for one man's fault be condemned, if guiltless?' Will any one of you, those of you born pure, join me? Or would you prefer to burn with the contaminated?"

When no one moved, Vince released me and said, in a voice all at once quiet and heavy, "'Abashed the devil stood and felt how awful goodness is,'"—He stared down Samuel with a hardened amber gaze, his pupils like the ancient things trapped within—"'and saw Virtue in her shape how lovely: and pined his loss.' That's also in *Paradise Lost,* I believe."

Samuel's eyes narrowed, and he curled his hand toward Vince, tossing him—as easily as a child would throw a doll—into the wall at his back, hard enough to crack the plaster. Then, helpless under Samuel's manipulations, he was pitched forward, landing with a grunt on his hands and knees at Samuel's feet.

He forced Vince's head back, pressing the muzzle of the gun to his temple. Wide, gilded eyes found mine, Vince's throat working, his hands loose at his sides.

"What's virtue to a bullet through your *head,* outcross?" Samuel hissed.

I pushed my way to the front of the crowd, shoving against arms as thick as the limbs of trees. "Samuel," I shouted, causing him to look up at me with something like amusement in his expression. "I challenge you."

His face twisted into something more contemptuous, paired with an emotion I couldn't identify. "You *challenge* me," he repeated, flatly. He tried to make it seem as if he found the situation hilarious, but even to me it seemed forced. "Challenge me to what, might I ask?"

"Cavea," I said, and Vince writhed in his grasp, beginning to say something to me before Samuel cut in.

He smirked and rubbed his chin thoughtfully. "You wish to challenge me to a Cavea *duel*, little girl? Seems a bit of a gamble, don't you think? And not one in your favor, I might add." His lips turned down into a scowl, and his hand fell from his face to grip the back of Vince's neck again. "Then again, I've never been one to risk victory, myself. You haven't thought this out nearly enough, I'm afraid. If I refuse, there will be no triumph lost. You will die. I will live. Everyone you care for will die. Now, help me see the reason in your request. Is there any incentive for me to *agree* to your childish games?"

"No," I said, my hands curling into fists at my sides. "Aside from the obvious."

"The obvious?" Samuel inquired, more for the sake of curiosity than anything else.

"I'll die. You'll live. But one day *you'll* die, too. The only difference is, *you* will die a liar, a murderer, *and*"—his eyes blazed blacker than black as he looked at me—"a pitiful coward."

For a moment Samuel didn't move, just stared at me with that bottomless gaze of his. Then, he smiled, a wide, terrible smile, and hauled Vince to his feet, the gun still pressed to his skull. "For that remark, I should kill you right now, Jennifer." He tucked the pistol back into the waistband of his pants, with a contemplative tilt to his head. "But I think we both know what would hurt you more: Watching someone you care for *bleed*. Any volunteers?"

Vince released an agonized shout as his arm twisted the wrong way with an audible popping sound, raised stiffly in the air at a grotesque angle. "Oh, Mr. Hallows. How noble of you."

"Stop!" I shrieked, my voice not even sounding like my own as I threw myself against the wall of Deadlocks, my hand reaching uselessly for Vince, who kneeled now on the floor, cradling his broken arm. "Please, stop hurting him."

"That's not up to me to decide, Jennifer," Samuel replied, peculiarly straight-faced. "It's for Vincent to decide. Well, go on, then. Hit me, outcross. If you can."

Vince stood, shakily, breathing hard as his arm hung limp at his side. He rushed at Samuel, winding back to cuff him with his good arm. But before Vince could even make contact, Samuel sidestepped him and wrapped his hand around his bicep, digging his fingers into the break so that he buckled and collapsed to his knees, shuddering in his effort not to cry out. Samuel's other hand shot out to grab Vince by the chin, and this time he *did* cry out, paralyzed by whatever it was Samuel was doing to him.

"Right now the blood is being denied from entering your brain," Samuel said, as evenly as a doctor delivering a diagnosis. "You'll be dead within moments, I'm sure."

I watched as Vince's movements began to slow, his eyelids lowering. Liam tried to fight the Deadlock restraining him, only to be tackled to the floor by two others of the same mass and might. "That's *my son!*" I heard him shout. "My son!" With is arms pinned behind him and his cheek pressed to the carpet, he stopped struggling, looking on bleakly as Vince began to slump. "Vincent," he whispered, hoarsely.

"Vince!" I cried out. "Vince, please. Do something! *Anything.*"

But he didn't respond—*couldn't* respond. A sob broke free from my chest as I realized that he would die. He was going to die and there was nothing I could do about it.

But then...then I sensed an aura, an aura just beyond the doors. I glanced around to see if anyone else noticed, and detected the slightest of changes in the faces of Natalia's guard and Natalia herself, and then in the faces of the Deadlocks. I supposed the rest were too terrified to notice and as for Samuel...I could only assume that, whatever he was doing, it was distracting him.

And then a dark figure appeared in the doorway, and I could barely blink before an object cut through the air, end over end, toward Samuel's head.

He ducked away from it, moving faster than I thought humanly possible, releasing Vince and standing to face his attacker. Vince took a gasping breath inward and fell forward onto his hands. The object—which I could now distinguish as a tomahawk—was lodged in the floorboards.

Gwen stepped from the shadows of the porch, into the bright glow of the room, and Natalia moved forward as well, astonished and furious. "Gwen, get out of here. *Now*. That's an order."

But Gwen just shook her head. "No. I'm not leaving." Her hand fumbled for something in her pocket, and only when she slipped it around her wrist did I realize it was the same device encircling Samuel's. His eyes widened when he saw it.

"Where did you get that?" he snapped.

"Where do you think?" She smiled in a manner both serene and defiant. "From your mercenary."

"Then I suppose you killed her." His face didn't change.

"No." Gwen took another step toward him. "But I can make up for that." Her hand shot out and the tomahawk flew back into her grasp.

He slid his hands into his pockets—an overconfident posture, I thought—as the tomahawk sliced through the air again, spinning even faster than before, designated to bury itself deep in his chest.

But, of course, it did not strike its target, but instead began to disintegrate into a fine, silver dust, rendered harmless as it struck Samuel like a fistful of glitter. He chuckled a little at this. "Best be careful with weaponry, young lady," he said, almost chiding her. "Wouldn't want to upset dear old Mom and Pop, would we?"

Gwen started a little at this, as if the thought had never occurred to her that she would be displaying her Sentry capabilities in front of her parents, parents who I was sure had been entirely oblivious up to this point. Her eyes flitted over to meet theirs, but their faces were frozen into identical masks of shock.

Two Deadlocks, at the slightest of nods from Samuel, descended on her while she was distracted, stripping her of her weapons as she kicked and writhed against their constraining arms. The bracelet fell to the floor in the struggle, unnoticed.

"A decent attempt, Farrier, but much like the others rather futile, no?" Samuel took a step back as another Deadlock grabbed Vince and wrapped a beefy forearm around his collarbone. Tarek lay on his back, his chest moving slowly as he stared up at the ceiling.

Samuel continued to take steps backward until he was outside of the room completely, and a Deadlock—presumably the captain of Samuel's guard—followed him to the door. "Make sure everyone here is escorted to the cellar, Damien. And if anyone tries to escape..." He placed his gun in the other man's hand, clapping him on the shoulder. "Take care of it."

The wind ruffled his copper hair, and he pushed it back, folding his hands neatly behind him. "If you all will excuse me, it seems as though I have larger game to hunt."

He turned and left, without another word. It was strange to think that after all the speech and ceremony that had followed his entrance, his exit—the moment he left everyone to die by his hand—would be so silent.

No one made a sound during the asphyxiating hush that followed, but it rose to a low, anxious murmur and an occasional whimper as the Deadlocks began jostling everyone—three to four at a time—through the door, to the side of the house, and down the steps into the cellar. I saw one put his arms under Tarek's, the other grabbing his ankles. There was nothing to do. There were too many Deadlocks to fight, and the bracelet…I'd lost sight of it when people had started to move around me. Without that bracelet, things really *were* hopeless.

A Deadlock appeared at my shoulder, shoving me forward without saying anything at all, a gun between my shoulder blades. Once outside, I could see that Vince was being led outside just in front of me, still cradling his arm, staggering some as he tried to keep his footing. The Deadlock in charge of him handled him roughly, ignoring his injury, and tossed him down the steps of the cellar as if he was nothing more than a sack of flour. Liam was a part of the group, and lurched forward to catch him before he struck the stone floor. Natalia and Gwen followed, and after them it was my turn. The Deadlock—I recognized him now as the captain who had spoken to Samuel before—grabbed my arm, pitching me forward. "She's the last of them. Seal it up, boys."

"You can't!" A Persuader I didn't recognize elbowed his way past me. "Please! I change my mind. Let me go. Let me join Samuel. Please, I don't want to die."

The captain eyed the man thoughtfully. "Alright, then leave."

The Persuader's face was bewildered. "Really? I can go?"

Damien stepped back, gesturing widely. "Of course. Be my guest."

"Wait a second." Another Persuader, a woman in her mid-thirties. I couldn't say I knew who *she* was, either. "I want to leave, too. I don't want to die because of…" She glanced at me, briefly, with no small amount of disgust. "Because of an *interbreed*. I'll even join Samuel if I have to."

The captain made a sort of bow. "Why, madam, how noble of you.

I'm sure there's room to be made for both of you."

The Persuaders ascended the stone steps, hardly pausing a second before making a run for it. Bleak-faced Sentries looked on, knowing they would have no such opportunity afforded to them. Damien waited a moment, his hand lifting to rub his chin as he watched them go, and then he pulled his gun and fired two, quick shots. There were several screams from within as the silhouetted bodies, now several yards away, fell, not moving again. "Room to be made in Hell, that is," Damien added, shrugging as if it all was just some funny misunderstanding.

The doors to the cellar slammed closed, and soon we all heard noises of something being moved to seal it up, something heavy. It was like a tomb now. A tomb filled with the living, though, in truth, we were all as good as dead. The clamp on my mind never lifted, only grew marginally fainter, so I supposed that meant they were still there, beyond the doors.

When I turned, I saw that half the room was filled with two dozen or so drums of gasoline, and that the other half was occupied by all the guests, everything grimly illuminated by a single, overhanging light.

I rushed over to Vince, helping him stand, Liam taking his apprentice's undamaged arm and sliding it over his shoulders. I felt a swell of relief fill me for just a second. "Vince," I whispered. "I'm so sorry. If I would've just—"

"Jenny," he said, interrupting me. The weak light above us made him look so pale. "Don't. I did what I had to do. Right now, we need to focus on getting everyone out of here. It's...it's almost midnight."

Gwen approached us, her stride purposeful and clipped, Natalia and her guard in tow. "How are we supposed to get out of here? We're running out of time."

Suddenly, her eyes flashed to Vince, and some sort of unspoken exchange passed between them. He shook his head. "I don't know if it's possible. It's too risky."

"You have to try," she said, pleading with him now. She reached for his hand, slipping something on his wrist. With a start, I saw that it was a bracelet. It was *the* bracelet, and somehow it would be our salvation.

For a moment they just stared at each other, amber against flint, obstinacy against desperation. Finally, he straightened, moving out from the circle of Liam's arm. "Fine," he said.

"What?" I demanded, looking between them. "What's the plan?"

"When the explosion went off," she began, speaking rapidly, "and Vince and I were in the car, somehow he protected us. He can teleport, but only short distances, and he can…well, we *think* he can widen that sphere to encompass others."

"But only by touch," he interjected.

"It seems a bit far-fetched. That everyone just holds hands and walks out of this alive," Liam said.

Natalia shook her head, moving away from us so that she stood in the center of the room with her hands folded crisply behind her back. Two Sentries—presumably of the sort Gwen had once called "Techies"—had taken to inspecting the detonation device, itself, exclaiming that dismantling it without Shifting and with such limited time would be impossible.

Natalia began to speak, raising her voice to be heard by everyone. "Now I know this may seem an odd request, but if everyone could just stop panicking for a moment—"

"Stop panicking?" Richard Farrier shouted, incredulous. "We're all going to *die* in,"—a glance at his watch—"thirteen minutes, and there's no way out."

This set everyone off even more, and the two Sentries resumed their efforts, fiddling gingerly with the wires, muttering obscenities.

I cleared my throat. "Everyone, please," I said, but it was lost in the din, too low to be heard. My hands folded into my sides. *"Everyone, please!"* I shouted, and dozens of pairs of eyes turned my way, stunned that I—an interbreed, a freak-of-nature—had the nerve, *the audacity*, to address them.

"Look," I said. "I know a lot of you probably hate me, hate me because I'm an *aberration* or because you think I'm the destruction of your society, but…if you could just listen to me—"

"Why should we?" one Sentry woman demanded. "It's *your* fault we're all trapped down here."

A noise of bitter agreement rose from several others, and Liam put a hand on my shoulder. "She didn't ask to be the victim in Samuel Locke's game. It's no one's fault but his, and his alone. Now listen to my daughter if you want to still be breathing at the end of this."

They went silent and, after a grateful nod to my father, I turned back to face them. "Okay. Now that I have your ears, I'd like to propose a way for us all to live."

"How?" One of the Techies stopped fiddling and looked up at me.

"There's no way I can disarm this bomb in less than thirteen minutes. No windows. No exit... We're trapped like rats in here."

"We're not," I said, and it took a moment for everyone to settle before I could continue. "We're going to have to trust another one of our society's *aberrations,* and we're going to *do* that because he's our only chance." I motioned to Vince, and Mrs. Farrier couldn't hide her scoff.

"Him?" she asked, gesturing dismissively to him. "An outcross is going to *save* us?"

A Sentry nodded. "For once, I agree with a Persuader."

Vince stood still for a moment, so still he didn't appear to be breathing. And then he disappeared, but only for a fraction of a second before reappearing just in front of the Sentry who had voiced his doubts a moment before. The Sentry gave a shout and took a staggering step backwards, but Vince was already gone, rematerializing beside Gwen, taking her arm. They both emerged in a different place in the room a moment later, and everyone took a sharp and collective breath inward.

"She can travel where I travel unharmed because her aura's linked with mine through touch," he said. "This...this ability that I have can be passed to anyone through physical contact, and I know it seems unbelievable—hell, it even seems unbelievable to *me*—but there's your proof. All the proof you need right in front of you. We don't have any other option and I think everyone knows that."

For a long while nobody said a word, just stared blankly at Vince, Gwen, and me, at Natalia and Liam, unsure if they could ever abandon everything they had ever known, everything they had ever been told by the people they trusted the most, even when the situation most called for it. After all, they had never placed any amount of faith on an outcross before, and neither had they once in their lives listened to an interbreed. A discouraged expression beginning to surface across Vince's face, and I took his free hand in mine.

When the stillness, the inaction, had become almost unbearable, Silas began to move across the room toward us. He stood level with Vince, not saying a word, and then after a moment placed a rough hand on my shoulder, the other clapping to Liam's. Natalia moved next to join hands with Gwen, and her loyal guards joined forearms and did the same.

Other Sentries began to file toward Natalia, Persuaders slowly toward Liam. Tentatively, they joined arms and placed hands to shoulders and to wrists, until only a few were left, a few that included Gwen's parents.

"If you think," Richard began, "that I would willingly put my life in the hands of some *goddamned outcross,* you are sadly mistaken."

A Sentry scoffed. "Joining hands and singing Kum Ba Ya isn't going to save our skins. We need to come up with a plan, not go *belly up* when there's only five minutes to spare!"

The remaining dissenters—three Persuaders and two Sentries—were clearly defined on either side of the room, somehow in perfect agreement and perfect *dis*agreement simultaneously.

Gwen's eyes were bright with tears. "Mom, Dad, *please.* What more do you need to be convinced? This is the only way—"

Isabel Farrier let loose a pained cry. "Gwendolyn, we do not wish to speak to you at this moment or...your father and I really do not wish to ever speak with you again, quite truthfully. That you would deliberately go behind our backs and do something like this is...our own daughter, a benefactor. A Sentry!" She laughed as if it were some cruel joke.

Gwen turned to her father. "Dad, please see reason—"

"Reason?" he repeated, incredulous. "The only *reason* I need to hear is the reason why you would betray everything you've ever known to throw your lot in with those murderers!"

Liam scowled at him. "Now, Richard, this is no time to be foolish. What have you to lose by believing us?"

"Only my sense of dignity, *Michael Cable,* of which you clearly have none!" he fired back.

"Two minutes!" someone in the crowd shouted.

Gwen was clearly agitated now. Terrified, actually. *"Just hold on to someone, will you?"* she shrieked.

"I would sooner die," Isabel sniffed, "than to place my trust on him. Or on you, as you have thoroughly ceded your right to it."

Tarek, seeming to awaken from his state of shock, pulled himself across the floor, gripping my ankle tightly. "Jenny," he said, in a choking voice. "Please don't let me die. I know I deserve it, but...please, I don't want to die."

I knelt close to him, not letting go of Vince's hand. *"No one here* deserves to die. I *forgive* you, Tarek. I forgive you."

At this, he lowered his head onto the floor. "How could you forgive me? It's because of me that this is happening—"

"No," I said. "It's because of Samuel Locke that this is happening."

He lifted his head to say something else, but the same person who had pronounced that it was two minutes to twelve shouted that it was now down to less than a minute.

"Mom, Dad, please," Gwen begged. "Just hold onto someone."

"Forty-five."

Richard took one step, his heavy brow crinkling with uncertainty.

"Thirty seconds."

His wife followed behind him, gripping his arm tightly.

"Twenty-five."

He reached a hesitant hand out toward a Persuader, and the other man extended his own toward him, straining, almost. "Come on," the Persuader urged. "Take my hand, Richard."

"Fifteen."

"Take it!" he said, louder.

"Ten seconds to midnight."

Gwen lurched in Natalia's grasp. "Dad, just take his hand!"

"Five. Four—"

"Dad!" she cried.

"Three. Two—"

The two were so close that just one more step would've put them in range of each other. Richard began to say something.

"One."

The room was engulfed in fire and a wrenching, splintering, booming sound filled my ears. It was too hot and loud, too bright for me to discern anyone from the blast.

When I opened my eyes at last, we all stood on the front lawn, the grass scorched some and littered with debris. And Richard Farrier, his wife in tow, held tightly onto the Persuader's hand and did not let go until the last of the flames had been chased upward into the night. The others, those who despite the evidence hadn't allowed themselves to trust in Vince's abilities, had disappeared almost instantly. I blinked and they were gone.

We all glanced around at the wreckage, the blackened panels of what was left of the walls, the nonexistent ceiling, the charred planks of wood and melted shards of glass and warped metal, and some even gave whoops of victory, of triumph, because they were alive against all odds, alive because tonight they had bet faith against instinct, because tonight they had gambled it all and won.

My eyes searched the lawn, sliding over the coughing, slightly singed figures on the far side of the grass, glancing from Liam, to Gwen standing uncomfortably with her parents, to the Sentry leader and her guards, before finally finding Vince, standing off to the side, his back to everyone else. I left Tarek in Natalia's care as I crossed the neatly trimmed grass.

I reached out to touch his shoulder. "I can do something about that arm, if you'd like—" He turned to me with the look of a haunted man, shaking visibly, and I understood. "You were terrified the whole time, weren't you? Of the fire?"

His mouth slid down at one corner, and he wrapped his good arm around his torso. "Absolutely petrified," he whispered, his eyes searching mine for something. He was expecting me to be ashamed of him, I realized, to be ashamed of his weakness. But I wasn't. I only felt a sense of pride that he had been so selfless and so brave and so *good.* Truly good, as I had known he was all along.

"You saved all our lives," I said, and his gaze softened.

"Not all of them." He took my hand, pressing his thumb to my palm. "Not the ones who wouldn't be convinced. And Samuel's still after Taylor. If he finds him, he *will kill him*, Jenny. You have to understand that."

I pulled my hand from his. "Not if we find him first."

Vince said something after that, but I didn't hear him. When I felt it, I suddenly didn't hear anything at all.

"Taylor," I said, and my mouth felt like it was filled with cotton. I knew this feeling. I knew it was his aura, calling out to me, hitting me like a physical blow to the chest. Somehow…I *knew.*

I looked off at the horizon, blotted with the black shapes of trees, and barely illuminated by the white face of the moon, and without realizing it I was running. Running in the direction of that opaque horizon. Vince called out my name, but I didn't turn.

The trees were too quiet. They were too close together, too dark.

I ran almost blindly through them, led only by the moonlight filtering through high branches in weak, blue shafts, tripping over roots and rocks, scraping my hands against the rough bark of the trees before regaining my footing.

It was difficult to follow only the presence of an aura, especially when

Taylor seemed to be everywhere all at once. I had only a general direction, a faulty compass, and no inked lines on a map to show me the way through.

My mind reached out, trying to grasp at anything at all, but it was like trying to grasp at fog. Useless and impossible. I had gone deep into the woods by now, I suspected. I could barely even hear the others anymore as they called out to me and, after a while, I couldn't hear them at all.

And then I felt it again, that pull, the calling. We had always been connected in some deep, nonphysical way, but I hadn't expected *this*, the force of his emotions dragging me deeper into the darkness. There was desperation and fear, pain and regret, and beneath all of it *hope*. Some part of him still hoped that I would find him, and some part of him dreaded it.

I knew immediately when I found him, knew it even before I saw the faint, yellow light, just ahead, and a bowed silhouette against it. He was bound with rope, around the ankles and upper torso, lashed to a tall, wide oak, his hair hanging into his face and sticking to his skin with sweat.

"Taylor." I could only whisper it hoarsely. The shock of finding him like that had rendered me all but mute.

My fingers pulled at the rope, trying to undo the knots. Taylor's head lifted, and his violet eyes met mine with surprise and momentary relief before it was quashed in an instant by his alarm. "Jenny, no," he mumbled, faintly. It seemed he'd been beaten badly before being lashed to the tree. His bottom lip was split, a dried line of blood across his chin, and the skin above his eye was swollen. "*Stop.* You have to get out of here."

My fingertips began to bleed, and I finally pulled my hands away from the knots. I looked around, for anything to cut him loose, but all I saw was a floodlight, casting a yellow glow on Taylor and me. "I don't have anything to cut the rope with. Did Samuel leave a knife or—?"

"You think I'm that careless?" a voice asked, amused and familiar and terrible in its icy tranquility. "Come, now, Jennifer. You know better than that."

"Samuel," I said, a cold tide washing over me.

Taylor looked at me, breathing shallowly, the rope too tight to allow for him to breath deeply. "Run," he said in a low voice, through his teeth. "Now. Go!"

"Oh, she's not going anywhere," Samuel said, stepping into the glow of the floodlight. There were ghoulish shadows cast across the indents of his face. "She's far too noble for that, of course. And, after all, the noble mind is predictable."

"Is that so?" I demanded, unsure where this sudden nerve was coming from. "Then how is it I'm not dead yet?"

Samuel tossed me a sneering expression, devoid of shock or disbelief, and my confidence faltered. Had he anticipated this, too? "How, indeed," he said.

"Face it, Samuel," I snapped, jabbing a finger at him. "You *lost.* Nearly everyone got out of there alive. And it's all because you made one, tiny miscalculation: You underestimated someone you thought was weak and incapable."

"Vincent," he said, slowly, "has always been my greatest oversight. That was something I came to understand a long time ago. Before he was born, I had allowed myself to believe that the threat he would pose at a later time would be minimal, negligent. I was wrong."

I looked at Taylor, but he appeared as perplexed as I was. "What are you talking about?"

Samuel smiled, and I knew. I could see it in his finely arched brow and sharply defined features, in the lilt of his voice and the line of his posture. I didn't know how I had missed it before, but suddenly it seemed so obvious.

He was Vince's father.

"Vince is your son," I said, at last. Samuel's eyes watched me expressionlessly. "But...how? How is that possible?"

Samuel sighed, starting to pace, his hands still clasped behind his back. Alarmingly, I realized Vince often performed the same gesture. "Well, I suppose I can spare you a little story of my past seeing as you're going to be *dead,* soon, anyway." He cleared his throat. "Once upon a time, long ago in a sprawling, English estate, there lived an outcrossed woman and her ignorant fool of a husband."

"Vince's parents," I reasoned.

"One of them," Samuel said with a smirk. "The woman—Amelia— was beautiful. She was wealthy. She was...bored, honestly, and desperately in need of a change of pace. And I gave that to her, for a time."

"She had an affair with you." There was a sick feeling in my stomach.

His eyes flashed, unexpectedly. "It was more than that. I loved her." Seeing my dubious look, he scowled and kicked the floodlight. It hit a root and flickered once before resuming its incandescence. "Don't look at me like that, child. You know nothing of what I'm capable of feeling."

"Hatred," I said, narrowing my eyes at him. He wasn't about to make me feel sorry for him, to make me see him as anything more than a monster. "Arrogance. Fear, maybe. But not love."

"I am not what I once was, who I used to be before I'd met her," he replied, looking up at the stars visible through the gaps in the browning leaves. A breeze blew through them, making me shiver and realize for the first time that I was out in the cold in nothing more than a party dress. "Love was burned out of me long ago, leaving only...vengeance, I suppose. Anger. I was angry with her."

"What did she do to you?" I asked, trying to keep my tone neutral, apathetic to his suffering. "Did she break your heart? That is, if you ever even had one to begin with."

"Don't tell me you didn't want revenge on your father after he left you. Don't stand there and pretend you and I are any different from each other." His hands unclasped and hung at his sides.

I could feel that I was starting to lose my temper, could feel that my frustration was growing and eclipsing all reason and clarity. "You murder and lie and manipulate others. You're a horrible man with a twisted vision and nothing else."

Samuel took a step toward me, and Taylor strained against his bindings. "Jenny, stop talking," he hissed.

But Samuel paused, thoughtful. "And you haven't *lied* or *manipulated* those around you? I find that hard to believe."

My mind, unwillingly, flashed to Vince and Taylor, how Vince had told me before the Embracement that he hated Taylor not because he was a Persuader and Taylor was a Sentry, but because Taylor had *me*. I'd strung both of them along without stopping to consider *their* feelings above my own, strung them along continually and unfeelingly. And then there was that boy on the street, how I'd assumed control of his mind without a second thought. The truth was right there in front of me: I was a liar. I was as manipulative as Samuel. Maybe, if I didn't die here tonight, I would also become a murderer.

My head lowered, and Samuel laughed at the flush of shame in my face. "Oh, but I haven't even gotten to the best part of my story, have I? Here's a little known fact about me you can take to the grave with you: I was born in a Sentry stronghold." My gaze snapped up to meet his, and he grinned. "Shocking, isn't it? Yes, I was born a Sentry. Vincent Mason. That was my name. My parents, operating under the belief that it was better I grow up alone than in Sentry hands, abandoned me on the stoop of some *dismal* children's home and I became a freak and a pariah among my peers. I didn't know what was wrong with me because, like you, I had no understanding of the Persuader world. And then the Wardens came for me when I was just a boy. I wanted to distance myself as far away as I could from my parents' memory, so I decided to become a Persuader on my eighteenth birthday. First chance I got, I got on a plane to London and six years later, I met Amelia Hallows. I fell in love. But, after a brief few months, she told me she had grown weary of my company." Something rare and *human* flickered in his gaze. "Ah, but there was a *twist*. She was with child, and that boisterous, insufferable husband of hers, Malcolm, assumed it was his. It was not. She told me I could never see my son. Never. The only time I ever laid eyes on him was from a distance. Eight years after that, I had finally worked up the nerve to seek my revenge."

"*You* started the fire," Taylor said, after a lapse of silence. The earth beneath my feet seemed to tilt a little when I finally connected the dots and came to the same conclusion. "The fire that killed his family. It was you."

My hands curled into fists at my sides. "His home. His only brother. How could you?"

"Half-brother," Samuel reminded me, as if it made a difference. "And how *could* I? Well, it's simple. She made a poor decision, and I was the reckoning."

"It doesn't work like that," I said, hotly. "You can't just kill people you dislike and justify it to yourself by saying they deserved it."

"Ah, but I didn't simply dislike Amelia. *I hated her.*" His eyes burned like in my nightmare. "Besides, isn't that what *you're* doing? Attempting to kill me because of your dislike for the things I do?"

"I'm *going* to kill you," I corrected. "And it won't be because I dislike you. It'll be because the world is better off without you in it."

He shed his suit jacket, rolling up the sleeve of his shirt. "You can certainly try."

I grasped his forearm, and his black gaze pulled me into darkness.

Cavea was cold and dark, darker than I ever remembered it being before. I stood before a gray, dreary Victorian with a wide veranda and broken, unlit windows set into its otherwise nondescript face. The sign above the door was faded, and I had to squint to read it.

ST. ALEXANDER'S HOME FOR CHILDREN

So this was where Samuel had grown up, though I could only assume that it appeared less maintained *here* than it was in reality. There were vines clawing their way up the side of it, and the front lawn was brown and pockmarked by crabgrass. Above me, I saw the violet portion of the sky threading through a deep maroon.

"Where are you, you coward?" I called, into the bleak, frigid air. Dead leaves danced around my ankles in a sudden wind, blowing through the gaping doorway of St. Alexander's.

So he wanted to play games, did he? I marched up the crumbling stone steps, through the doors, looking around to see that the inside of the place was much of the same: Gray and dreary and in disrepair. The lampshades were coated in dust, and the lamps themselves seemed nonfunctional. The hallways echoed only loneliness and neglect. I concluded that this was a cold place, devoid of any nurturing or warmth.

I found a groaning set of stairs at the end of the hallway, following them up into the next floor, where a row of doors lined either side.

Only one of them was open, the one at the end of the hall.

Inside, the room looked as if it hadn't been lived in in years. Decades. The mattress was gone, leaving only the bedframe and twisted springs. There was the outline of a rectangle staining one of the walls, leaving me to suppose there had been a mirror there, once. The floors were bare, bare except for three, glass marbles, directly in the center.

The marbles started to levitate, spinning in the air like a tiny solar system. I reached out to touch them, but they blew away into dust before I could.

Samuel stepped out of the shadowy far corner of the room, his hands in his pockets. "The marbles were how I practiced. After a while, I learned to keep my abilities a secret, to only use telekinesis when no one else was around. I locked the door and laid them on the bed, and then I stared at them until my eyes itched, stared at them until I couldn't stare any longer. That was when they started to move."

I looked at him steadily, keeping a distance between us. "Why are you telling me this?"

He shrugged, holding out his hand. The glass dust hovered in the air, compressing in on itself until it formed three, solid marbles once again. "Fair distraction, wouldn't you agree?"

When my eyes flashed back to him, he had vanished.

The back of my neck prickled, and I whirled to see him standing just behind me, a knife in his hand. His hand shot out, as fast as a viper's strike, drawing the edge of the blade across my cheek.

I gasped, more in surprise than pain, reeling away from him, my hand clasped to my bleeding face.

He wiped the thin line of red dripping from its point on the sleeve of his shirt. "Jennifer, you aren't a fighter. Let's be reasonable here. You wish to win our little game, but I've had the winning hand from the start."

I shook my head, slowly. "It isn't a game."

I threw out my hand, Shifting Samuel off his feet and into the long hallway. But before he hit the floor, he disappeared again, vanishing in a black vapor.

I cried out as a barb of pain laced up the side of my arm, stumbling into the doorframe as I turned to see Samuel, having reappeared behind me again. I gripped my arm, my fingers coming away red.

"You really must be more aware of your surroundings, Jennifer," Samuel murmured, taunting me.

Then his face changed, drawing tight at the corners of his mouth. "Wait, just a moment." His long fingers wrapped around my neck, pinning me to the wall as he spoke. "Ah, so the rumors are true. Your face appears to no longer bear injury. Such a shame, I was quite proud of the precision of it."

I struggled uselessly against him, my hands wrapping around his in an attempt to pry it off. When I tried to Shift him, his mind put up a wall, deflecting it, scattering it around him. "Hm," he clucked, shaking his head. "I was going to go easy on you, but now I'm rather curious about the *extent* of your powers."

His grip tightened, and I could hear the crunch of my windpipe being crushed beneath his fingers.

With a scoff, he tossed me to the floor. "Alright, then. Heal yourself, interbreed. Go on. I'd be quick about it, were I you."

I writhed and shuddered uncontrollably at his feet, my nails scratching at the wooden floorboards, my lungs feeling as if they would burst inside of me. My vision began to blur and darken, swimming with spots, all the thoughts in my head beginning to slow.

No.

No, I *wouldn't* die. Not here, not at his hands.

I cleared my mind of everything except the action itself, the *healing*. My eyes closed, my hands curling into my chest. After a moment, I heard another popping sound, and I took a gasping breath inward, dragging myself unsteadily to my feet.

Samuel clapped his hands three times, smirking at me. "Oh, very impressive. Someone with your talent could be quite *useful,* I'm sure. Alright. Here's an idea: We stop this whole childish endeavor before I end up killing you, and you work for me. No one gets hurt. How does that sound to you?"

I frowned, rubbing my neck. "You don't get it, do you? It's not about *my* life. It's about the lives you'll *take* if I fail. It's about what's right."

"What's right?" Samuel demanded, clearly amused. "Oh, you poor, deluded thing. 'Right' and 'wrong' are human constructs, designed only to keep one from his potential. There is no good. There is no evil. There is only life and death, power and weakness. Every man thinks his purpose to be a necessary one. The only difference is, the ones who perceive it to be *noble* are the ones who end up dead."

"Then it's a good thing I don't think of killing you as noble," I said, sinking to one knee. "Only *necessary.*"

Leaping for him, I drove his discarded knife up toward his chest, and he only managed to move out of the way of a lethal blow, the blade sinking deep into his left shoulder. With a shout, his hand cracked across my face, so hard flashes of light burst in my vision, sending me to the floor.

He released a strangled grunt as he pulled the knife from his shoulder, starting for me without the confident smile from before. There was only anger and malice in his face now. "Don't think I was done with you," he hissed. "We've only just started."

His foot came down on my ankle, and I heard the bone snap like a dry twig under his heavy sole, heard my own scream, distantly. My lip started to bleed from where I'd bitten down on it. Samuel pulled me upright, his hand gripping my hair, almost ripping it from my scalp. He pressed the knife to my skin. "Let's see you heal yourself when I slit your throat."

"Get away from her," snarled a voice from over his shoulder.

Taylor materialized beside him, throwing him off of me, into a bare table, the flimsy legs snapping under his weight and the momentum of his fall.

Taylor offered a hand to help me up, mindful of my shattered ankle. "How are you here right now?" I demanded, and the question was met with a sudden ripping sound.

We looked toward the window on the other side of the room, where the red-violet sky was visible. The lower half began to change rapidly, Sentry blue spreading across the other shades like a bruise. The ground trembled slightly, as if we were standing atop a minor earthquake. "I don't know," Taylor whispered, his face as awestruck as I felt. "I just...touched your arm and—"

"While this is a poignant reunion." Samuel brought a broken piece of the table leg down over Taylor's head with a cracking sound, and Taylor was knocked to the floor.

He sprung to his feet, losing no time in going on the offensive against Samuel, who appeared to be just as martially capable, if not more so. Samuel's knee drove into Taylor's side, but his opponent still was not so easily incapacitated. Stumbling to the side, he caught Samuel in the jaw with a left hook, causing him to spin away, blood dribbling down his chin, with an expression that for once was not utterly cool and collected. Without the mask, there was only pure hatred, hatred and the sort of evil I could never have imagined before seeing it in Samuel Locke's black eyes, not even in my darkest nightmares. He brought the table leg down again, and this time Taylor had the mind to lift an arm to defend himself. The leg broke in two over it, and he hissed in the pain, drawing his arm back toward his body. Samuel tossed the broken half aside, a new object materializing between them out of thin air, metallic in look and weight, like a cue stick in shape but more pointed at the end.

Before I could even reach out to him, Samuel Shifted the weapon at Taylor, driving it underneath of his ribs, through his body completely, all in the flutter of an eye. It stuck in the wall behind him, vibrating like a tuning fork.

Taylor staggered, coughing blood in a fine spray, crumpling to the ground with a hole in his back. A crimson pool formed around his body as he laid very still, his hands scrabbling at his chest weakly.

I didn't scream. Or cry. Or drag Taylor into my arms and lay my head against his. I didn't do any of the things I felt like doing. Instead, I looked at Samuel, a strange calm beginning to wash over me, my arms rigid at my sides, my palms facing the floor.

And the room collapsed into pieces.

23
WHAT IS NECESSARY

TAYLOR

Samuel's eyes were like the eyes of Death, itself, as I tumbled to the floor, my hands warm with blood as they grasped at the hole in my chest. It was about the size of a silver dollar, maybe larger. A silver dollar, like the kind my great aunt used to give me for my birthday when I was a kid. An odd thought, but one I couldn't manage to dislodge from my brain for some reason.

Jenny looked down at me with wide eyes, eyes that hardened as her gaze turned to Samuel. The rumbling in the floorboards and the ripping sound of the sky ceased all at once, a silent pressure beginning to build around Jenny as her hands closed into fists.

And then the room around us fell inward, splitting apart into spear-like shards that hovered around us. The sky was now completely visible, appearing as though it were shattering into pieces, as well, multi-faceted and multi-colored like the skylight in the Cable mansion. All that remained of the small bedroom was the floor; the ceiling and all of the walls were in parts and pieces around us. My vision darkened, and my lungs felt as if they would spill out of the wound in my chest with the rest of me. The pain was the only thing missing. I only felt numb, as if it hadn't happened at all, which scared me more than anything else did.

Samuel turned in a slow circle, and for the first time he actually looked genuinely surprised, surprised and awestruck and...almost afraid. "This is...unexpected," he said, drawing a hand across his chin. It shook.

Jenny stared on, impassive. I could hear the *crack* of her ankle as the two pieces of bone melded themselves back together.

He pointed a finger at her, looking half wild. "If you don't stop this now, you'll be pursued by the others. Wherever you go they'll find you. And when they do, don't think they won't make you *suffer* for what you've done."

"Suffer?" Jenny shook her head, her hair whipping around her face as it tangled in the sudden gust of wind. Her eyes found mine again, and I couldn't hold my head up anymore to fully meet her gaze. "Whatever torture you have planned for me, I don't think you could make me suffer more," she whispered. I realized in that moment that she thought I was dead, and this belief caused an almost imperceptible change to come over her. In her expression, I saw coldness. I saw grief. I saw vengeance.

The pointed fragments circling slowly around us like a saw-toothed carousal froze. For a moment, everything was still. Straining to look at her, I saw that Jenny didn't appear to be seeing anything at all, not even Samuel as he took a step toward her.

It was his last step, his last breath inward, his last blink of astonishment as the spear-like slivers of wood and metal and glass sliced through him as easily as a hand would reach through fog.

He staggered back a few steps, pinpricks of light shining through his perforated body, before falling backwards, over the edge of the building where the floorboards ended, striking pavement two stories below. The red faded from the Cavea sky.

Jenny, as if coming out of a trance, blinked and rushed to my side, gently pulling me into her lap as tears began to streak down her face. It was such a strange sight, Jenny crying. So strange, yet beautiful in a way. "Taylor..." she murmured, my name nearly inaudible through the sobbing hitch in her voice.

"Jenny..." My voice was hoarse, each breath shallower than the last. "Promise you'll stay right here. Promise me."

"I promise. Of course I promise." Her eyes grew large and bright, and her fingers curled around mine tightly. "I thought you were d-dead," she hiccuped, pressing a hand to her face.

"I still have some things I want to say to you."

Jenny looked up into the sky, as violet and blue began to thread together into one, into a shade that reminded me of the cornflowers Jenny's mom used to grow in her garden. She looked back to me. "What kinds of things?"

"An apology, for one," I replied, smiling a little. "I never should have...left. N-never." My lungs constricted and I coughed again.

Her brow creased in anxiety. "Don't give up on me, Taylor. Please. Stay with me." She lifted my shirt, which was sticking to my skin with blood and perspiration, pressing her hands to the hole in my chest. I could feel the effects of her healing ability, but it didn't feel as if it was enough. It felt like an act done in vain. Futile.

"I forgive you," she whispered, fervently. "If I could forgive you a million times I would, and I can only hope you can forgive *me* for...for everything I've done. For everything I haven't done."

She bent to touch her lips to mine, gently, for just a moment, before pulling away with misery written across her face, misery in every line of her body. "I'm too late, aren't I? To tell you the truth. To tell you that I love you." She shook her head, pushing the hair back from my forehead. "I'm too late."

My sight tunneled into darkness, into an oblivion darker than the black of Samuel's eyes, darker than the clouds that had started to gather in the broken sky above us, but not before I whispered to her, "Too late? I would've waited forever to hear you say that."

VINCE

When I found her, she had her back against a tree, cradling Taylor's motionless body in her arms.

Her eyes said everything as they stared up at me, and at the same time they held nothing at all within them. Excavated tunnels, wells filled with a loss too profound to communicate.

Samuel lay on his back just a few feet from them, equally motionless. I stooped next to him, reaching down to check his pulse. His skin was cold.

"Samuel's dead." Jenny was standing over me now. Her voice held no human emotion, no inflection at all. "I made sure of it."

I stood to face her, noting the rigid line of her shoulders as she looked back at me. "Taylor—"

"Taylor isn't dead," she snapped, her eyes bright.

I felt a wave of sorrow stir inside of me. I hadn't been particularly close with Taylor, but Jenny had been, and I felt somehow extremely close to her. I wondered at what point her pain had become mine. "I'm so sorry, Jenny—"

"He isn't."

After a moment, her face collapsed in on itself, and she fell into my arms, her body trembling. "He isn't dead," she repeated over and over against my shoulder. "He can't be dead."

"I know, I know," was what I said to her, and we were both lying to ourselves. Taylor *was* dead. And I *didn't* know, didn't know how she felt. I couldn't know because, as she had said herself, I'd never really had friends, so I couldn't lose them.

When Natalia and Gwen finally caught up to us, Jenny was irreconcilable, gasping for breath as she grieved the loss of a boy I think she might have loved. I may not have been entirely certain what love was supposed to look like, but if pressed to define it I would've described "love" as the looks that passed between them. They led her away from the forest, away from the bodies, and I found Liam by the charred remnants of the house, staring in the direction of fast-approaching daybreak, where the sky looked silent and bruised.

Well after they'd gone, Liam and I trekked back to the tree where I'd found them earlier. He stood next to me as the morning sun rose, a light drizzle starting to fall. We both stared at the place before the tree, the place where Taylor *should* have been.

Should've been, and yet was not.

"Did you search everywhere?" I gasped, after we had looked in every place conceivable to look, in every crevice and in every hidden nook within a half-mile radius. When our shoes had struck the asphalt of the road at the outer edge of the woods, we'd turned around and regrouped back at the same place

Liam nodded. "I did. He was nowhere to be found."

Without looking at him, I demanded, "Then where *is* he?"

Liam sighed, bowing his head. "I don't know. There were probably others Samuel came here with. Other Purists. *His* body is gone, as well."

"I don't understand. What would be the purpose of that?"

"Insanity has no purpose," he replied, turning to walk away from me.

Maybe he was right, but the answer didn't satisfy me, not really. I followed him, not looking behind me.

EPILOGUE

LIAM

"I'm sorry, Mr. Cable. It's out of my hands. I can't help you."

"You mean you won't."

The Warden was young, maybe only twenty-five, and he sat with his hands folded on the desk. He fidgeted in his chair, looking uncomfortable. "Look, my only job is piecing together exactly what happened a few days ago. Interviewing witnesses. Collecting evidence. Beyond that, I have absolutely no authority."

I leaned forward in my chair, bracing my palms against the armrests. "Mr. O'Brien, the government has turned a blind eye to the Purists and their criminal activities for too long. Samuel Locke could still be alive. He could be out there right now, as dangerous as ever. Taylor Ross—"

"Is very likely dead, as is Mr. Locke," the Warden interrupted, with an impatient tone to his voice. "And even if they're alive, the Adjudication has made it very clear that the kidnapping of a Persuader is one thing, the kidnapping of a rogue something entirely else. Whether he lives or dies isn't really a major concern of theirs with so many other cases to attend to. As for Samuel, if he's safe in Purist hands the Adjudication knows better than to take direct action against them. With the numbers of Persuader kind dwindling rapidly, with the bloodlines thinning, their cause has been gaining more momentum now than ever. To go against them would be…unwise."

I slammed my hands down on the desk in front of him, launching to my feet, and he appeared only mildly startled by it. "God dammit, how you bastards can just sit here at your desks and twiddle your thumbs as blatant criminals run loose in the streets, vindicated by the cowardice of their own government? You're supposed to protect your citizens but all you people do is protect yourselves."

O'Brien looked away from me, his expression never changing. "Again, I'm sorry, Mr. Cable. I will not go against my superiors."

I pushed violently away from the desk, straightening. "To hell with your superiors, and to hell with you. If Locke is alive, the blood he spills will be on your hands, too. And even if he's not, there are others who will take his place, others you could've prevented from seizing power while you had the chance." I had made it all the way to the door before I turned back, taking in O'Brien's pale face, the movement of his throat as he swallowed. I pitied him, pitied him for his weakness, and also for his naivety. If he thought he could push this matter off to the side forever, he was wrong. "By the way, whether someone lives or dies—rogue or not—should *always* be the Adjudication's concern. Giving some people priority over others is exactly what's wrong with our government."

"I wonder if it really ought to be *your* concern, Mr. Cable," the Warden said, arranging stacks of paper on his desk into neat piles. "Seems like a lot of trouble for a dead rogue or a rogue in Purist custody. If he's no longer a threat, why pursue him? Forgive me if I can't see the reason for it."

I paused. My hand rested on the door now, and I stood half in and half out of the room. "Forgive me if don't *know* the reason," I said, and I left him.

JENNY

Vince took a deep breath, exhaling it in a cloud of white. "So Samuel...was Sentry-born. An orphan. A madman. Anything else?"

I had detailed to him everything Samuel had told me in the woods that night, but I had left out one part. The part about his mother, and the part about him being the *son* of that madman. I couldn't bear to tell him the truth, not after everything he had been through, not after everything his real "father" had done. "A murderer," I said. "A Purist. A monster."

Vince nodded, because he could only agree, agree and wince as his arm struck the wall behind him. Laura had attended to Vince by putting the arm up in a sling, but there was nothing she could do for the injuries *I* had sustained, myself, as they were less than physical. I felt certain there would always be a lingering darkness around my heart, because I had taken someone else's life. Taken it without even thinking about it, as if it were the most natural thing in the world. Even if it was justified, in doing it, I felt as if I had killed a part of myself. My innocence, maybe. No, that didn't seem right. It seemed like…like what had died in me was something more important than that.

Gwen was visible at the end of the driveway, speaking in subdued tones with Liam, a battered suitcase clutched in her hand. As I had come to learn, her parents had cut her off and disowned her after the night she faced down Samuel. They thought themselves generous, generous because they had arranged a negotiation in which Gwen wouldn't be tried for her crimes but rather would be forced to sever any and all ties with the stronghold immediately. I couldn't even imagine what that would be like, being cast out of your home and stripped of your identity all at once like that. Liam had arranged for her to stay at the mansion with us for the time being, which *I* was thrilled about because it would mean I could spend time with another girl my age, while Vince remained…anxious about the arrangement, to say the least. Tarek was beside them, twirling a leaf in his hands absently. For the time being, he would also stay with us, since we had no idea who else might come for him, and for what reasons.

"Do you want me to do something for that?" I asked, gesturing to Vince's arm.

He shook his head. "No, I want to be reminded of what happened, for now. I want it to heal on its own. I've always had to heal on my own."

"Well…" I touched his wrist, gently. "You don't *have* to, you know."

"I know," he said, his gaze flickering to meet mine. "Just like you don't have to search for Taylor alone, either."

"What are you talking about?" I released my hold on him, trying to make my face expressionless, revealing nothing. Of course, I had never really been any good at that.

Vince's face moved a little as if he meant to smile, but it fell back into a frown, as any levity at all had been absent ever since a few nights before. "You know what I'm talking about, Jenny. You don't believe he's gone, and you haven't believed it ever since I told you his body had gone missing."

I bit my lip, hesitant for fear that he would dismiss me as insane. "I can feel it," I admitted at last, looking off toward the burning noon sky. The clouds hung low, as if I could reach out and touch them. "He's alive."

"It could be just wishful thinking," Vince warned me.

"It's not," I said, still staring into the orange-yellow glow as my breath puffed out in front of me. "When he's away I can feel it. I can feel it like some sort of...pull. And it's *still there*. I have to follow it. I have to find him. You *know* I have to."

After a moment, Vince sighed, running a hand through his thick, black curls. "Well, then I guess wherever you go, I'm going with you. Far too dangerous to do alone."

I turned to smile at him, and this time he smiled back. "Thank you, Vince. I don't think I could do it without you."

I allowed myself the tiniest amount of faith that it wasn't my imagination, that at some point it would all start to make sense. I allowed myself to believe that the world would one day crack open to reveal a perfect pearl of everything it'd hidden from me.

And here was the gravity of it all: I chose to let myself hope, however *wishful* my thinking was, just as my mother had chosen to hope before her passing. She didn't hope for health, or for life, but for a daughter that would remember all the things she had imparted to her during what limited time they had together. And I remembered. I remembered everything.

And that, in itself, gave me hope.

ABOUT THE AUTHOR

Erin Caine wrote *Wicked Game* while still in high school with a goal of having it published before graduation. She lives in the Southern Maryland area with her parents and two siblings. Coming from a family that encourages musical and artistic expression, she draws and plays the piano as well as writes. Her mother is a teacher and her father works for the D.C. Metropolitan Police Department. In 2013, she won first place in a statewide short-story competition at Balticon, in 2014 received the Lorraine Hansberry Award for A.P. Language and Composition, and in 2015 received the Wanda Trollinger Award for English. She plans to attend Washington College in the fall.

For updates and news regarding *Wicked Game* and future projects, visit
erincaine3.tumblr.com